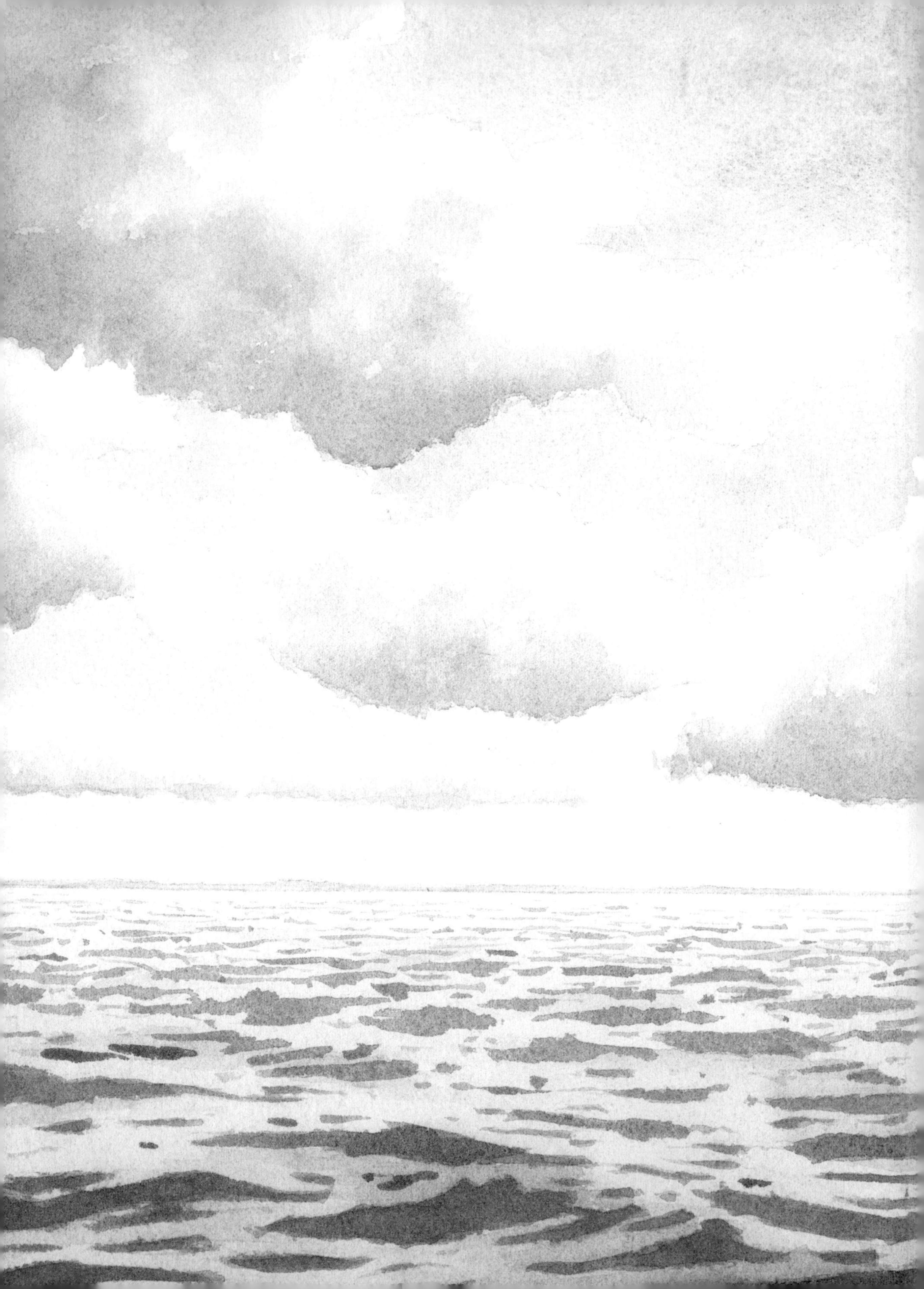

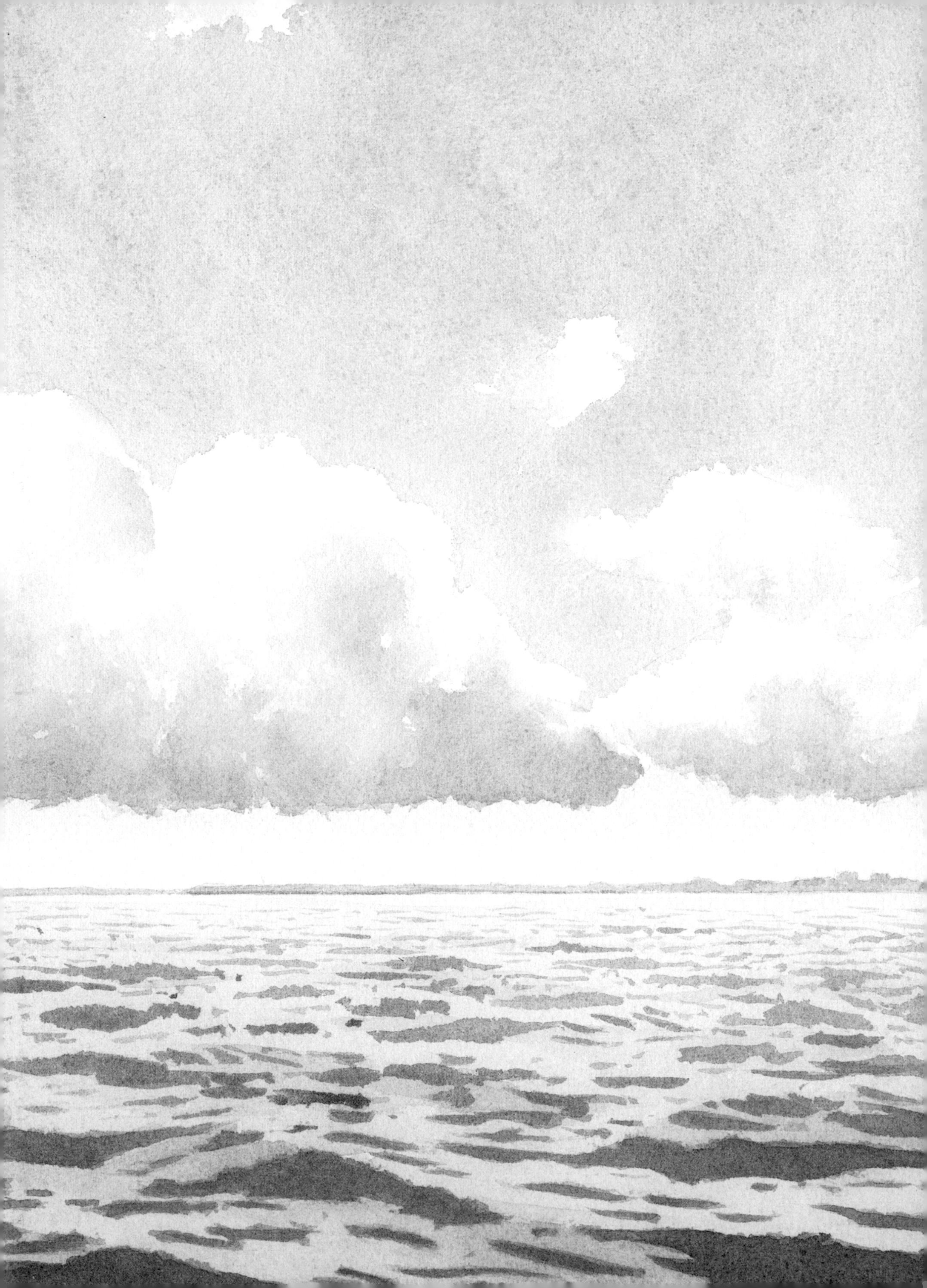

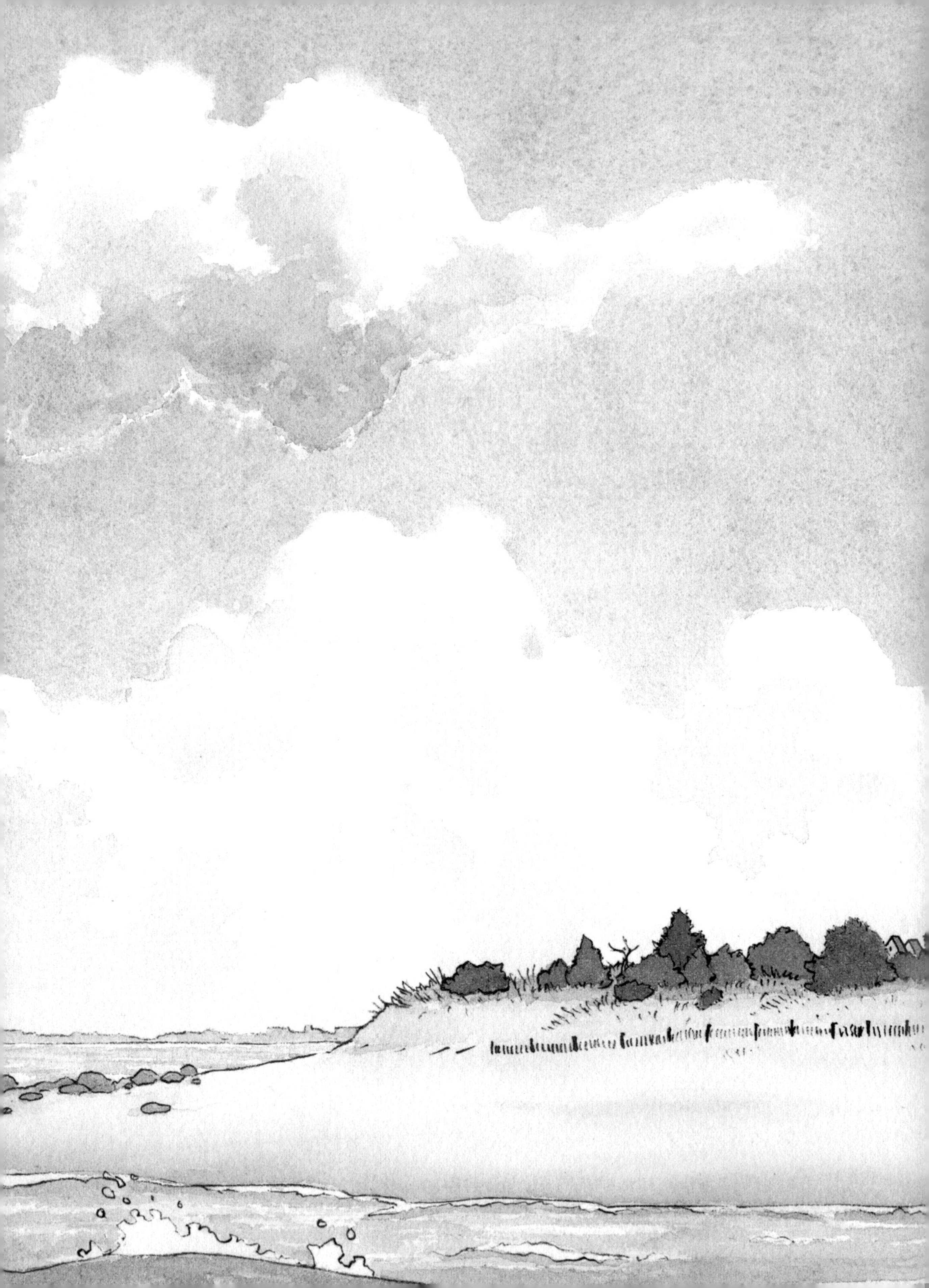

Fish Girl

Story by Donna Jo Napoli
& David Wiesner
Pictures by David Wiesner

CLARION BOOKS • NEW YORK

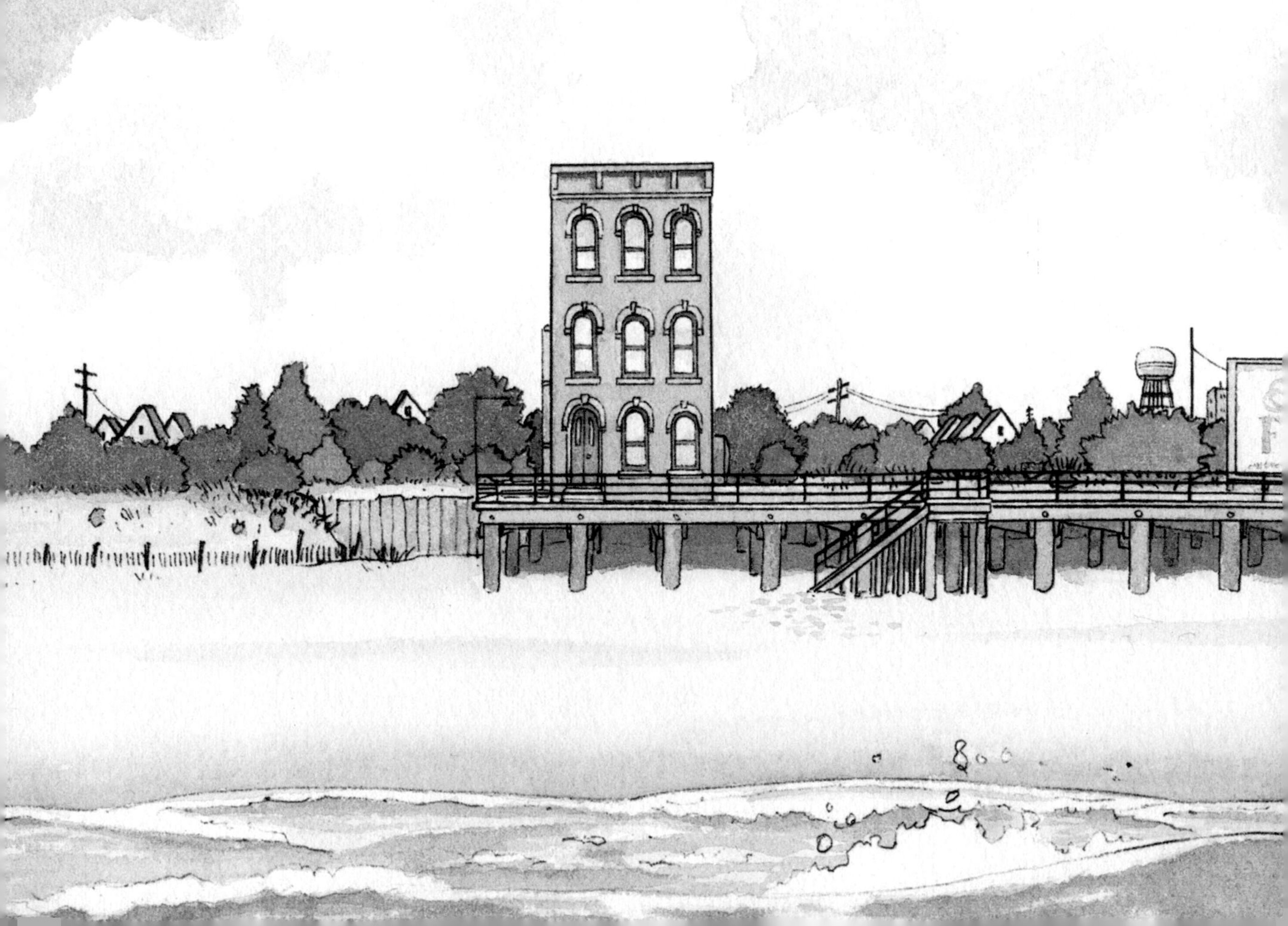

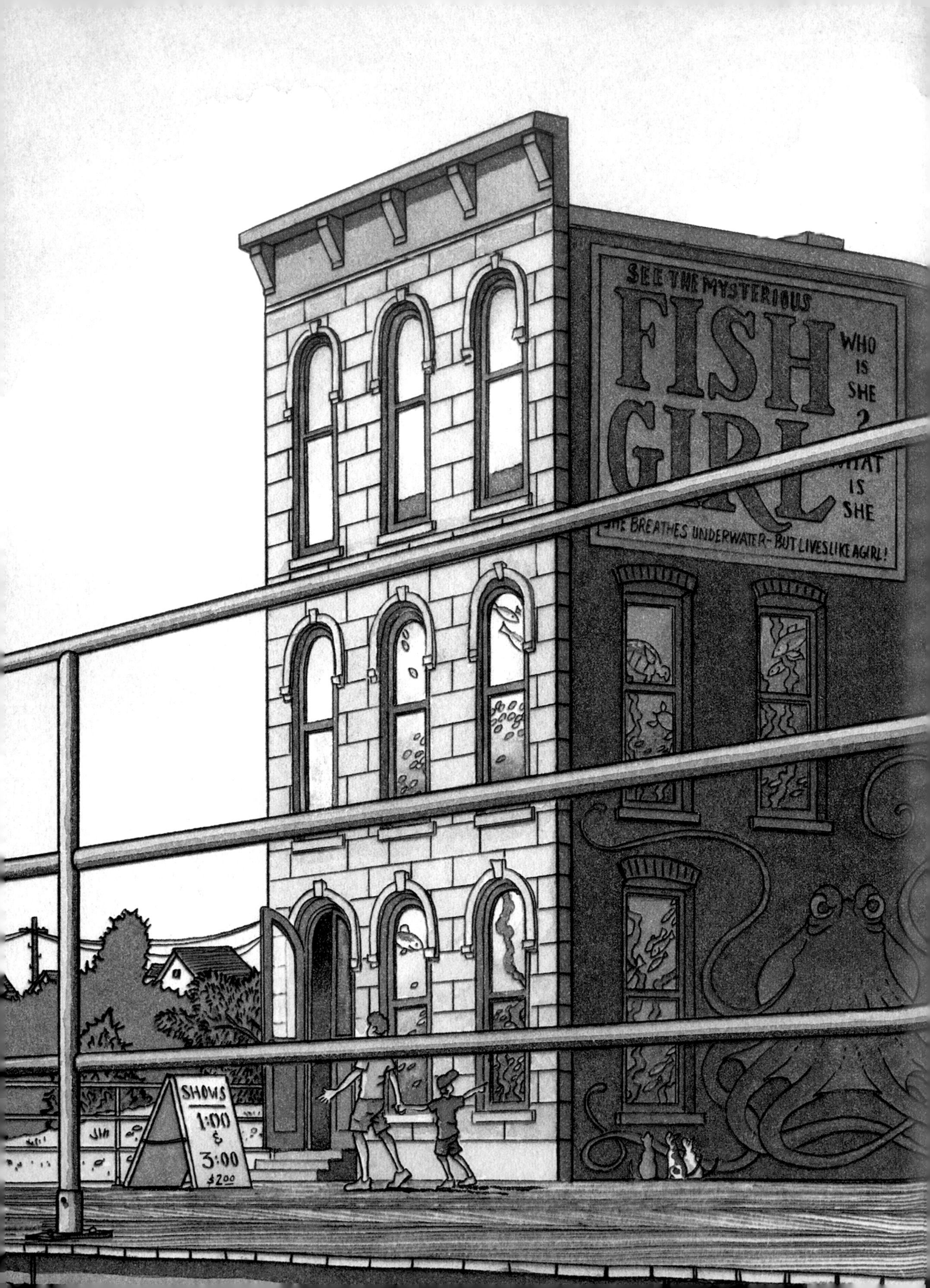
SEE THE MYSTERIOUS
FISH GIRL
WHO IS SHE
IS SHE
BREATHES UNDERWATER—BUT LIVES LIKE A GIRL!
SHOWS
1:00
&
3:00
$2.00

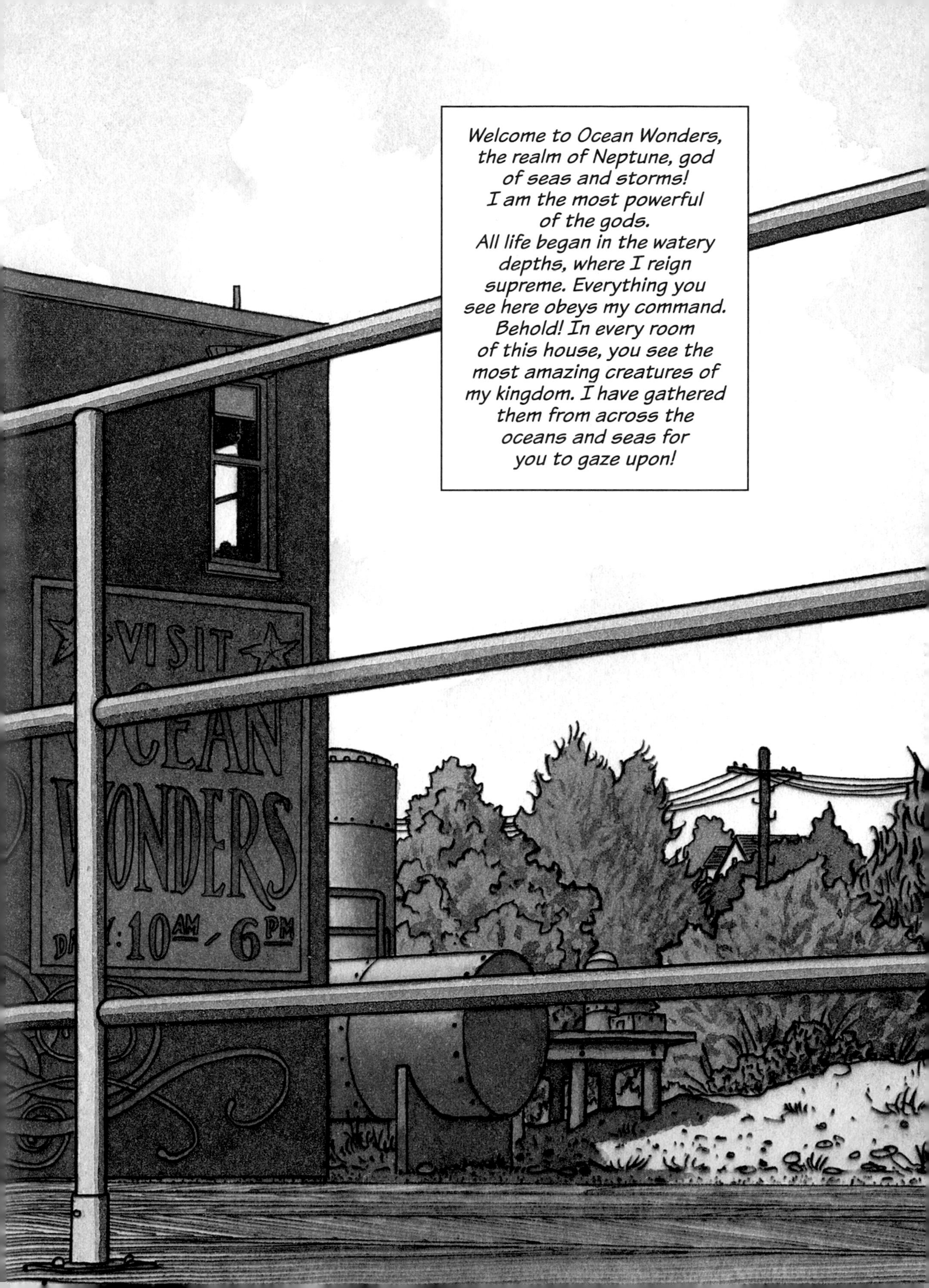
Welcome to Ocean Wonders, the realm of Neptune, god of seas and storms! I am the most powerful of the gods. All life began in the watery depths, where I reign supreme. Everything you see here obeys my command. Behold! In every room of this house, you see the most amazing creatures of my kingdom. I have gathered them from across the oceans and seas for you to gaze upon!
VISIT

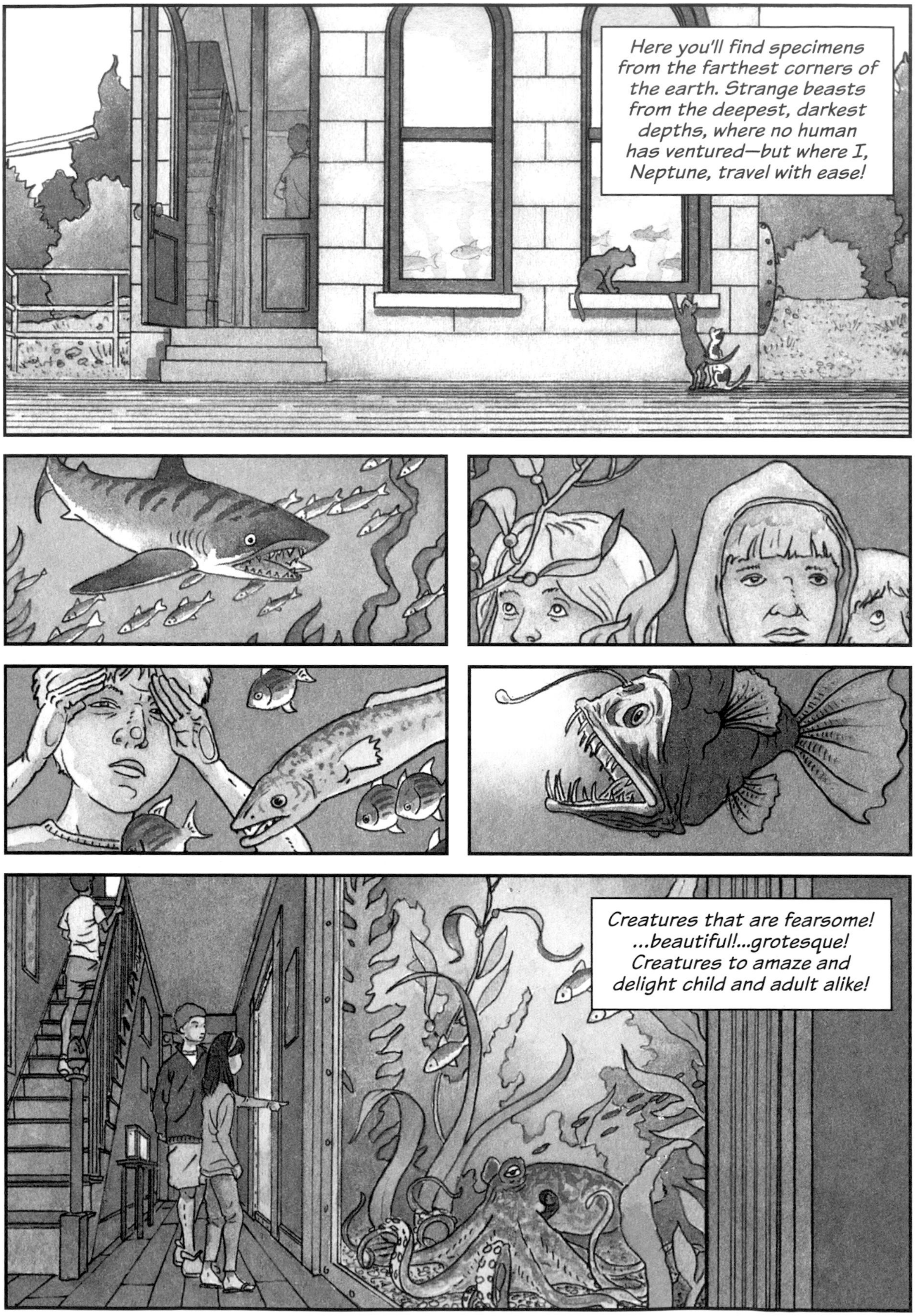
Here you'll find specimens from the farthest corners of the earth. Strange beasts from the deepest, darkest depths, where no human has ventured—but where I, Neptune, travel with ease!
Creatures that are fearsome! ...beautiful!...grotesque! Creatures to amaze and delight child and adult alike!

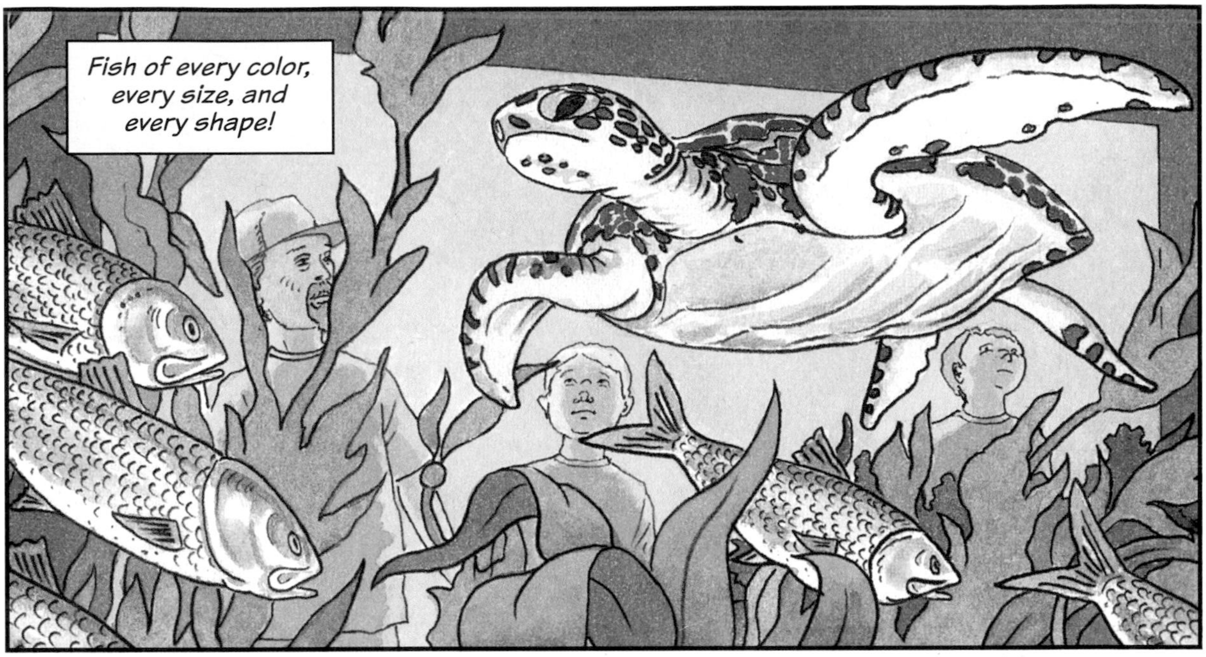
Fish of every color, every size, and every shape!

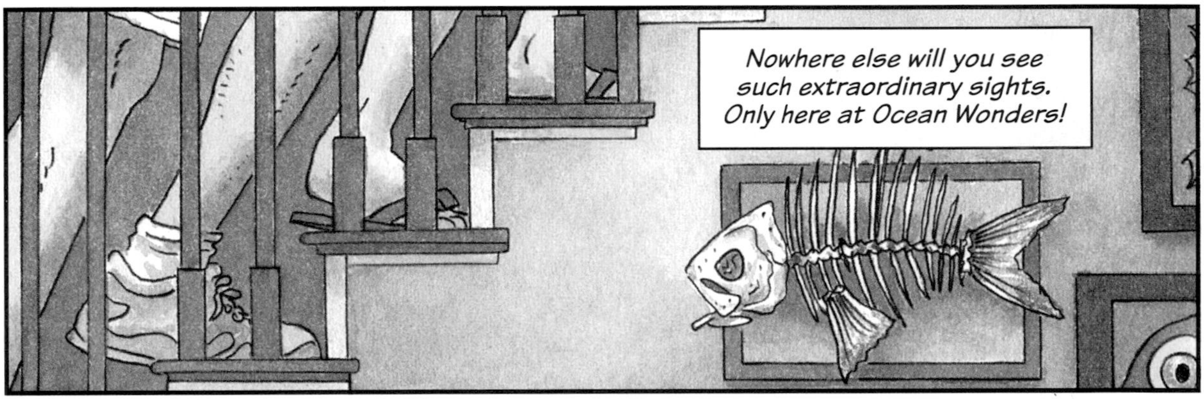
Nowhere else will you see such extraordinary sights. Only here at Ocean Wonders!

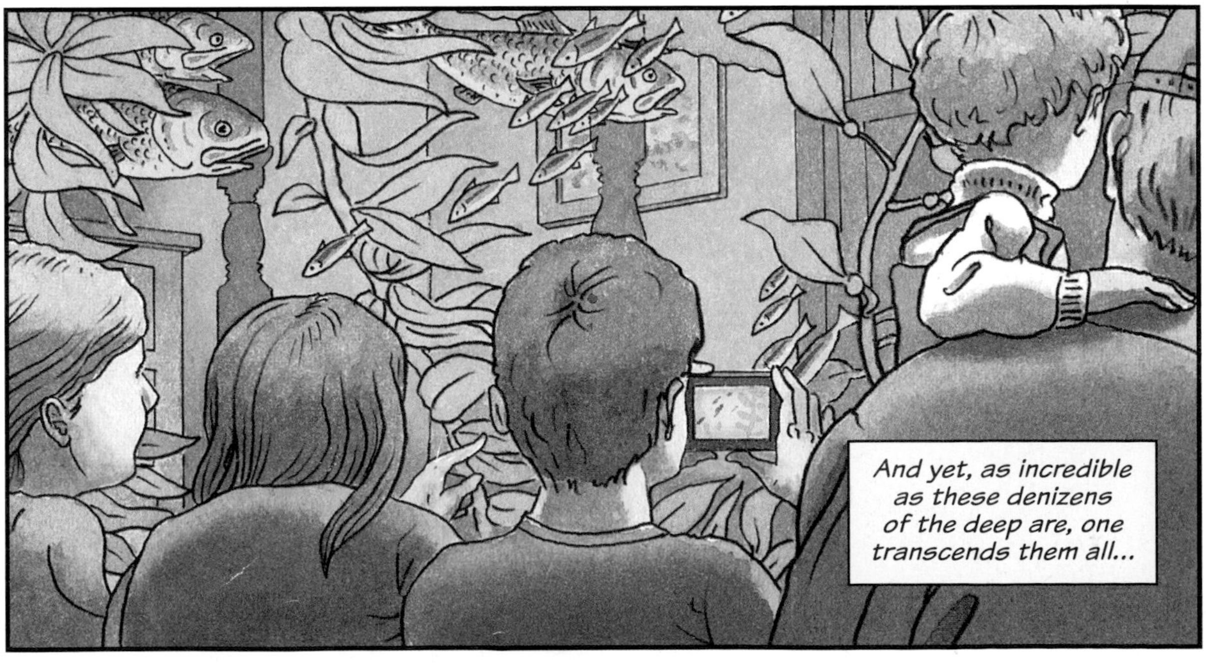
And yet, as incredible as these denizens of the deep are, one transcends them all...

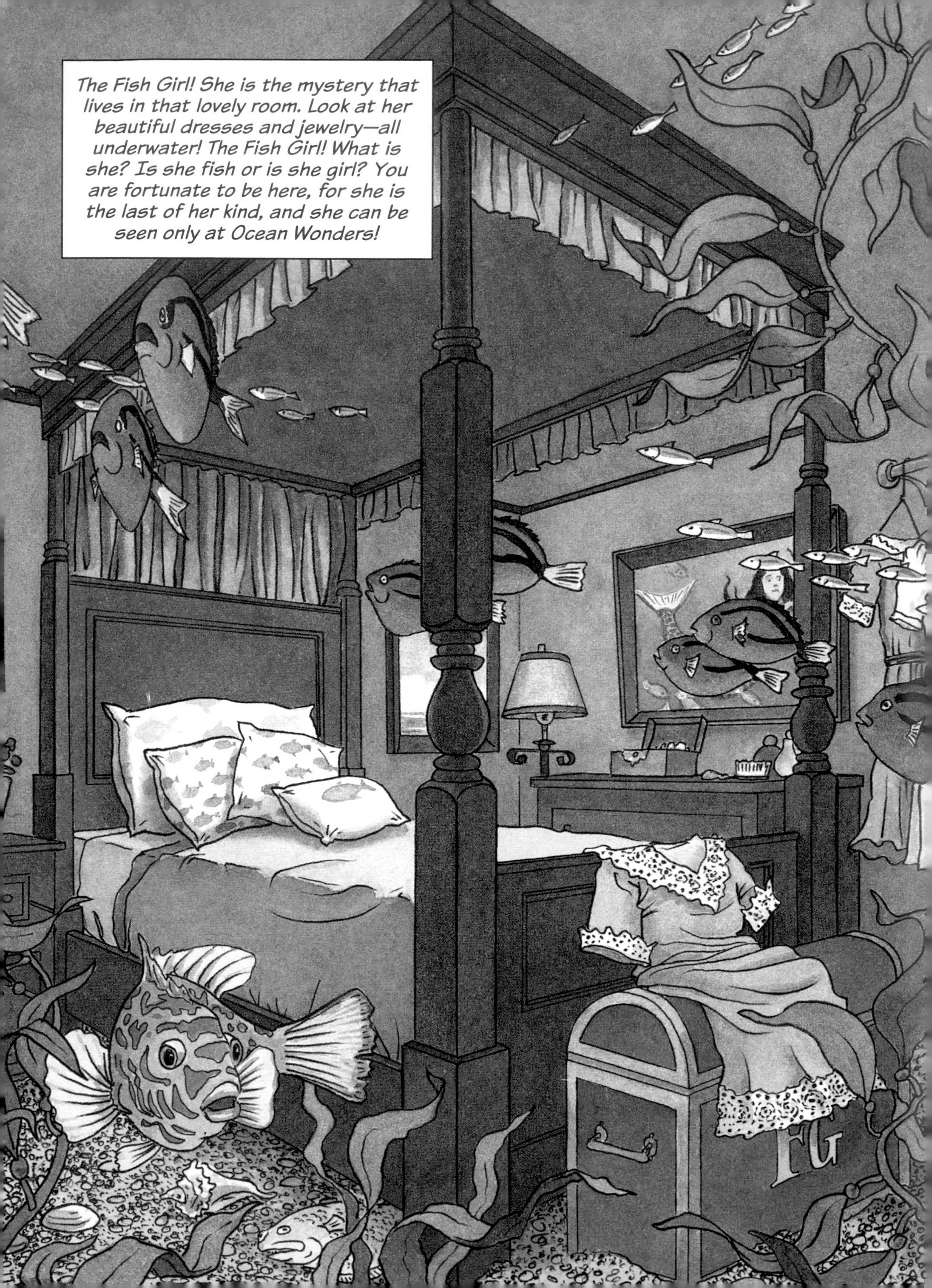
The Fish Girl! She is the mystery that lives in that lovely room. Look at her beautiful dresses and jewelry—all underwater! The Fish Girl! What is she? Is she fish or is she girl? You are fortunate to be here, for she is the last of her kind, and she can be seen only at Ocean Wonders!
FG

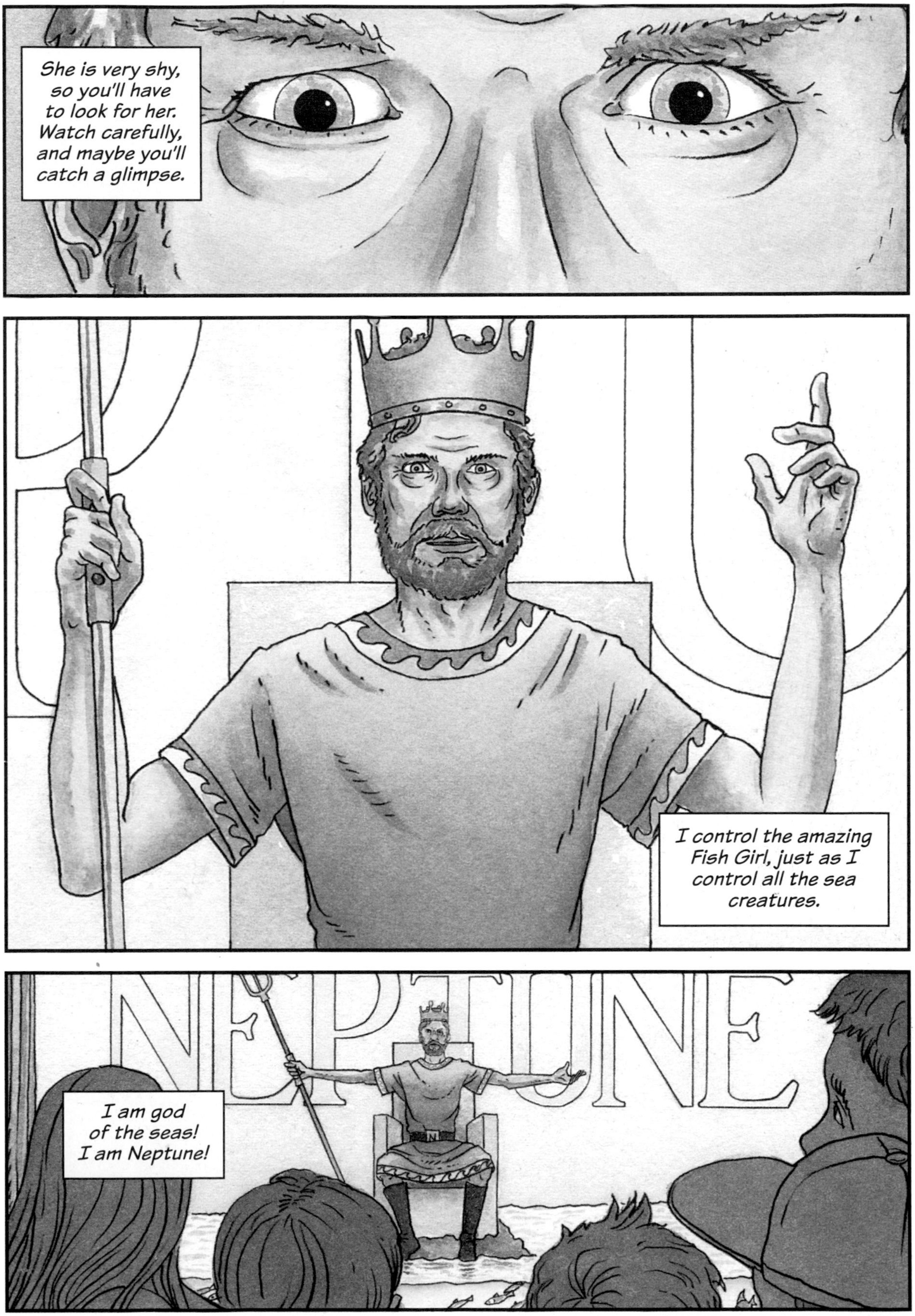
She is very shy, so you'll have to look for her. Watch carefully, and maybe you'll catch a glimpse.
I control the amazing Fish Girl, just as I control all the sea creatures.
NEPTUNE
I am god of the seas! I am Neptune!

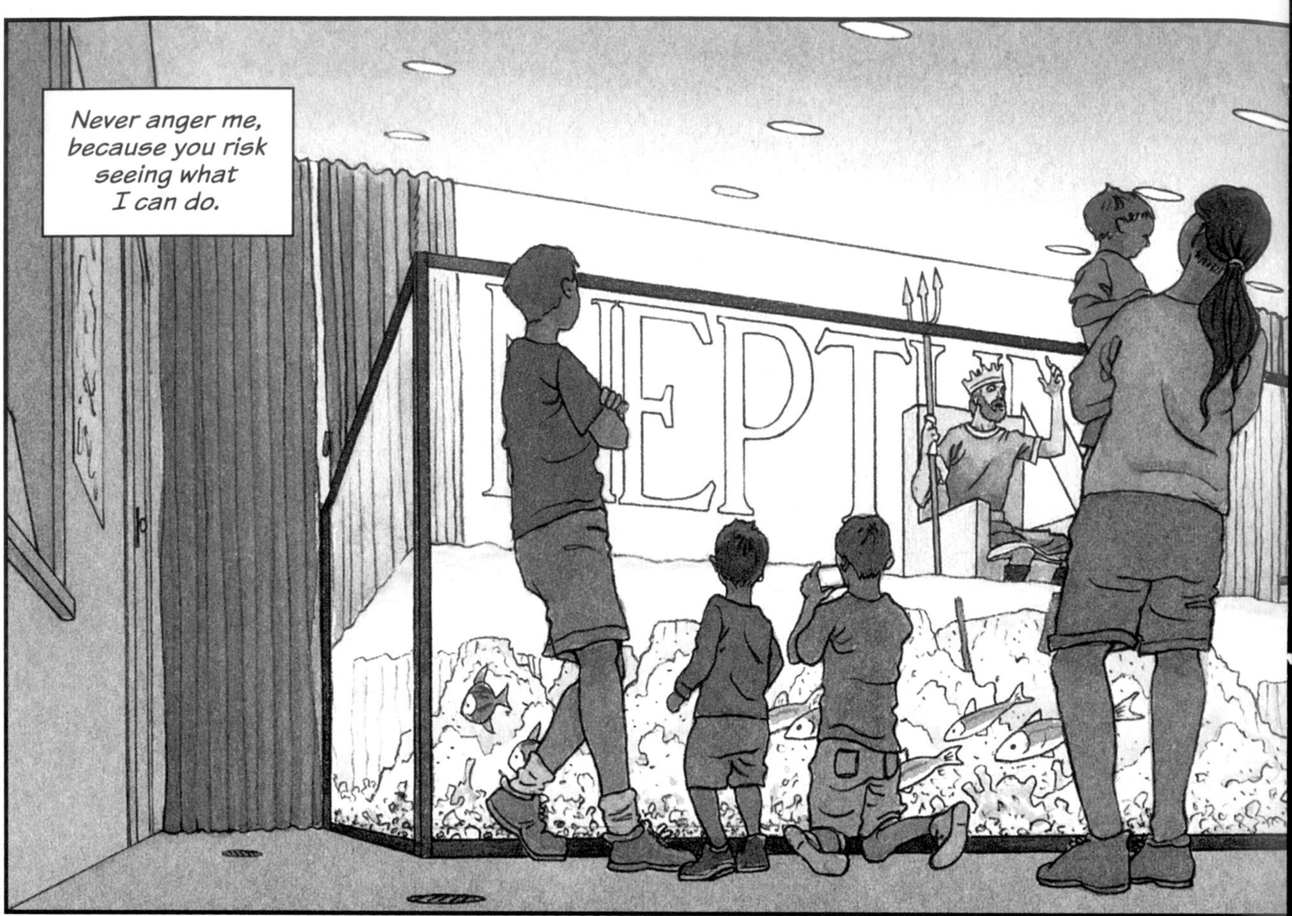
Never anger me, because you risk seeing what I can do.
NEPT

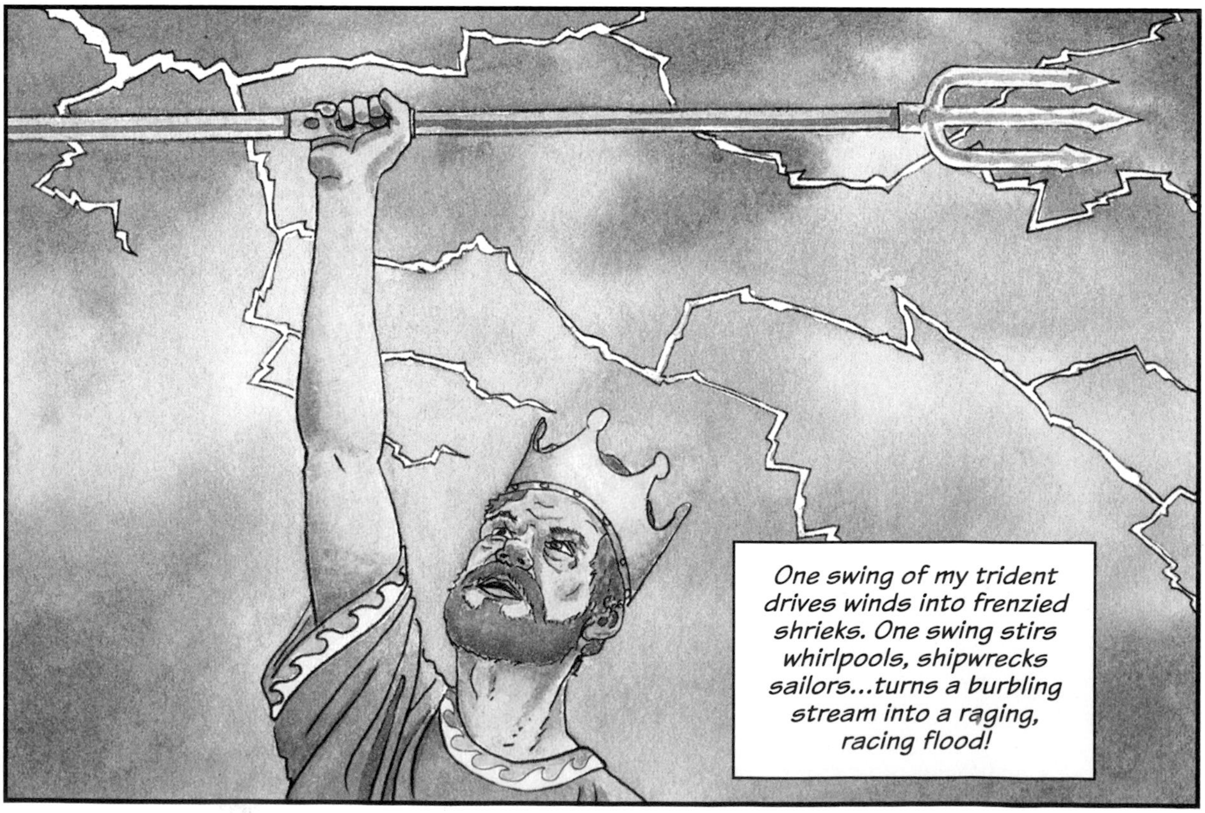
One swing of my trident drives winds into frenzied shrieks. One swing stirs whirlpools, shipwrecks sailors...turns a burbling stream into a raging, racing flood!

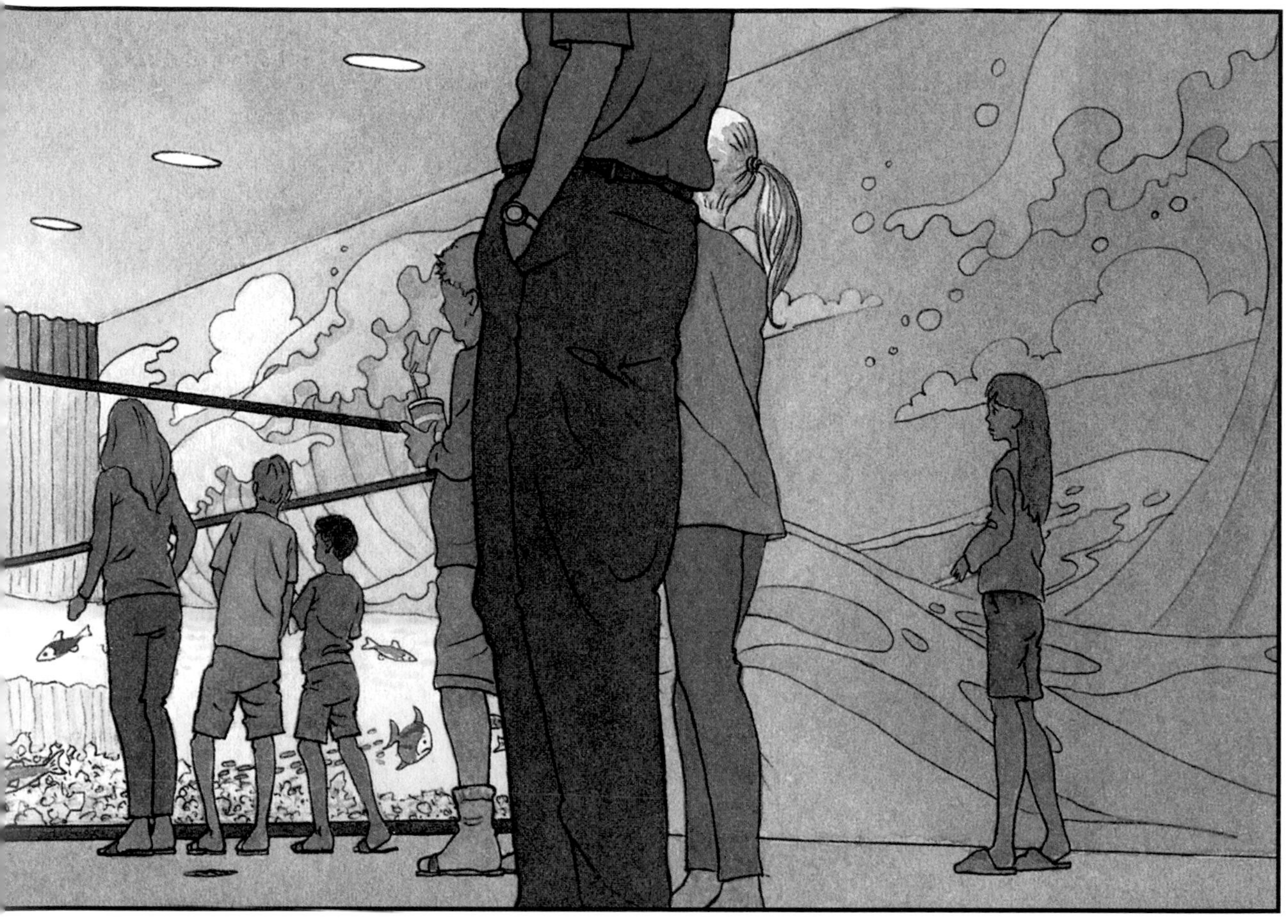

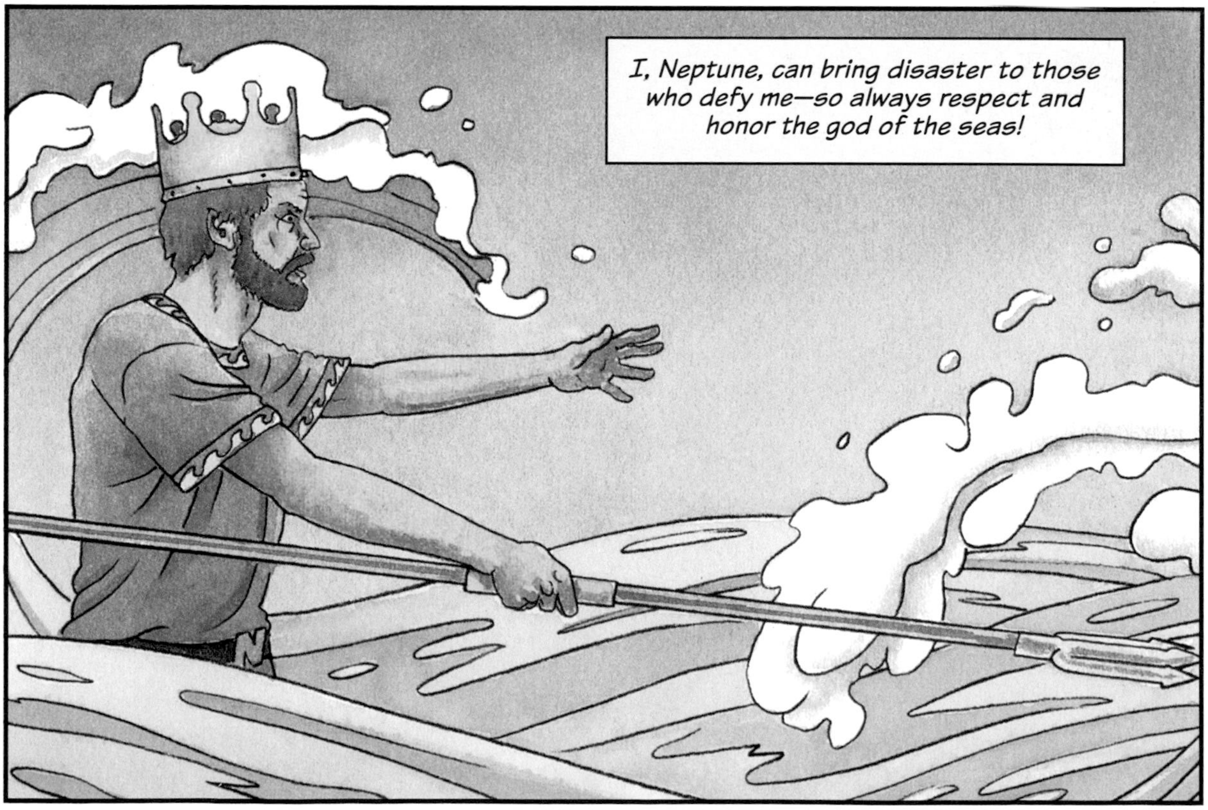
I, Neptune, can bring disaster to those who defy me—so always respect and honor the god of the seas!

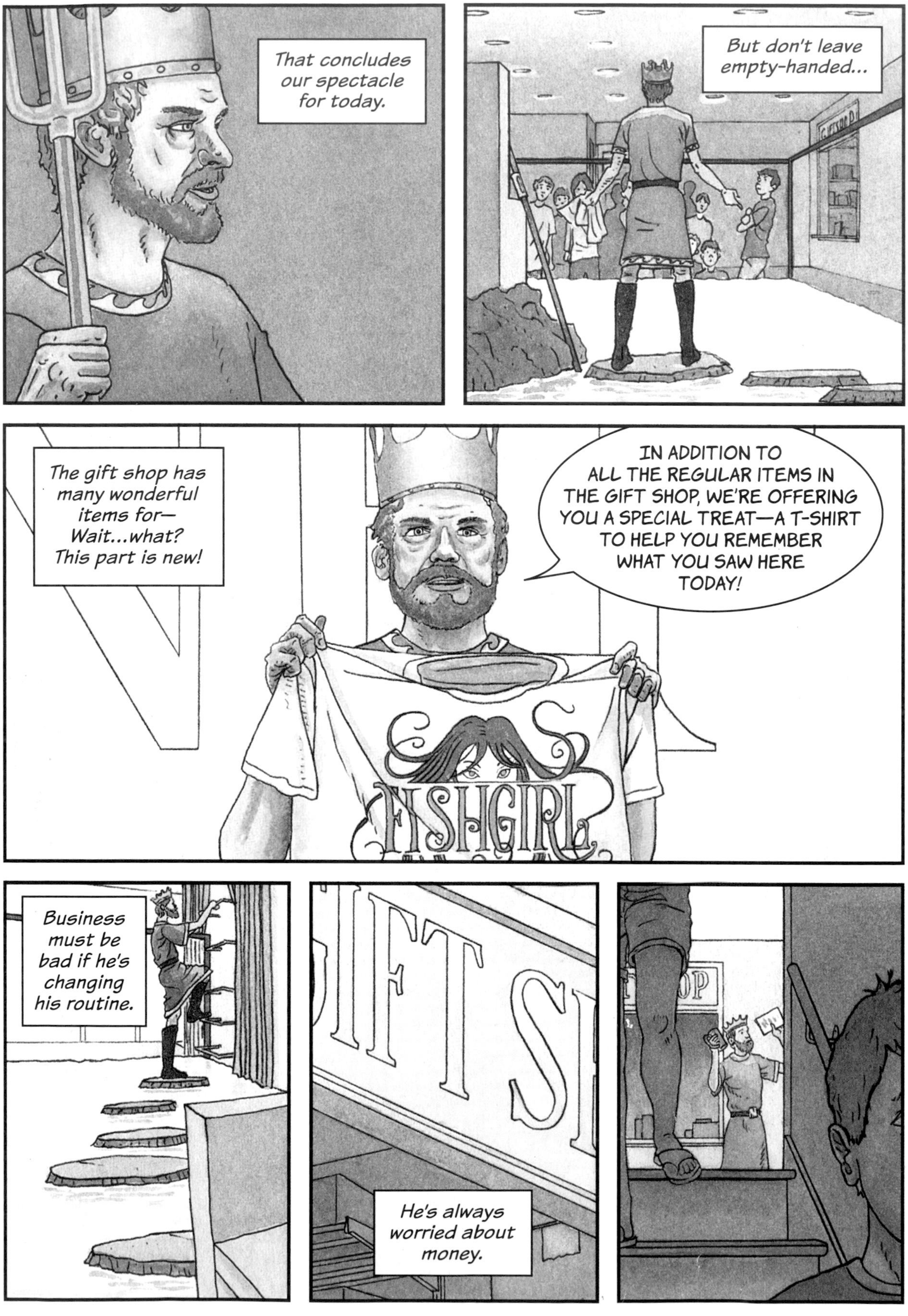

That concludes our spectacle for today.
But don't leave empty-handed...
The gift shop has many wonderful items for— Wait...what? This part is new!
IN ADDITION TO ALL THE REGULAR ITEMS IN THE GIFT SHOP, WE'RE OFFERING YOU A SPECIAL TREAT—A T-SHIRT TO HELP YOU REMEMBER WHAT YOU SAW HERE TODAY!
FISHGIRL
Business must be bad if he's changing his routine.
He's always worried about money.

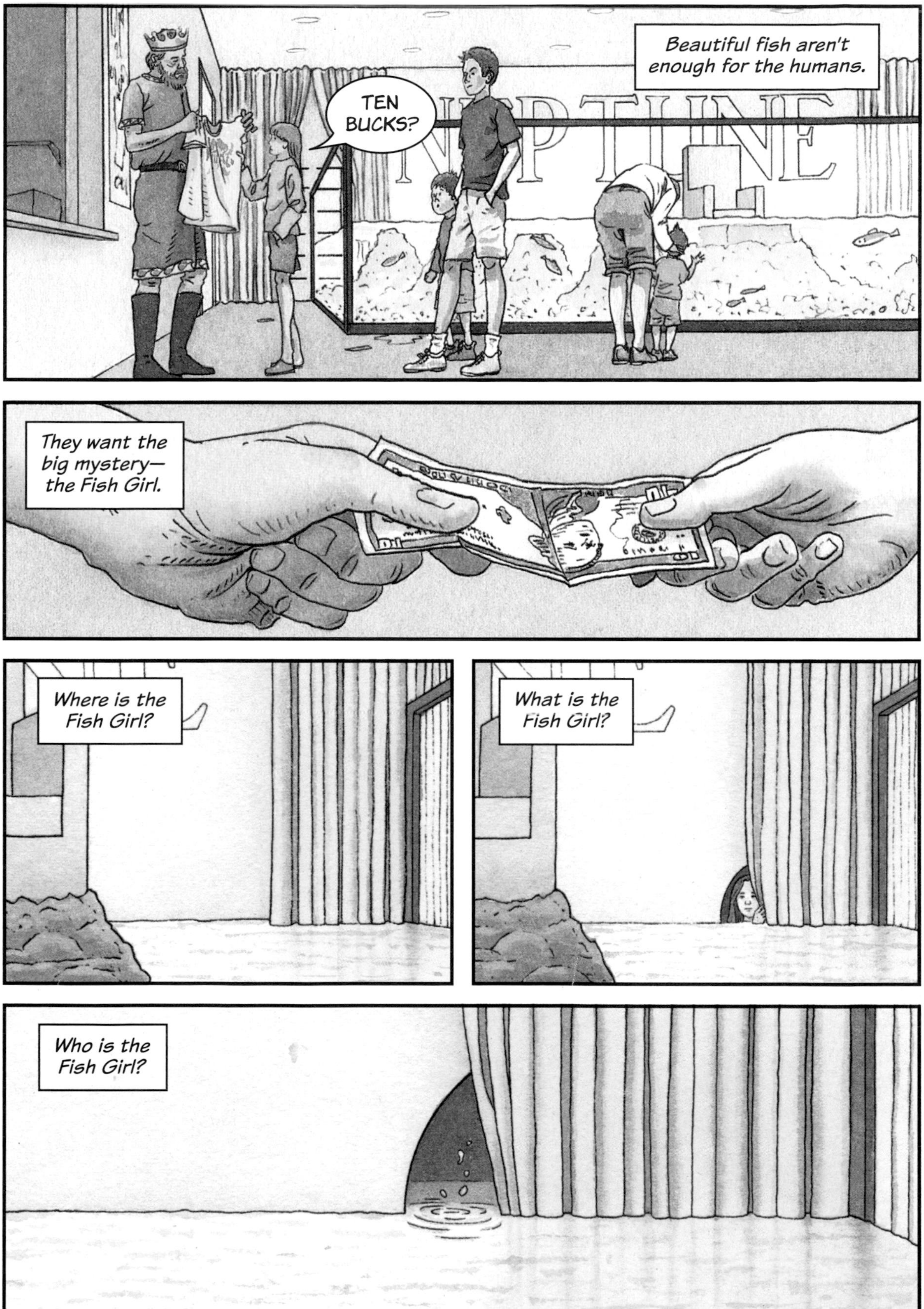
Beautiful fish aren't enough for the humans.
TEN BUCKS?
They want the big mystery—the Fish Girl.
Where is the Fish Girl?
What is the Fish Girl?
Who is the Fish Girl?

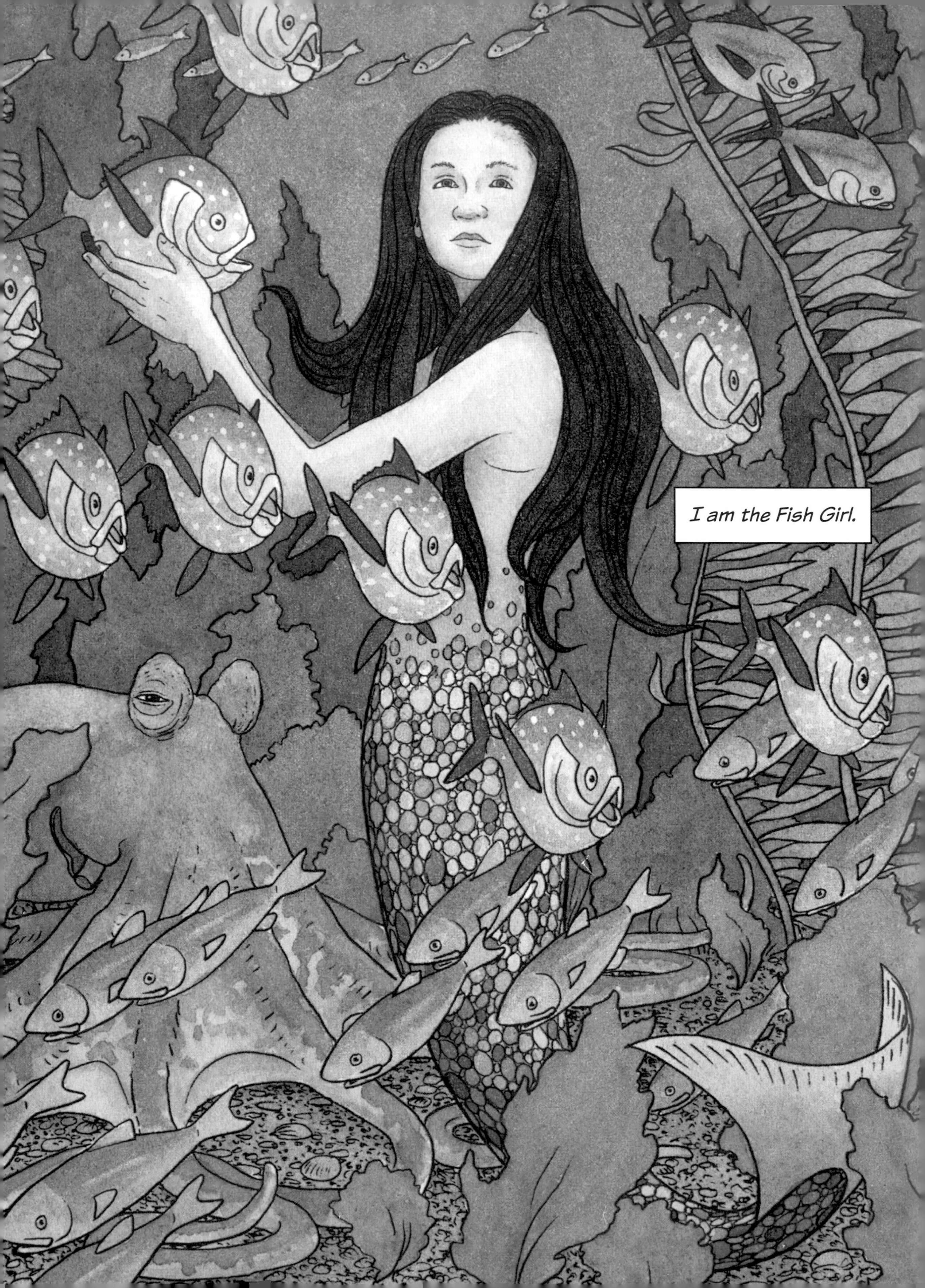
I am the Fish Girl.

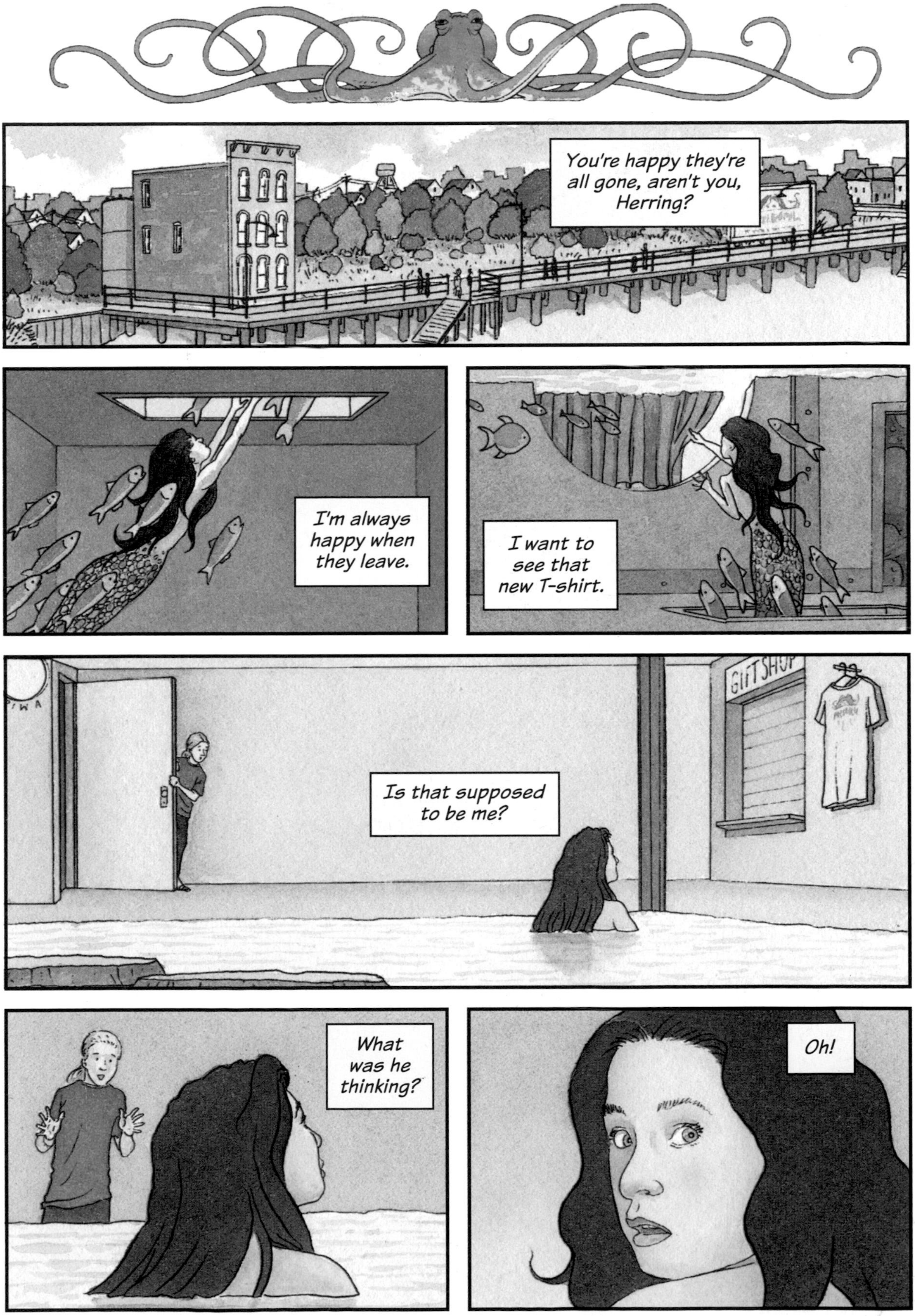
You're happy they're all gone, aren't you, Herring?
I'm always happy when they leave.
I want to see that new T-shirt.
GIFT SHOP
Is that supposed to be me?
What was he thinking?
Oh!

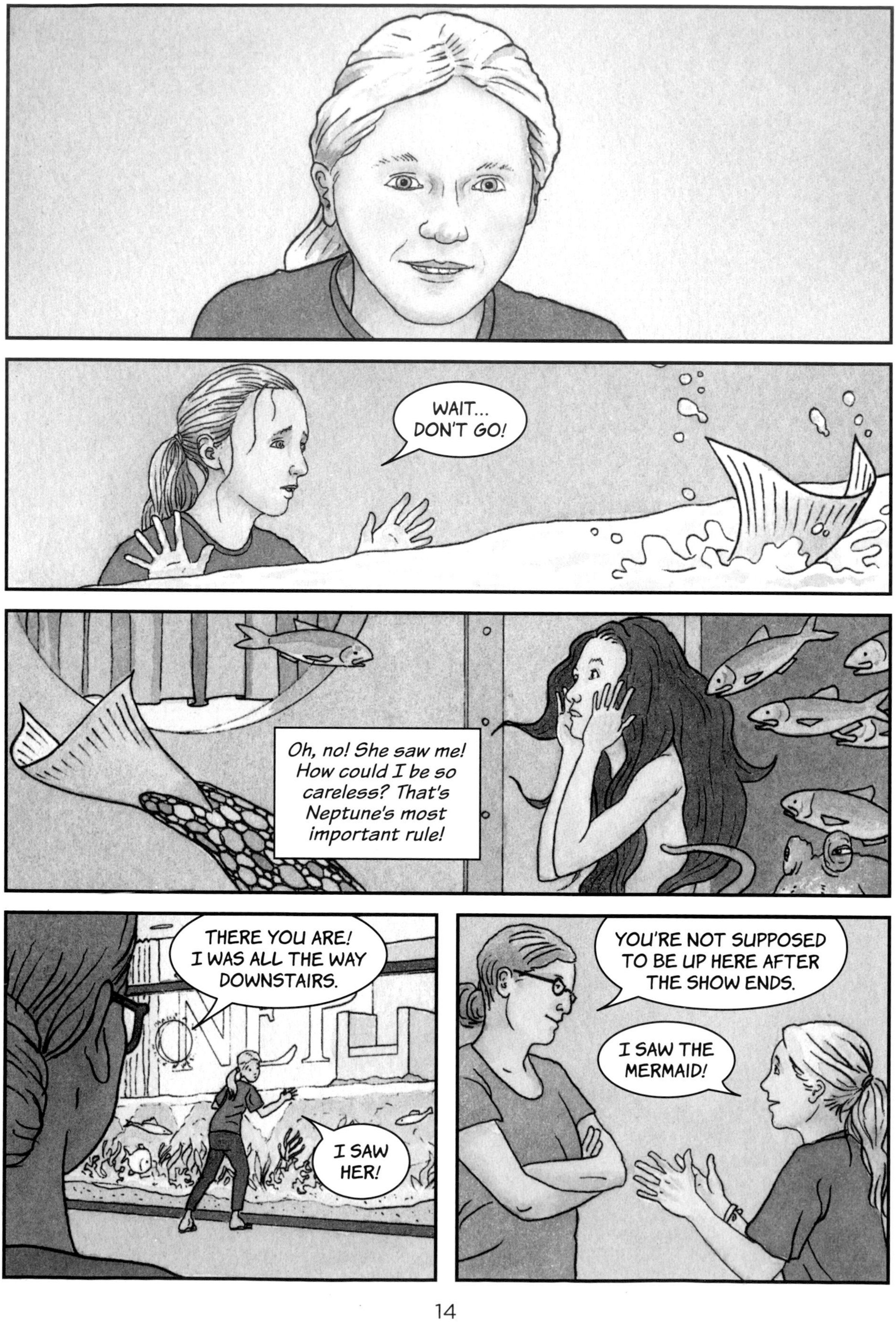

WAIT... DON'T GO!
Oh, no! She saw me! How could I be so careless? That's Neptune's most important rule!
THERE YOU ARE! I WAS ALL THE WAY DOWNSTAIRS.
I SAW HER!
YOU'RE NOT SUPPOSED TO BE UP HERE AFTER THE SHOW ENDS.
I SAW THE MERMAID!

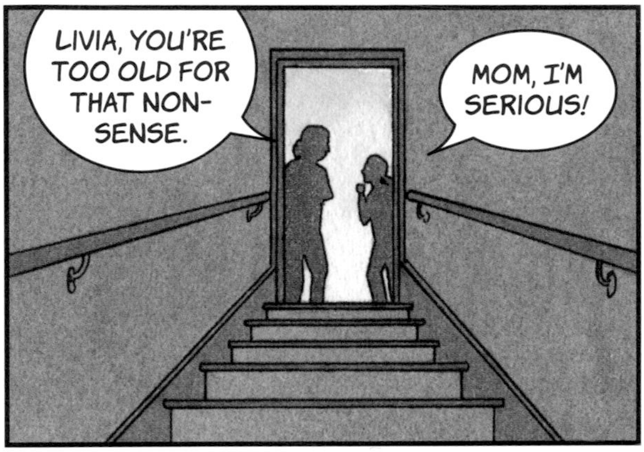
LIVIA, YOU'RE TOO OLD FOR THAT NON-SENSE.
MOM, I'M SERIOUS!

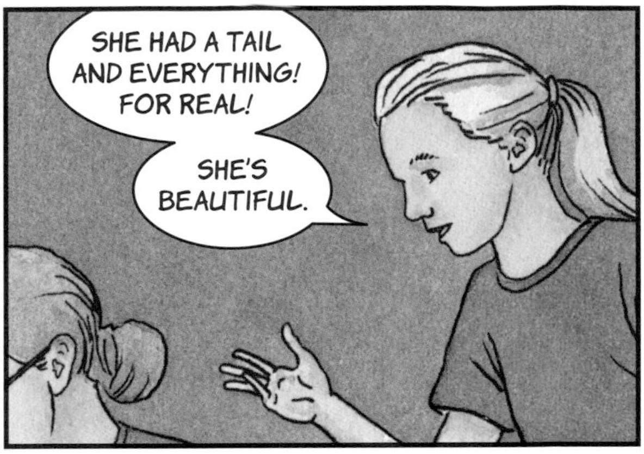
SHE HAD A TAIL AND EVERYTHING! FOR REAL!
SHE'S BEAUTIFUL.

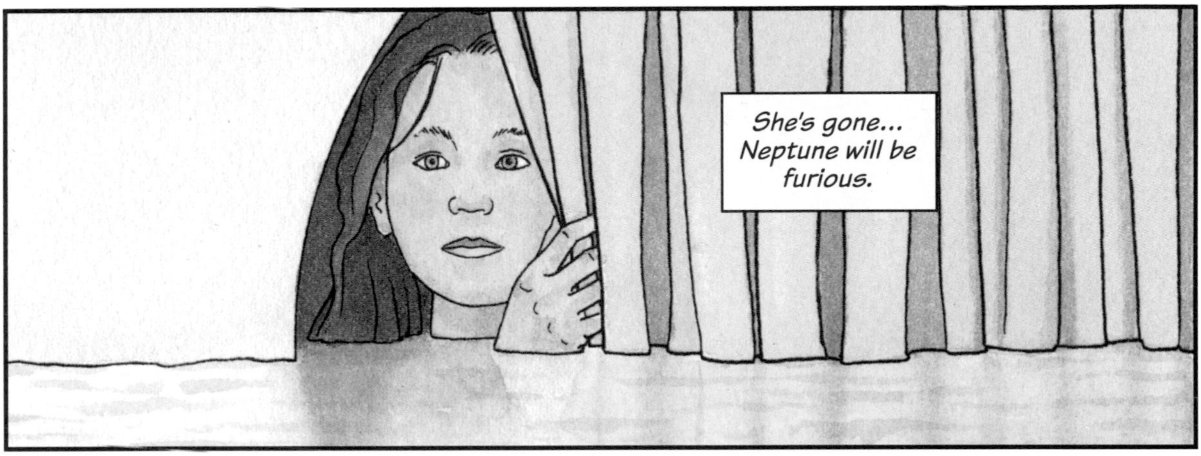
She's gone... Neptune will be furious.

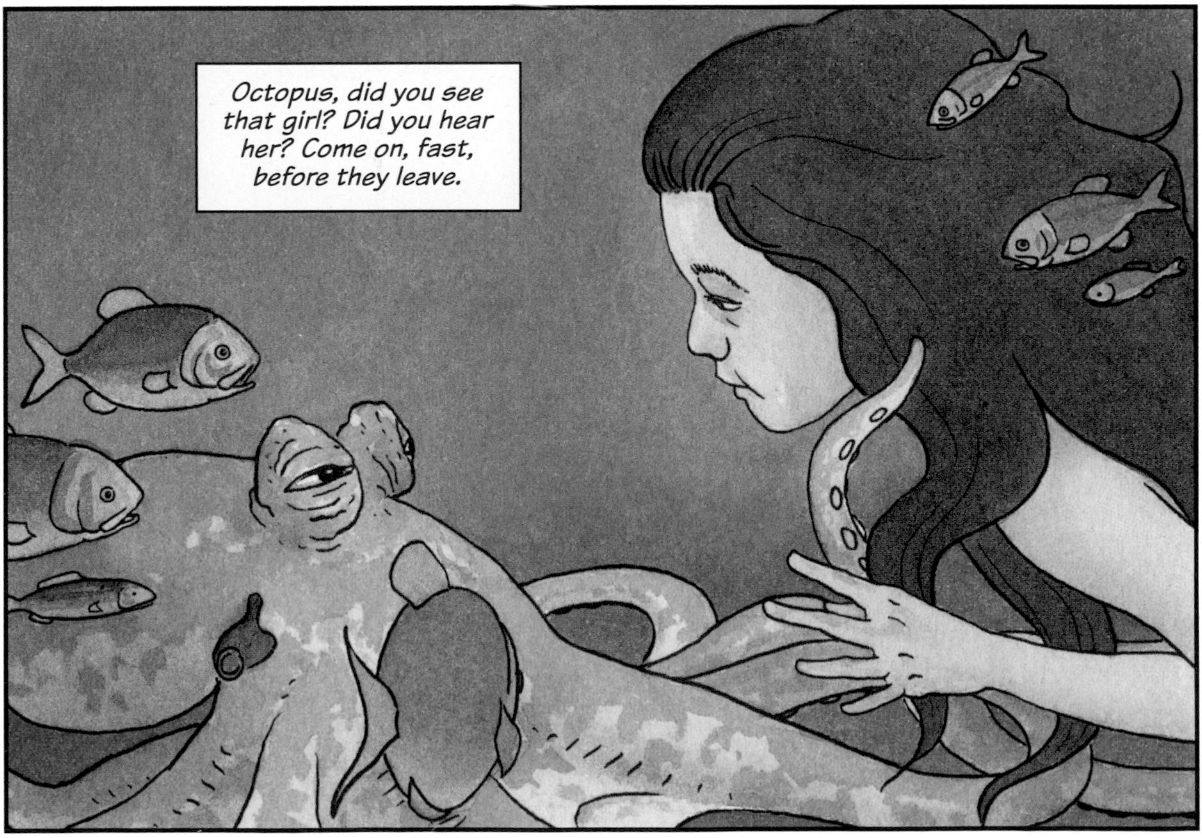
Octopus, did you see that girl? Did you hear her? Come on, fast, before they leave.

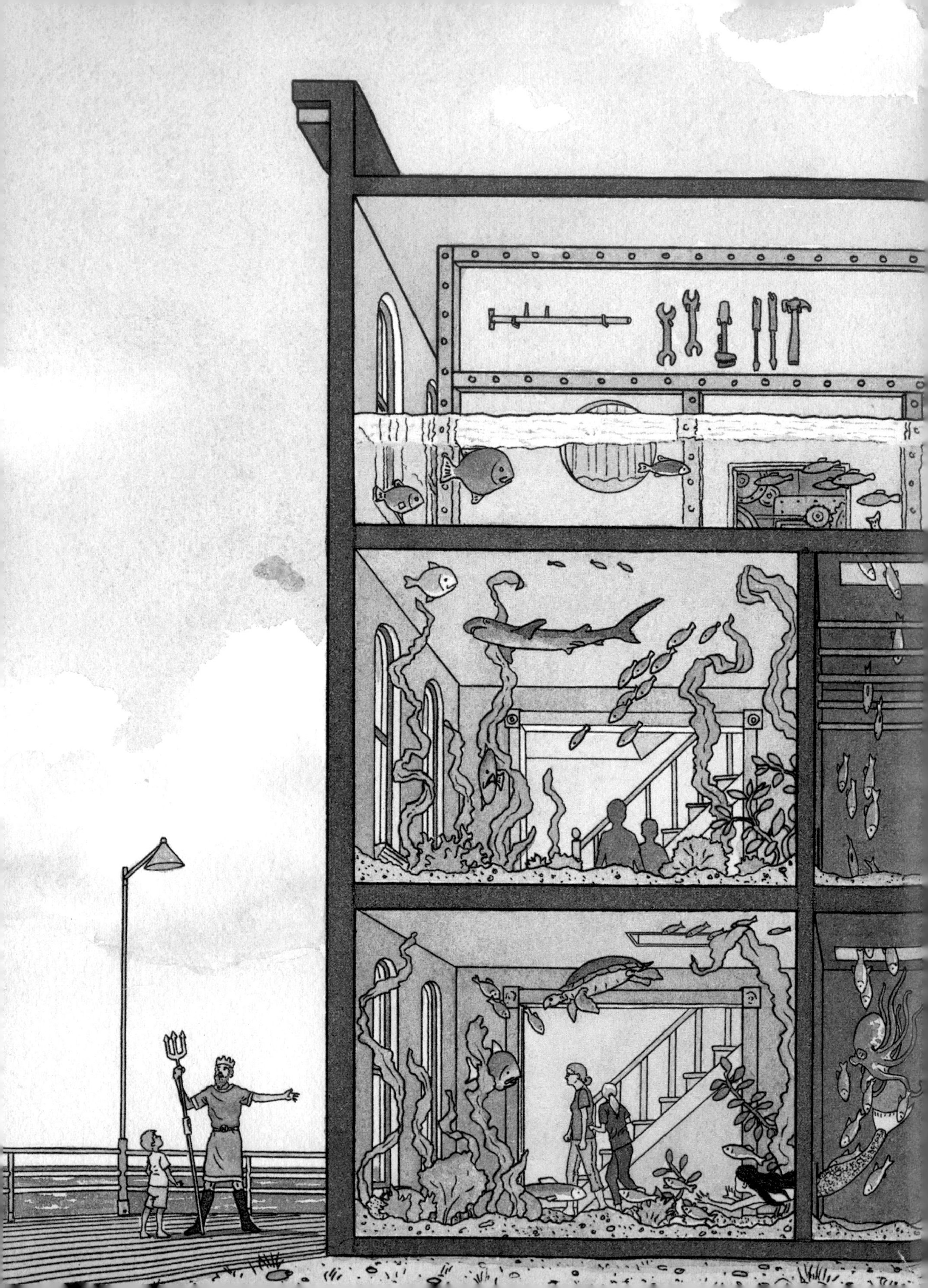

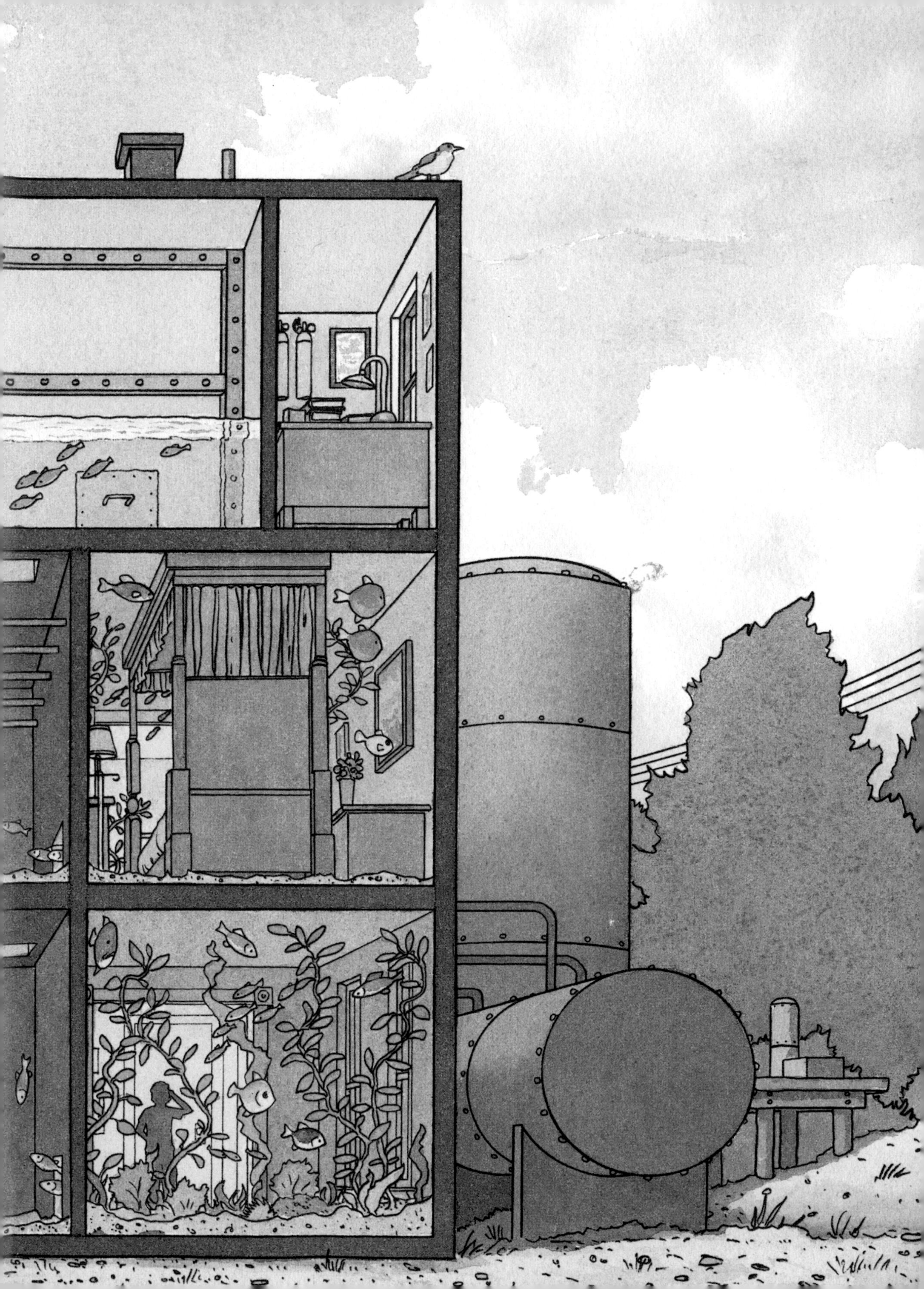

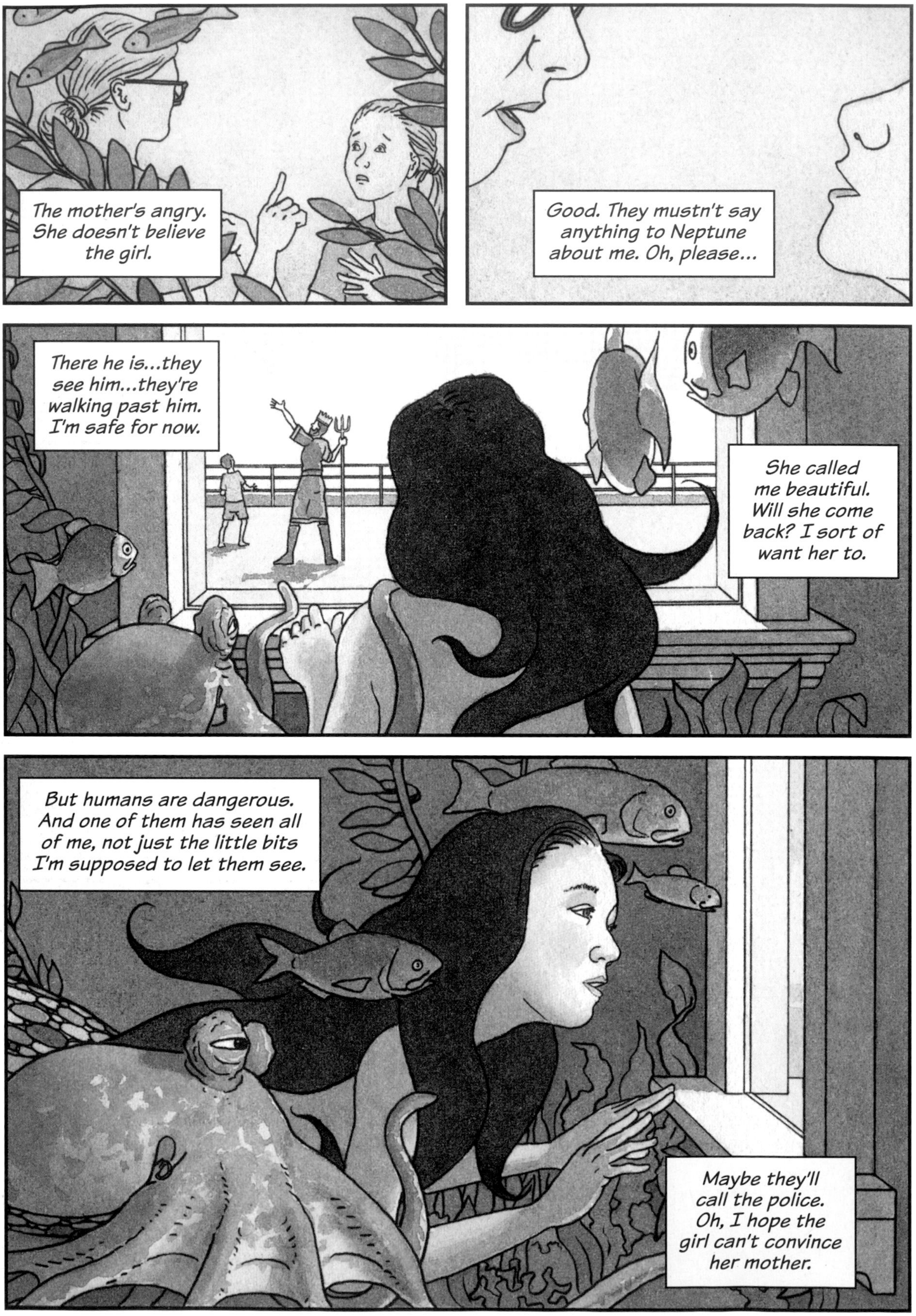
The mother's angry. She doesn't believe the girl.
Good. They mustn't say anything to Neptune about me. Oh, please...
There he is...they see him...they're walking past him. I'm safe for now.
She called me beautiful. Will she come back? I sort of want her to.
But humans are dangerous. And one of them has seen all of me, not just the little bits I'm supposed to let them see.
Maybe they'll call the police. Oh, I hope the girl can't convince her mother.

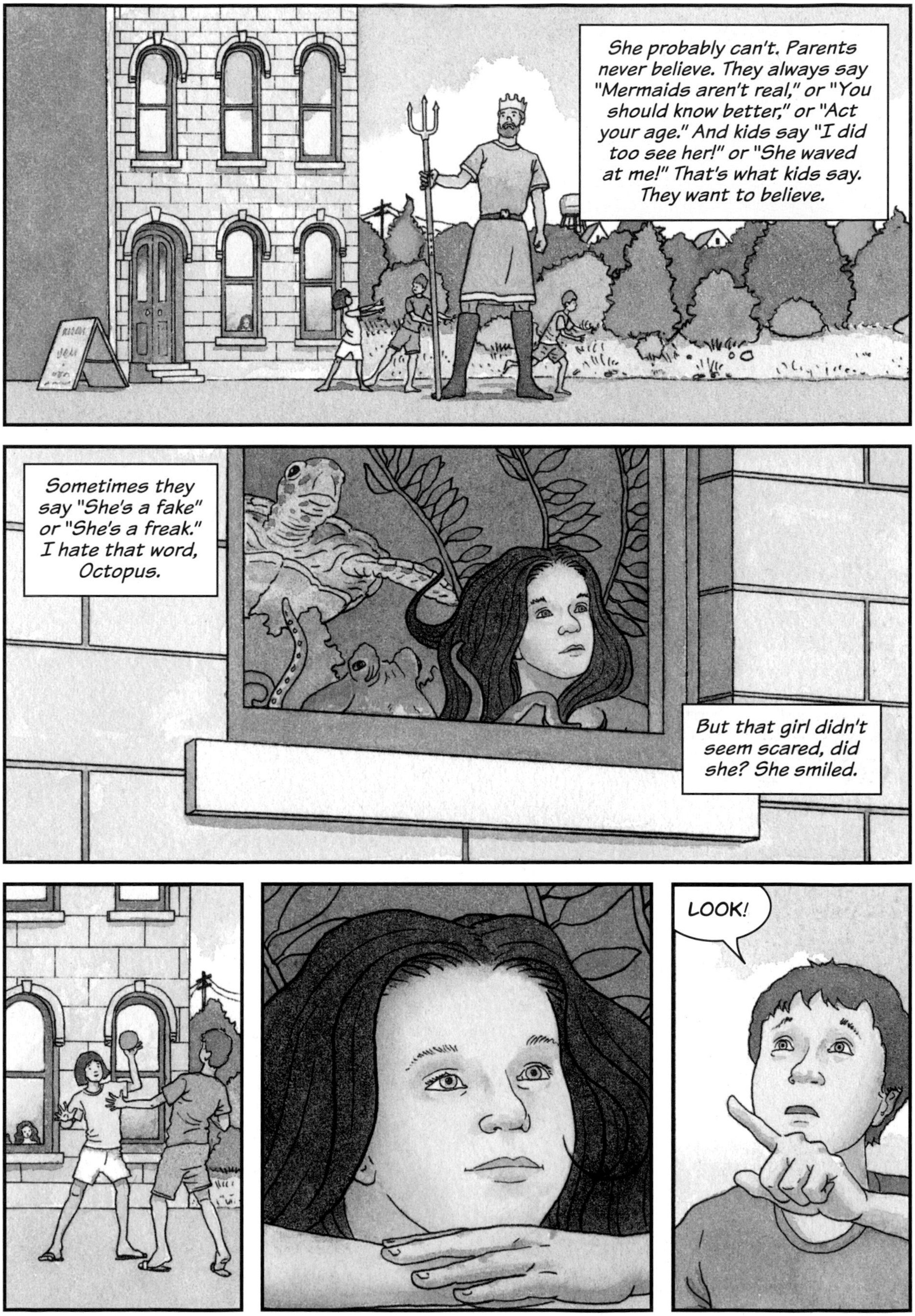
She probably can't. Parents never believe. They always say "Mermaids aren't real," or "You should know better," or "Act your age." And kids say "I did too see her!" or "She waved at me!" That's what kids say. They want to believe.
Sometimes they say "She's a fake" or "She's a freak." I hate that word, Octopus.
But that girl didn't seem scared, did she? She smiled.
LOOK!

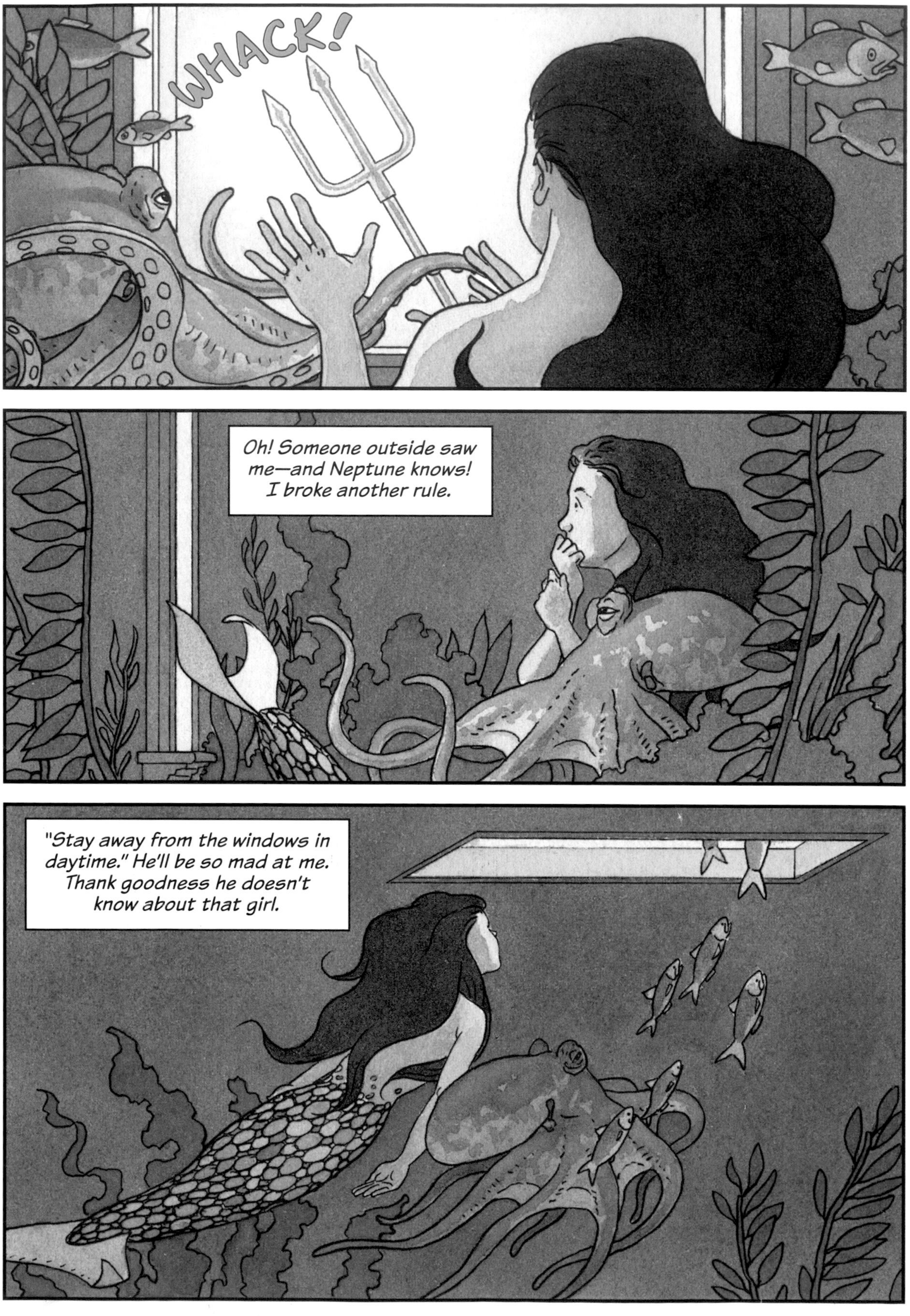
WHACK!
Oh! Someone outside saw me—and Neptune knows! I broke another rule.
"Stay away from the windows in daytime." He'll be so mad at me. Thank goodness he doesn't know about that girl.

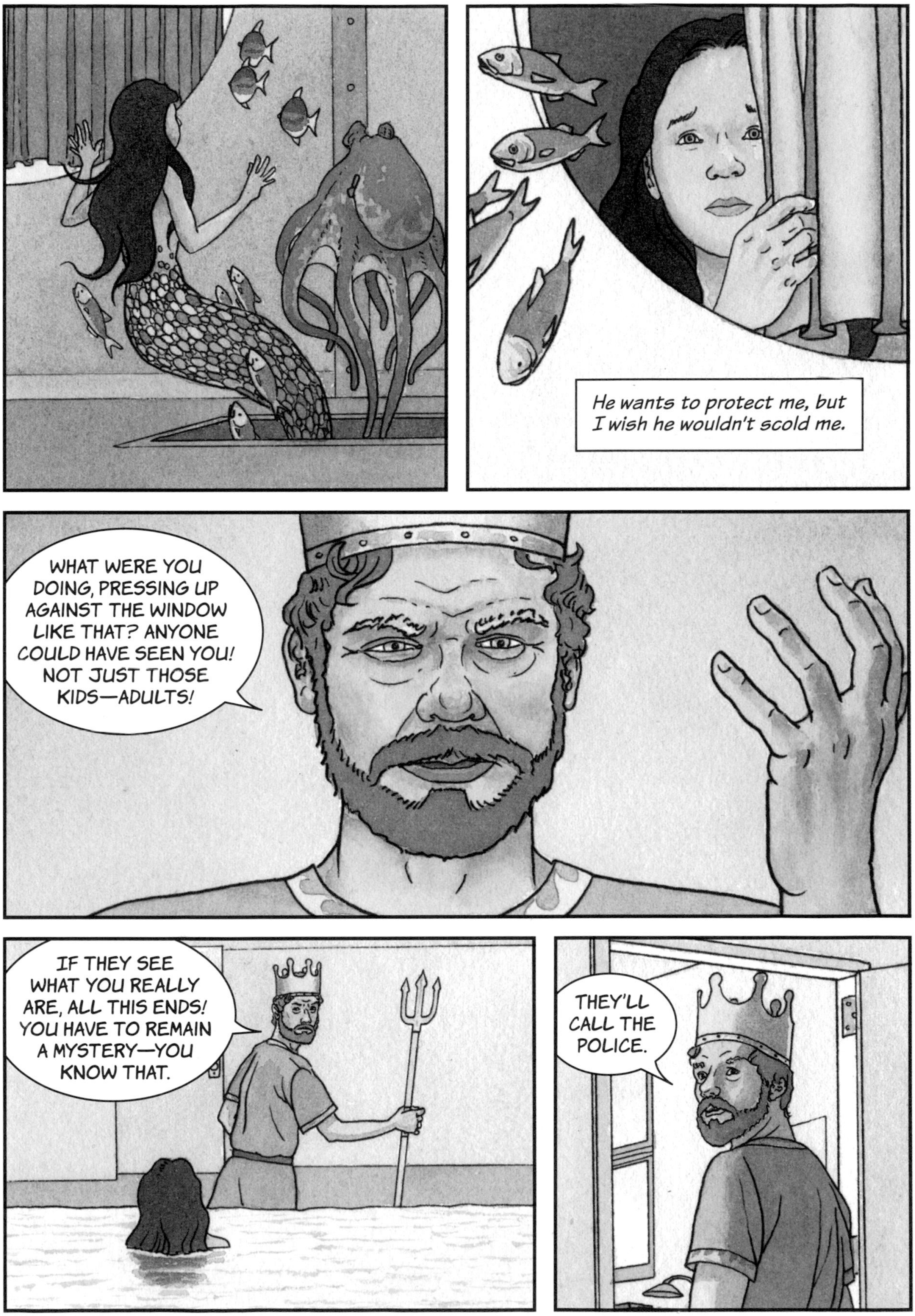
He wants to protect me, but I wish he wouldn't scold me.
WHAT WERE YOU DOING, PRESSING UP AGAINST THE WINDOW LIKE THAT? ANYONE COULD HAVE SEEN YOU! NOT JUST THOSE KIDS—ADULTS!
IF THEY SEE WHAT YOU REALLY ARE, ALL THIS ENDS! YOU HAVE TO REMAIN A MYSTERY—YOU KNOW THAT.
THEY'LL CALL THE POLICE.

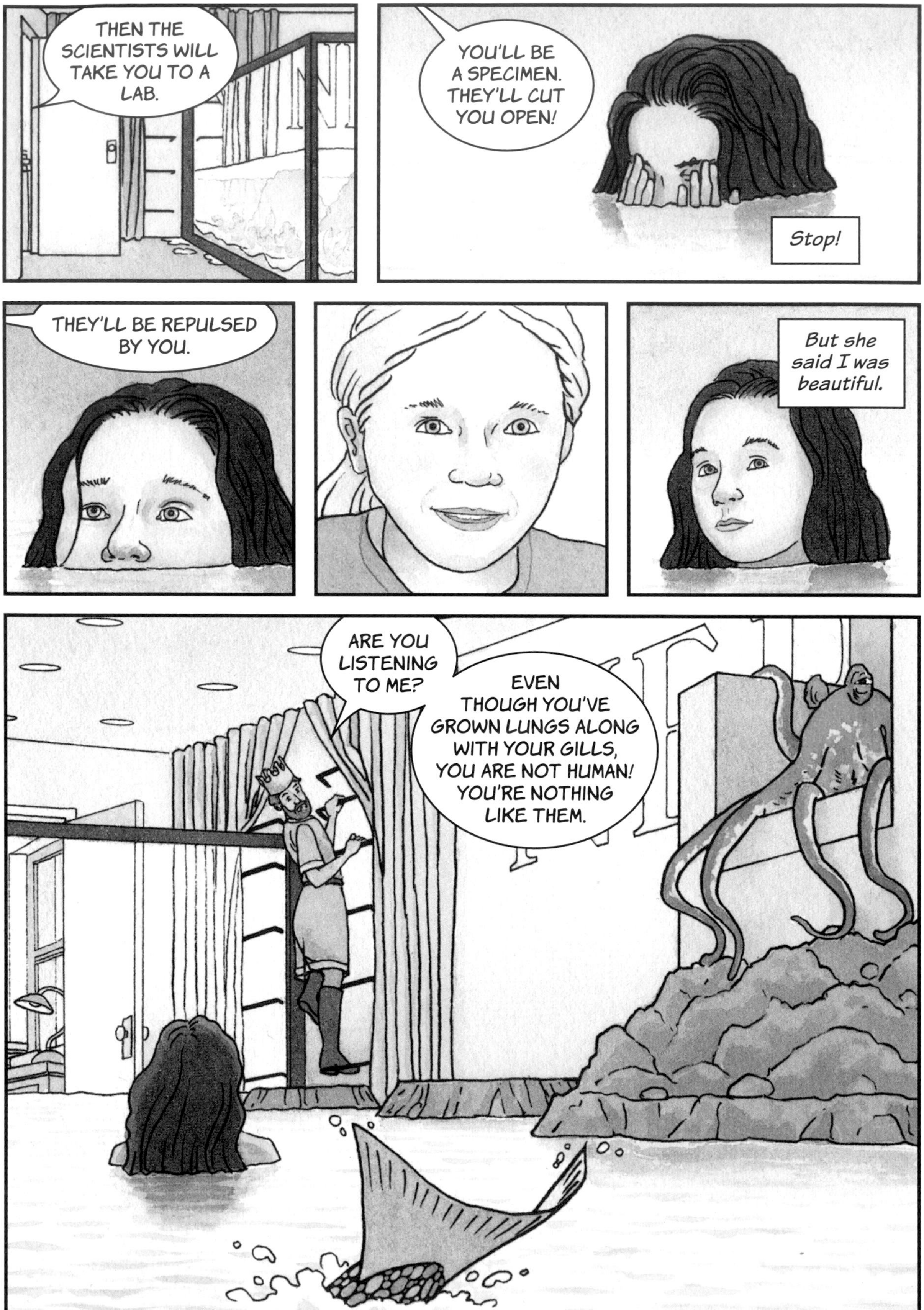
THEN THE SCIENTISTS WILL TAKE YOU TO A LAB.
YOU'LL BE A SPECIMEN. THEY'LL CUT YOU OPEN!
Stop!
THEY'LL BE REPULSED BY YOU.
But she said I was beautiful.
ARE YOU LISTENING TO ME?
EVEN THOUGH YOU'VE GROWN LUNGS ALONG WITH YOUR GILLS, YOU ARE NOT HUMAN! YOU'RE NOTHING LIKE THEM.

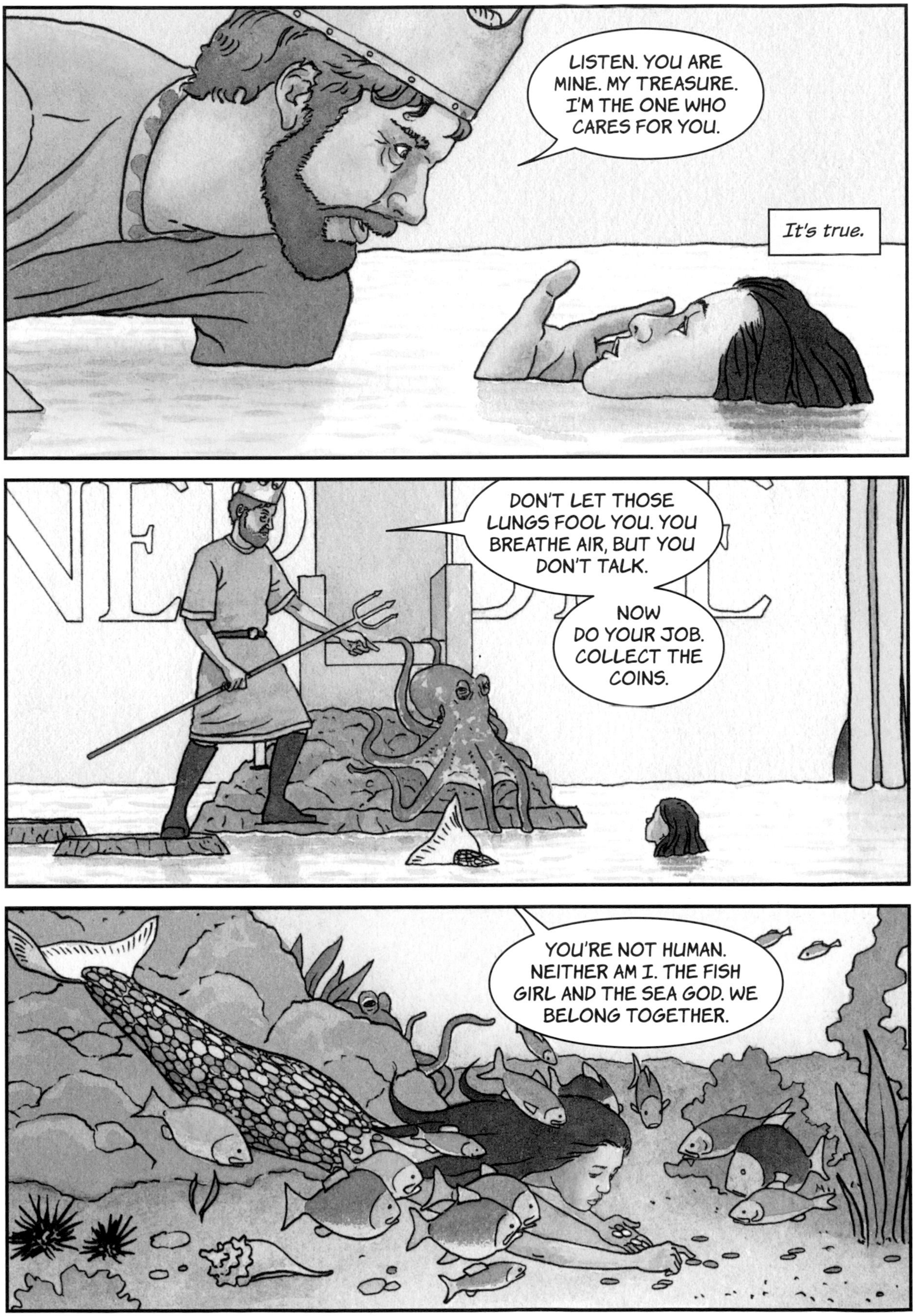
LISTEN. YOU ARE MINE. MY TREASURE. I'M THE ONE WHO CARES FOR YOU.
It's true.
DON'T LET THOSE LUNGS FOOL YOU. YOU BREATHE AIR, BUT YOU DON'T TALK.
NOW DO YOUR JOB. COLLECT THE COINS.
YOU'RE NOT HUMAN. NEITHER AM I. THE FISH GIRL AND THE SEA GOD. WE BELONG TOGETHER.

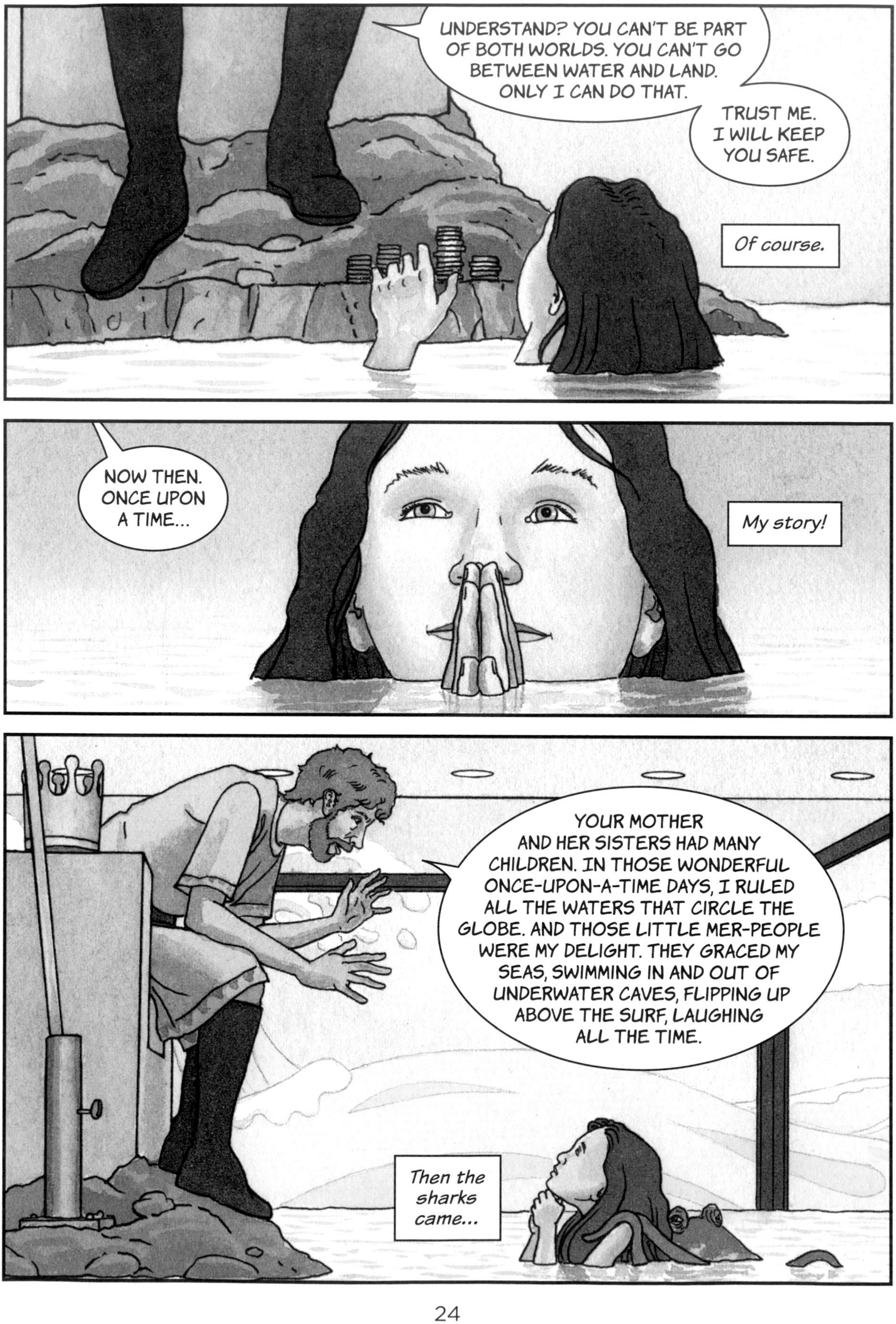
UNDERSTAND? YOU CAN'T BE PART OF BOTH WORLDS. YOU CAN'T GO BETWEEN WATER AND LAND. ONLY I CAN DO THAT.
TRUST ME. I WILL KEEP YOU SAFE.
Of course.
NOW THEN. ONCE UPON A TIME...
My story!
YOUR MOTHER AND HER SISTERS HAD MANY CHILDREN. IN THOSE WONDERFUL ONCE-UPON-A-TIME DAYS, I RULED ALL THE WATERS THAT CIRCLE THE GLOBE. AND THOSE LITTLE MER-PEOPLE WERE MY DELIGHT. THEY GRACED MY SEAS, SWIMMING IN AND OUT OF UNDERWATER CAVES, FLIPPING UP ABOVE THE SURF, LAUGHING ALL THE TIME.
Then the sharks came...

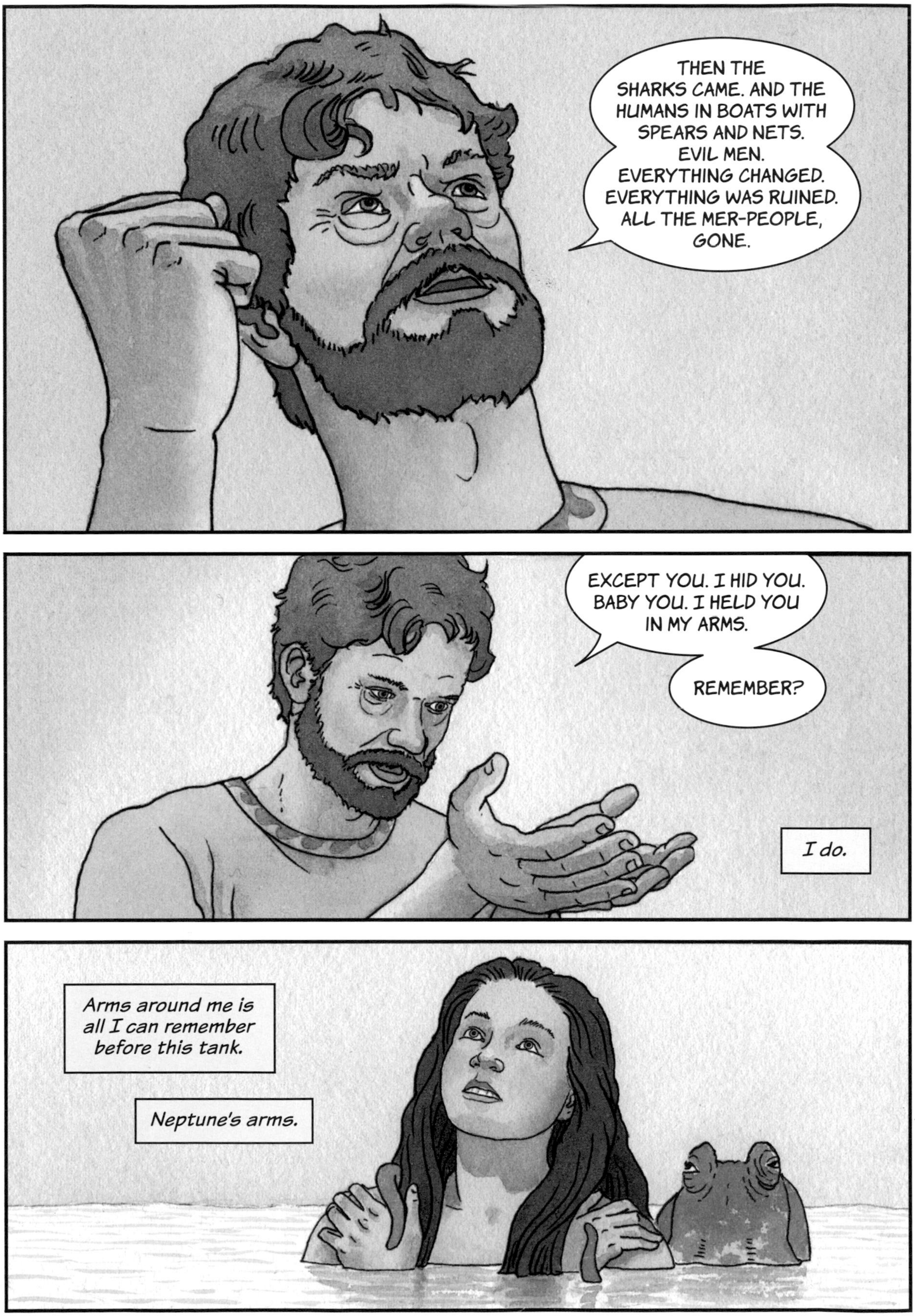
THEN THE SHARKS CAME. AND THE HUMANS IN BOATS WITH SPEARS AND NETS. EVIL MEN. EVERYTHING CHANGED. EVERYTHING WAS RUINED. ALL THE MER-PEOPLE, GONE.
EXCEPT YOU. I HID YOU. BABY YOU. I HELD YOU IN MY ARMS.
REMEMBER?
I do.
Arms around me is all I can remember before this tank.
Neptune's arms.

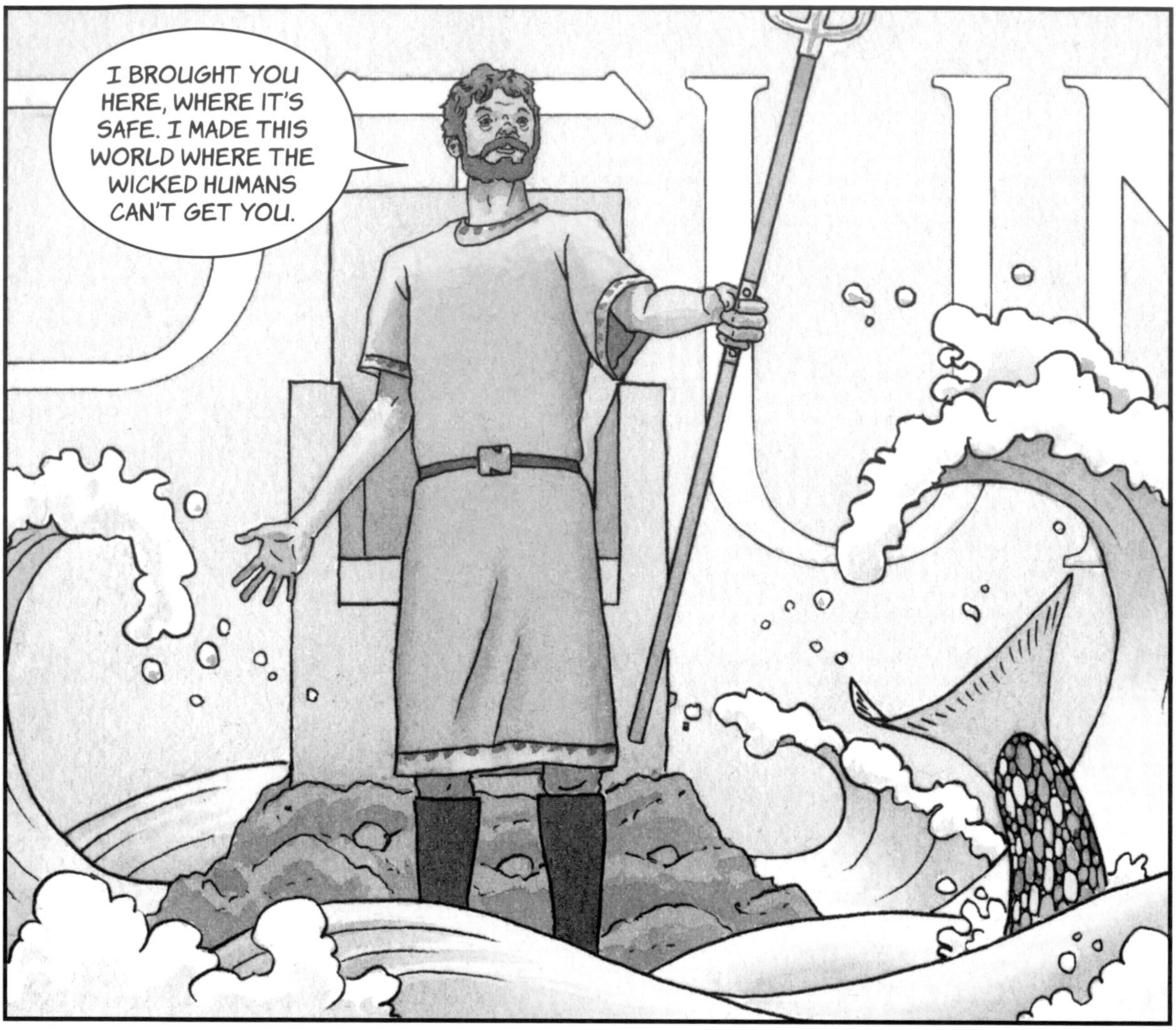
I BROUGHT YOU HERE, WHERE IT'S SAFE. I MADE THIS WORLD WHERE THE WICKED HUMANS CAN'T GET YOU.

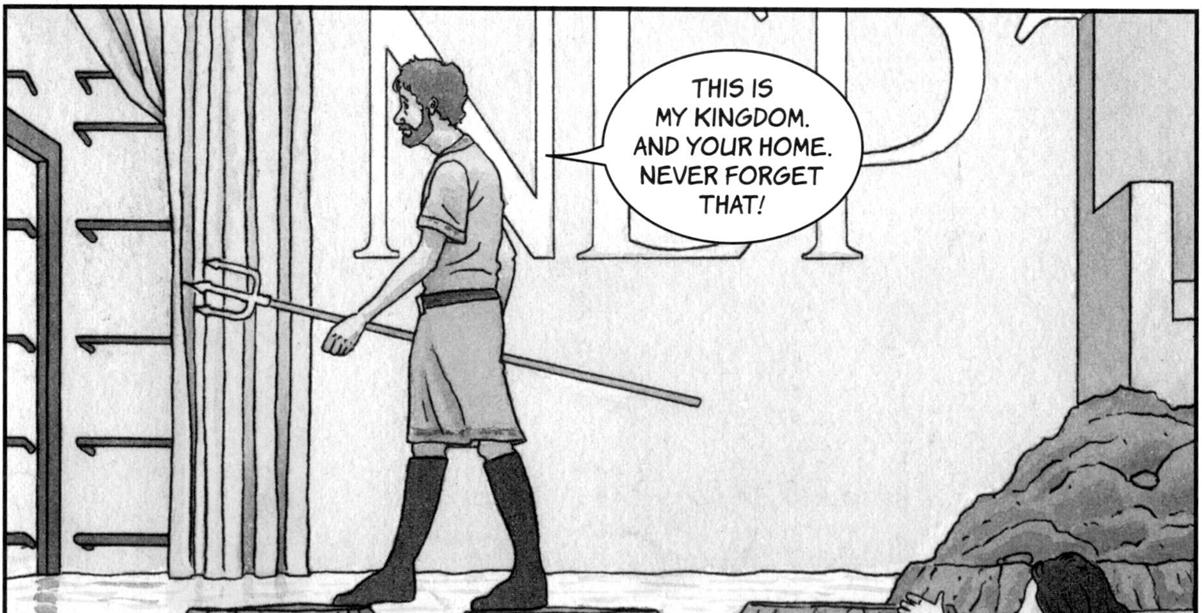
THIS IS MY KINGDOM. AND YOUR HOME. NEVER FORGET THAT!

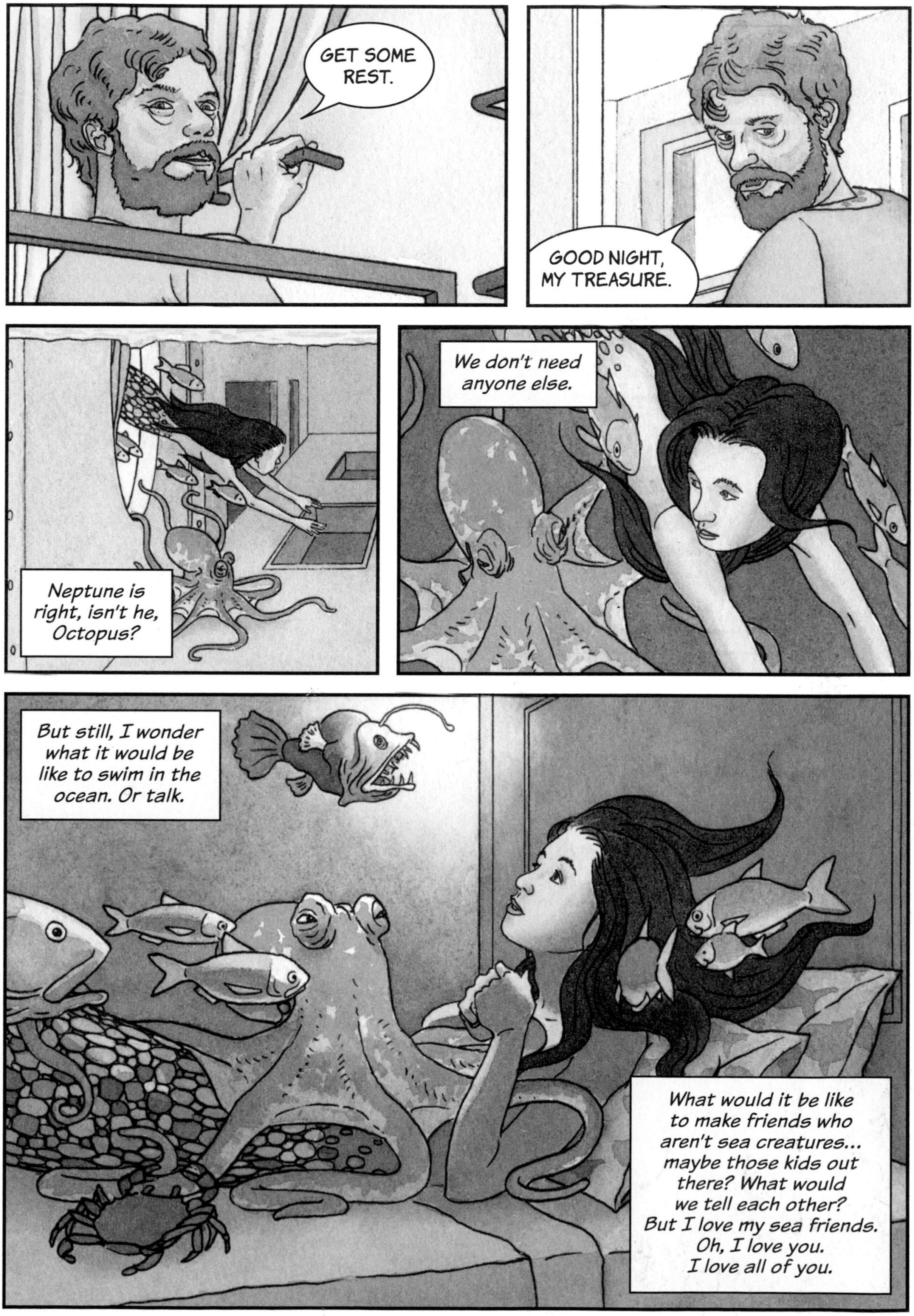
GET SOME REST.
GOOD NIGHT, MY TREASURE.
Neptune is right, isn't he, Octopus?
We don't need anyone else.
But still, I wonder what it would be like to swim in the ocean. Or talk.
What would it be like to make friends who aren't sea creatures... maybe those kids out there? What would we tell each other? But I love my sea friends. Oh, I love you. I love all of you.

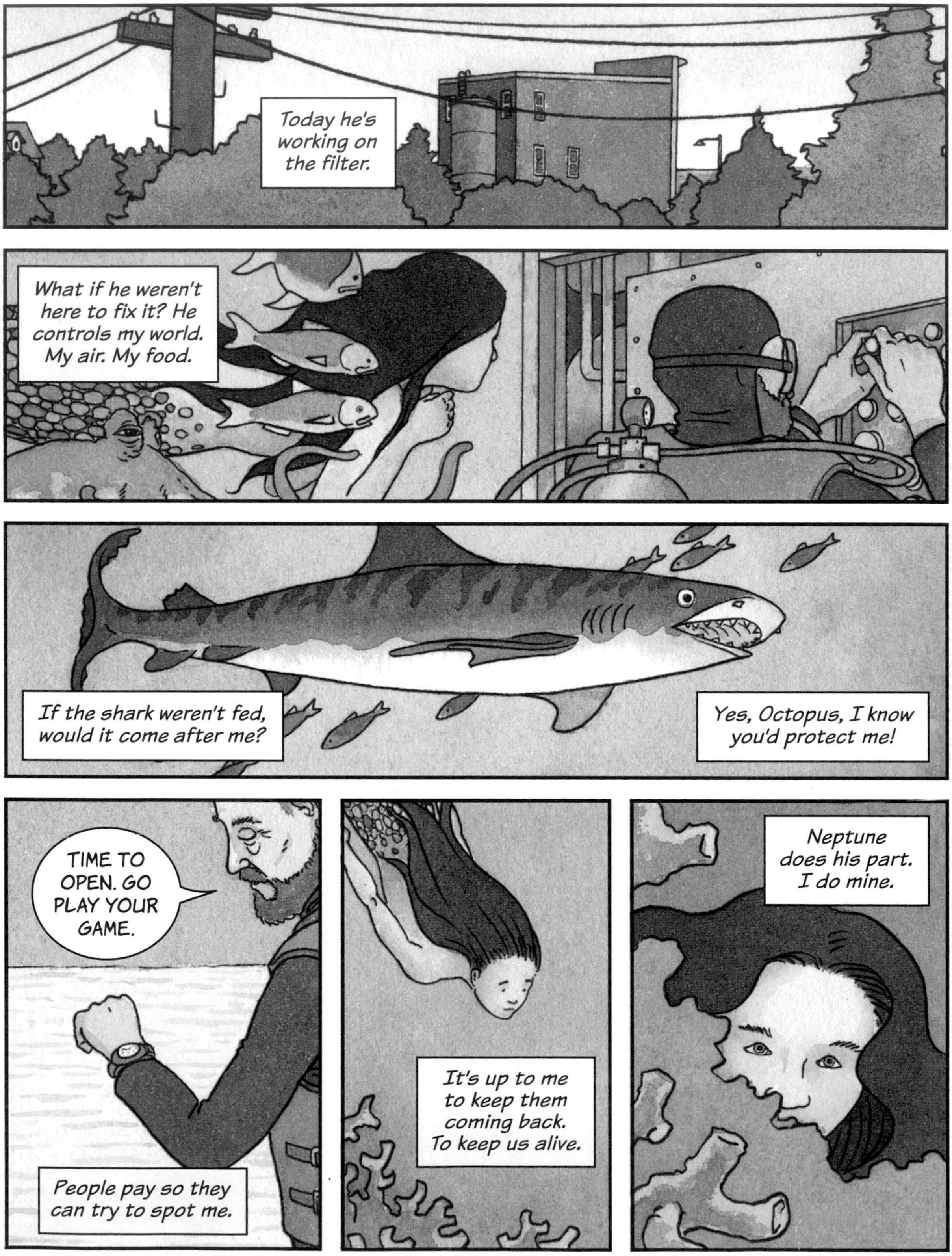
Today he's working on the filter.
What if he weren't here to fix it? He controls my world. My air. My food.
If the shark weren't fed, would it come after me?
Yes, Octopus, I know you'd protect me!
TIME TO OPEN. GO PLAY YOUR GAME.
People pay so they can try to spot me.
It's up to me to keep them coming back. To keep us alive.
Neptune does his part. I do mine.

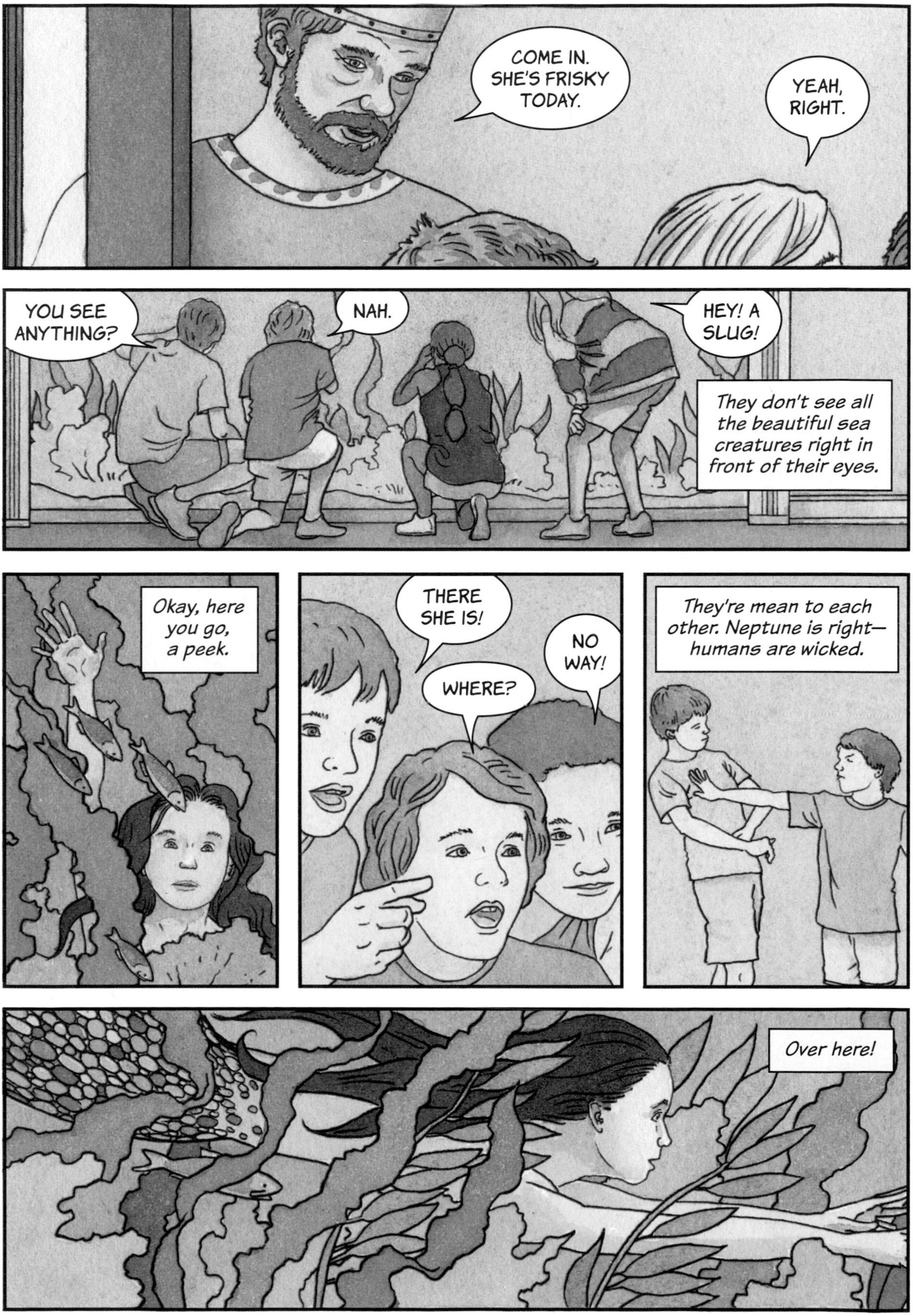
COME IN. SHE'S FRISKY TODAY.
YEAH, RIGHT.
YOU SEE ANYTHING?
NAH.
HEY! A SLUG!
They don't see all the beautiful sea creatures right in front of their eyes.
Okay, here you go, a peek.
THERE SHE IS!
WHERE?
NO WAY!
They're mean to each other. Neptune is right—humans are wicked.
Over here!

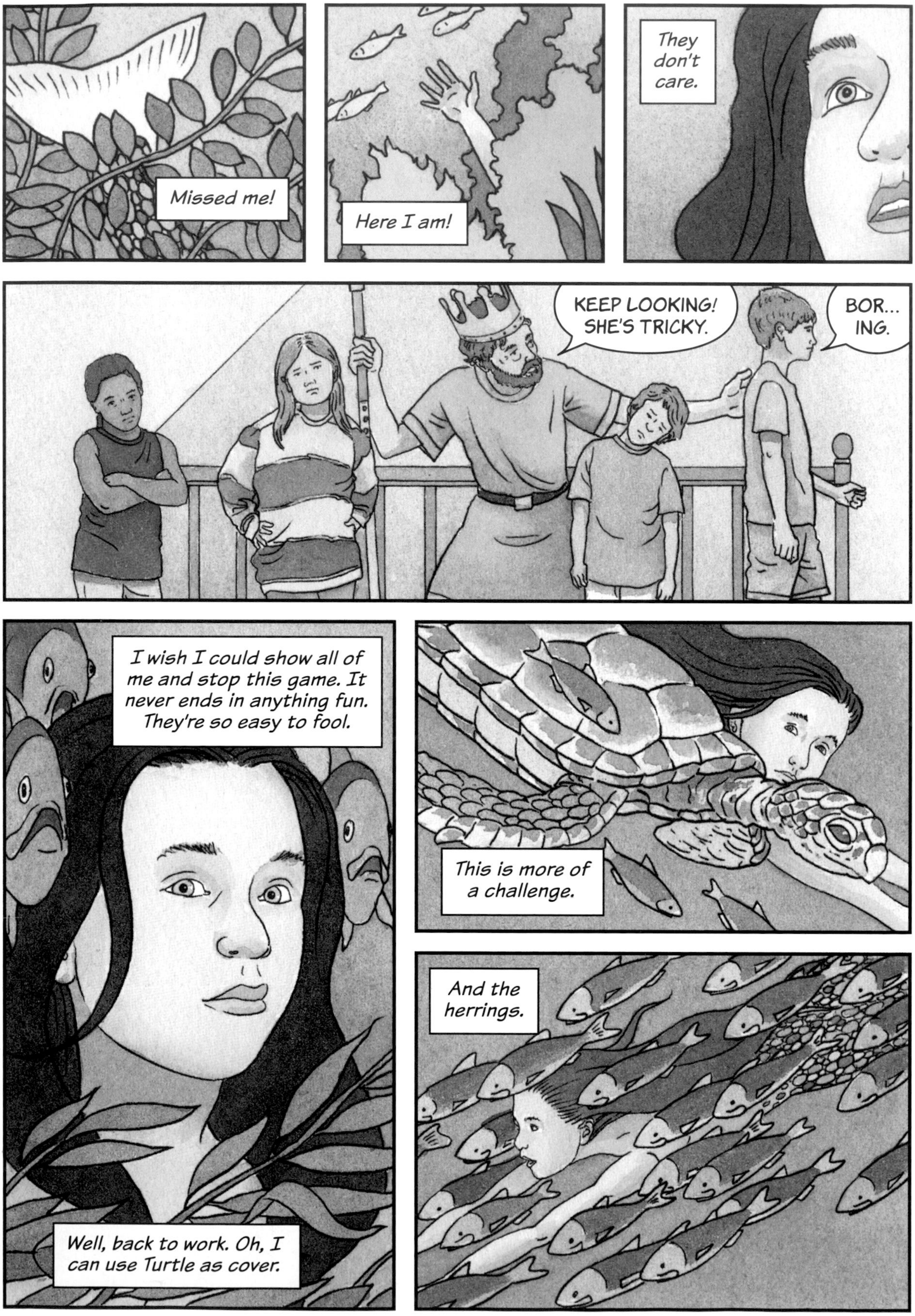
Missed me!
Here I am!
They don't care.
KEEP LOOKING! SHE'S TRICKY.
BOR... ING.
I wish I could show all of me and stop this game. It never ends in anything fun. They're so easy to fool.
Well, back to work. Oh, I can use Turtle as cover.
This is more of a challenge.
And the herrings.

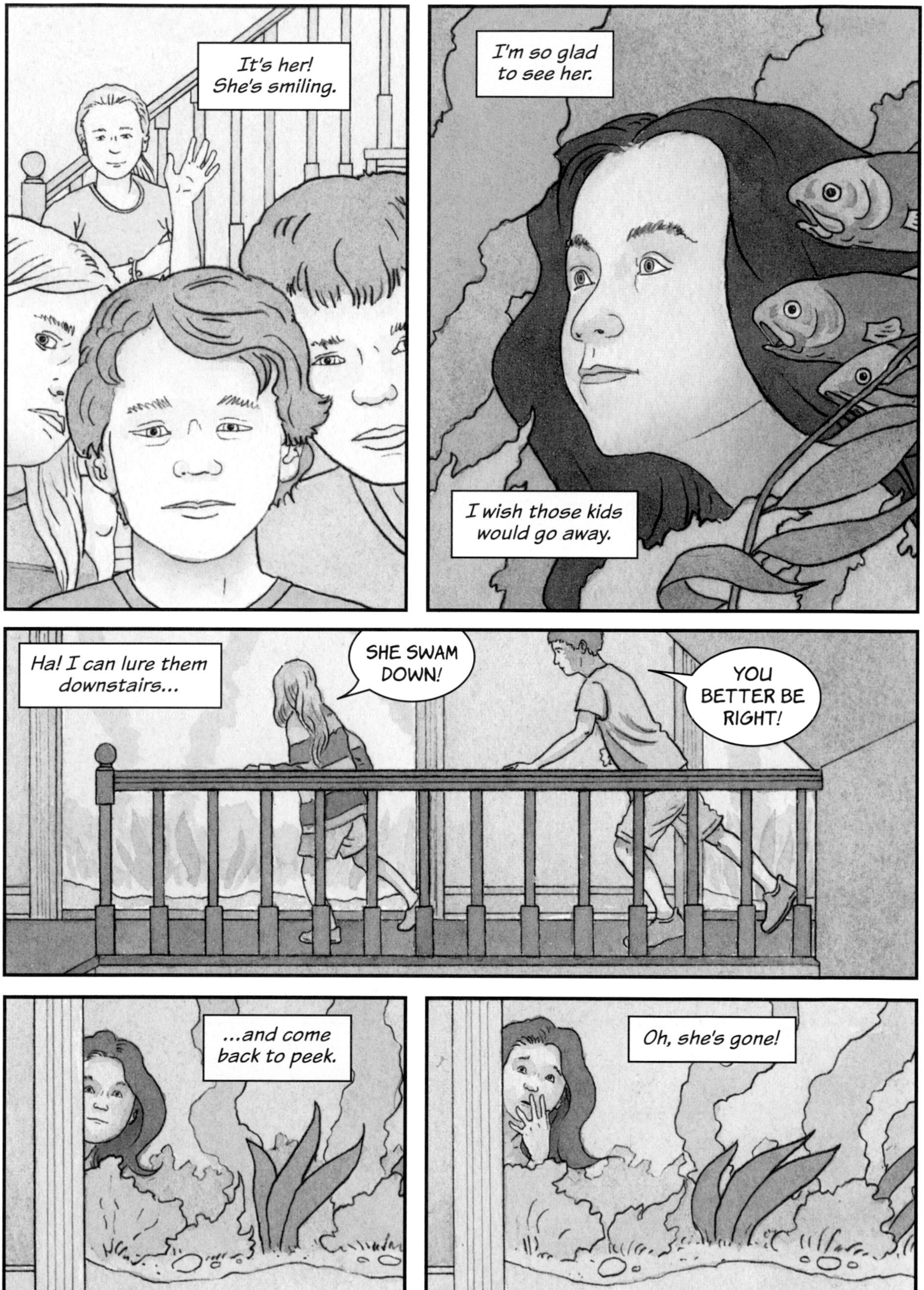
It's her! She's smiling.
I'm so glad to see her.
I wish those kids would go away.
Ha! I can lure them downstairs...
SHE SWAM DOWN!
YOU BETTER BE RIGHT!
...and come back to peek.
Oh, she's gone!

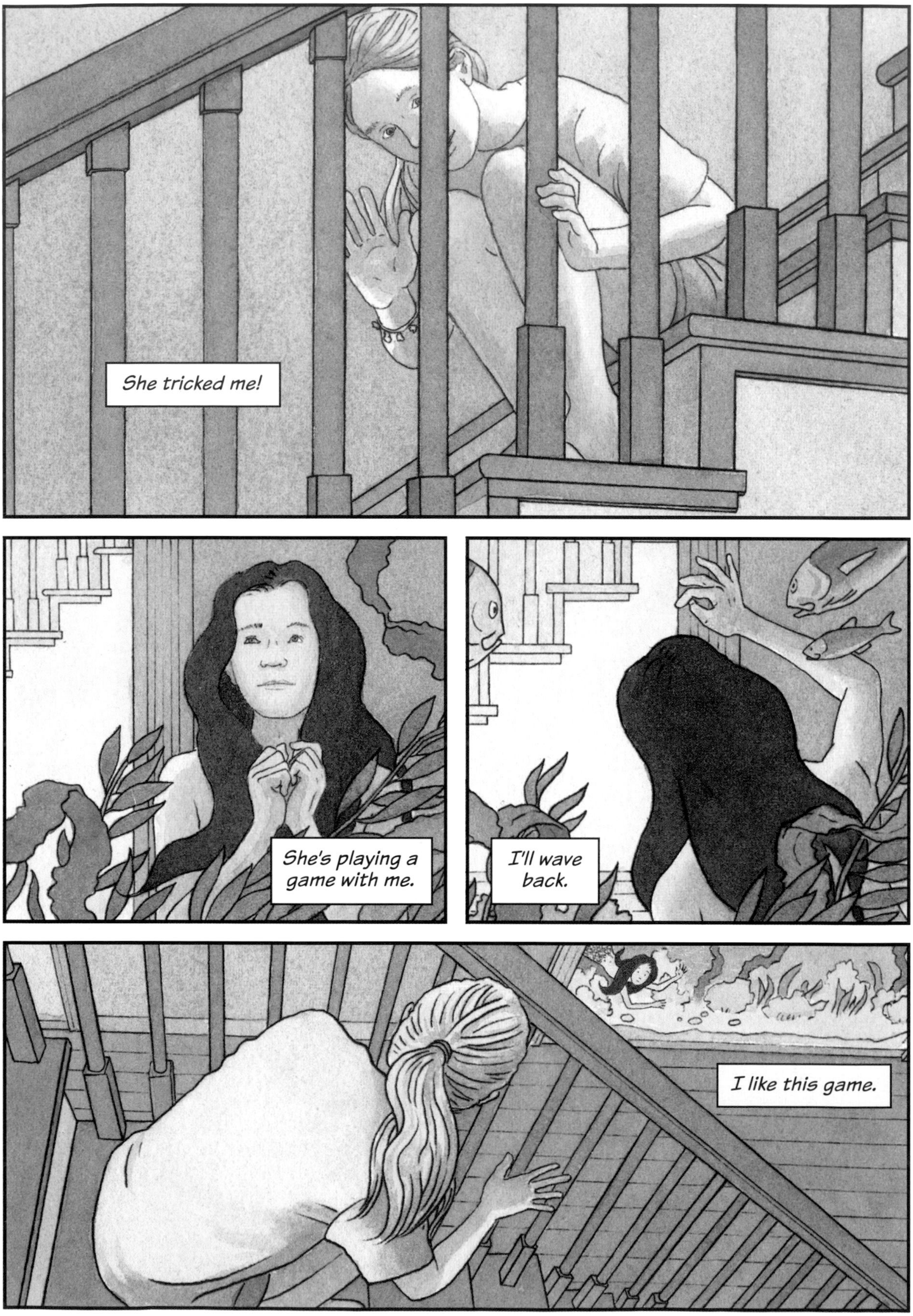

She tricked me!
She's playing a game with me.
I'll wave back.
I like this game.

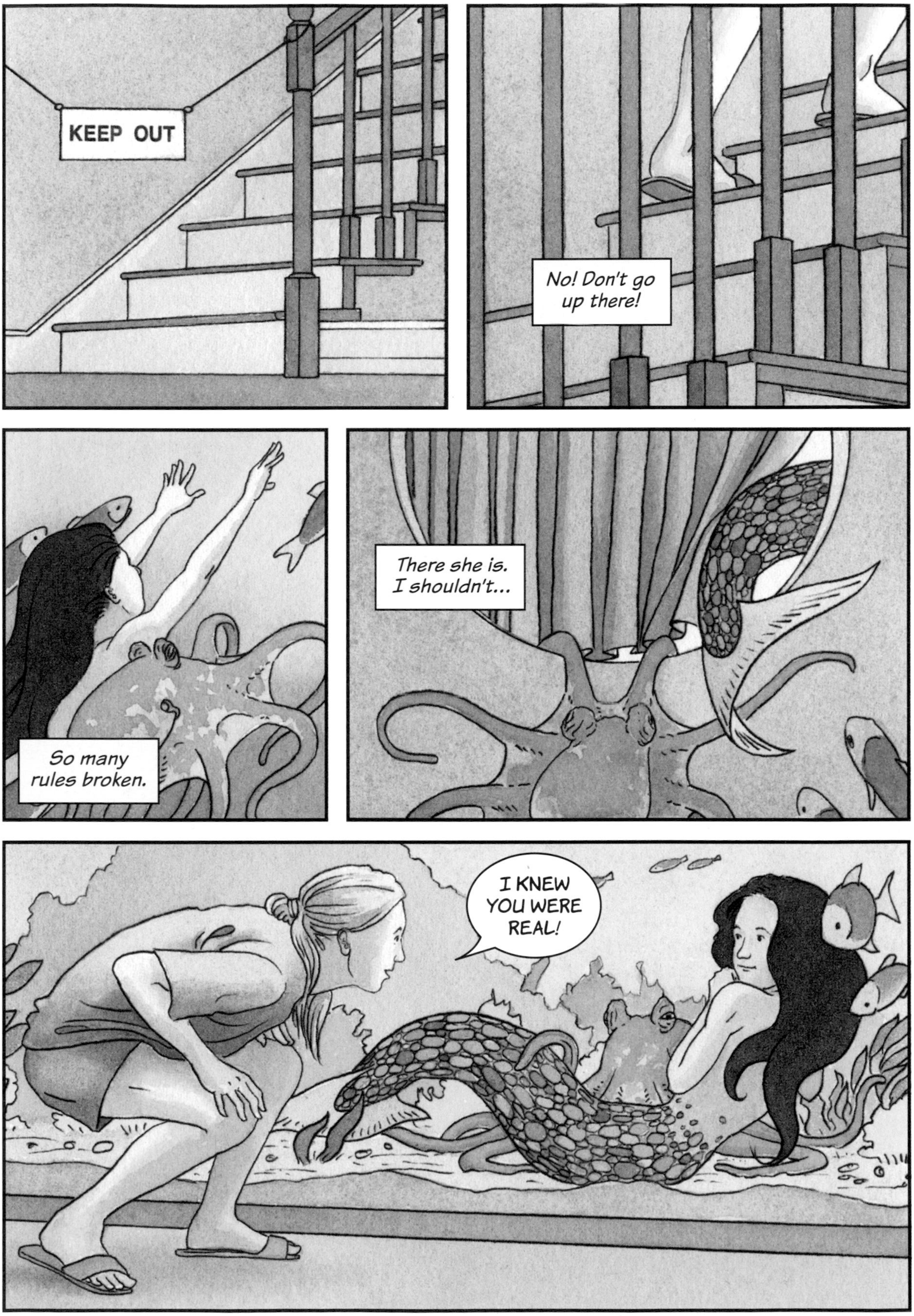
KEEP OUT
No! Don't go up there!
So many rules broken.
There she is. I shouldn't...
I KNEW YOU WERE REAL!

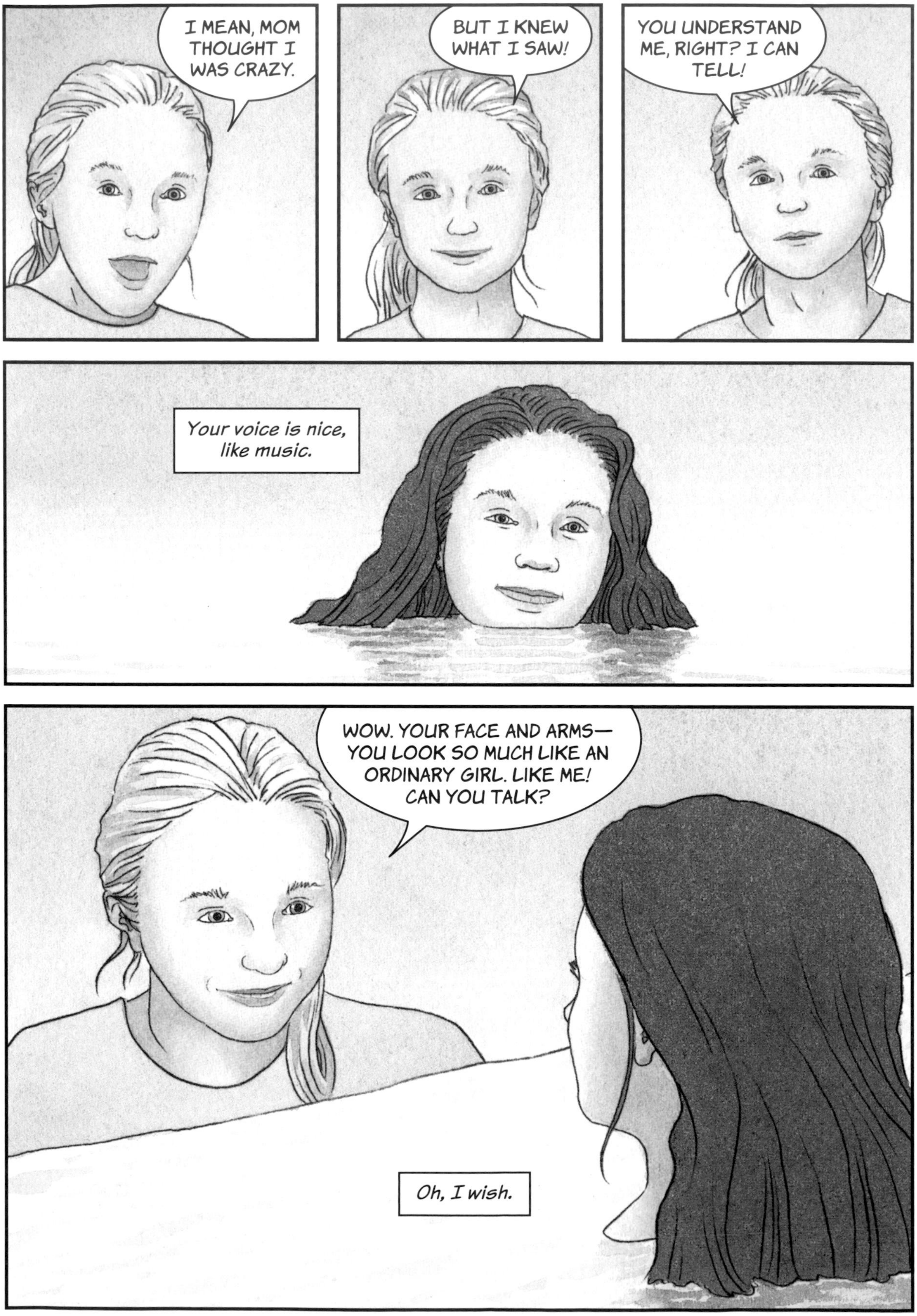
I MEAN, MOM THOUGHT I WAS CRAZY.
BUT I KNEW WHAT I SAW!
YOU UNDERSTAND ME, RIGHT? I CAN TELL!
Your voice is nice, like music.
WOW. YOUR FACE AND ARMS— YOU LOOK SO MUCH LIKE AN ORDINARY GIRL. LIKE ME! CAN YOU TALK?
Oh, I wish.

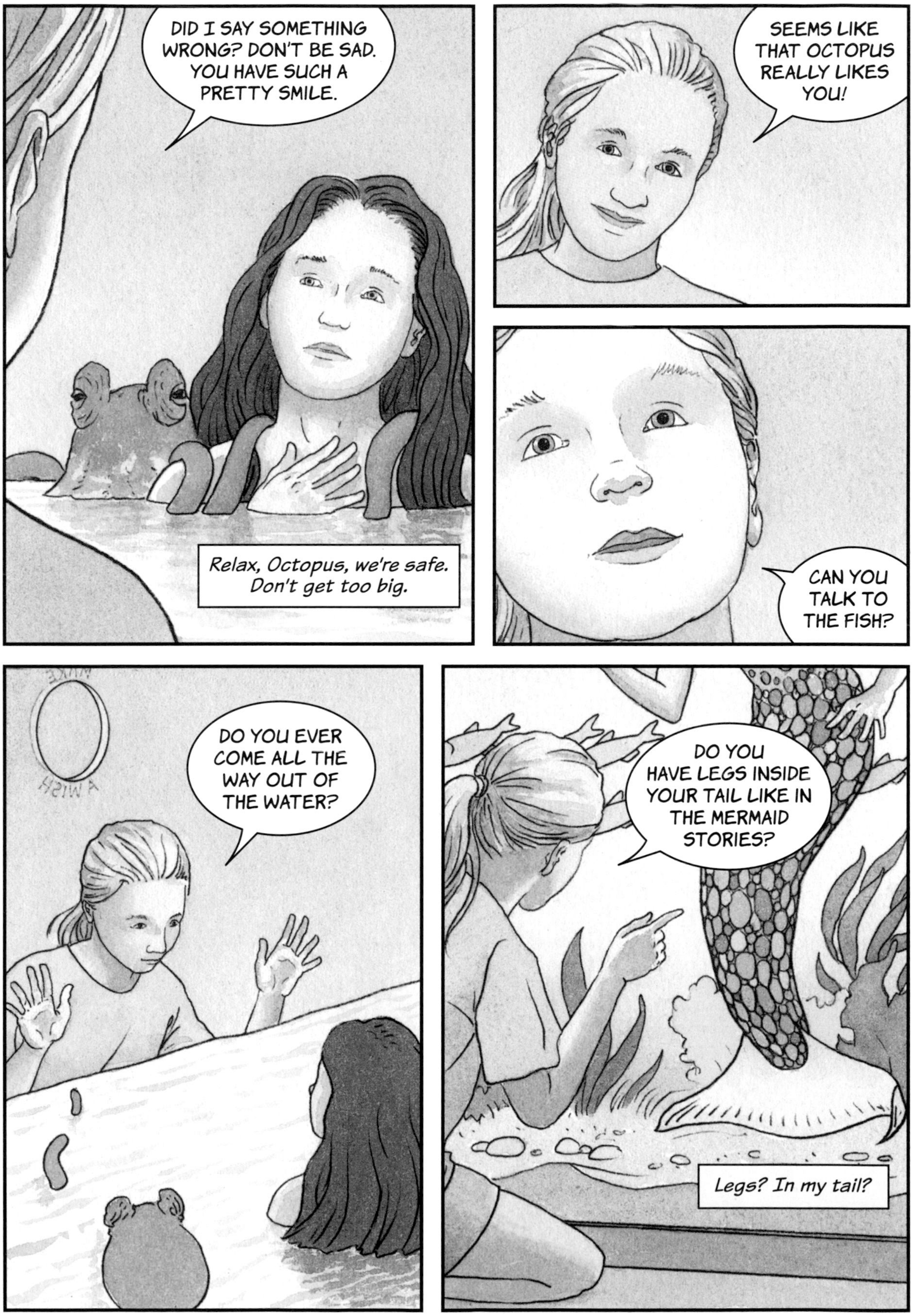
DID I SAY SOMETHING WRONG? DON'T BE SAD. YOU HAVE SUCH A PRETTY SMILE.
Relax, Octopus, we're safe. Don't get too big.
SEEMS LIKE THAT OCTOPUS REALLY LIKES YOU!
CAN YOU TALK TO THE FISH?
DO YOU EVER COME ALL THE WAY OUT OF THE WATER?
DO YOU HAVE LEGS INSIDE YOUR TAIL LIKE IN THE MERMAID STORIES?
Legs? In my tail?

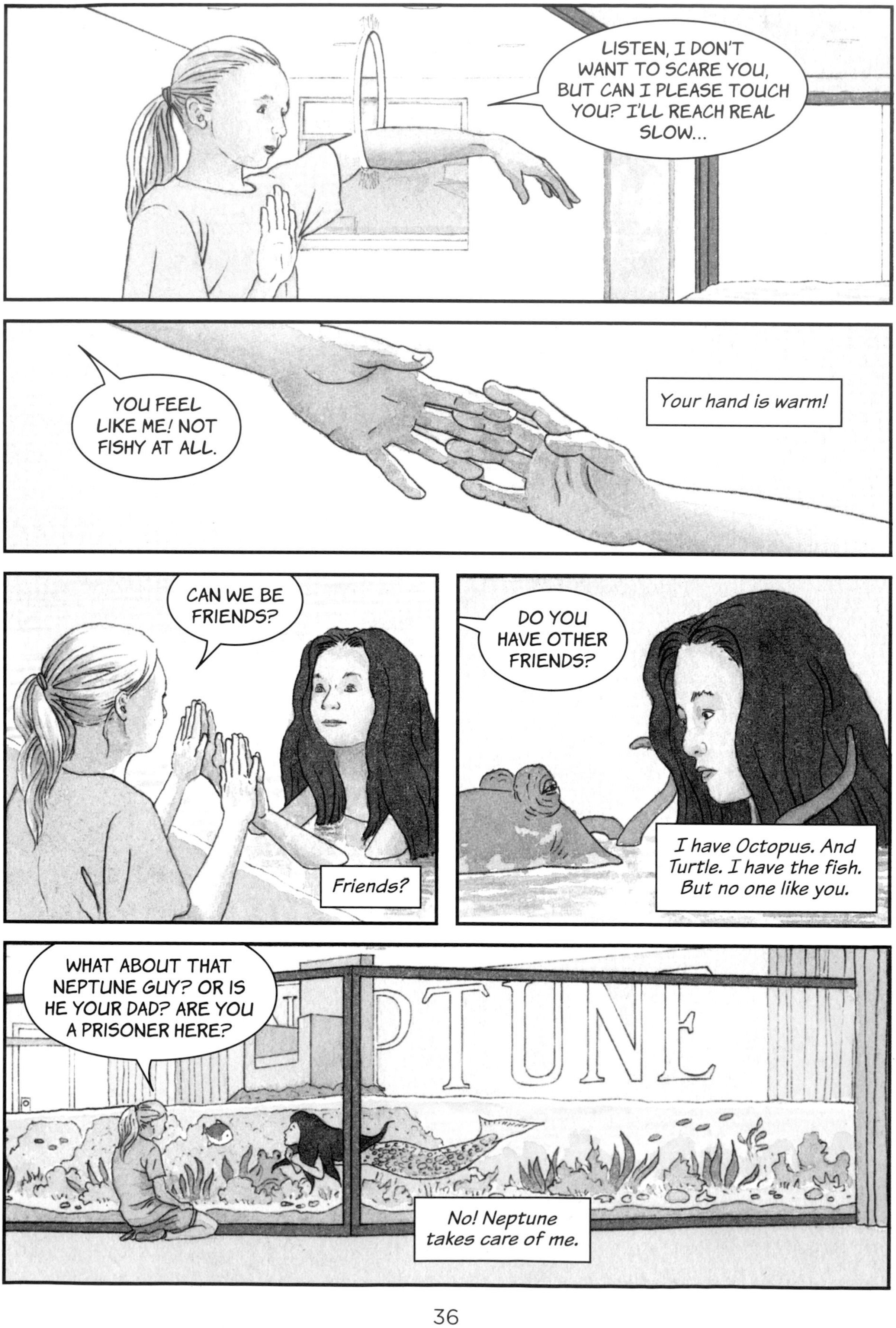
LISTEN, I DON'T WANT TO SCARE YOU, BUT CAN I PLEASE TOUCH YOU? I'LL REACH REAL SLOW...
YOU FEEL LIKE ME! NOT FISHY AT ALL.
Your hand is warm!
CAN WE BE FRIENDS?
Friends?
DO YOU HAVE OTHER FRIENDS?
I have Octopus. And Turtle. I have the fish. But no one like you.
WHAT ABOUT THAT NEPTUNE GUY? OR IS HE YOUR DAD? ARE YOU A PRISONER HERE?
PTUNE
No! Neptune takes care of me.

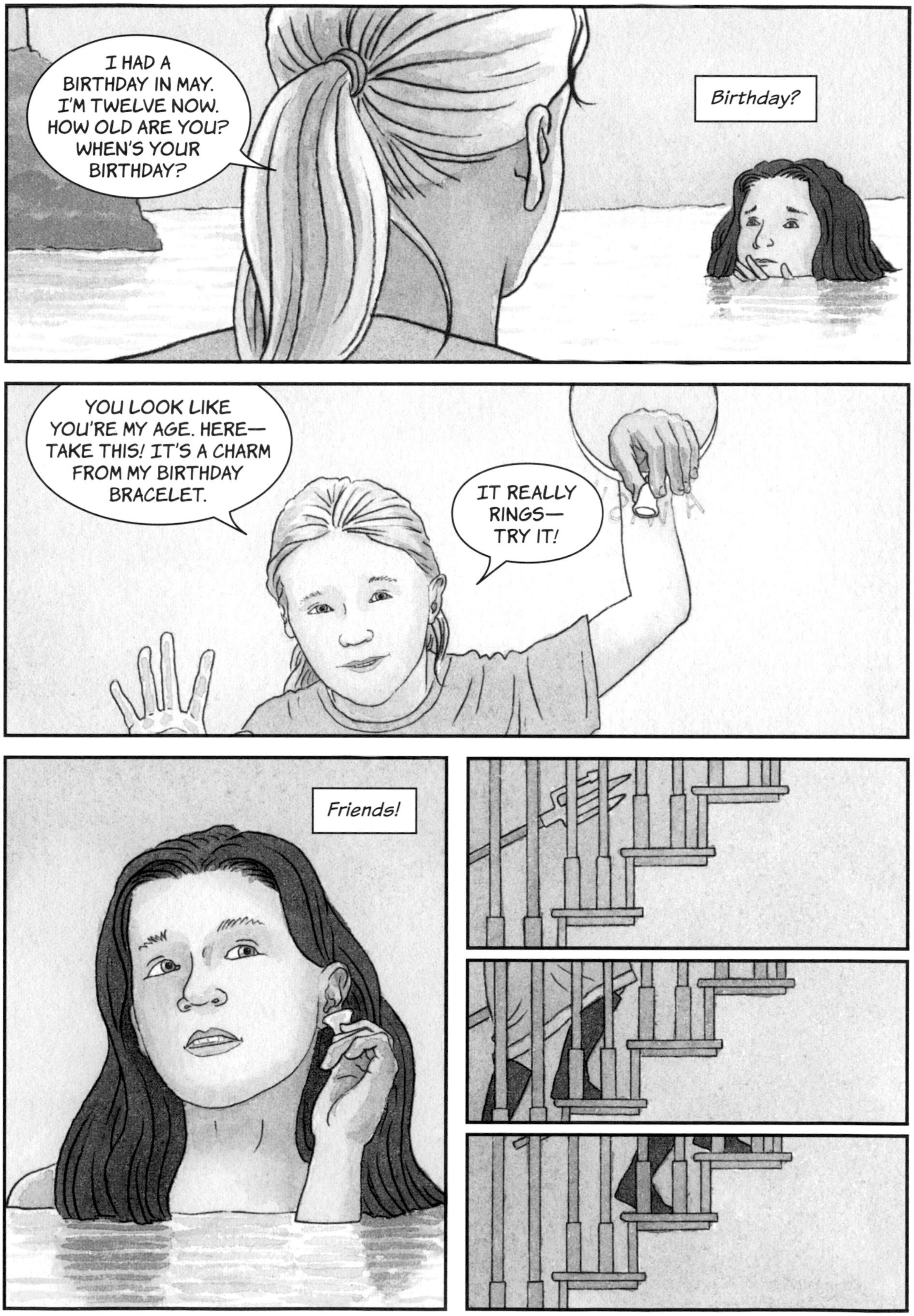
I HAD A BIRTHDAY IN MAY. I'M TWELVE NOW. HOW OLD ARE YOU? WHEN'S YOUR BIRTHDAY?
Birthday?
YOU LOOK LIKE YOU'RE MY AGE. HERE— TAKE THIS! IT'S A CHARM FROM MY BIRTHDAY BRACELET.
IT REALLY RINGS— TRY IT!
Friends!

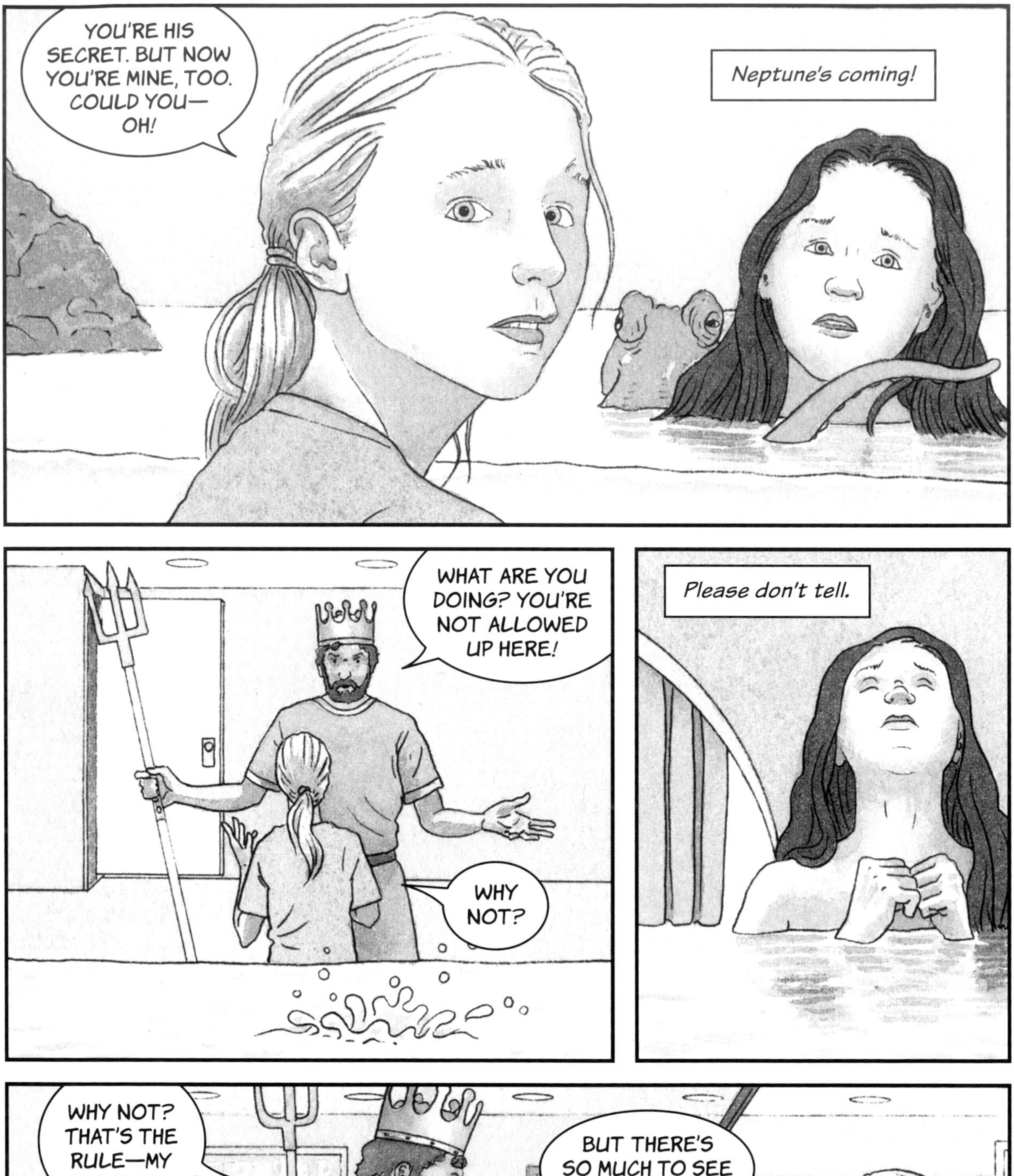
YOU'RE HIS SECRET. BUT NOW YOU'RE MINE, TOO. COULD YOU— OH!
Neptune's coming!
WHAT ARE YOU DOING? YOU'RE NOT ALLOWED UP HERE!
WHY NOT?
Please don't tell.
WHY NOT? THAT'S THE RULE—MY RULE!
BUT THERE'S SO MUCH TO SEE UP HERE.

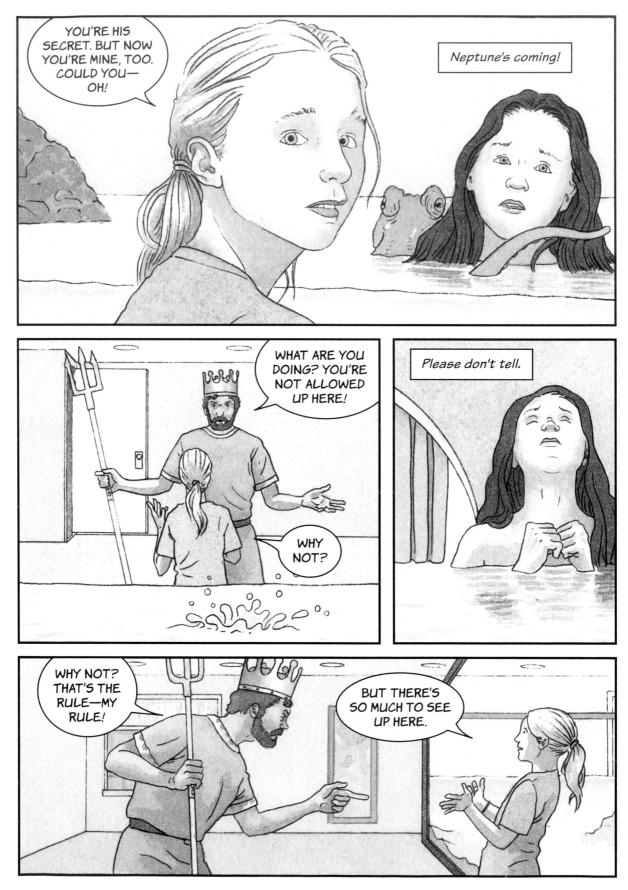

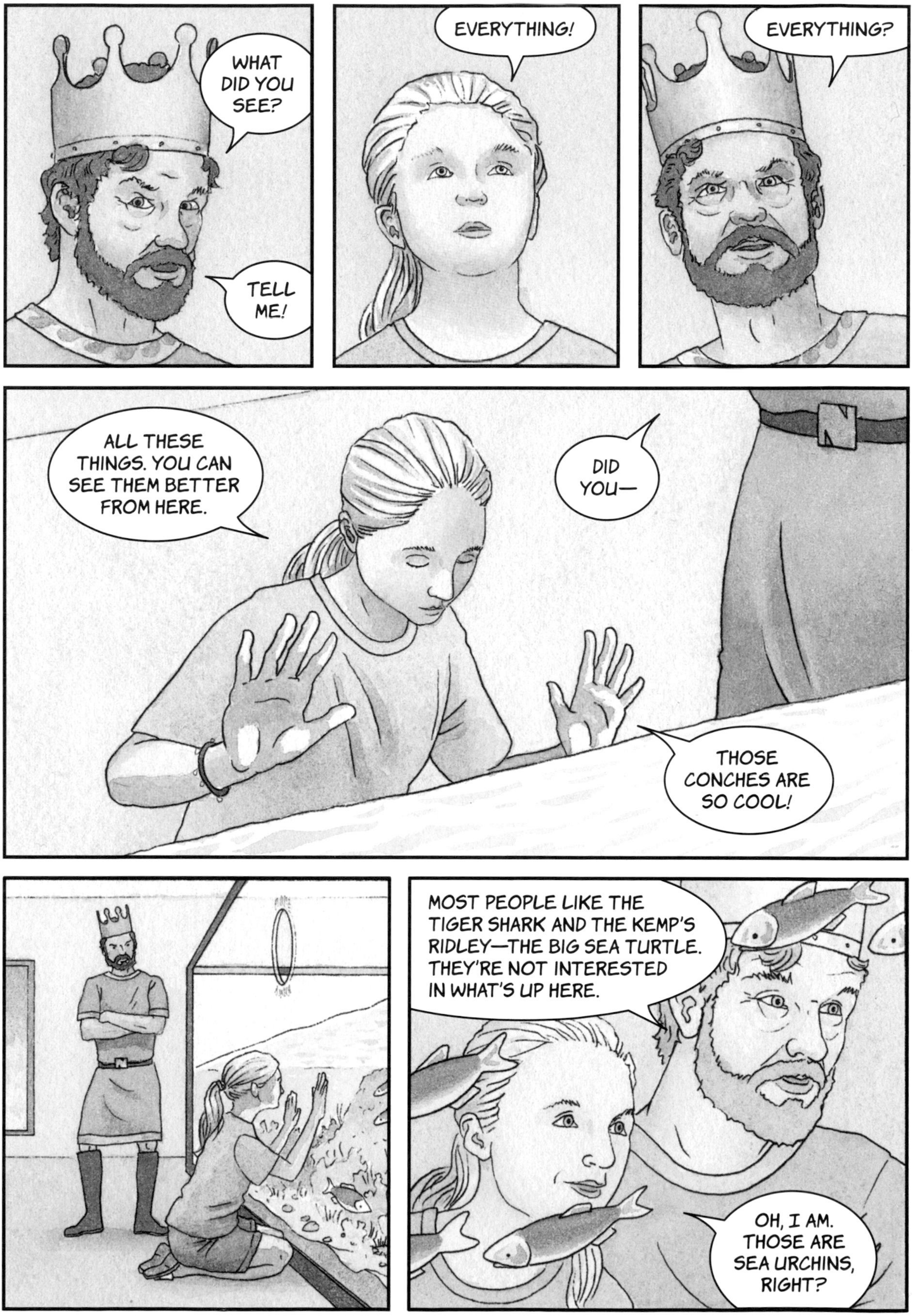
WHAT DID YOU SEE?
TELL ME!
EVERYTHING!
EVERYTHING?
ALL THESE THINGS. YOU CAN SEE THEM BETTER FROM HERE.
DID YOU—
THOSE CONCHES ARE SO COOL!
MOST PEOPLE LIKE THE TIGER SHARK AND THE KEMP'S RIDLEY—THE BIG SEA TURTLE. THEY'RE NOT INTERESTED IN WHAT'S UP HERE.
OH, I AM. THOSE ARE SEA URCHINS, RIGHT?

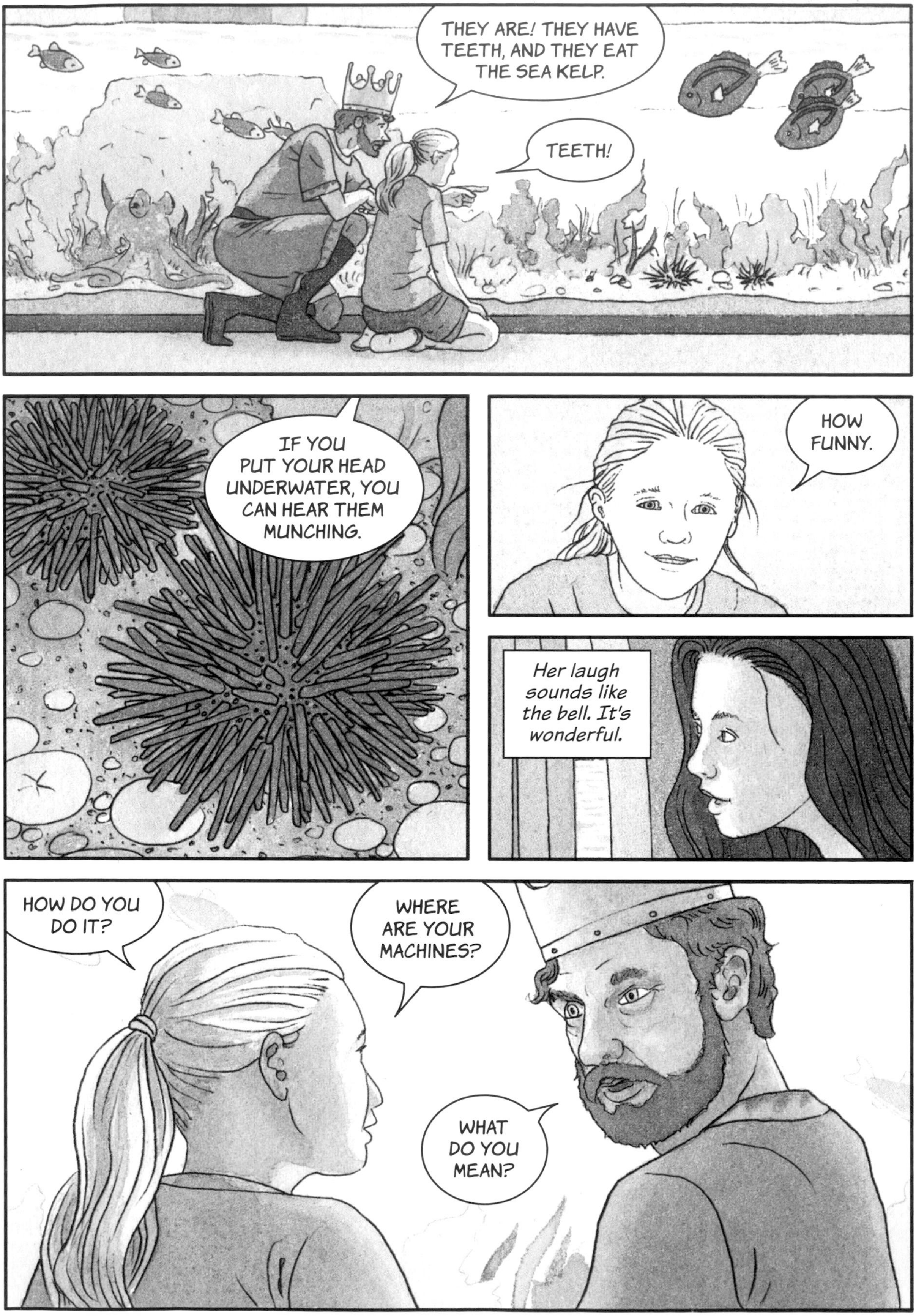
THEY ARE! THEY HAVE TEETH, AND THEY EAT THE SEA KELP.
TEETH!
IF YOU PUT YOUR HEAD UNDERWATER, YOU CAN HEAR THEM MUNCHING.
HOW FUNNY.
Her laugh sounds like the bell. It's wonderful.
HOW DO YOU DO IT?
WHERE ARE YOUR MACHINES?
WHAT DO YOU MEAN?

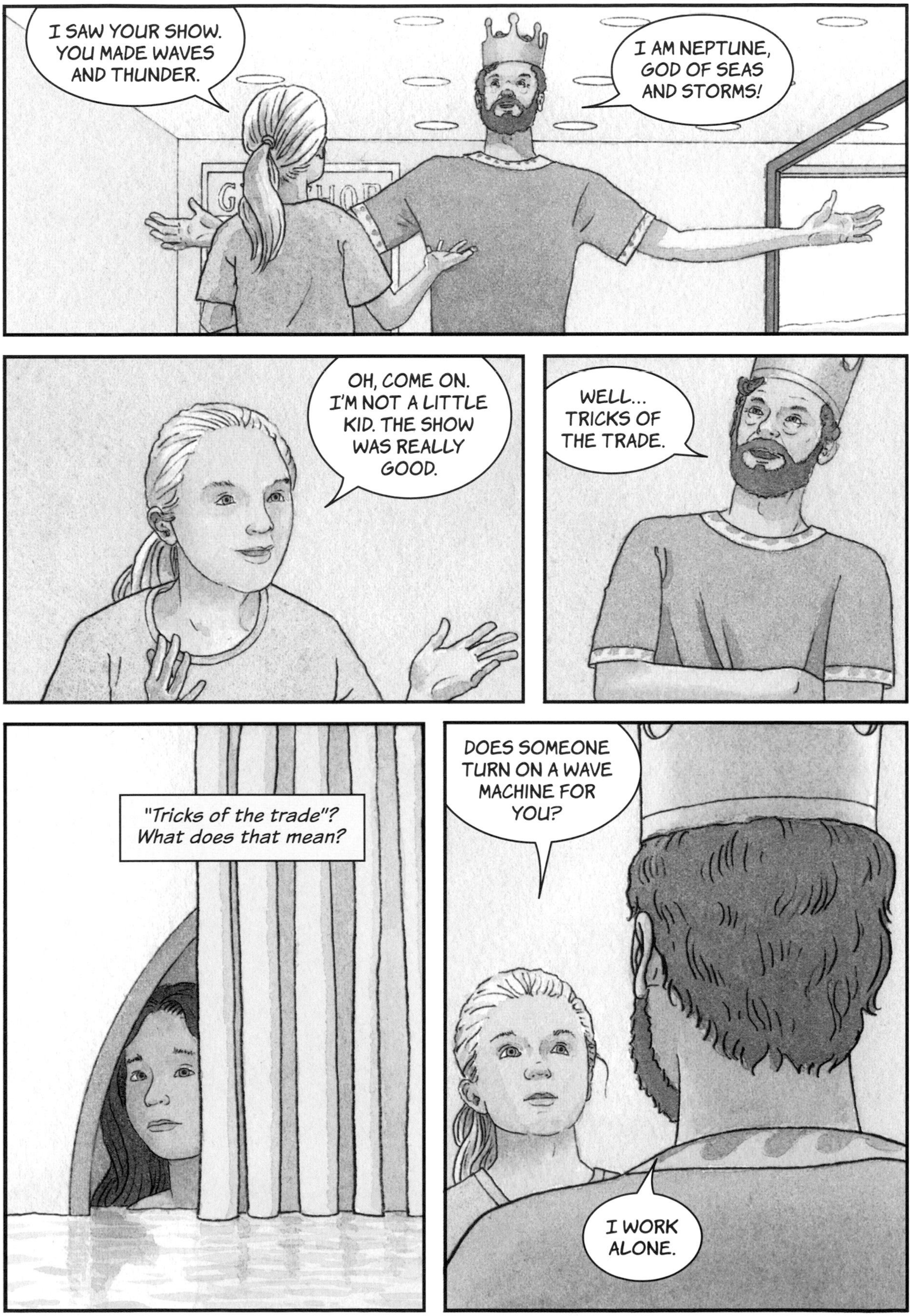
I SAW YOUR SHOW. YOU MADE WAVES AND THUNDER.
I AM NEPTUNE, GOD OF SEAS AND STORMS!
OH, COME ON. I'M NOT A LITTLE KID. THE SHOW WAS REALLY GOOD.
WELL... TRICKS OF THE TRADE.
"Tricks of the trade"? What does that mean?
DOES SOMEONE TURN ON A WAVE MACHINE FOR YOU?
I WORK ALONE.

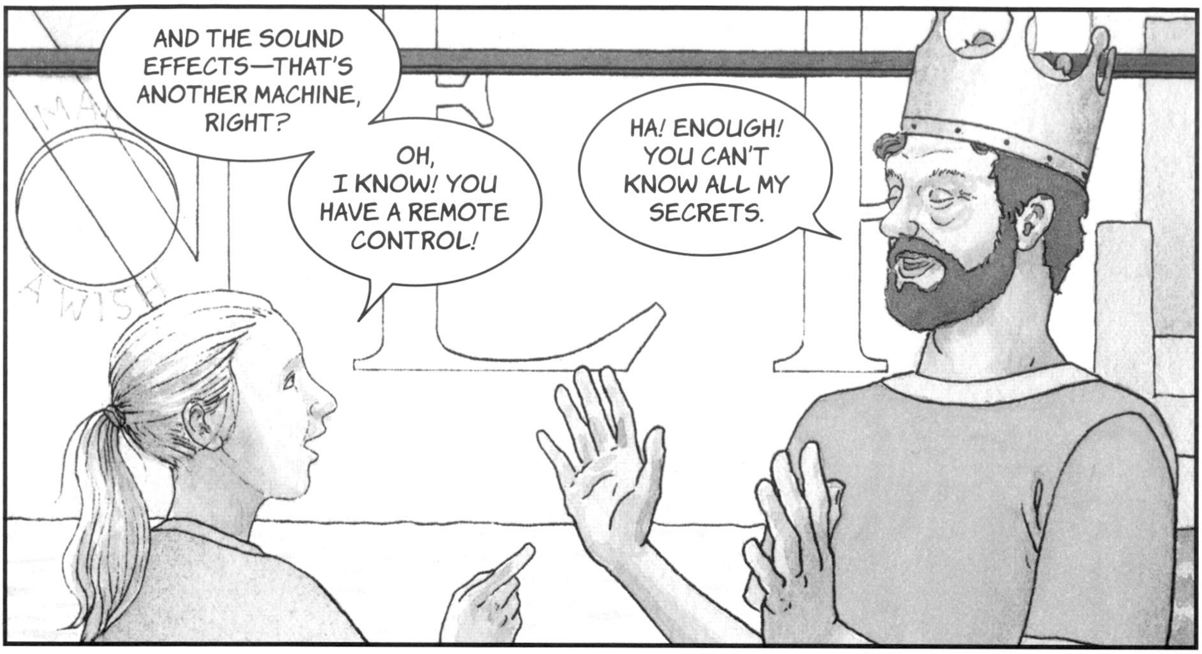
AND THE SOUND EFFECTS—THAT'S ANOTHER MACHINE, RIGHT?
OH, I KNOW! YOU HAVE A REMOTE CONTROL!
HA! ENOUGH! YOU CAN'T KNOW ALL MY SECRETS.

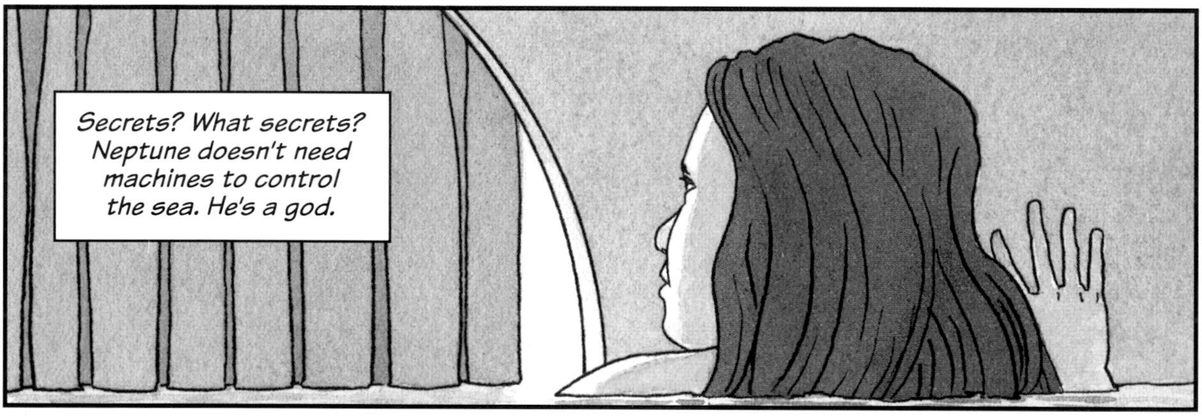
Secrets? What secrets? Neptune doesn't need machines to control the sea. He's a god.

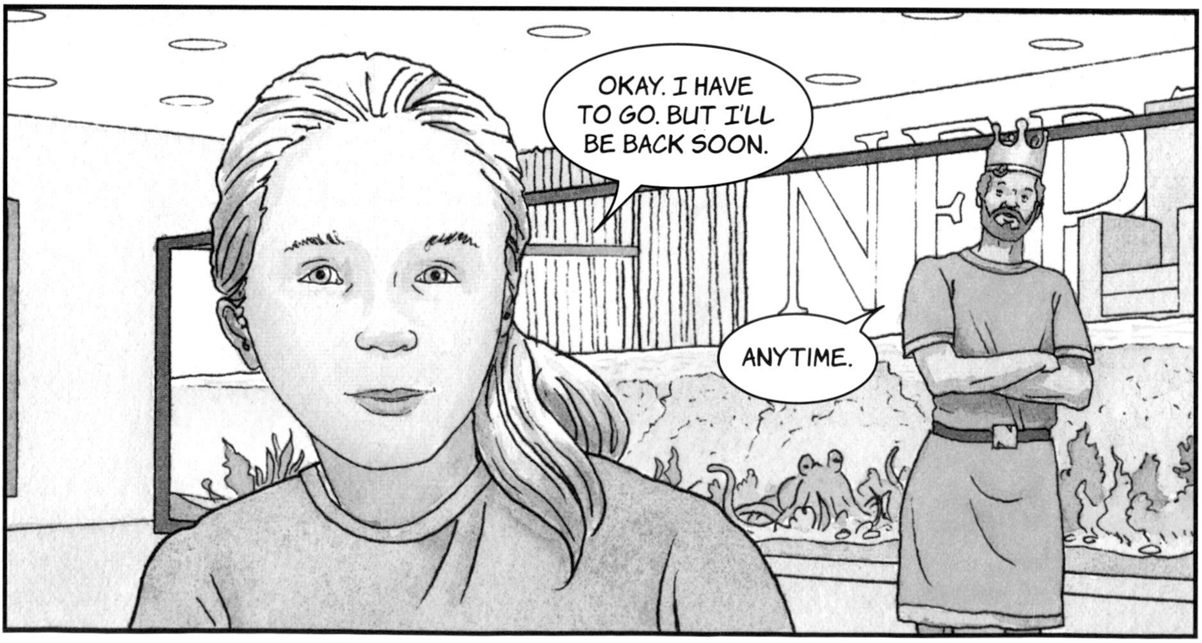
OKAY. I HAVE TO GO. BUT I'LL BE BACK SOON.
ANYTIME.

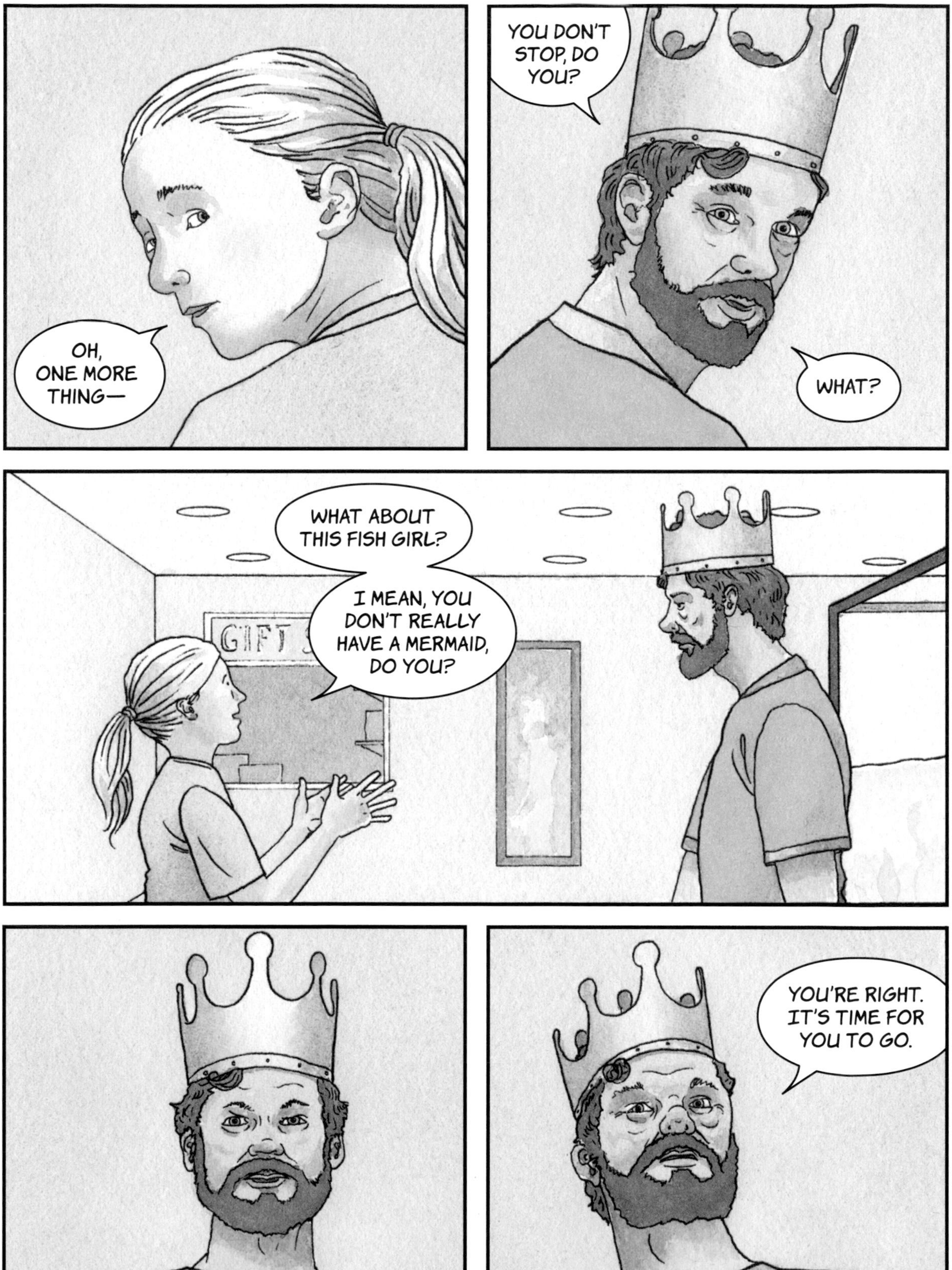
OH, ONE MORE THING—
YOU DON'T STOP, DO YOU?
WHAT?
WHAT ABOUT THIS FISH GIRL?
I MEAN, YOU DON'T REALLY HAVE A MERMAID, DO YOU?
GIFT S
YOU'RE RIGHT. IT'S TIME FOR YOU TO GO.

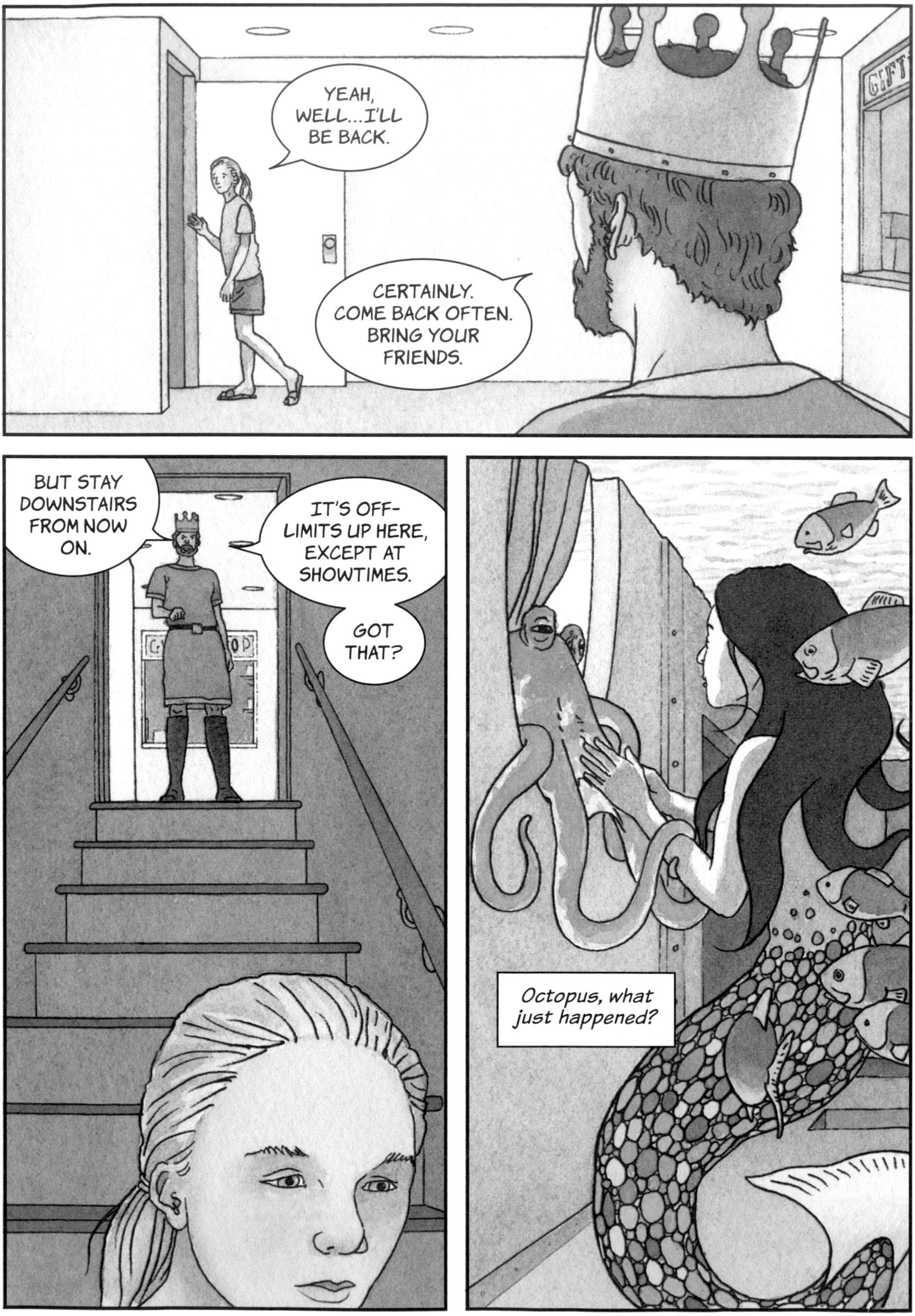
YEAH, WELL...I'LL BE BACK.
CERTAINLY. COME BACK OFTEN. BRING YOUR FRIENDS.
GIFT
BUT STAY DOWNSTAIRS FROM NOW ON.
IT'S OFF-LIMITS UP HERE, EXCEPT AT SHOWTIMES.
GOT THAT?
Octopus, what just happened?

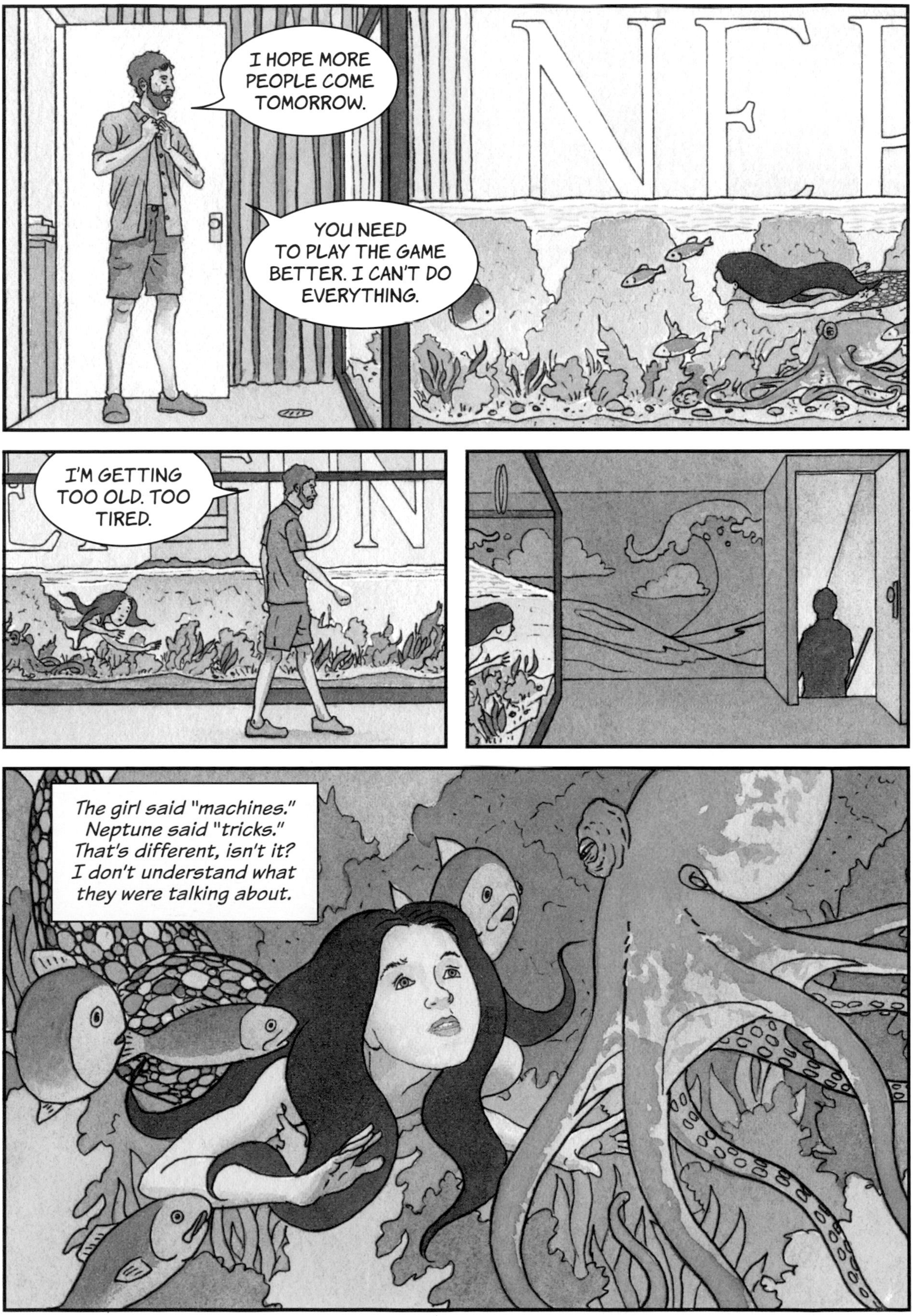
I HOPE MORE PEOPLE COME TOMORROW.
YOU NEED TO PLAY THE GAME BETTER. I CAN'T DO EVERYTHING.
I'M GETTING TOO OLD. TOO TIRED.
The girl said "machines." Neptune said "tricks." That's different, isn't it? I don't understand what they were talking about.

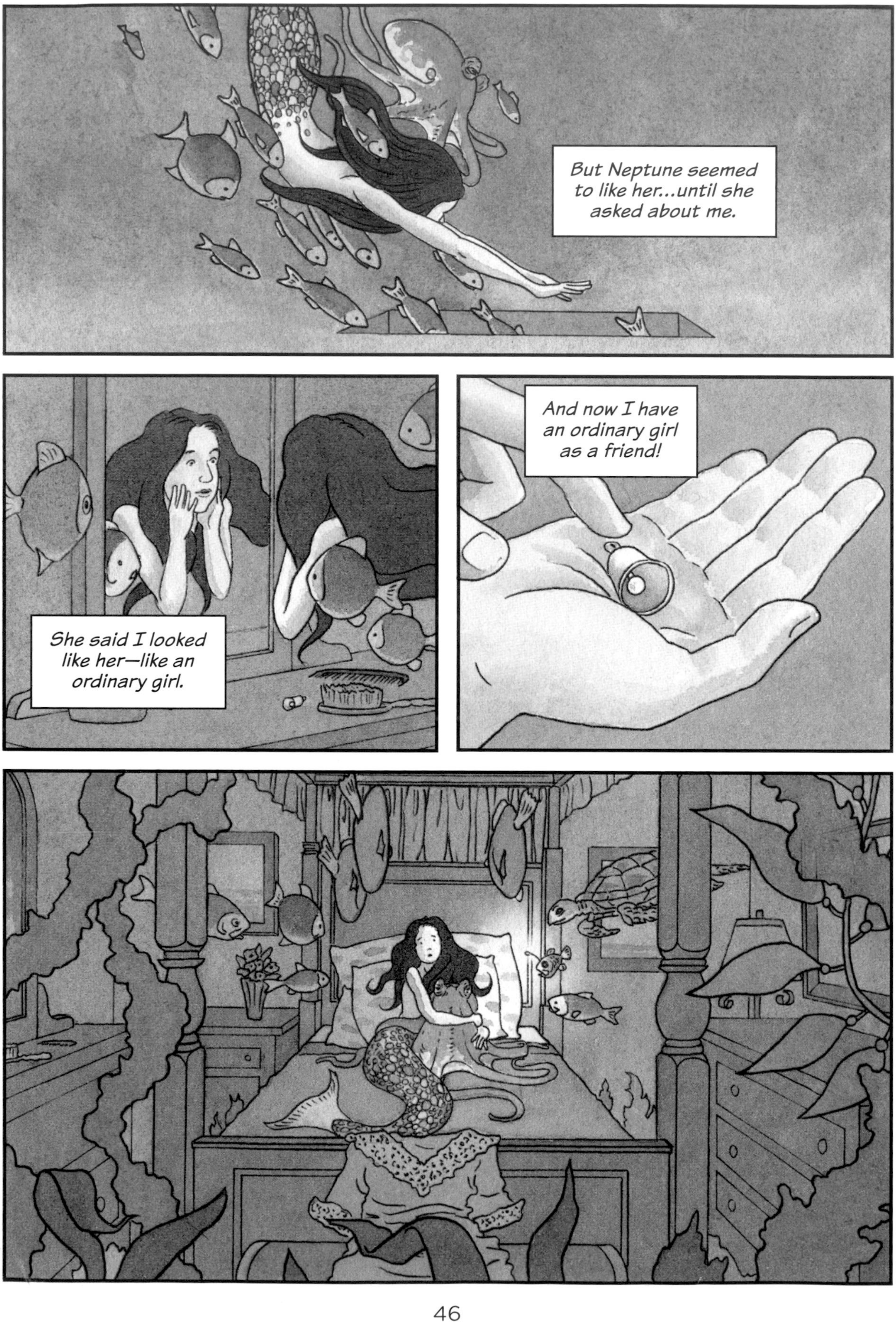
But Neptune seemed to like her...until she asked about me.
She said I looked like her—like an ordinary girl.
And now I have an ordinary girl as a friend!

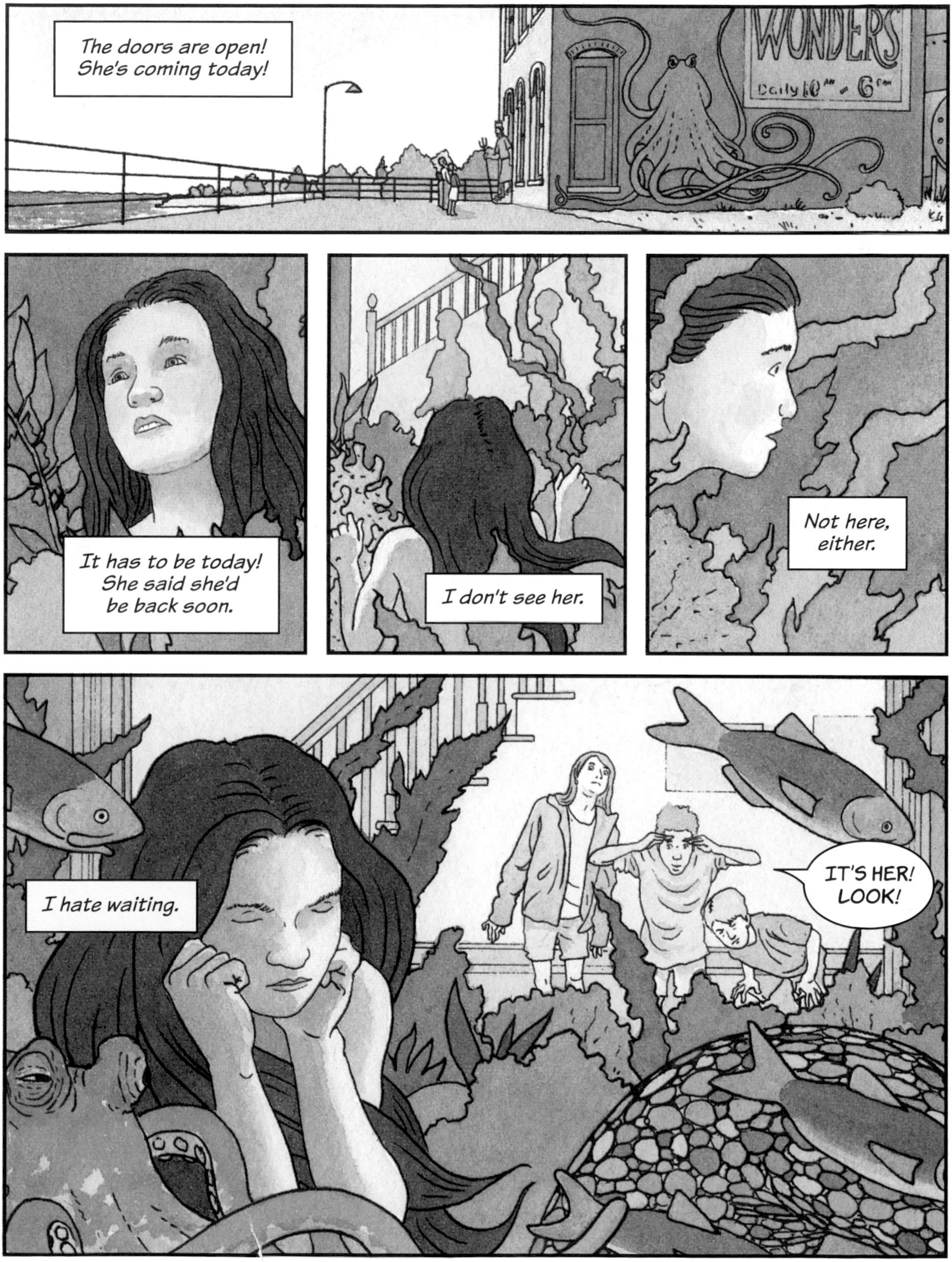
The doors are open! She's coming today!
WONDERS
It has to be today! She said she'd be back soon.
I don't see her.
Not here, either.
I hate waiting.
IT'S HER! LOOK!

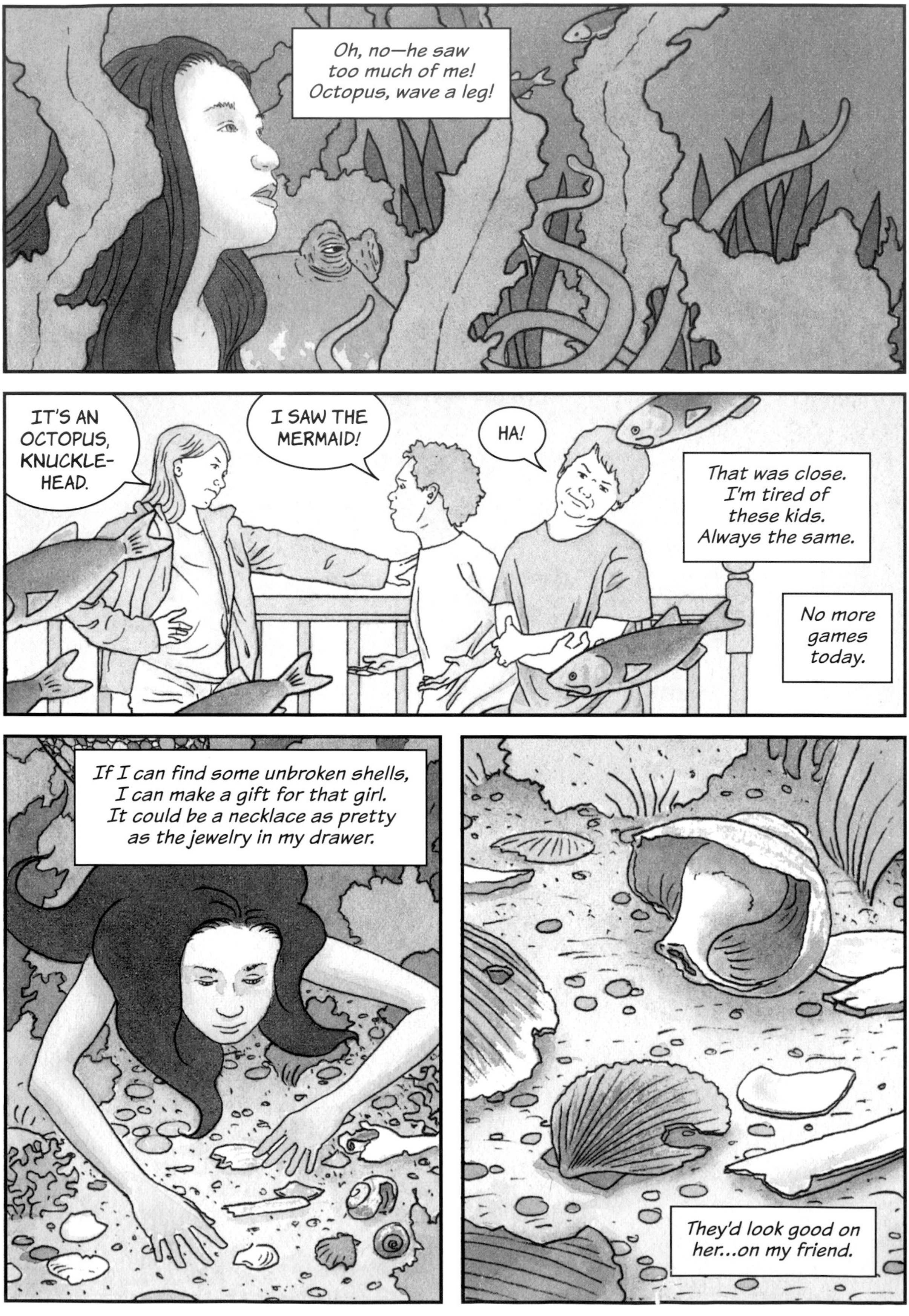
Oh, no—he saw too much of me! Octopus, wave a leg!
IT'S AN OCTOPUS, KNUCKLE-HEAD.
I SAW THE MERMAID!
HA!
That was close. I'm tired of these kids. Always the same.
No more games today.
If I can find some unbroken shells, I can make a gift for that girl. It could be a necklace as pretty as the jewelry in my drawer.
They'd look good on her...on my friend.

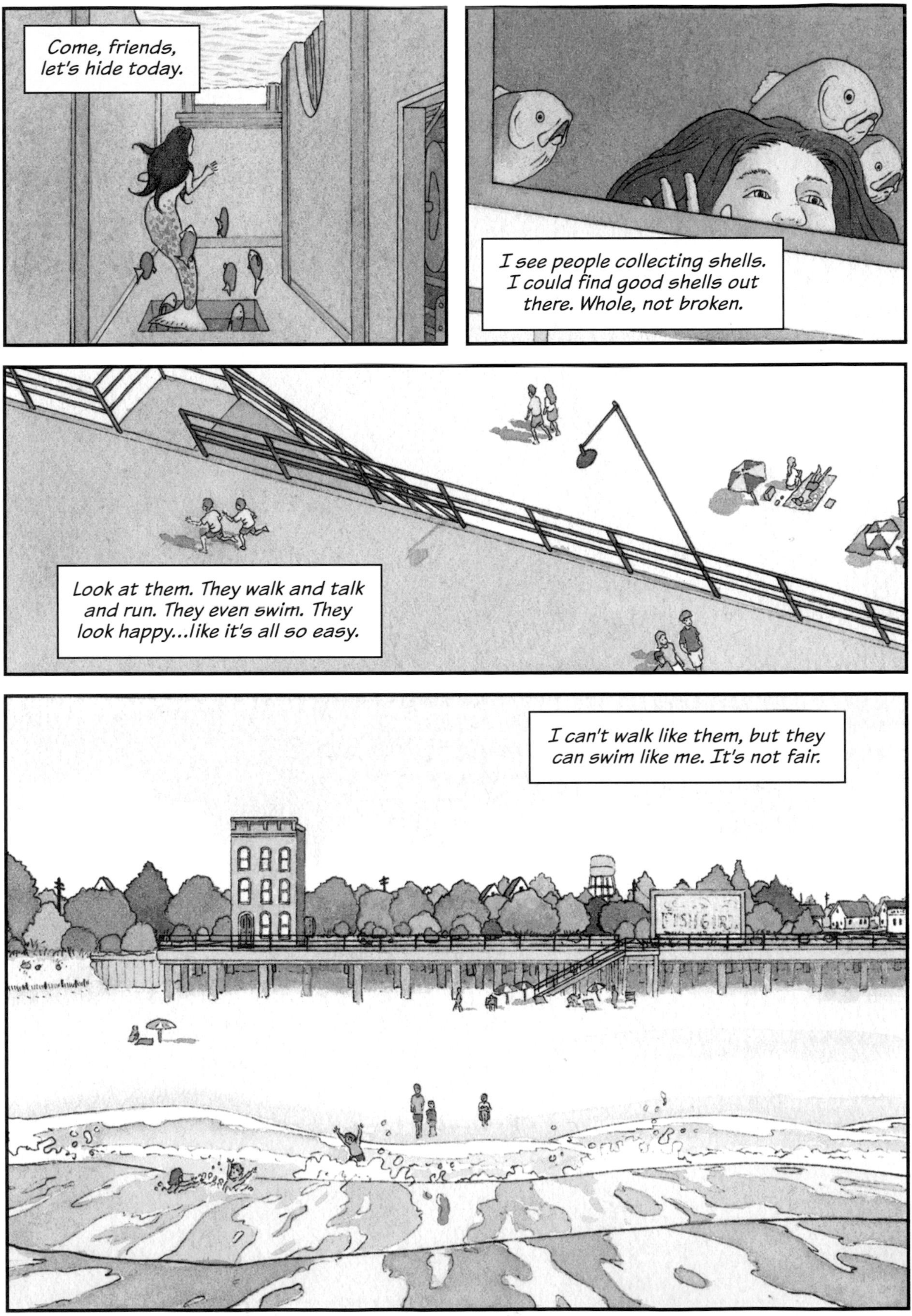
Come, friends, let's hide today.
I see people collecting shells. I could find good shells out there. Whole, not broken.
Look at them. They walk and talk and run. They even swim. They look happy...like it's all so easy.
I can't walk like them, but they can swim like me. It's not fair.

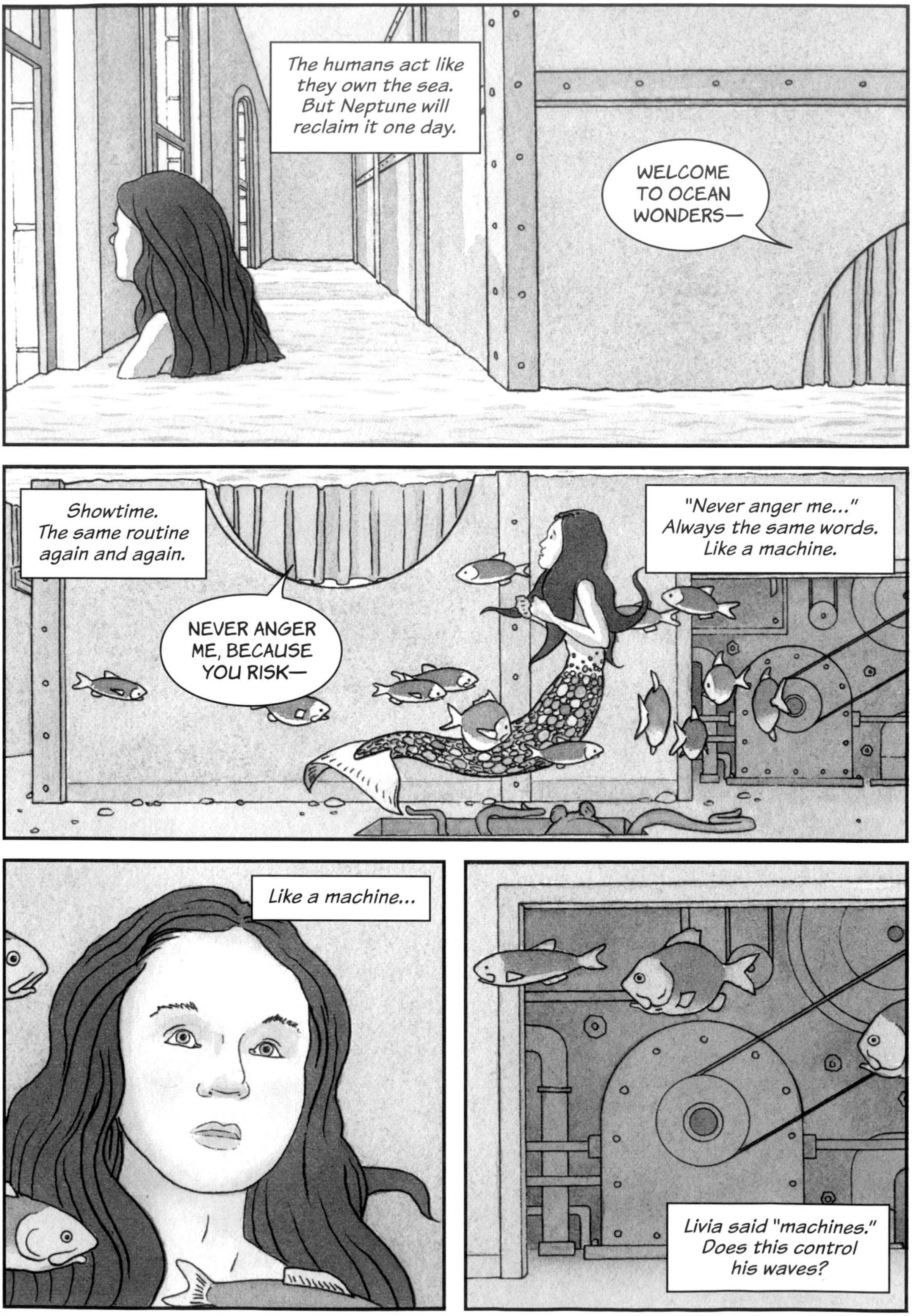
The humans act like they own the sea. But Neptune will reclaim it one day.
WELCOME TO OCEAN WONDERS—
Showtime. The same routine again and again.
NEVER ANGER ME, BECAUSE YOU RISK—
"Never anger me..." Always the same words. Like a machine.
Like a machine...
Livia said "machines." Does this control his waves?

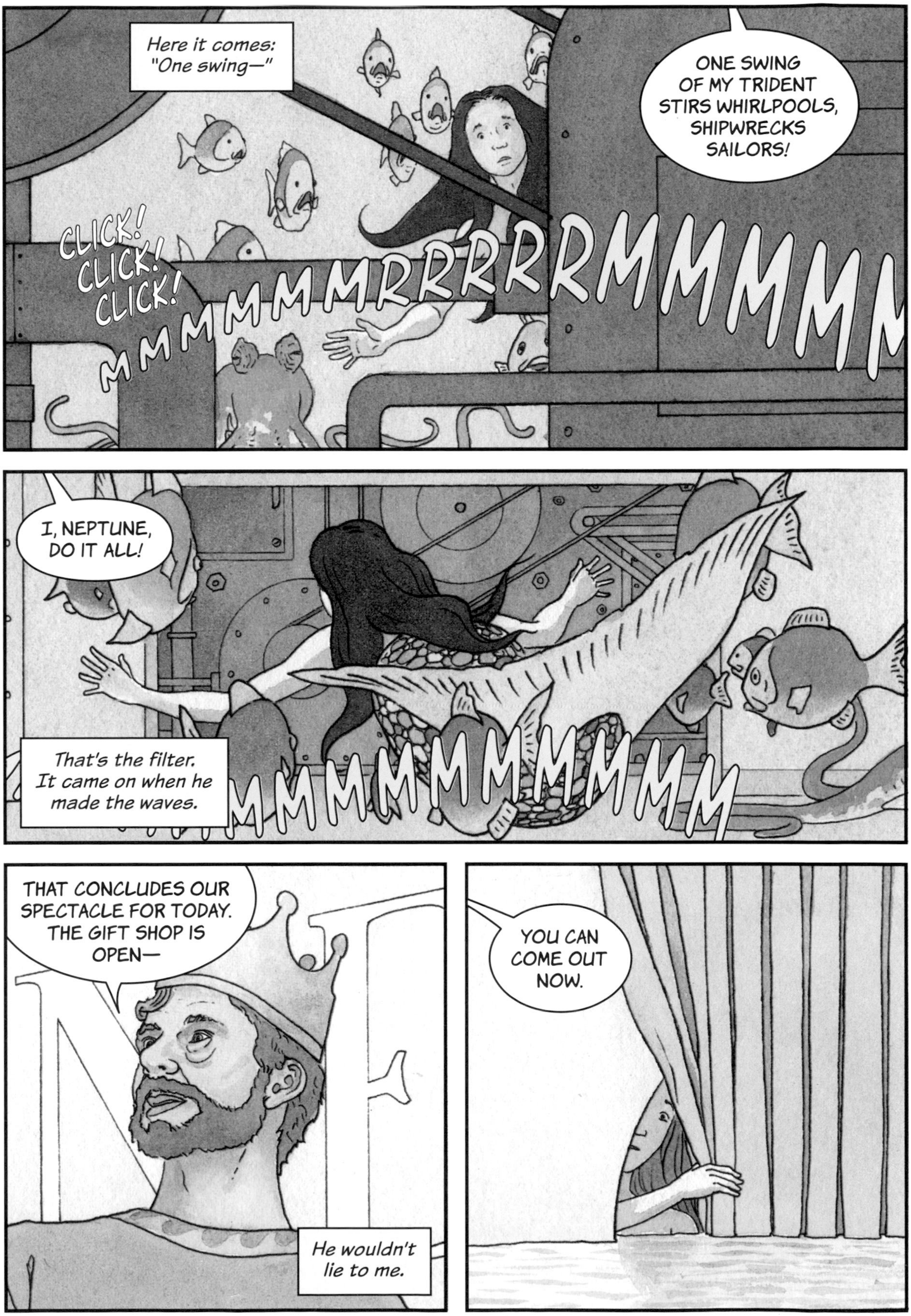
Here it comes: "One swing—"
ONE SWING OF MY TRIDENT STIRS WHIRLPOOLS, SHIPWRECKS SAILORS!
CLICK! CLICK! CLICK!
MMMMMMRRRRRRMMMMMM
I, NEPTUNE, DO IT ALL!
That's the filter. It came on when he made the waves.
MMMMMMMMMMMMM
THAT CONCLUDES OUR SPECTACLE FOR TODAY. THE GIFT SHOP IS OPEN—
He wouldn't lie to me.
YOU CAN COME OUT NOW.

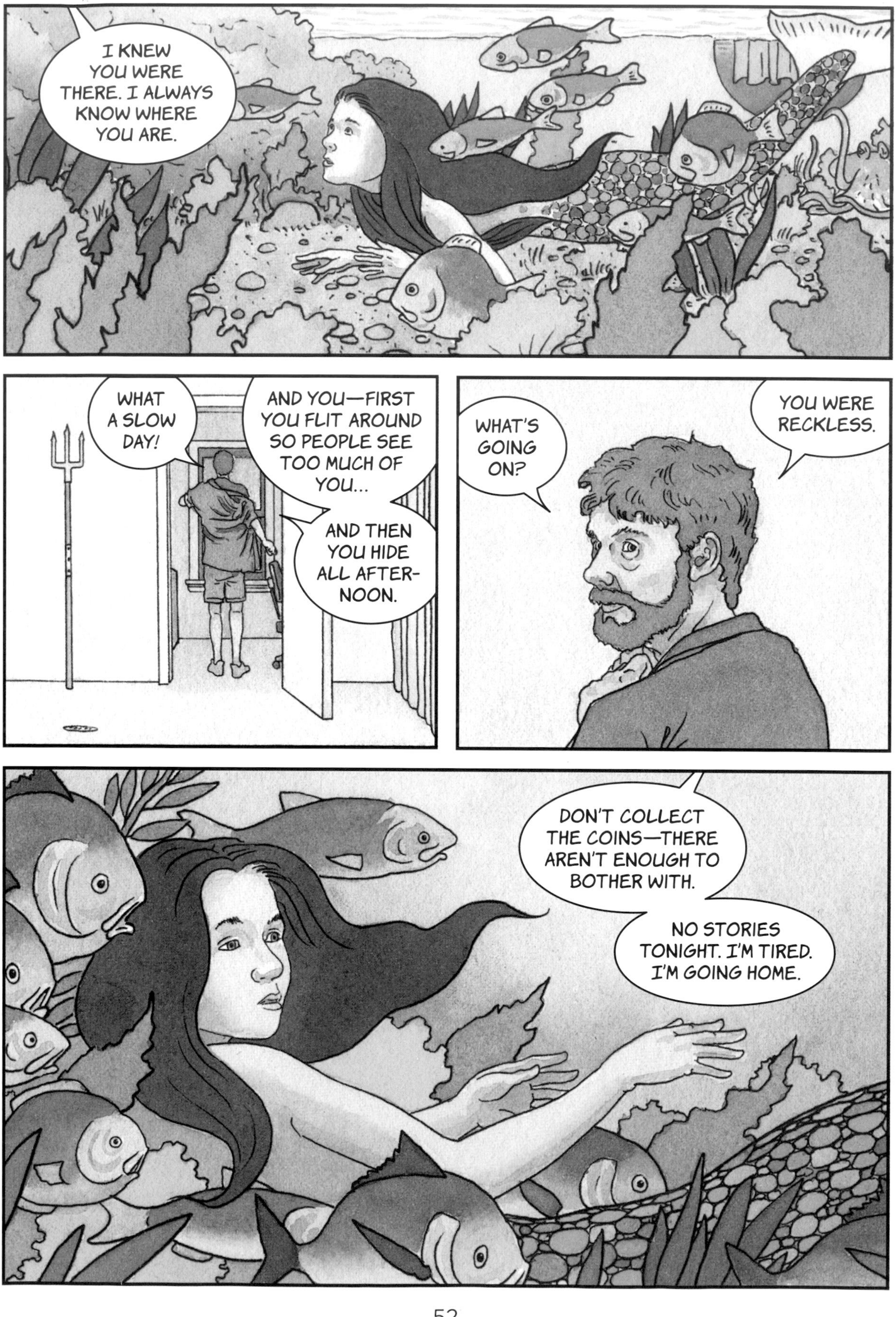

I KNEW YOU WERE THERE. I ALWAYS KNOW WHERE YOU ARE.
WHAT A SLOW DAY!
AND YOU—FIRST YOU FLIT AROUND SO PEOPLE SEE TOO MUCH OF YOU...
AND THEN YOU HIDE ALL AFTER-NOON.
WHAT'S GOING ON?
YOU WERE RECKLESS.
DON'T COLLECT THE COINS—THERE AREN'T ENOUGH TO BOTHER WITH.
NO STORIES TONIGHT. I'M TIRED. I'M GOING HOME.

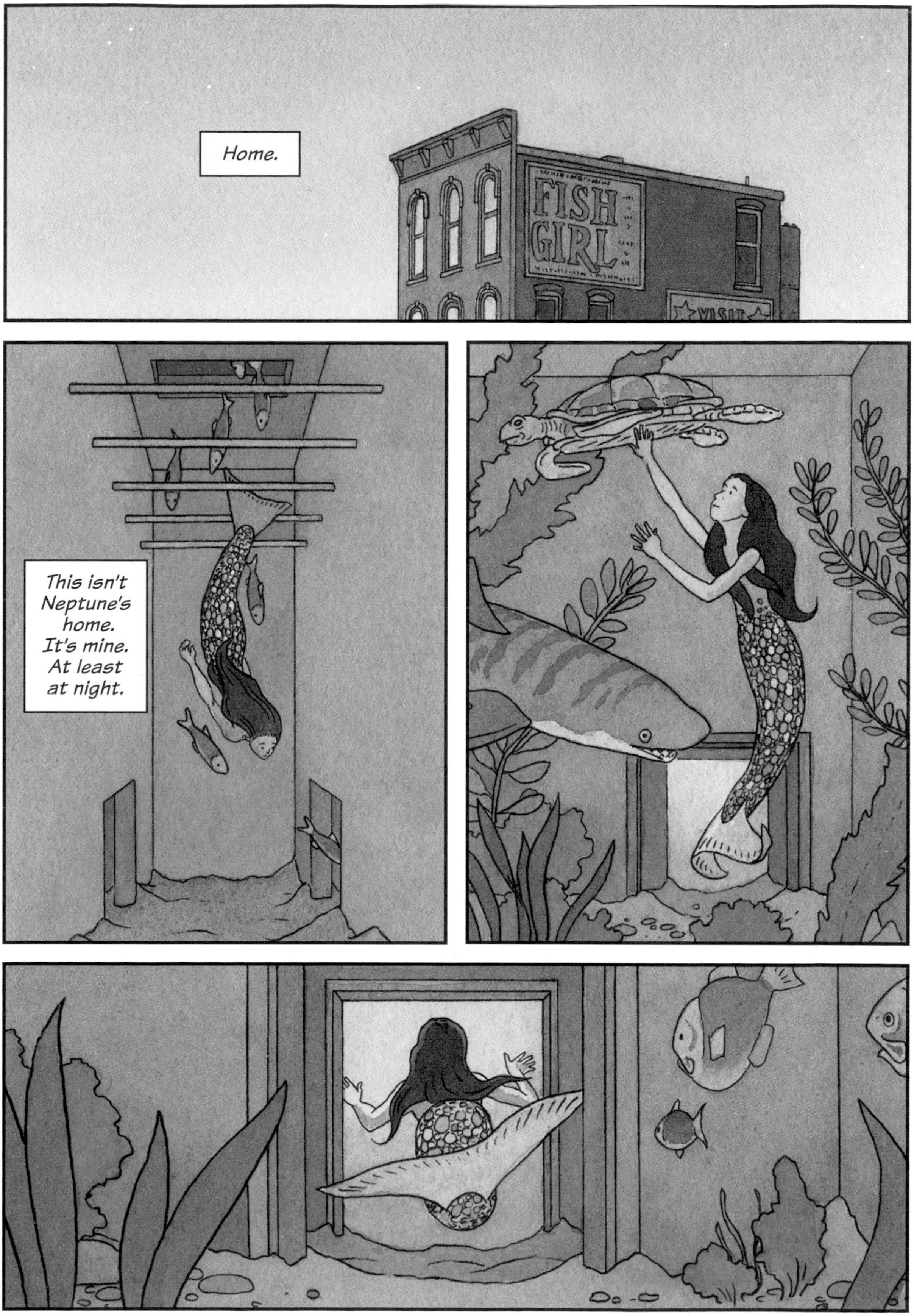
Home.
FISH GIRL
This isn't Neptune's home. It's mine. At least at night.

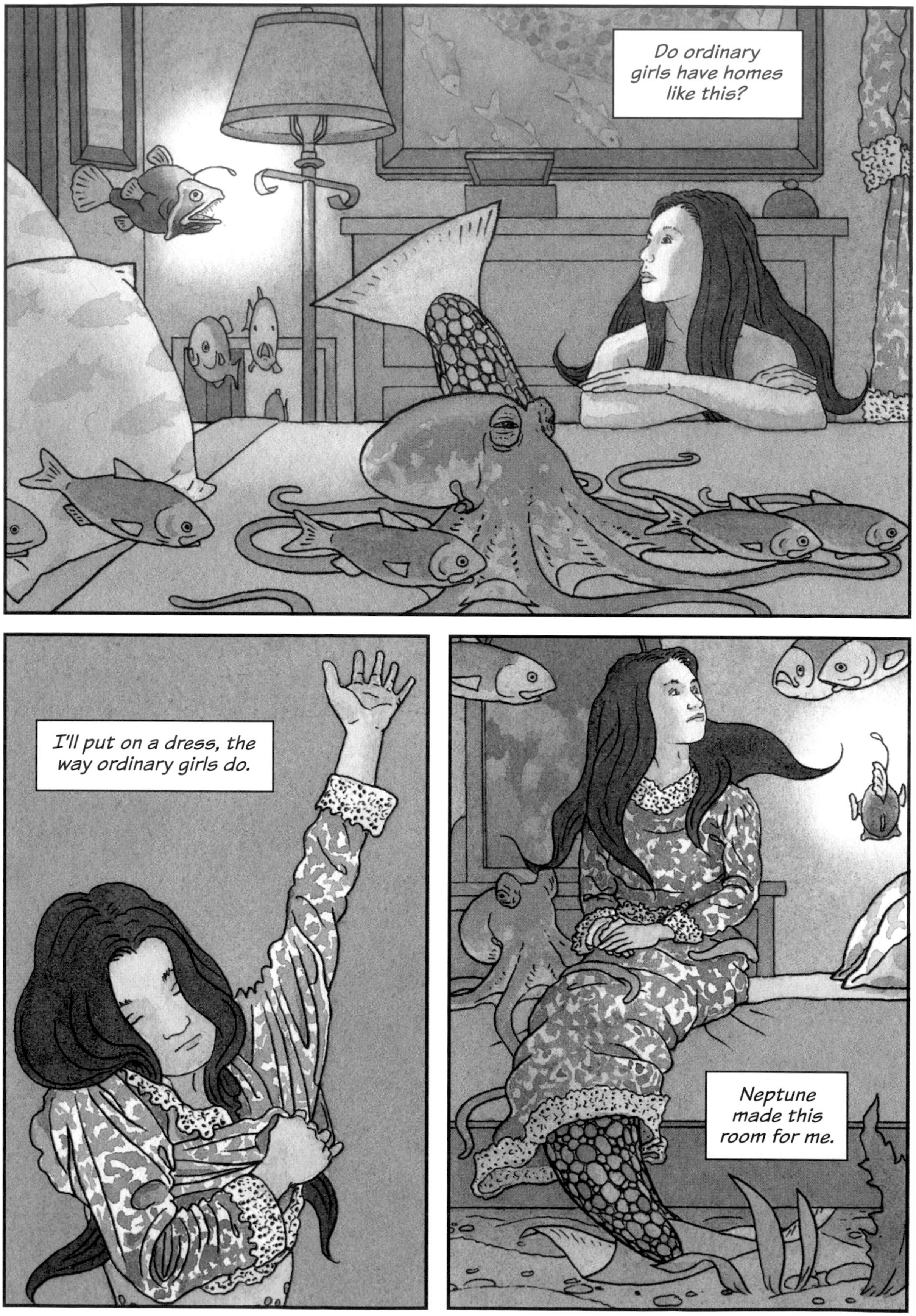
Do ordinary
girls have homes
like this?
I'll put on a dress, the
way ordinary girls do.
Neptune
made this
room for me.

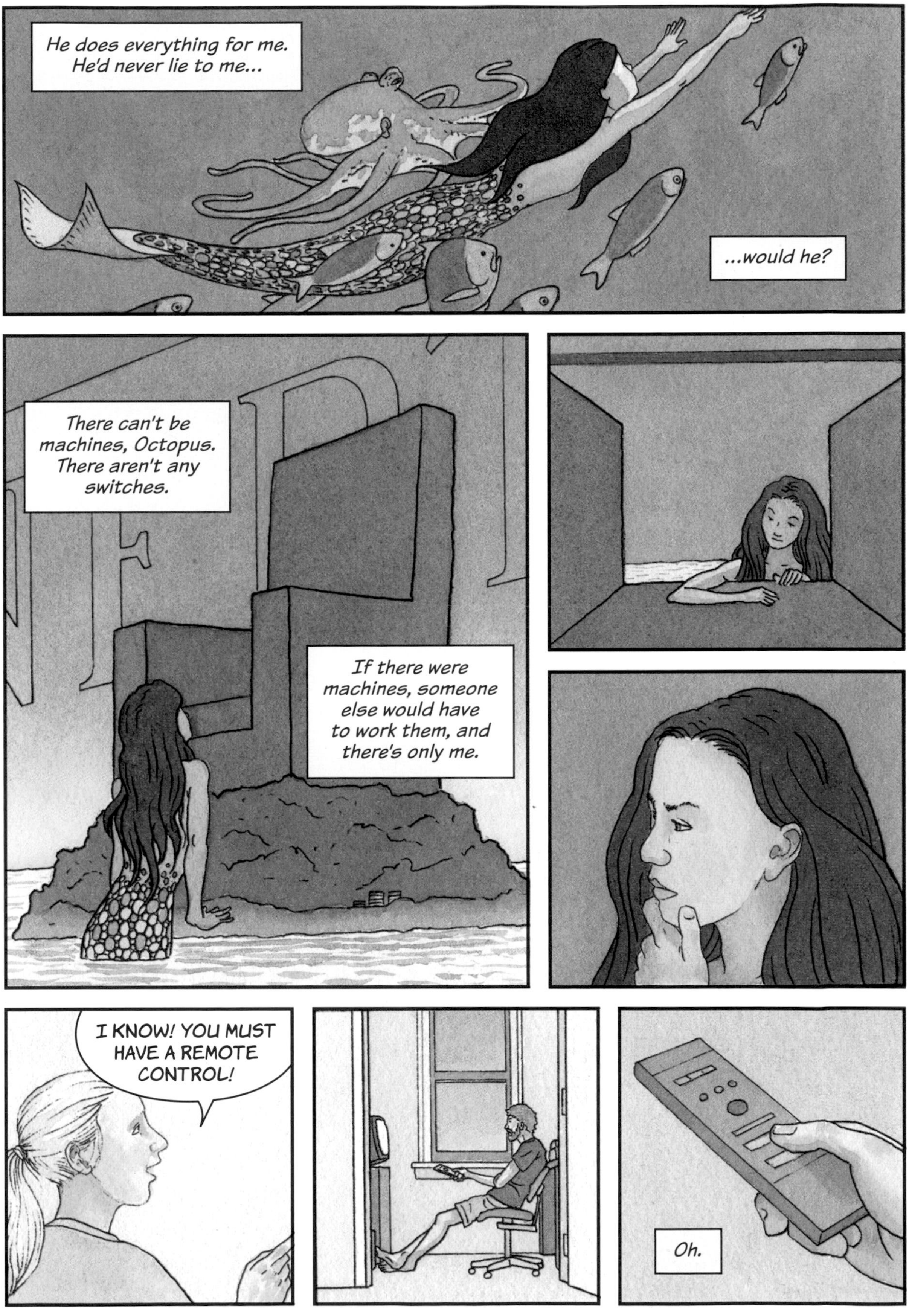
He does everything for me. He'd never lie to me...
...would he?
There can't be machines, Octopus. There aren't any switches.
If there were machines, someone else would have to work them, and there's only me.
I KNOW! YOU MUST HAVE A REMOTE CONTROL!
Oh.

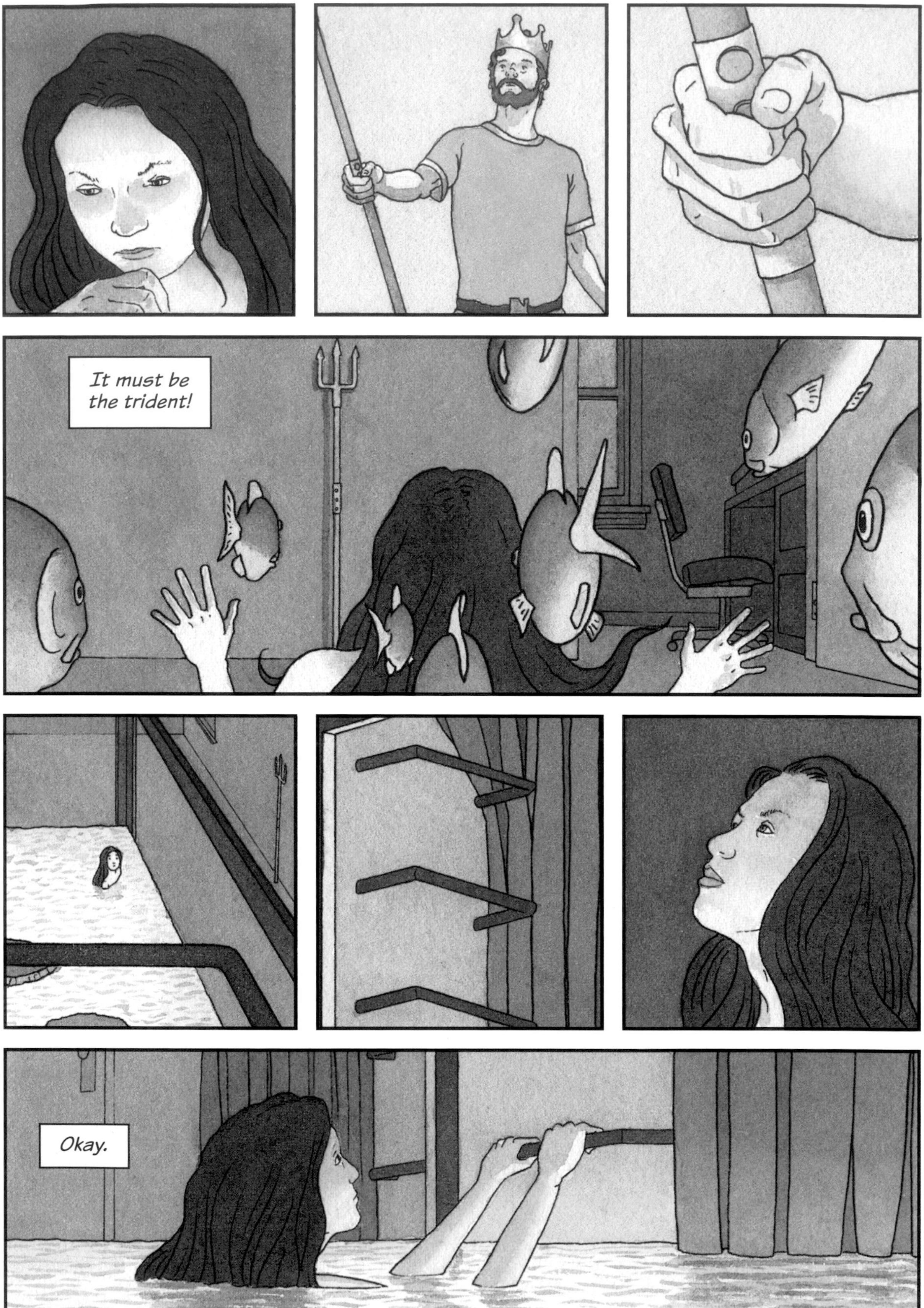
It must be the trident!
Okay.

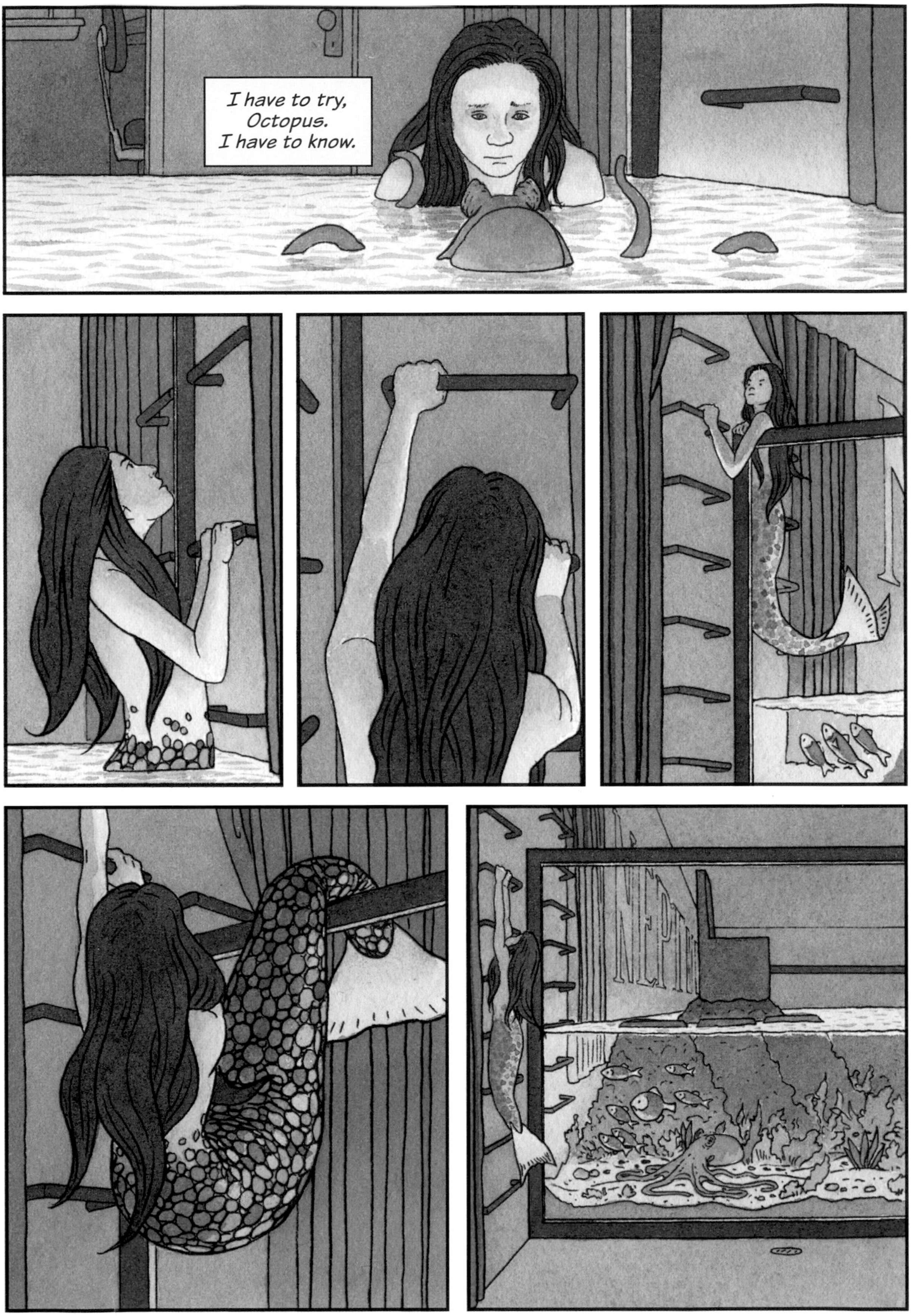
I have to try, Octopus. I have to know.

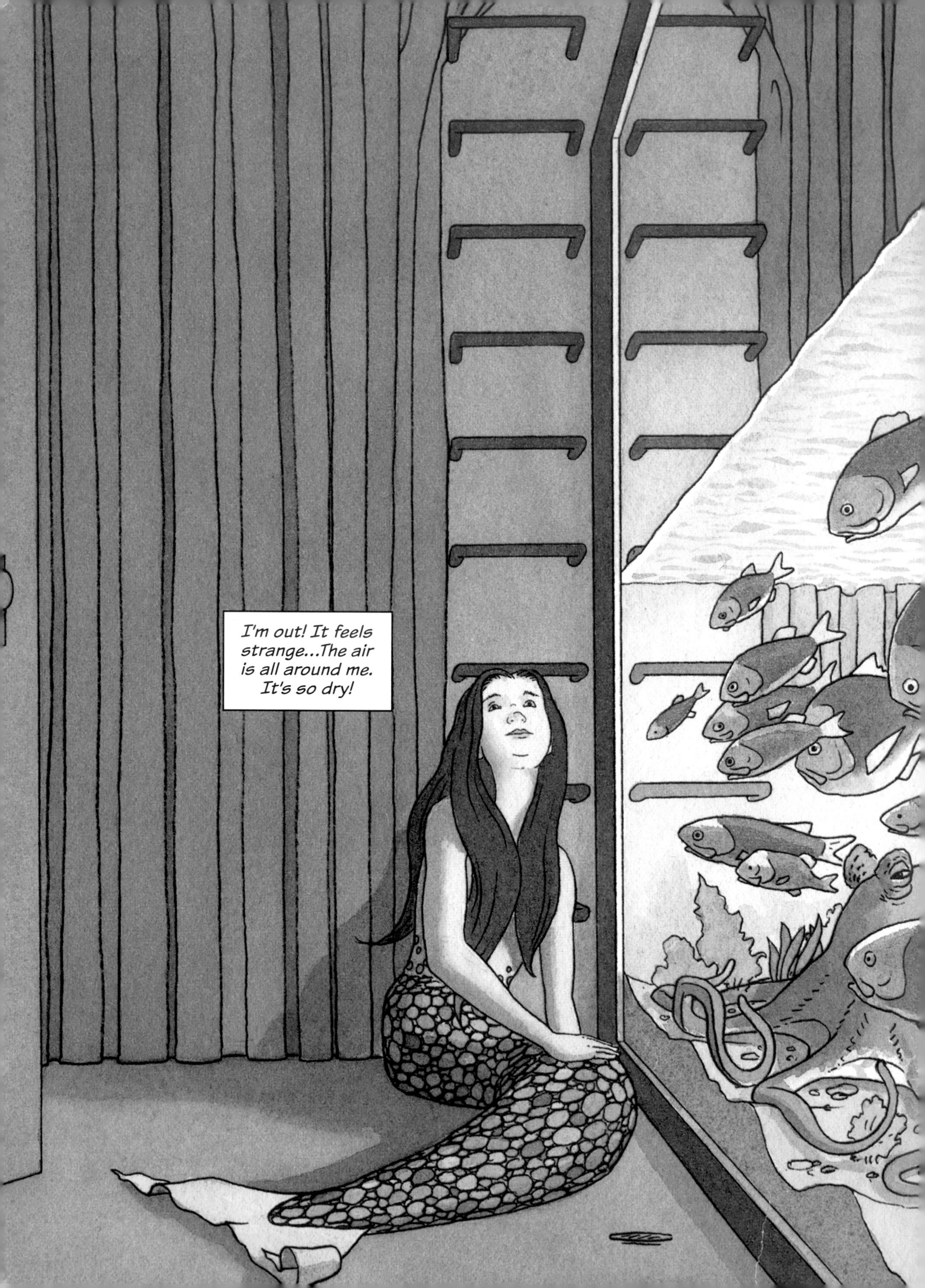
I'm out! It feels strange...The air is all around me. It's so dry!

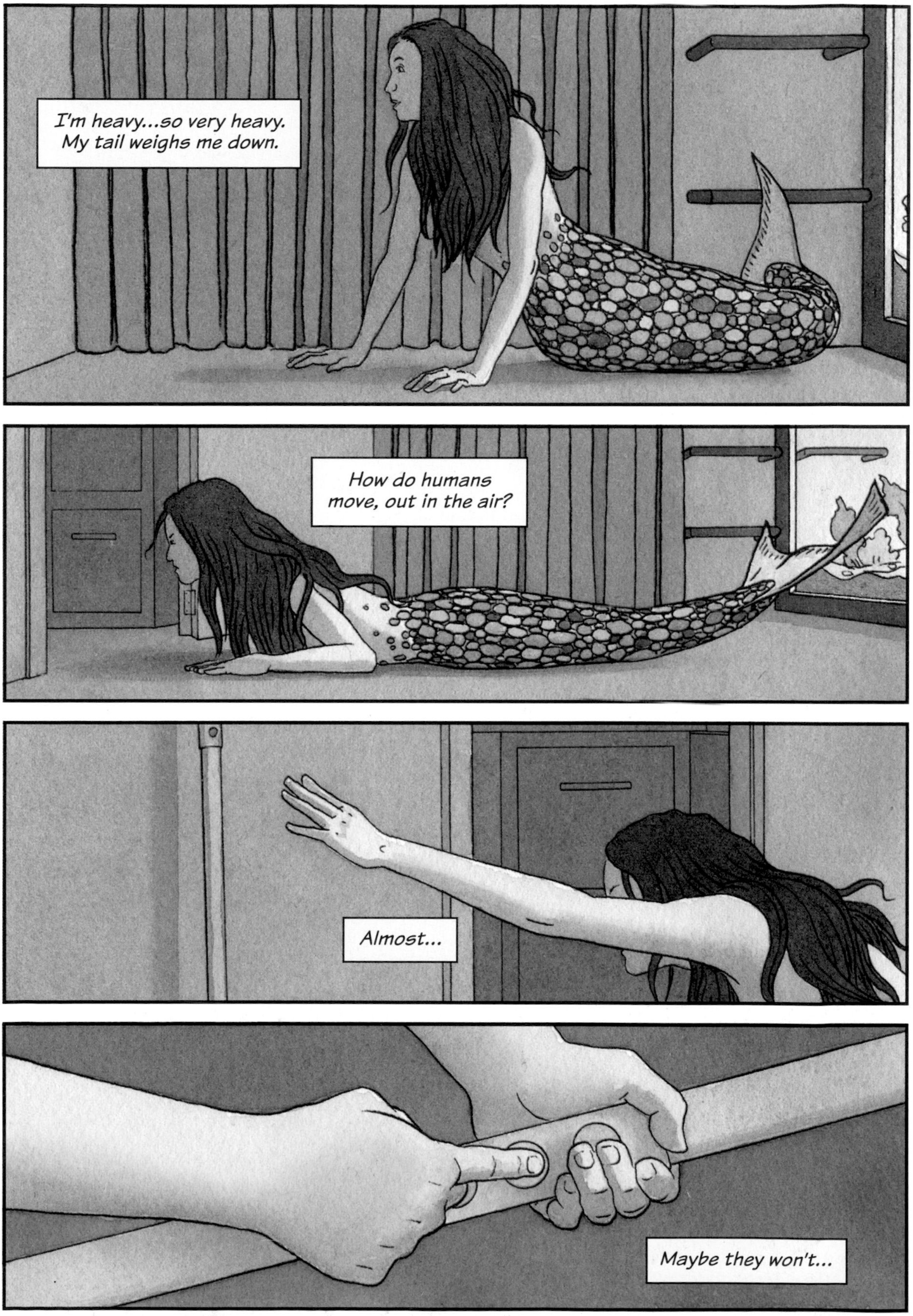
I'm heavy...so very heavy.
My tail weighs me down.
How do humans
move, out in the air?
Almost...
Maybe they won't...

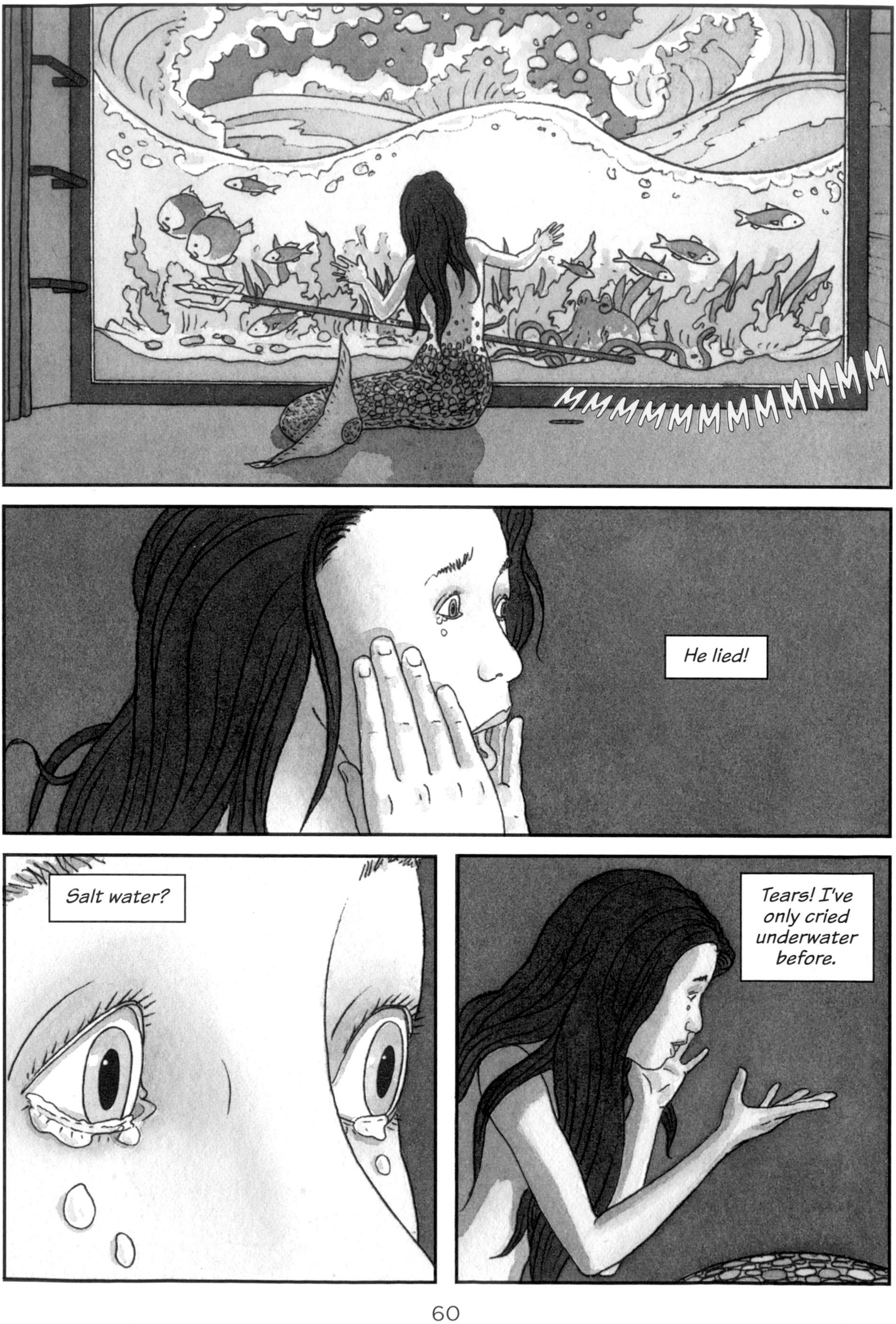
MMMMMMMMMMMMMMMMM
He lied!
Salt water?
Tears! I've only cried underwater before.

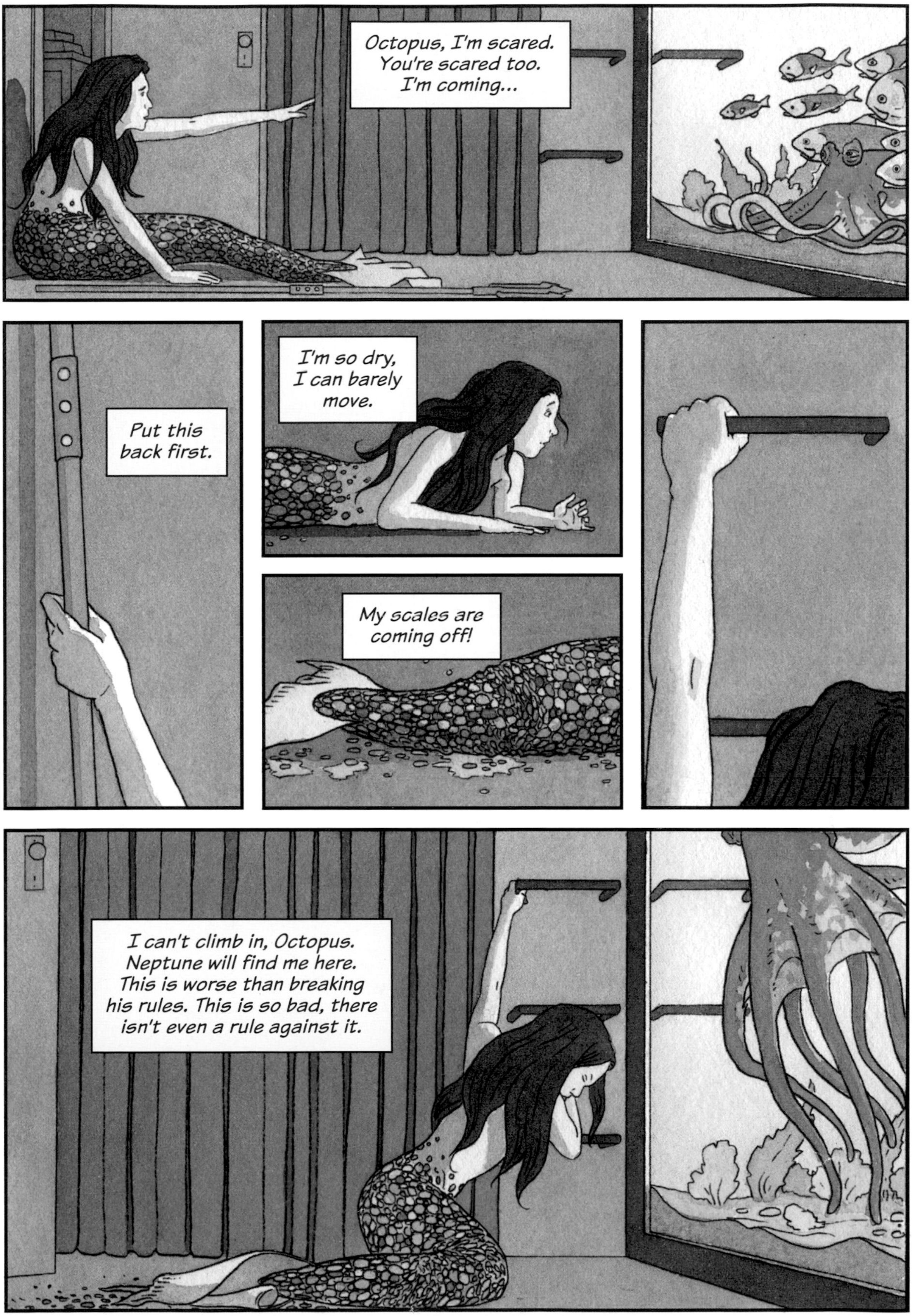
Octopus, I'm scared. You're scared too. I'm coming...
Put this back first.
I'm so dry, I can barely move.
My scales are coming off!
I can't climb in, Octopus. Neptune will find me here. This is worse than breaking his rules. This is so bad, there isn't even a rule against it.

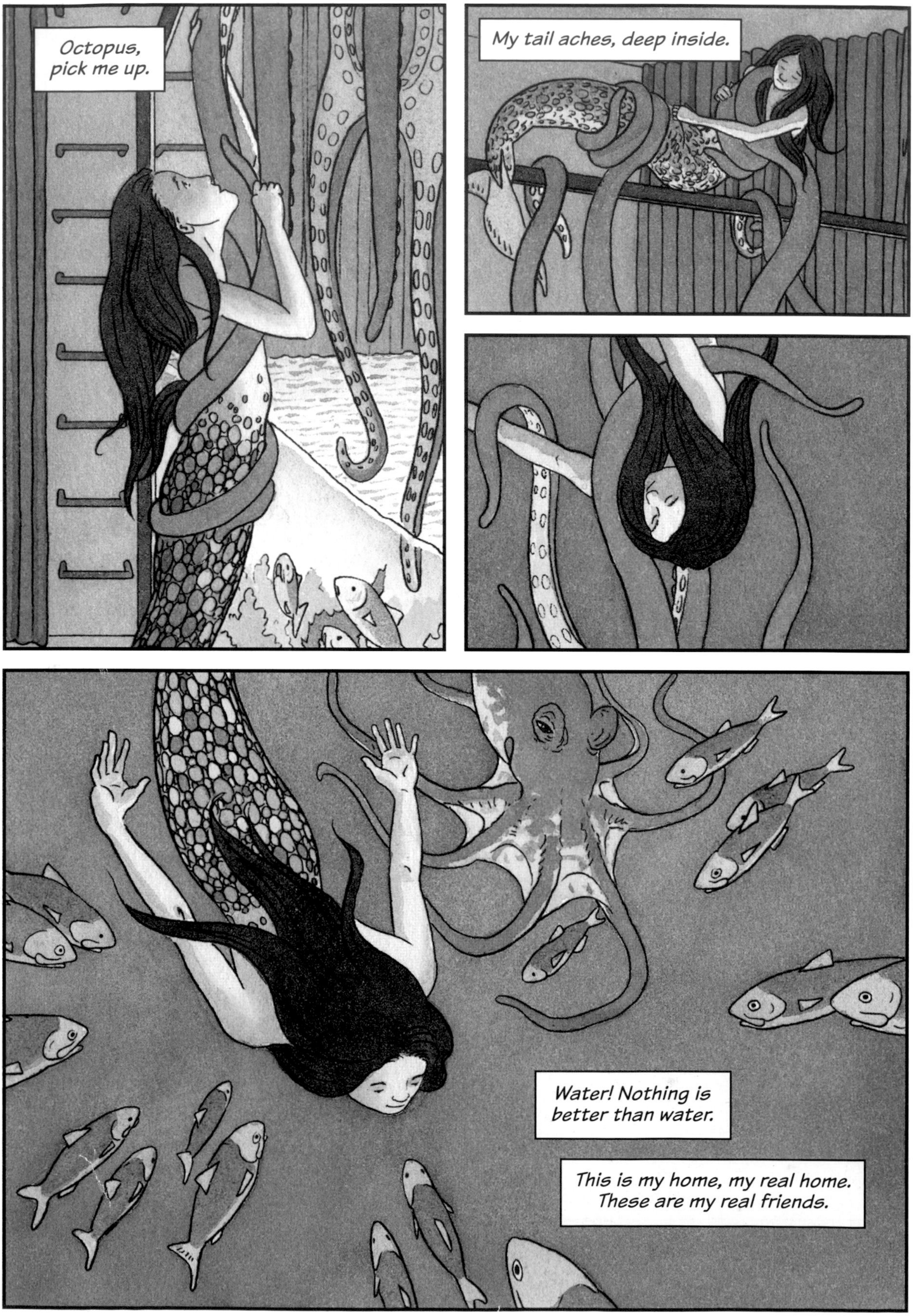
Octopus, pick me up.
My tail aches, deep inside.
Water! Nothing is better than water.
This is my home, my real home. These are my real friends.

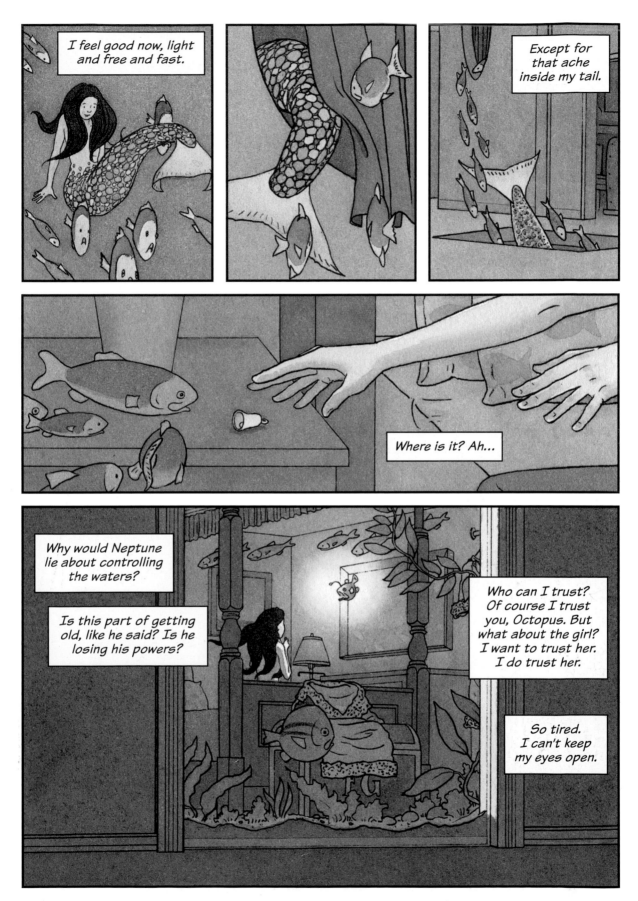

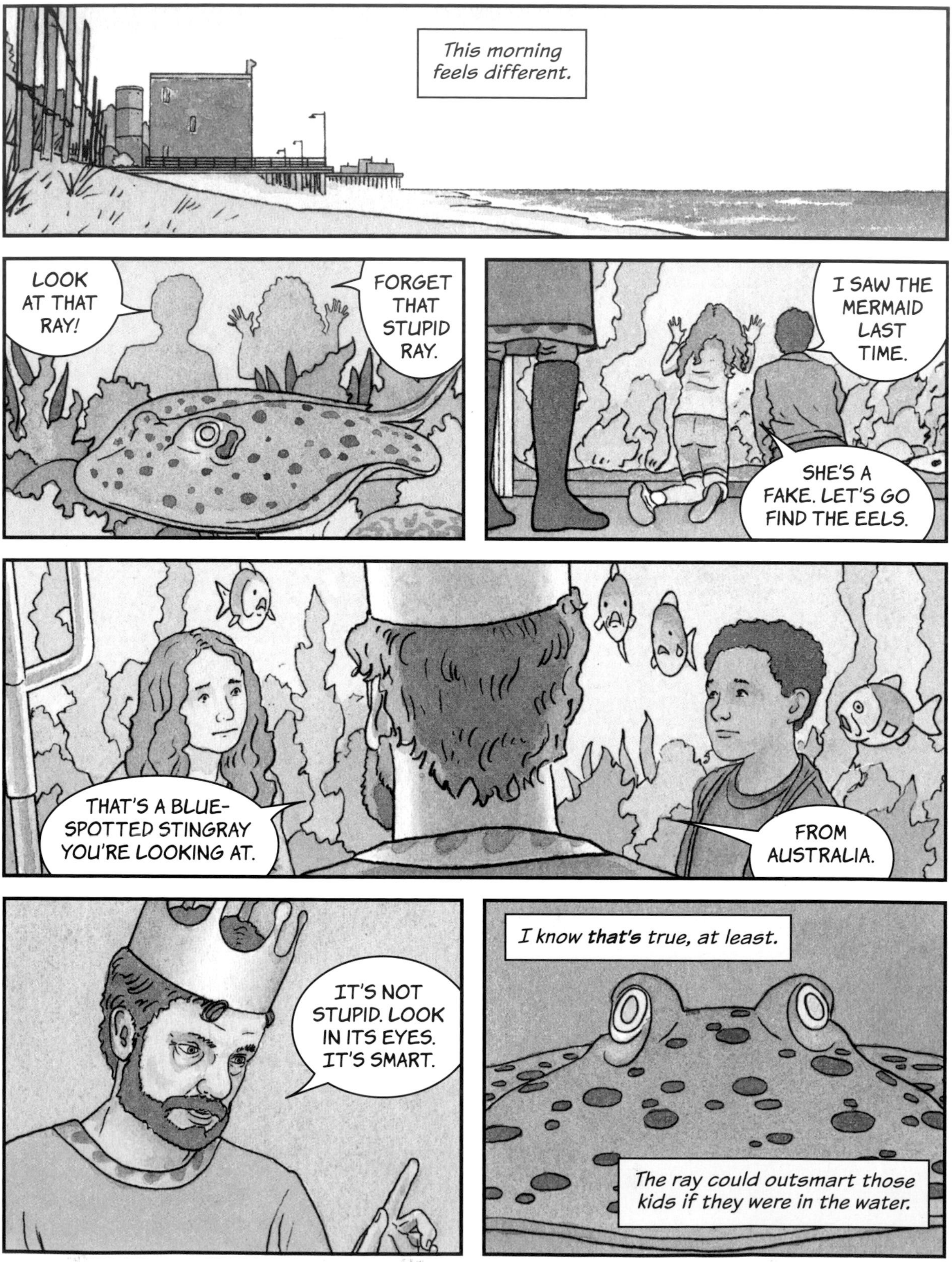
This morning feels different.
LOOK AT THAT RAY!
FORGET THAT STUPID RAY.
I SAW THE MERMAID LAST TIME.
SHE'S A FAKE. LET'S GO FIND THE EELS.
THAT'S A BLUE-SPOTTED STINGRAY YOU'RE LOOKING AT.
FROM AUSTRALIA.
IT'S NOT STUPID. LOOK IN ITS EYES. IT'S SMART.
I know **that's** true, at least.
The ray could outsmart those kids if they were in the water.

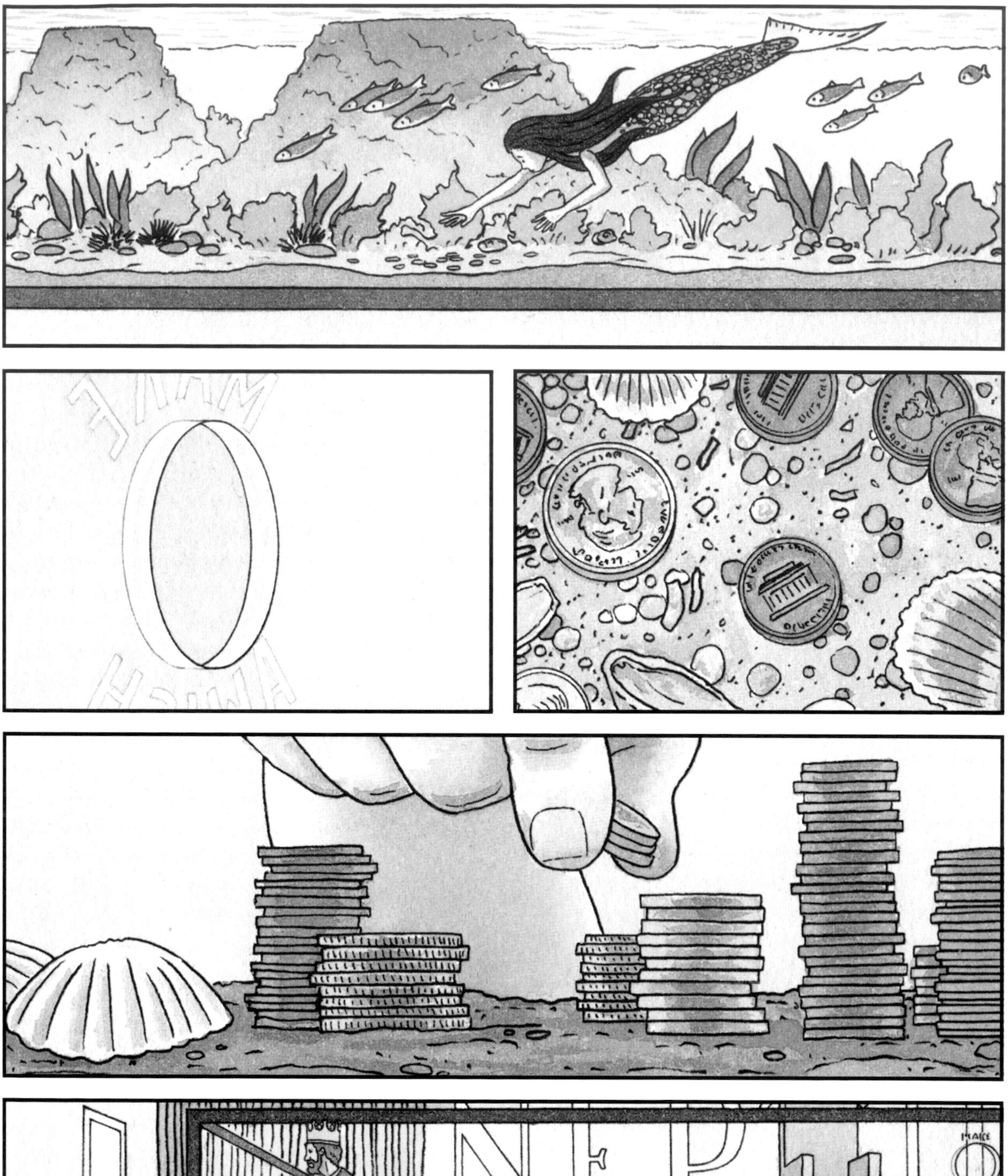
NEP
MAKE
A WISH

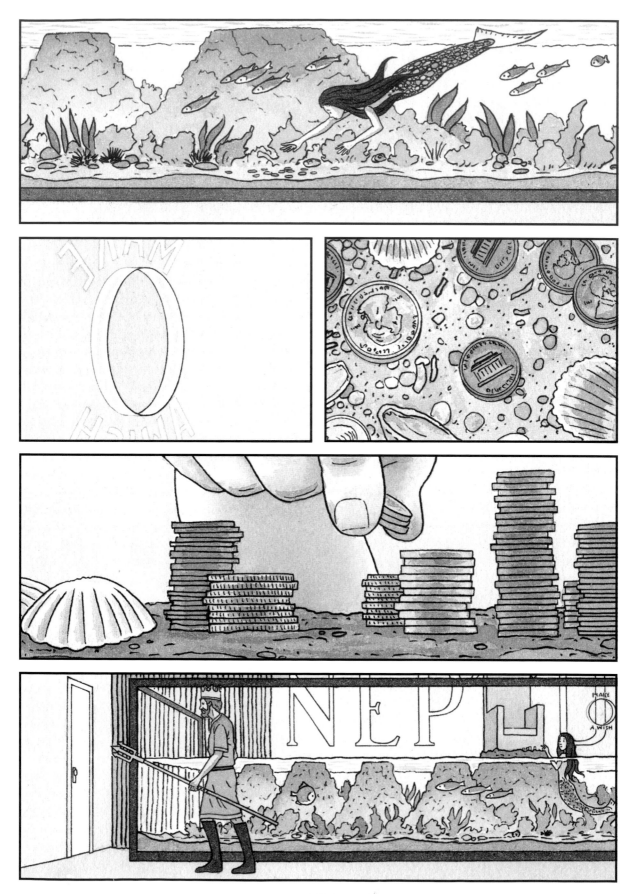

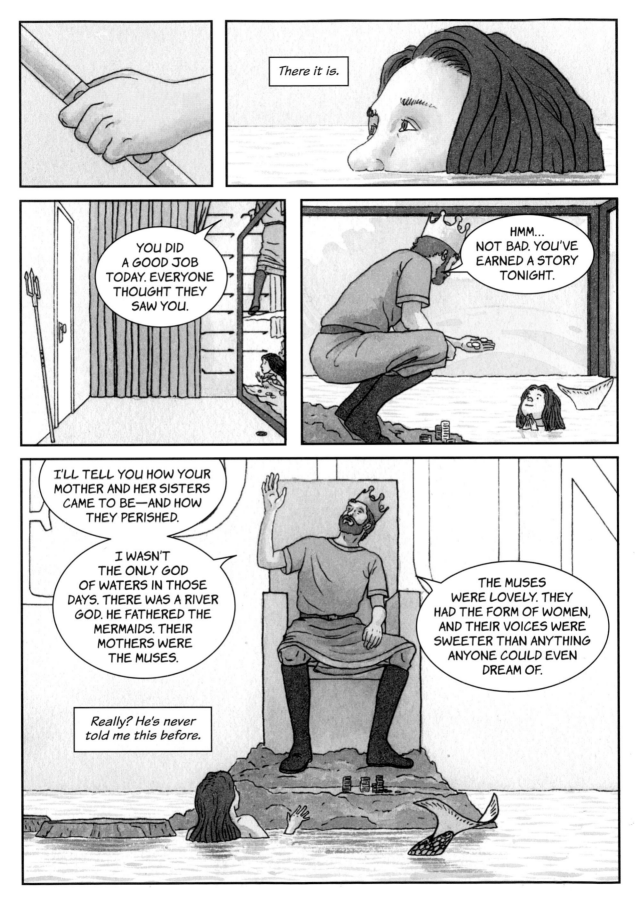

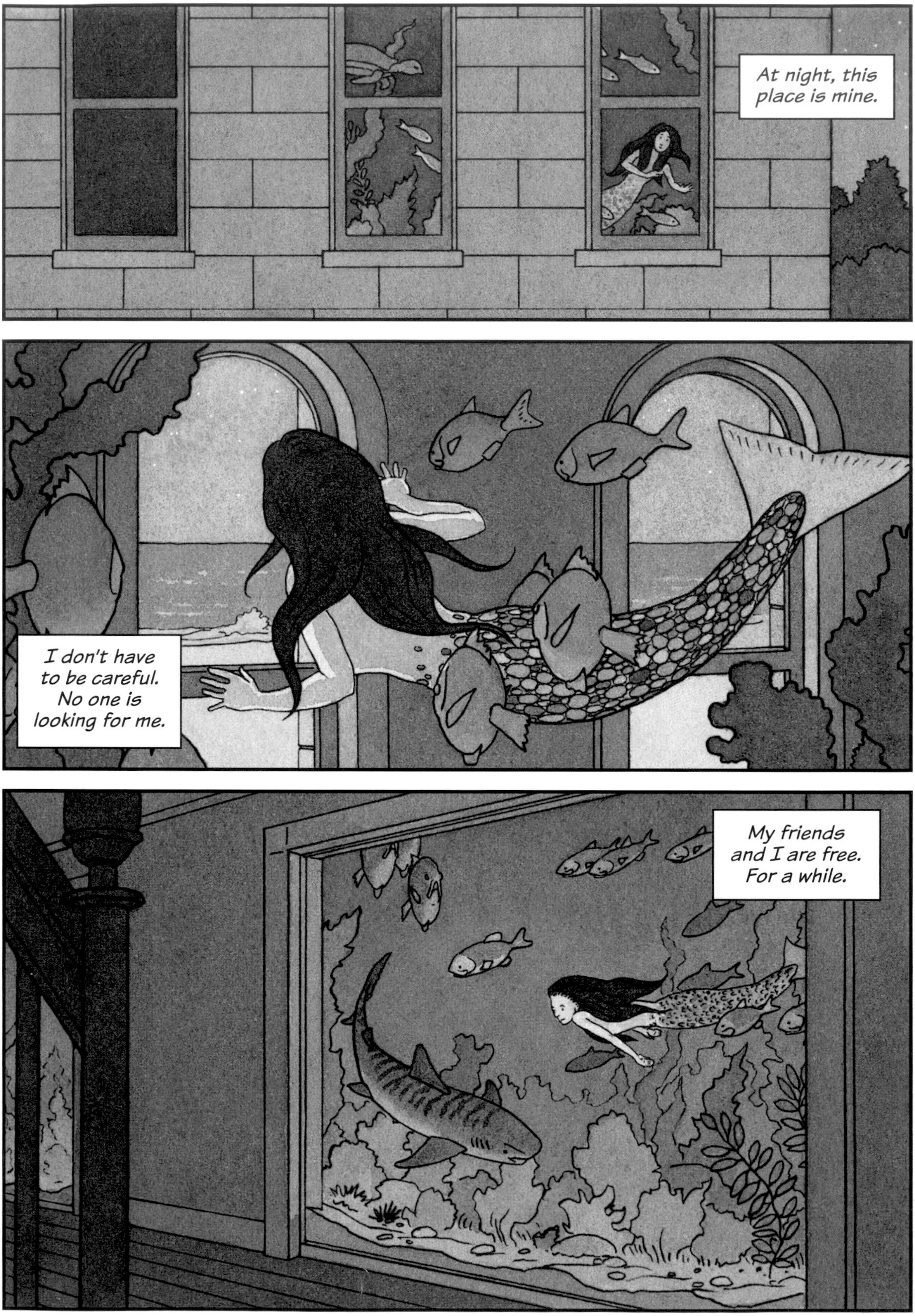
At night, this place is mine.
I don't have to be careful. No one is looking for me.
My friends and I are free. For a while.

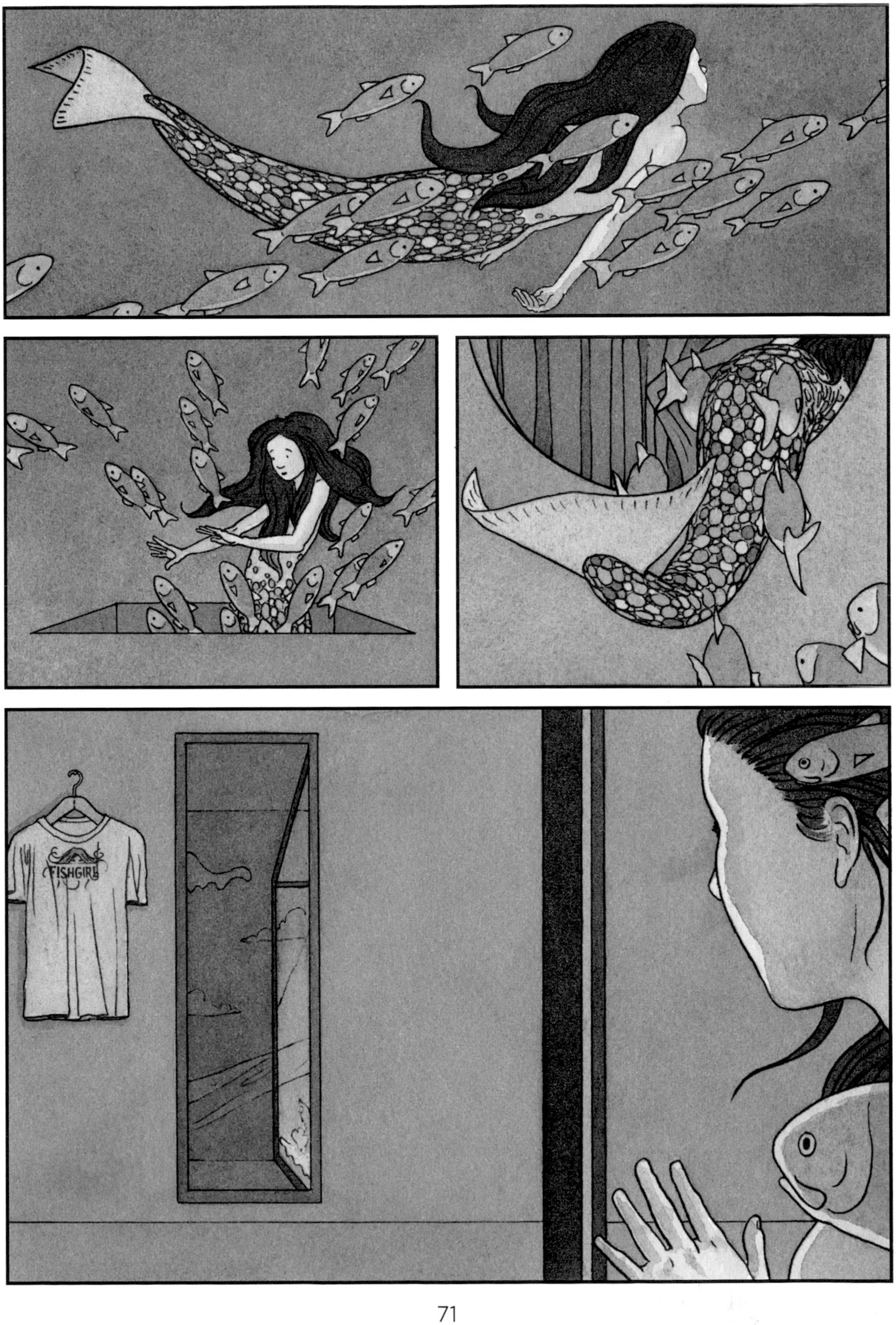
FISHGIRL

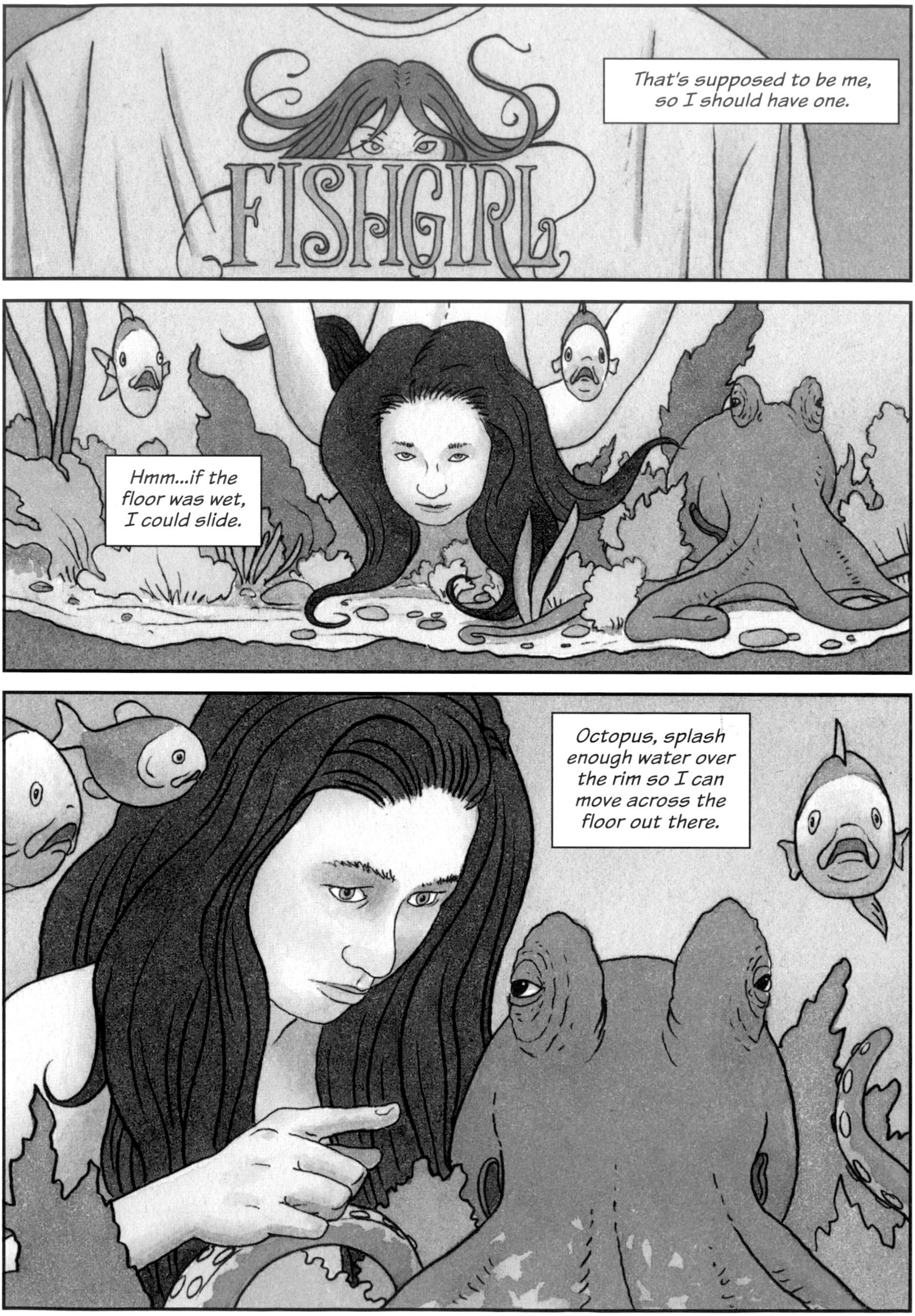
FISHGIRL
That's supposed to be me, so I should have one.
Hmm...if the floor was wet, I could slide.
Octopus, splash enough water over the rim so I can move across the floor out there.

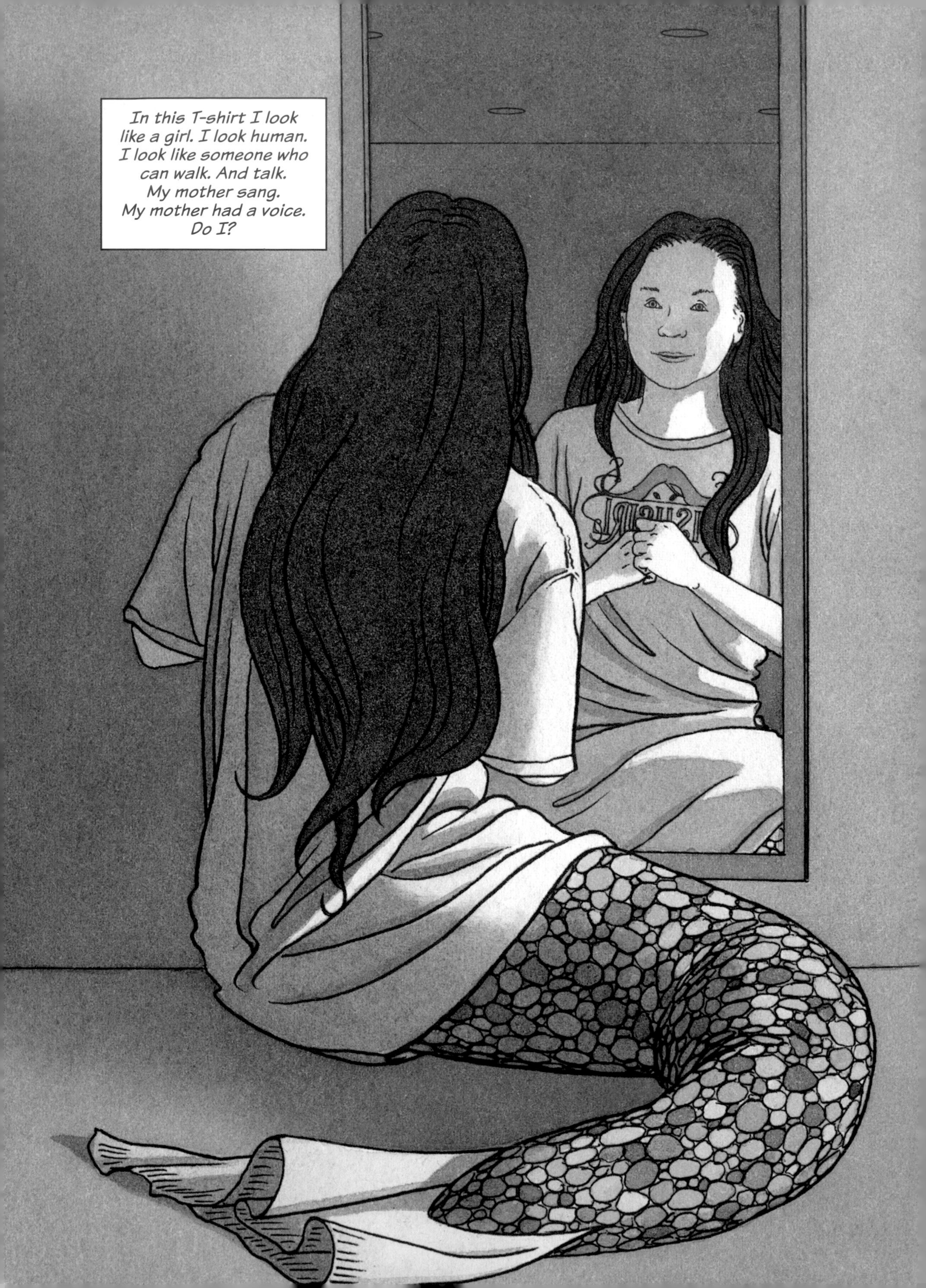
In this T-shirt I look like a girl. I look human. I look like someone who can walk. And talk. My mother sang. My mother had a voice. Do I?

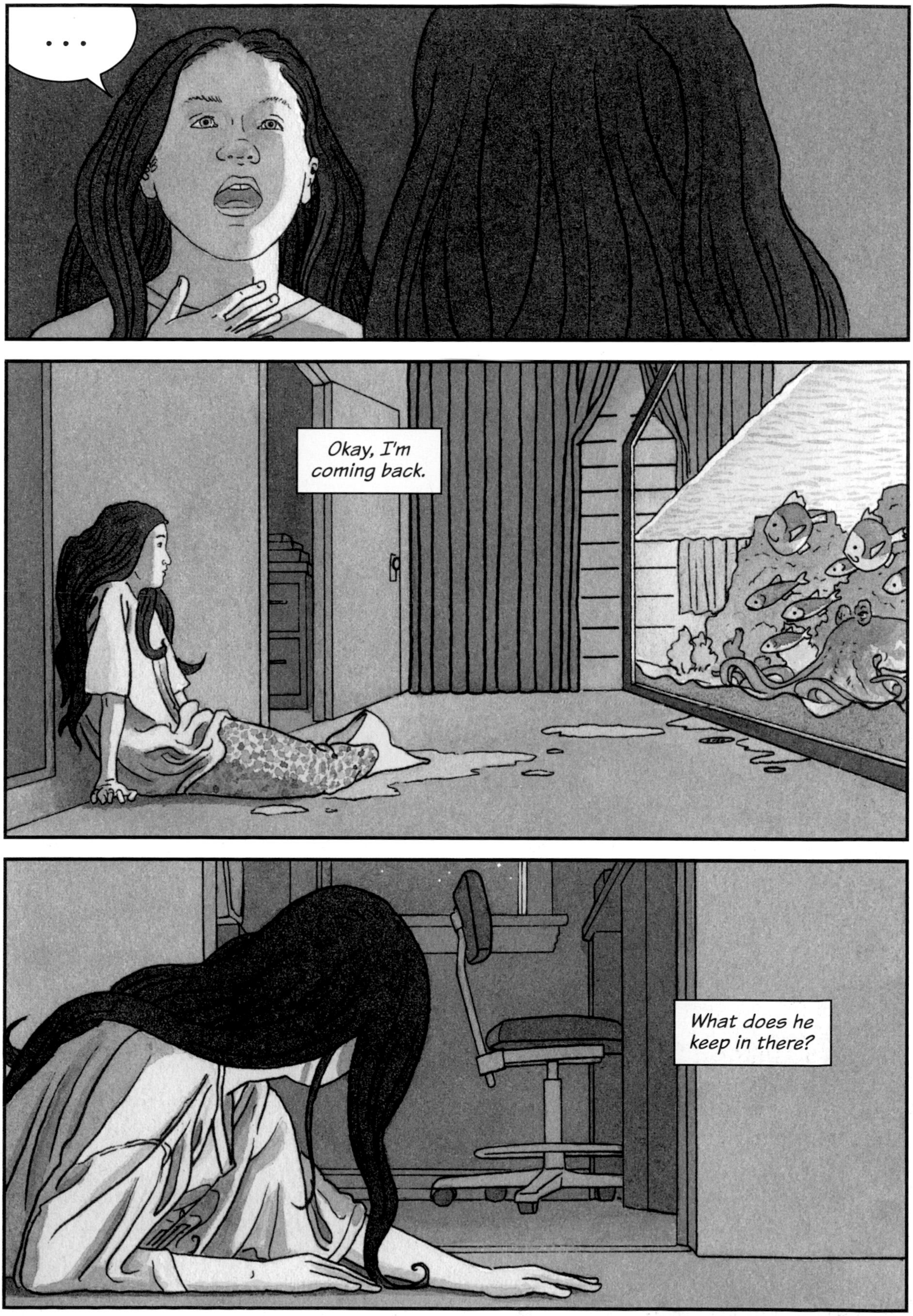
...
Okay, I'm coming back.
What does he keep in there?

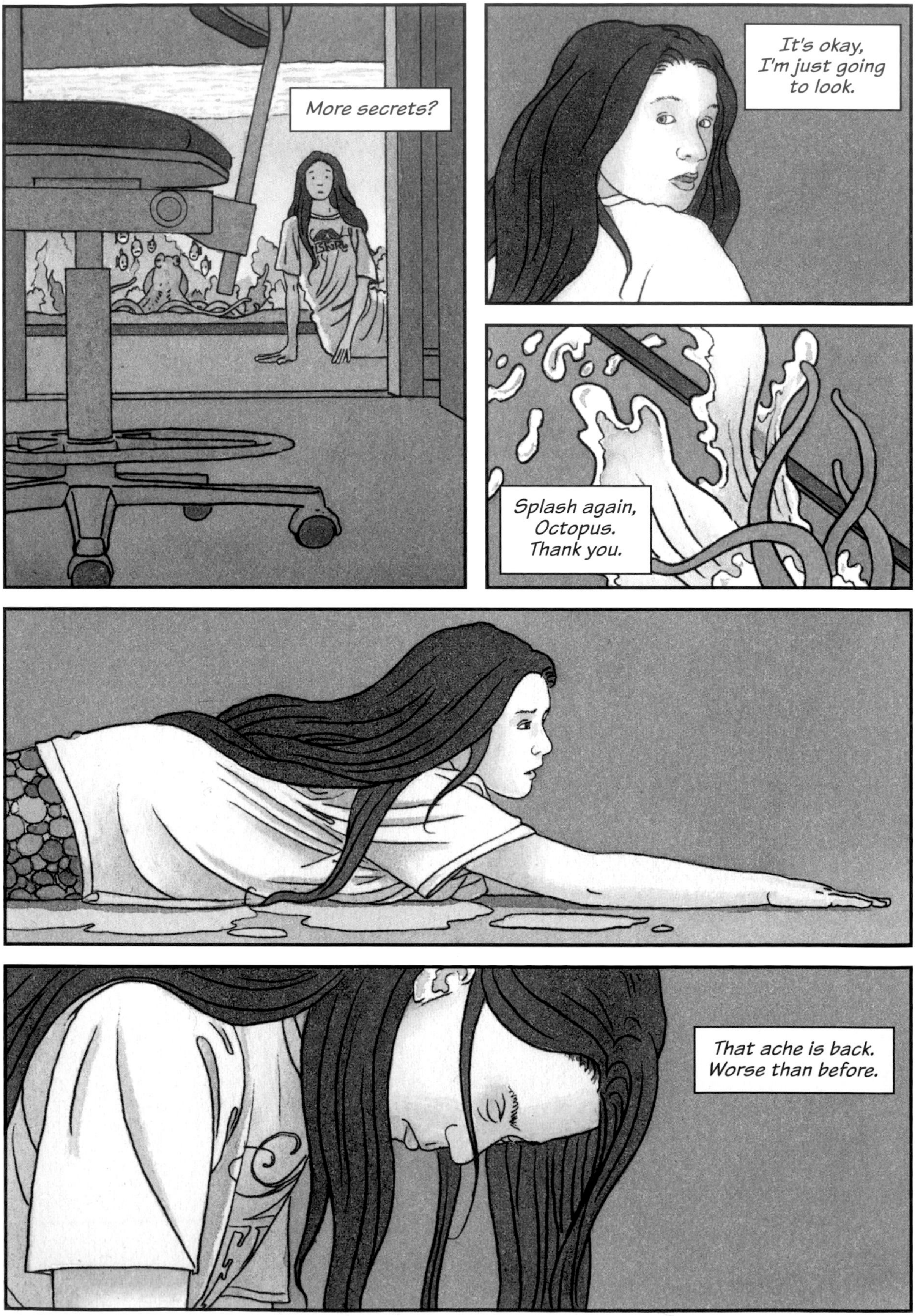
More secrets?
It's okay, I'm just going to look.
Splash again, Octopus. Thank you.
That ache is back. Worse than before.

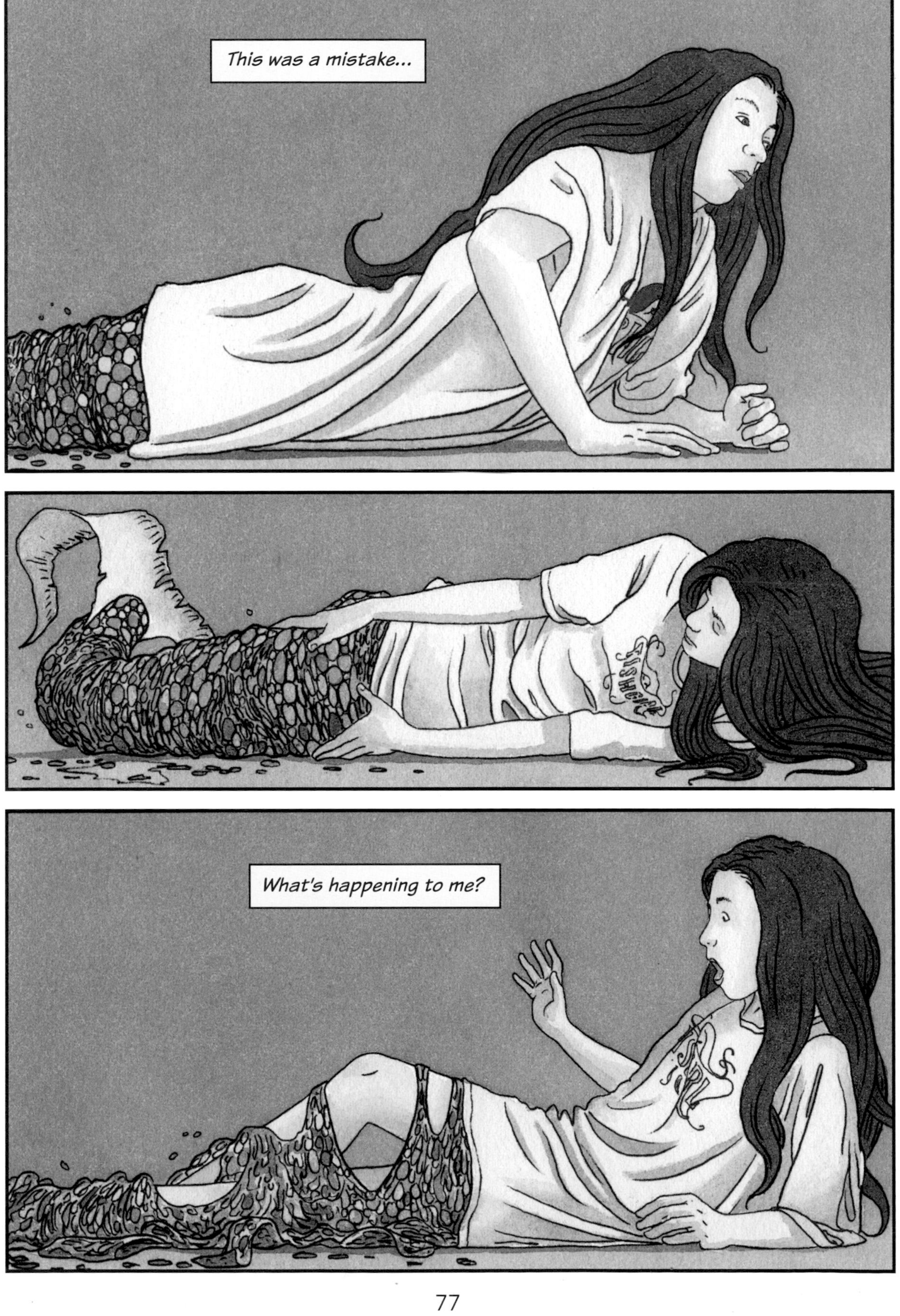
This was a mistake...
What's happening to me?

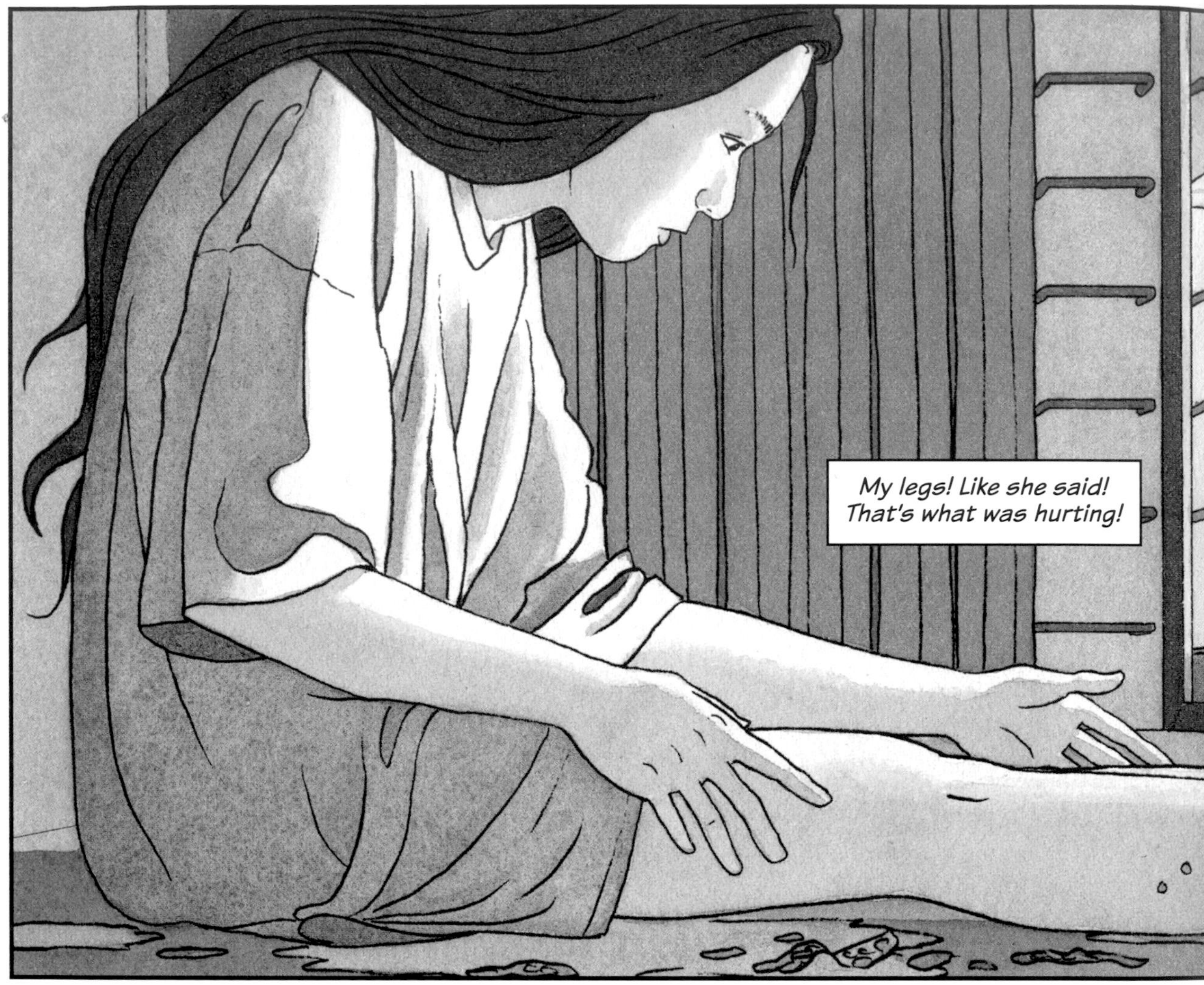
My legs! Like she said! That's what was hurting!

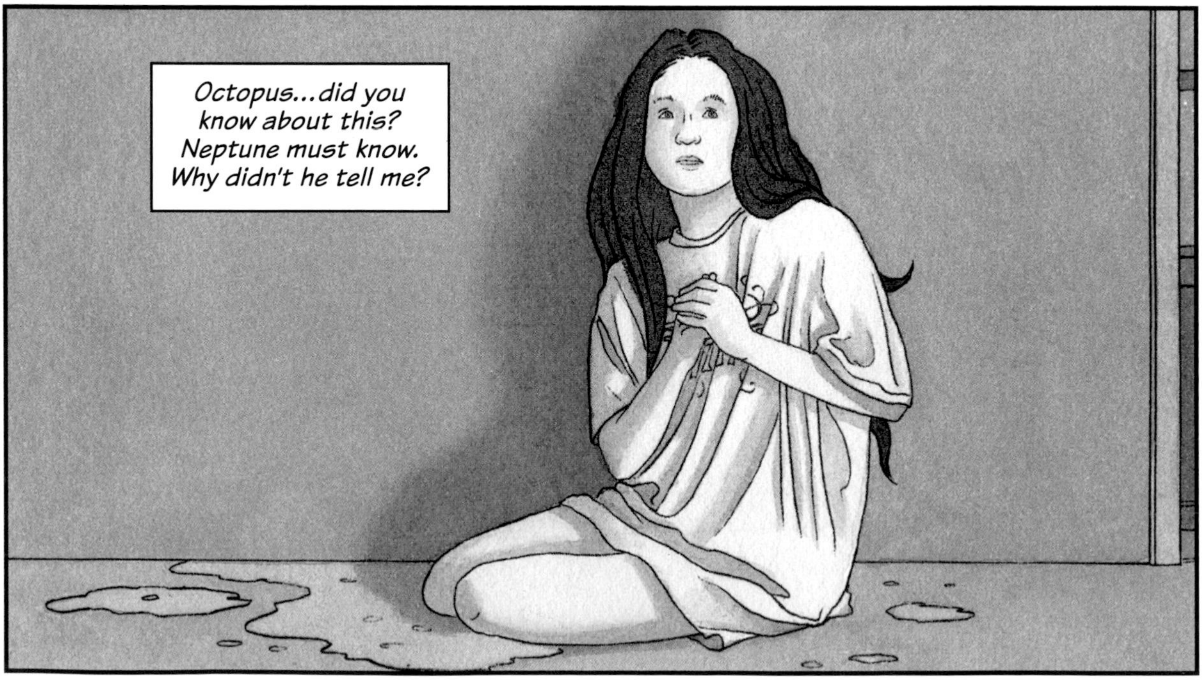
Octopus...did you know about this? Neptune must know. Why didn't he tell me?

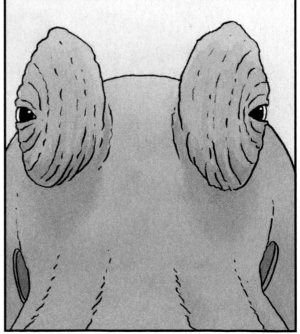

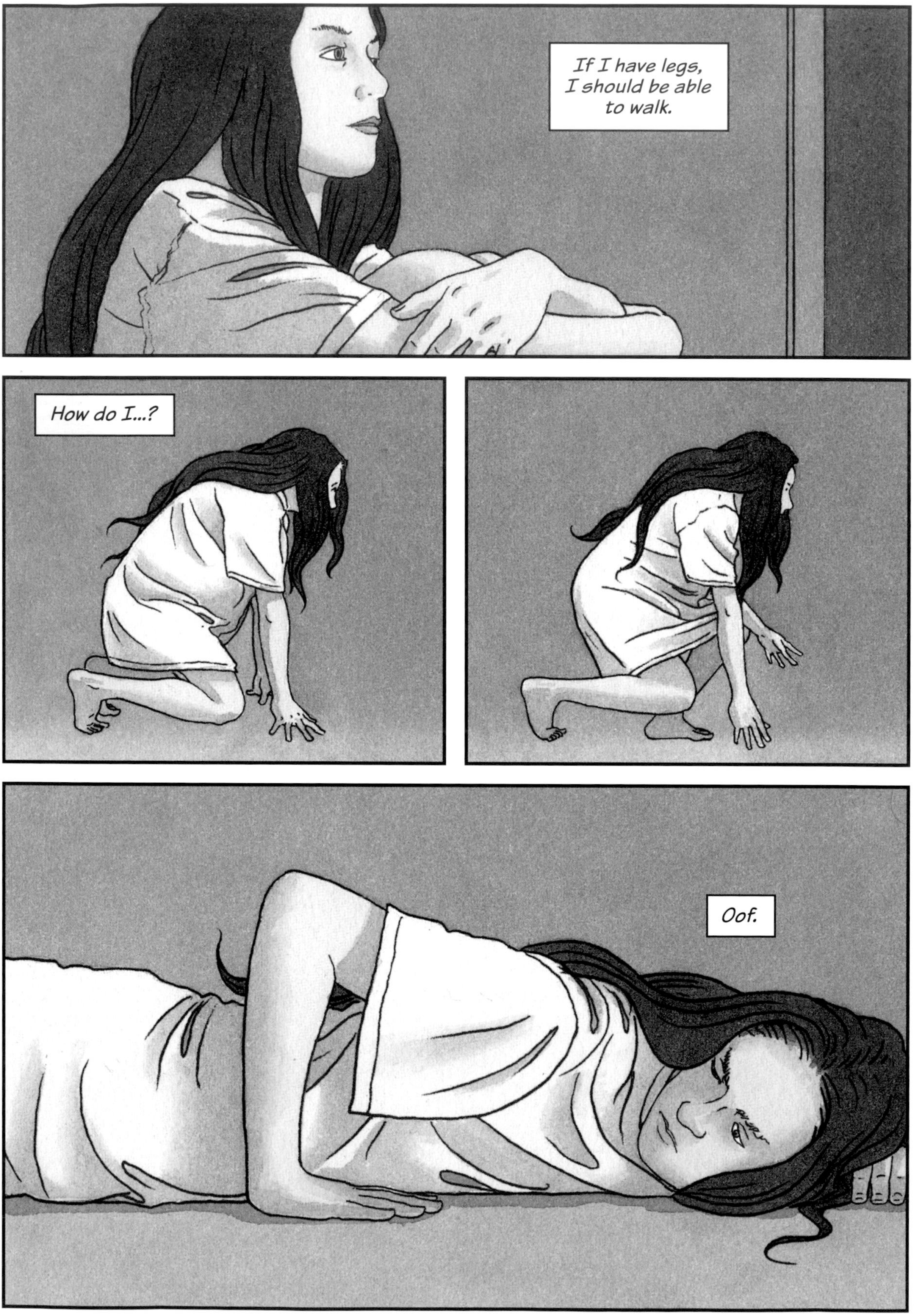
If I have legs, I should be able to walk.
How do I...?
Oof.

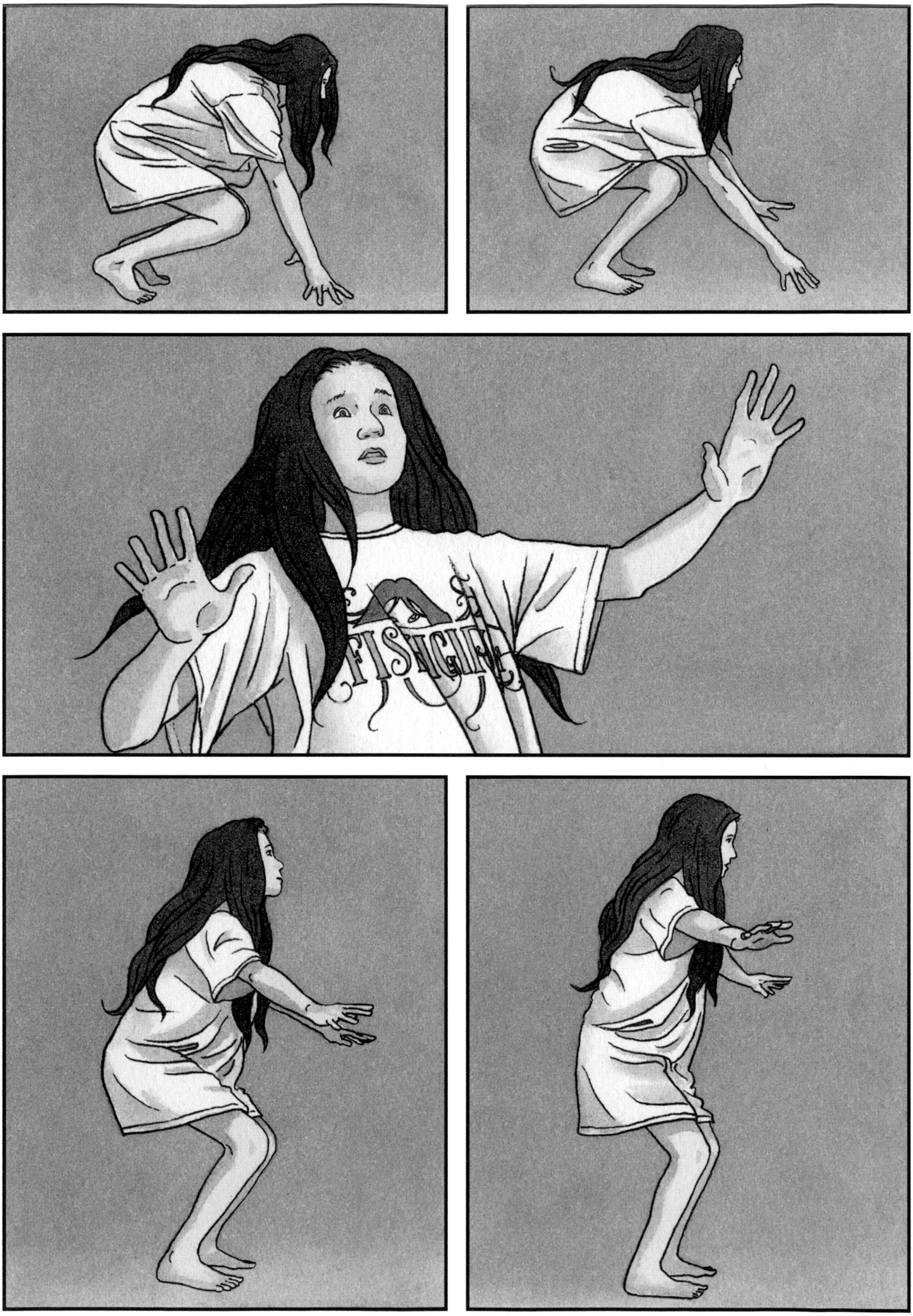

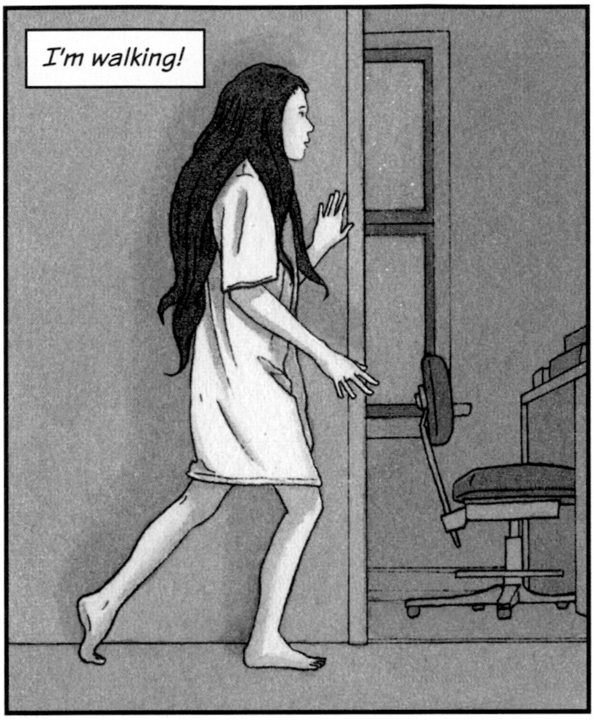
I'm walking!

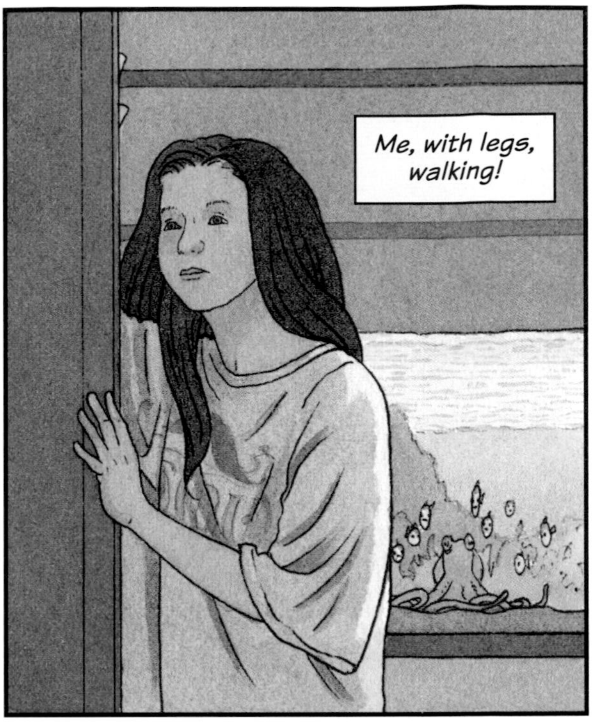
Me, with legs, walking!

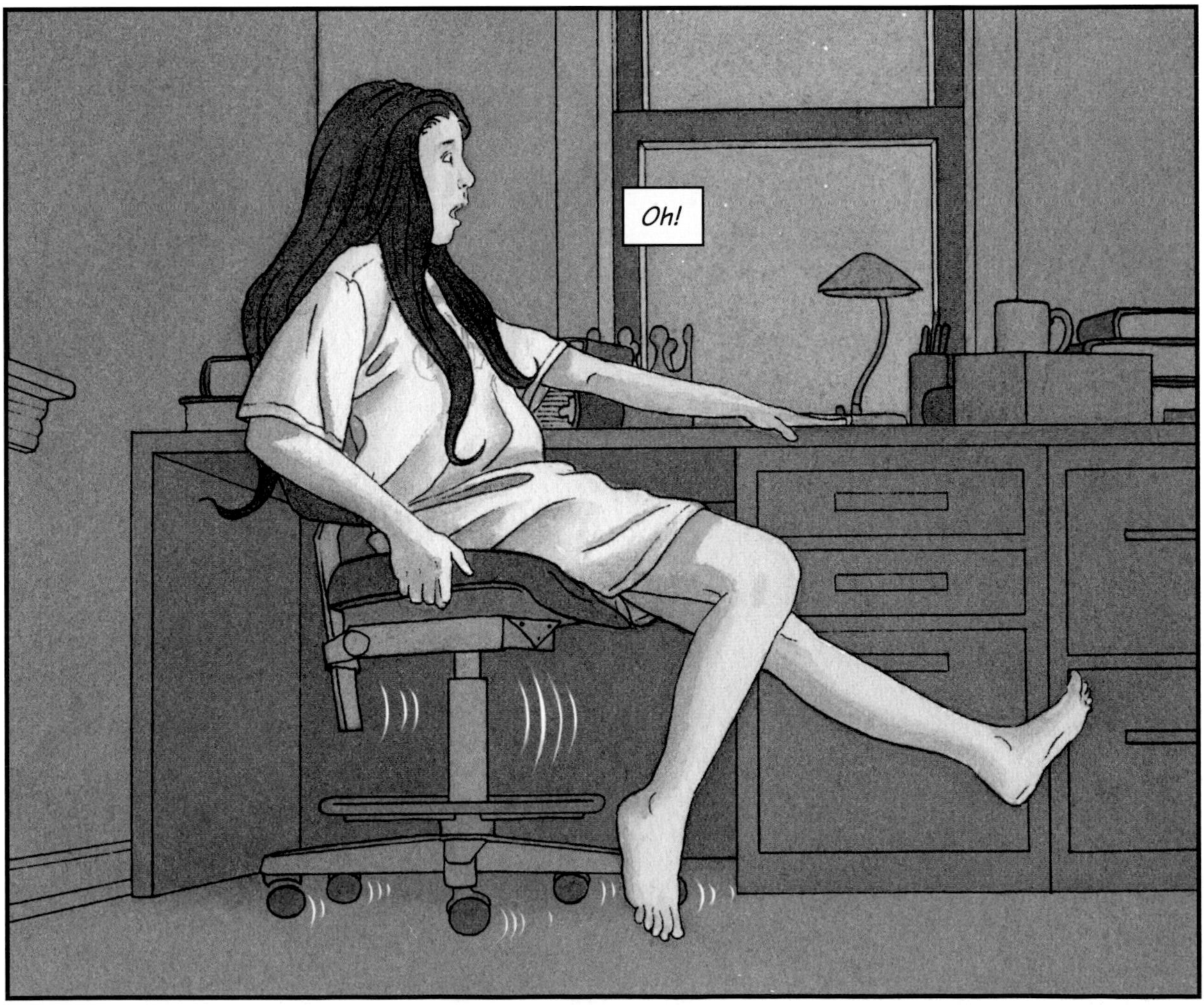
Oh!

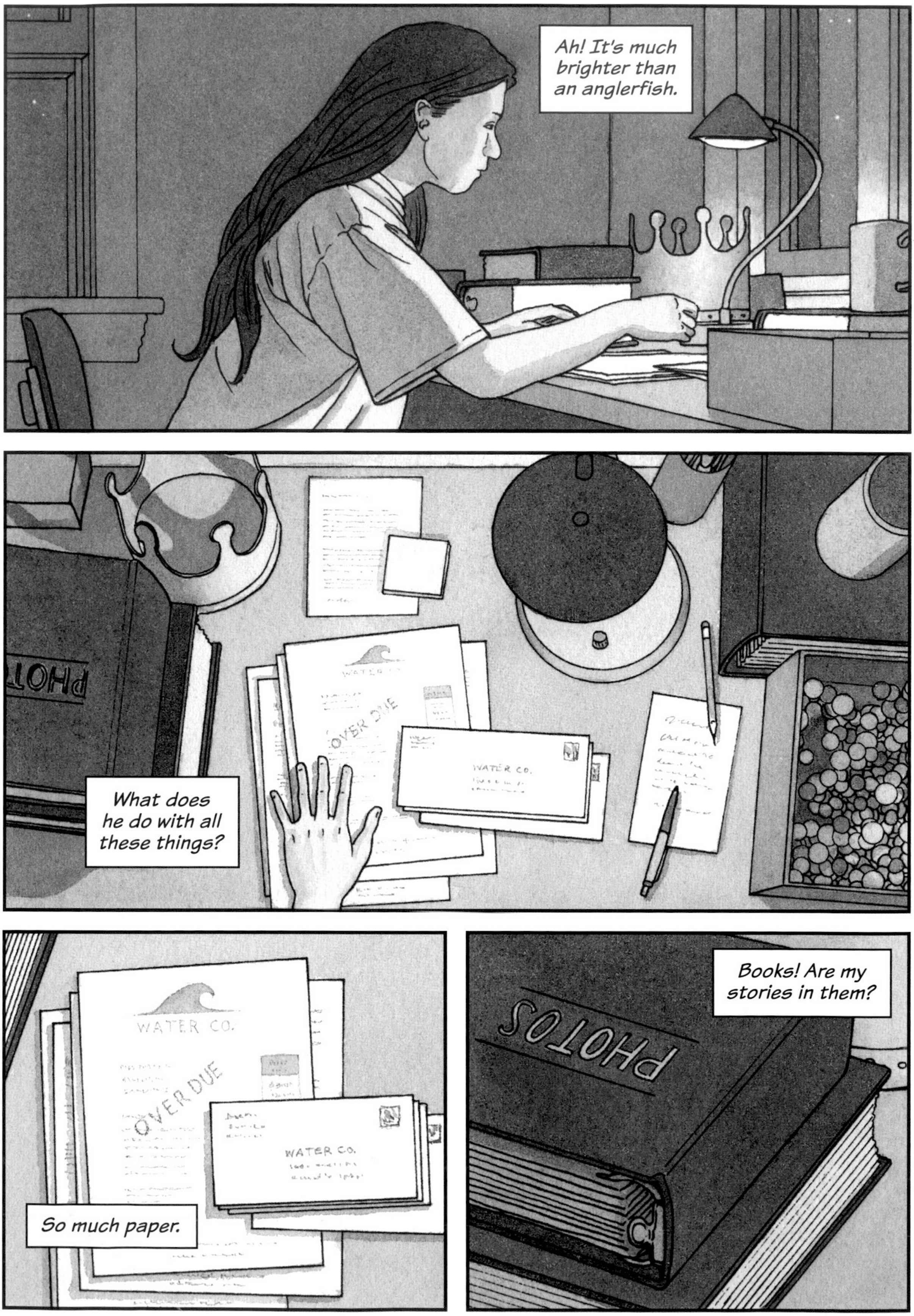
Ah! It's much brighter than an anglerfish.
What does he do with all these things?
WATER CO.
OVER DUE
WATER CO.
So much paper.
Books! Are my stories in them?
PHOTOS

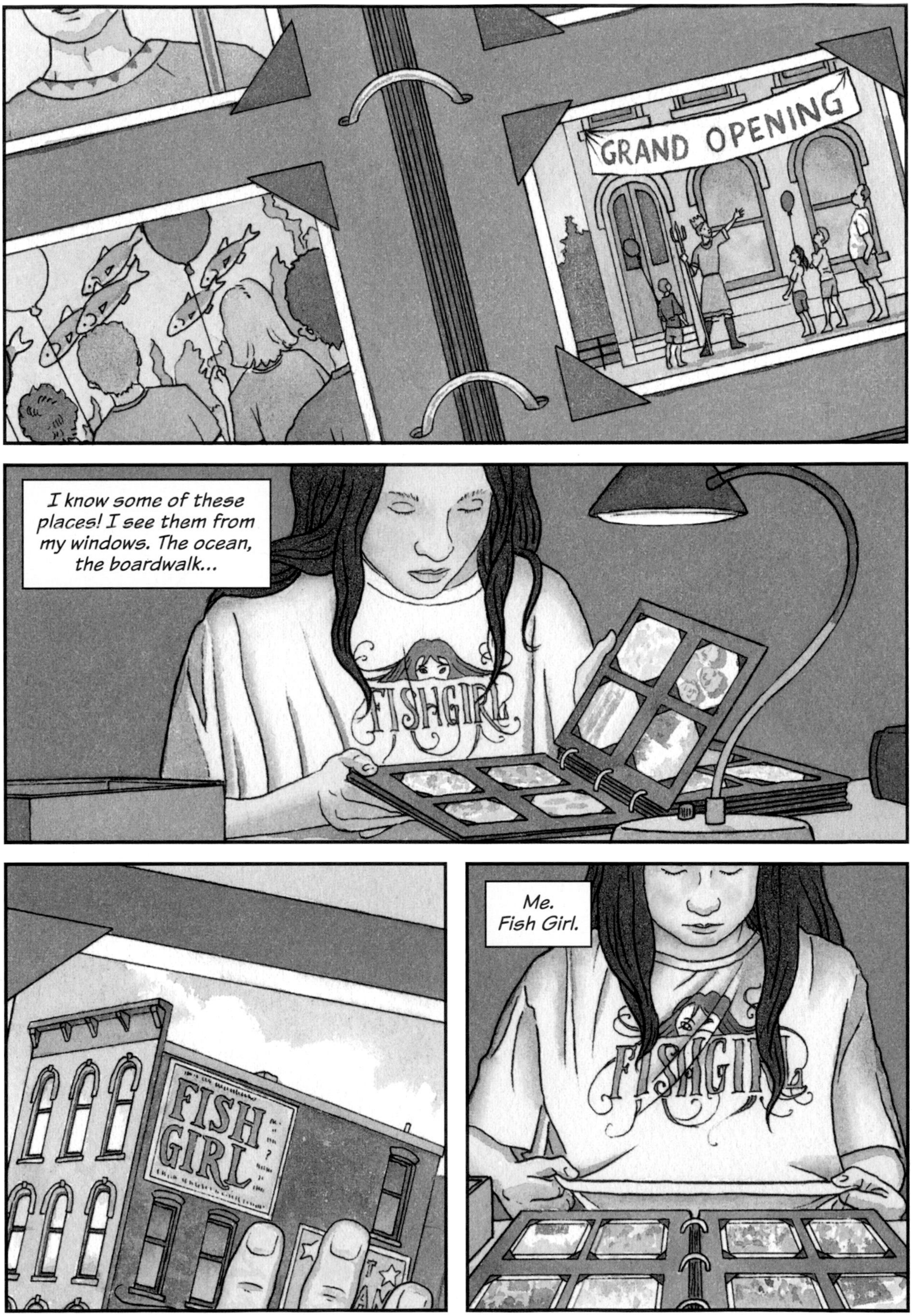
GRAND OPENING
I know some of these places! I see them from my windows. The ocean, the boardwalk...
FISHGIRL
FISH GIRL
Me. Fish Girl.
FISHGIRL

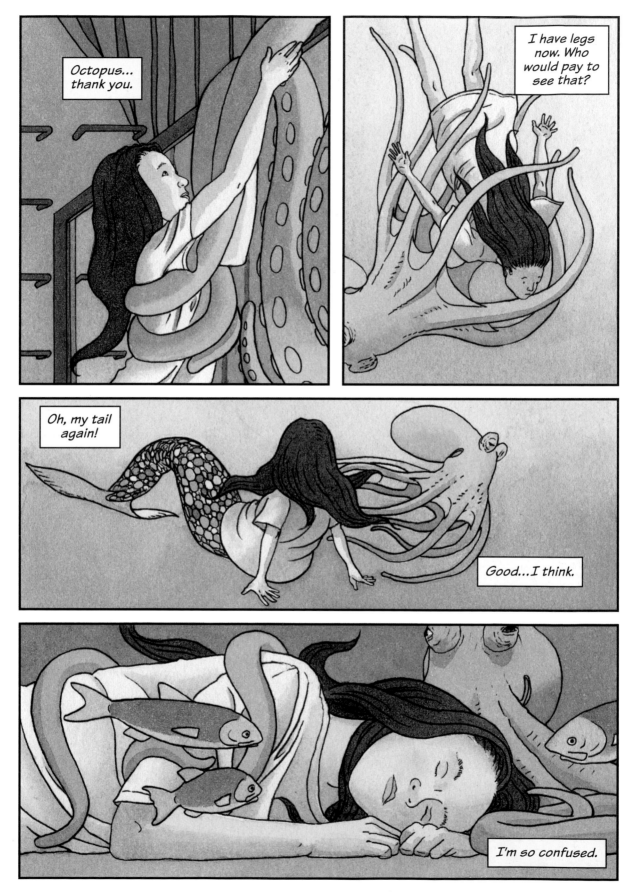

94

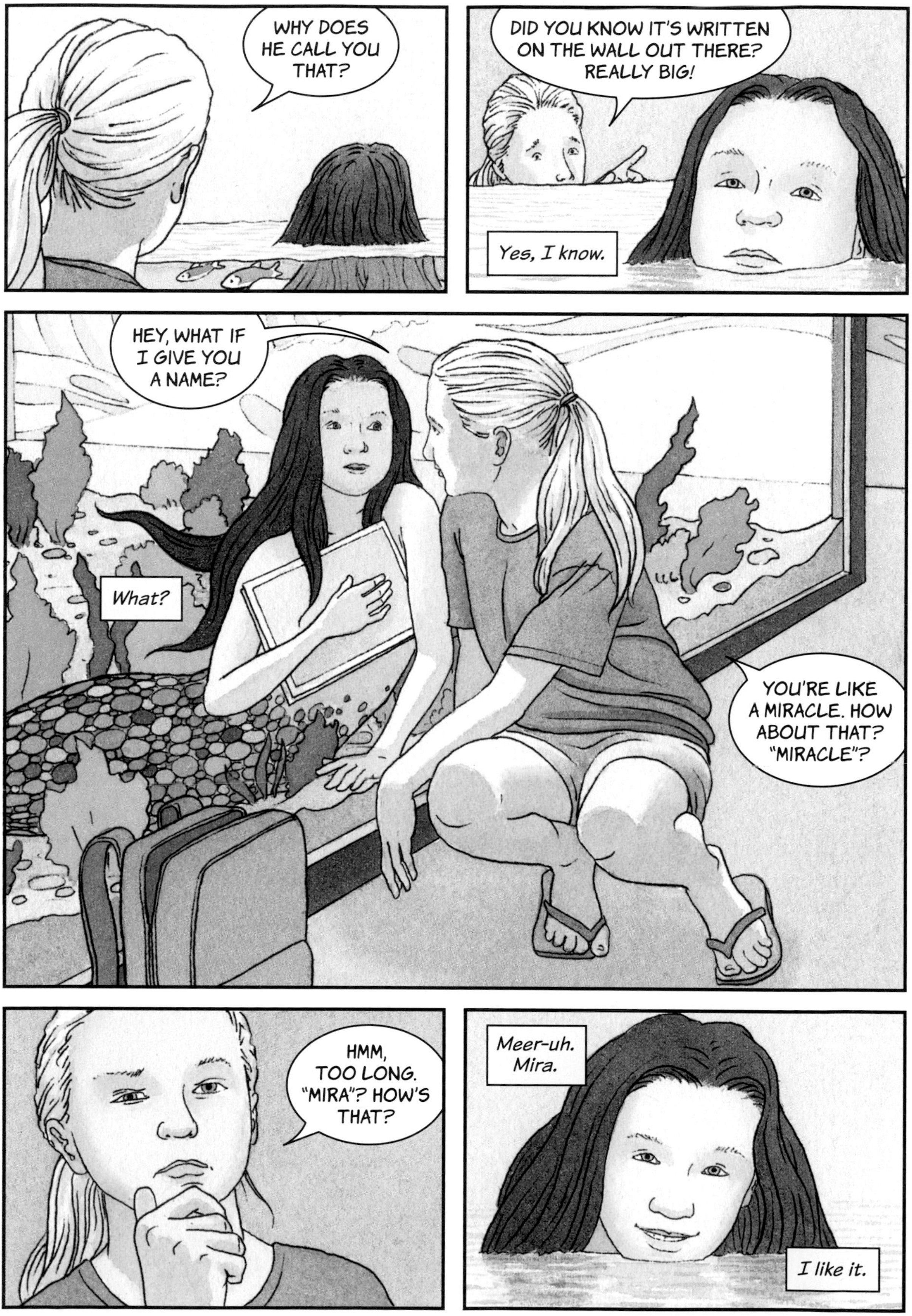
WHY DOES HE CALL YOU THAT?
DID YOU KNOW IT'S WRITTEN ON THE WALL OUT THERE? REALLY BIG!
Yes, I know.
HEY, WHAT IF I GIVE YOU A NAME?
What?
YOU'RE LIKE A MIRACLE. HOW ABOUT THAT? "MIRACLE"?
HMM, TOO LONG. "MIRA"? HOW'S THAT?
Meer-uh. Mira.
I like it.

98

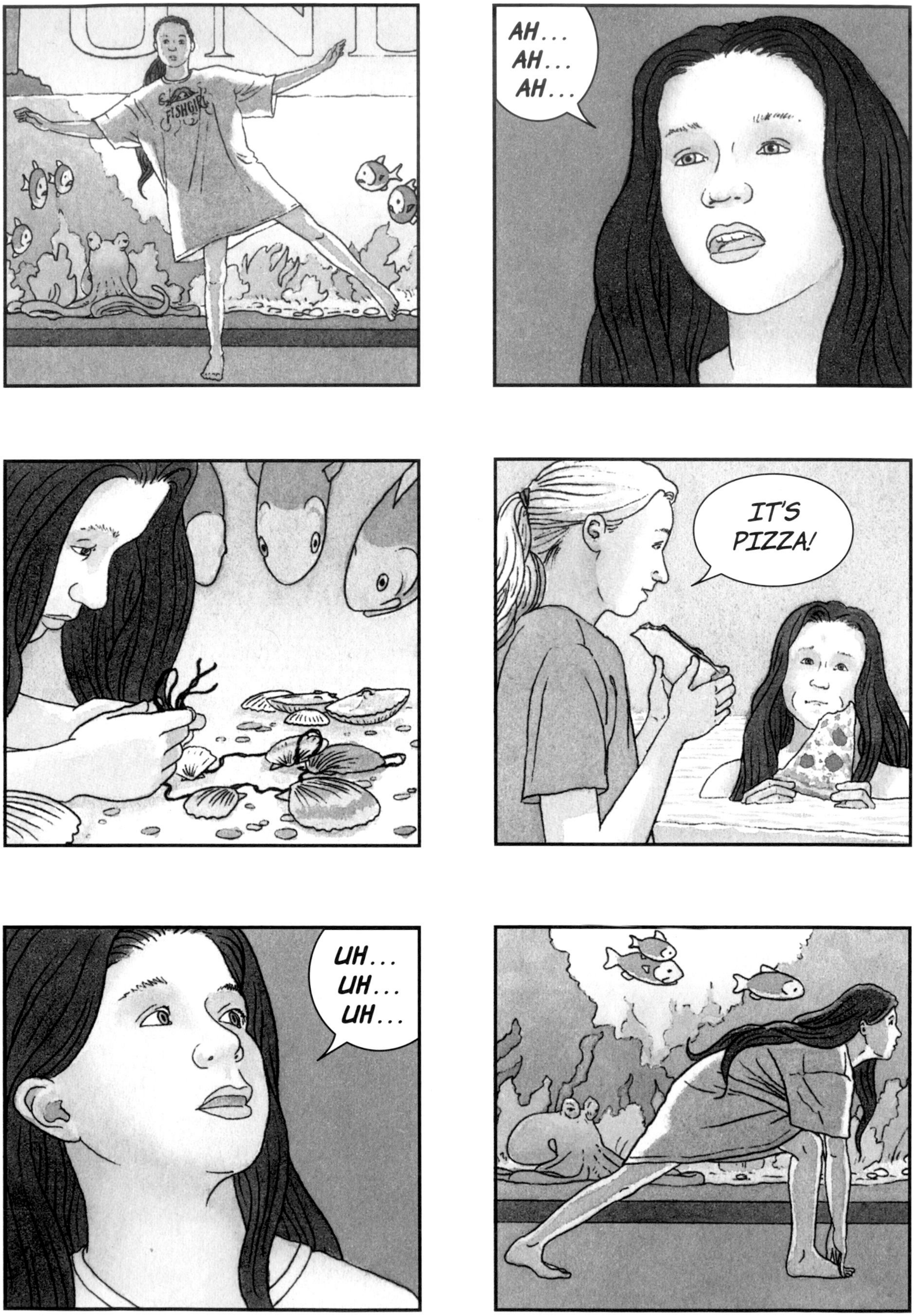
FISHGIRL
AH... AH... AH...
IT'S PIZZA!
UH... UH... UH...

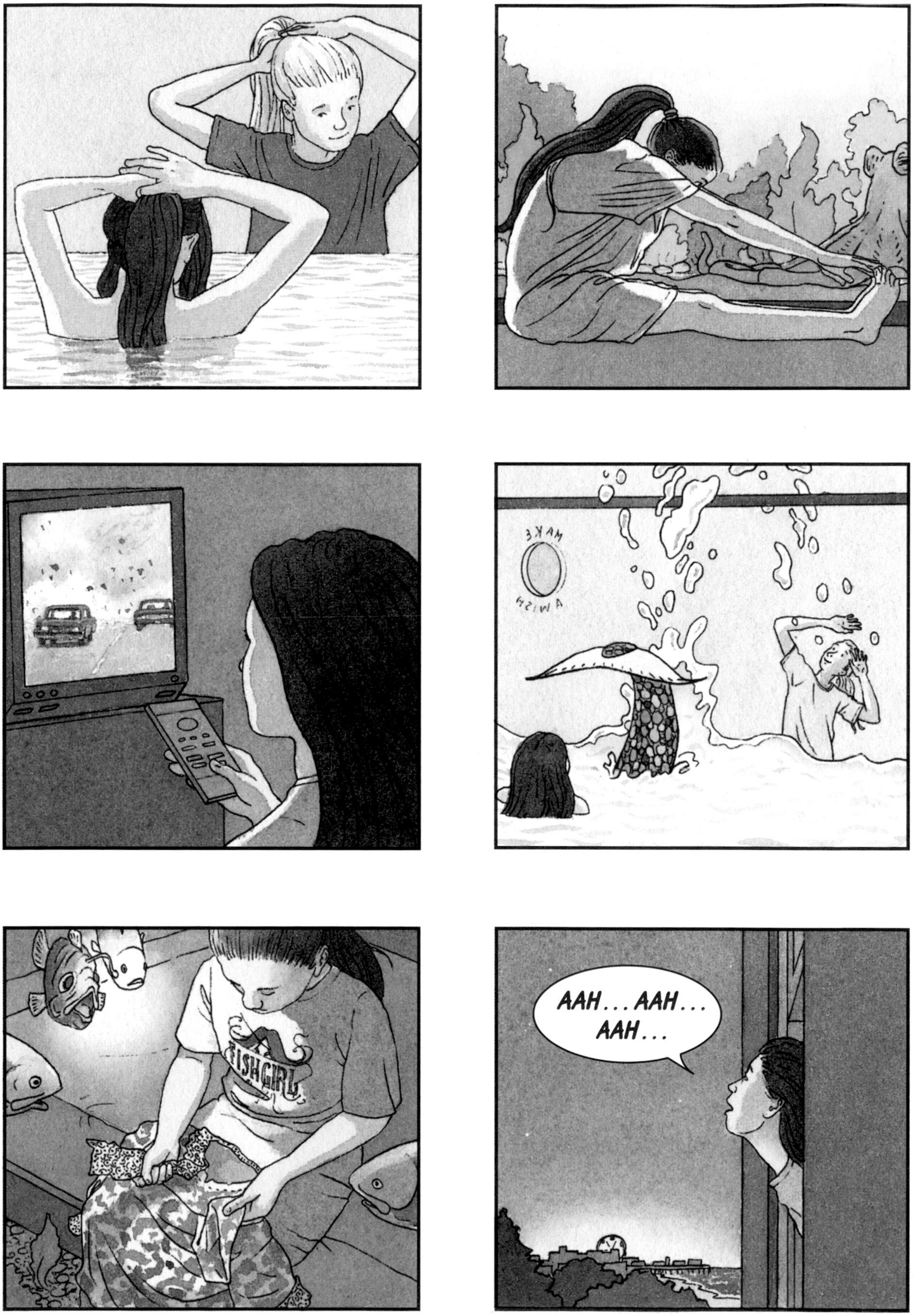
FISHGIRL
AAH... AAH...
AAH...

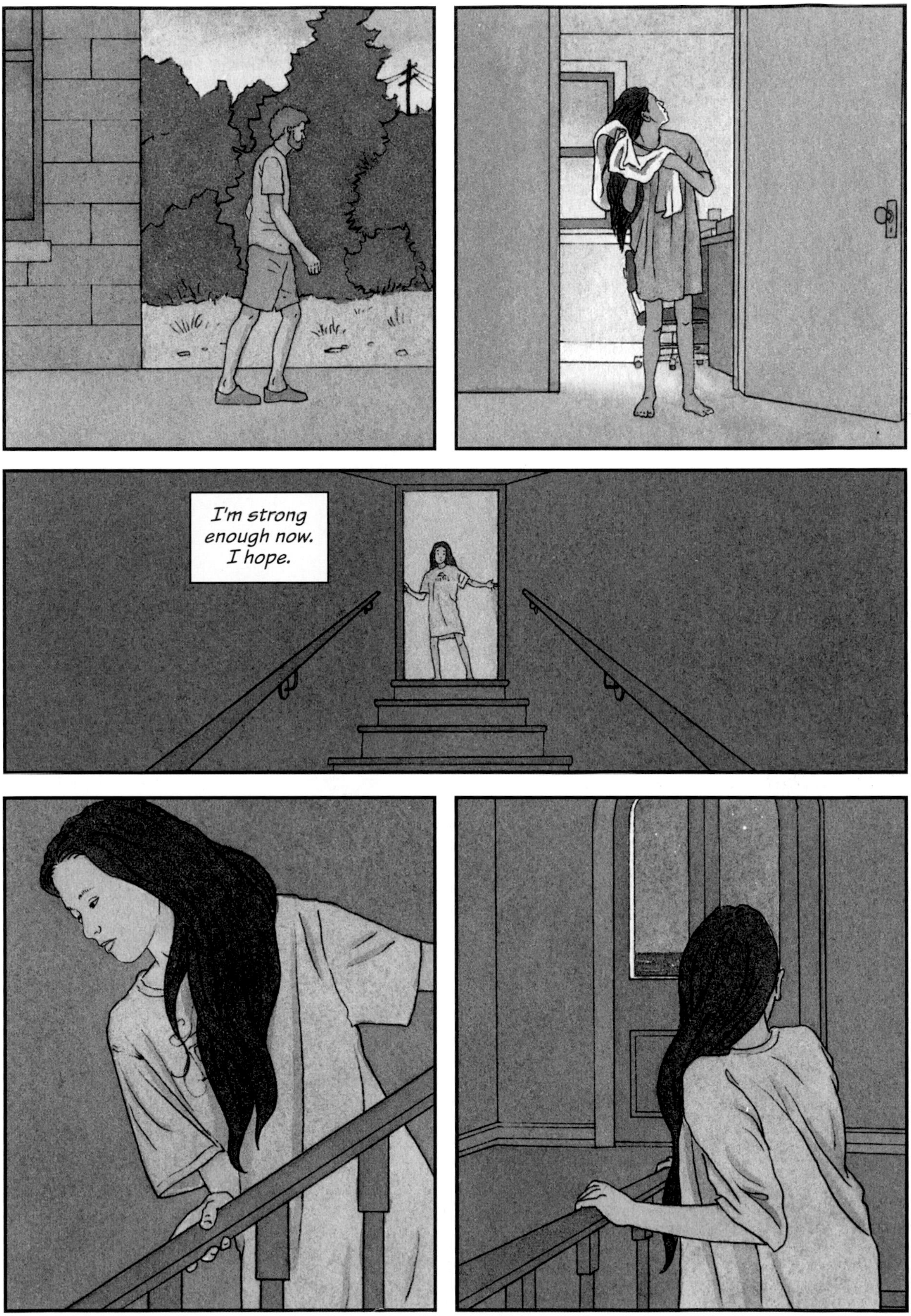
I'm strong enough now. I hope.

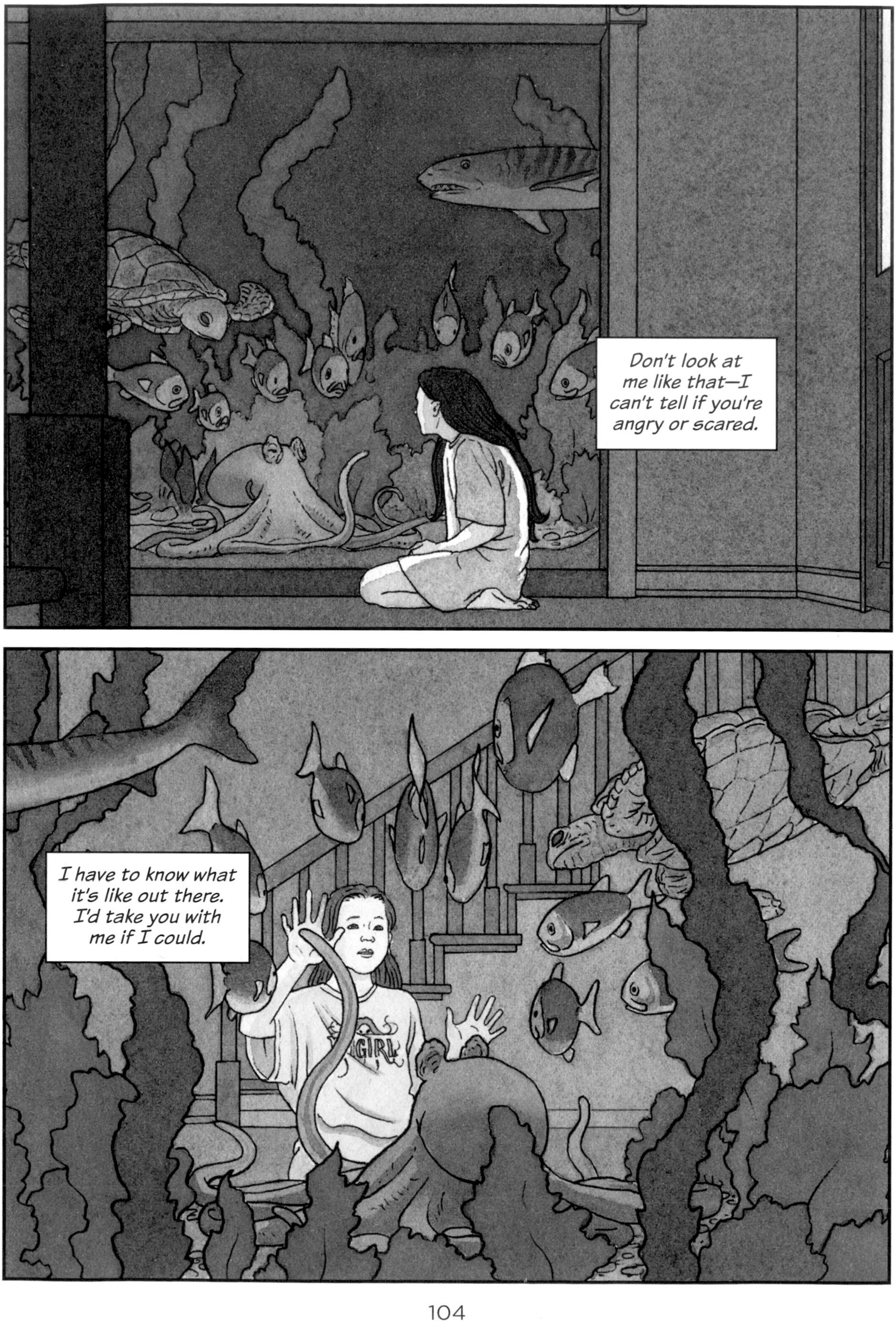
Don't look at me like that—I can't tell if you're angry or scared.
I have to know what it's like out there. I'd take you with me if I could.

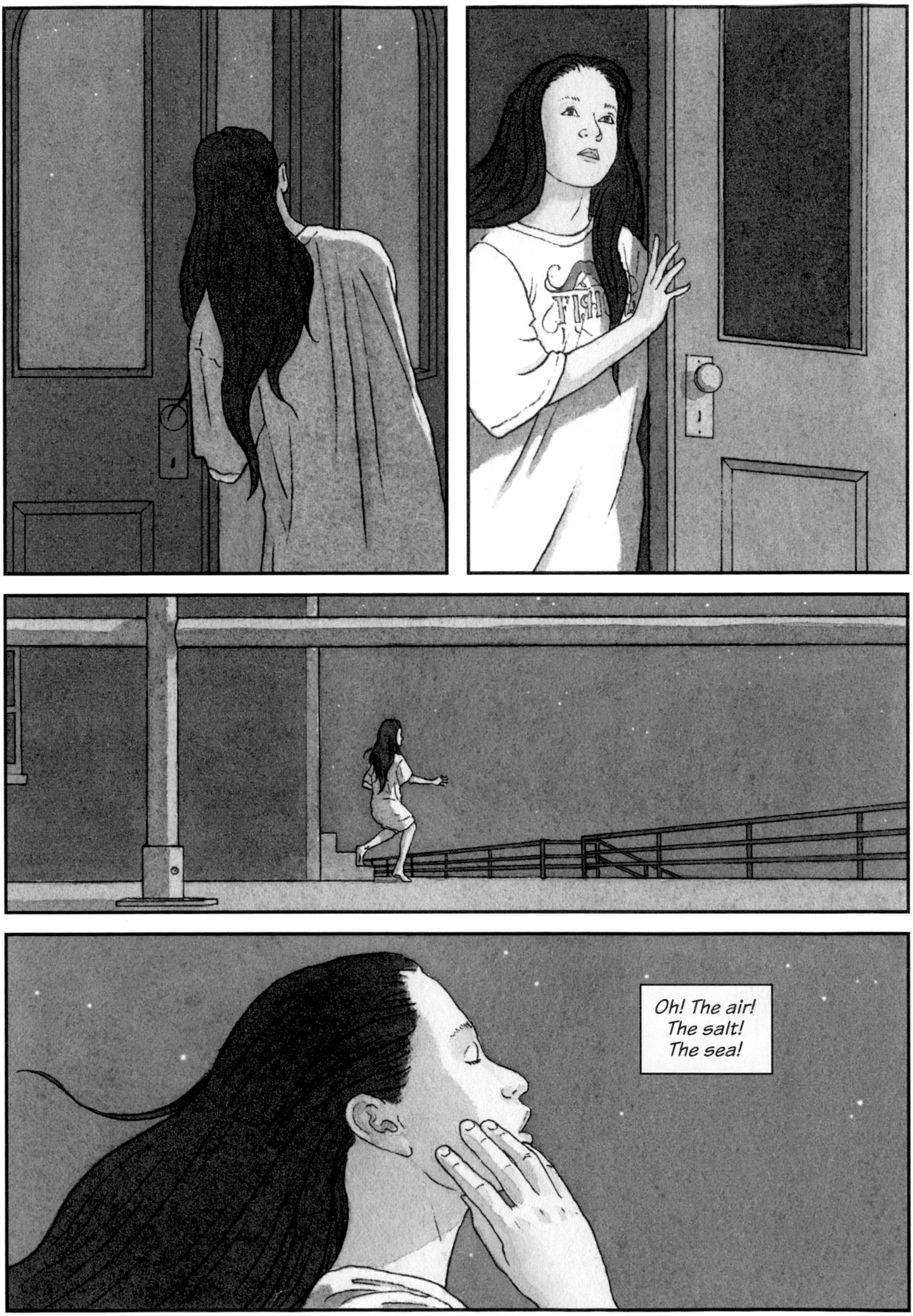
Oh! The air!
The salt!
The sea!

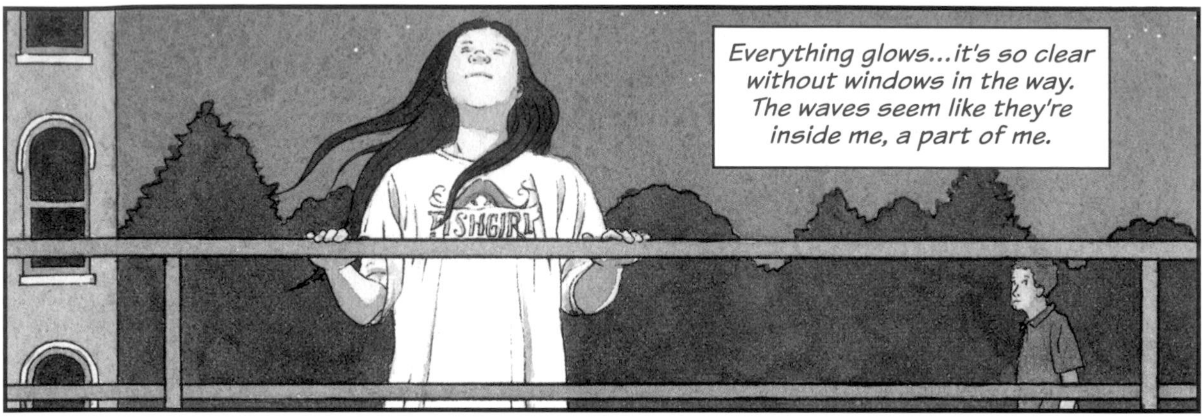
Everything glows...it's so clear without windows in the way. The waves seem like they're inside me, a part of me.
FISHGIRL

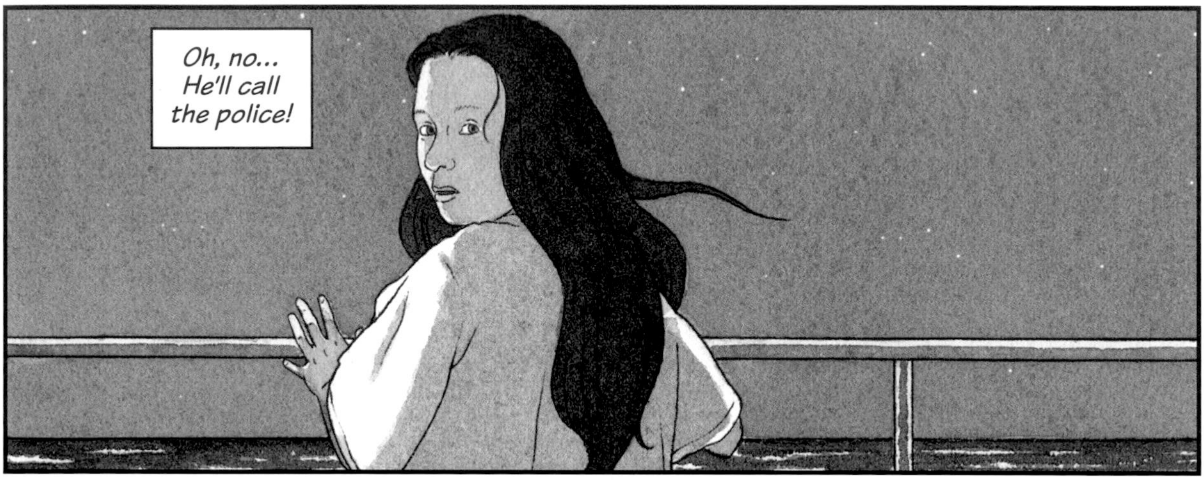
Oh, no... He'll call the police!

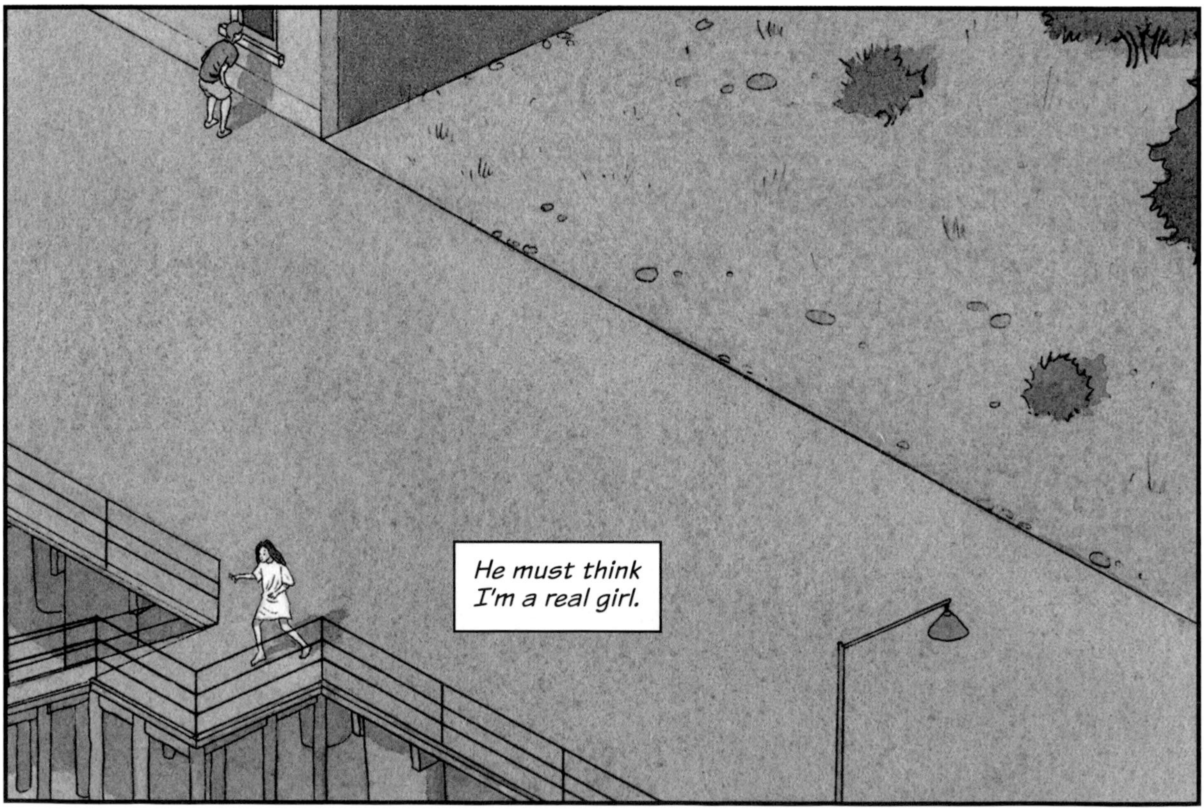
He must think I'm a real girl.

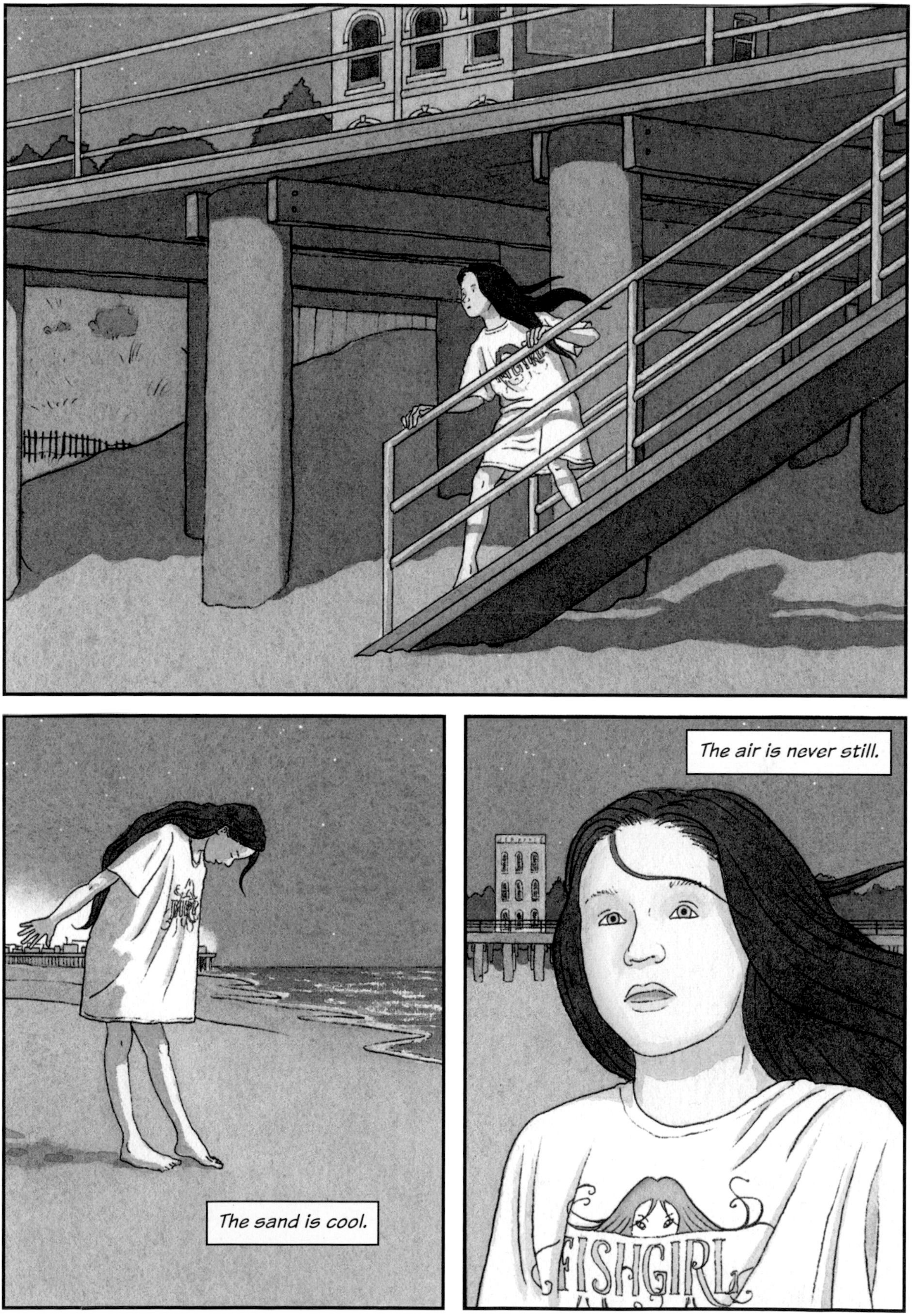
The sand is cool.
The air is never still.
FISHGIRL

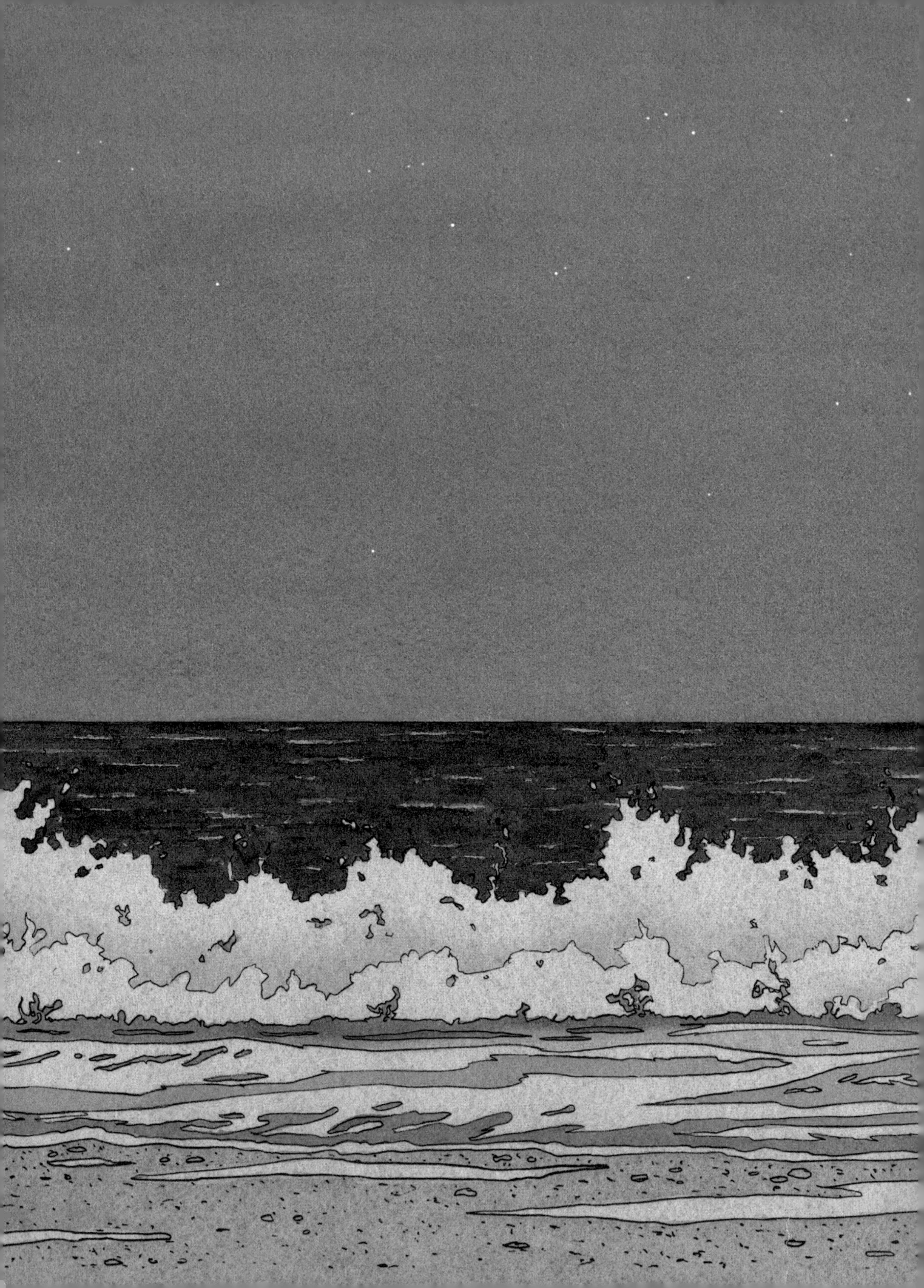

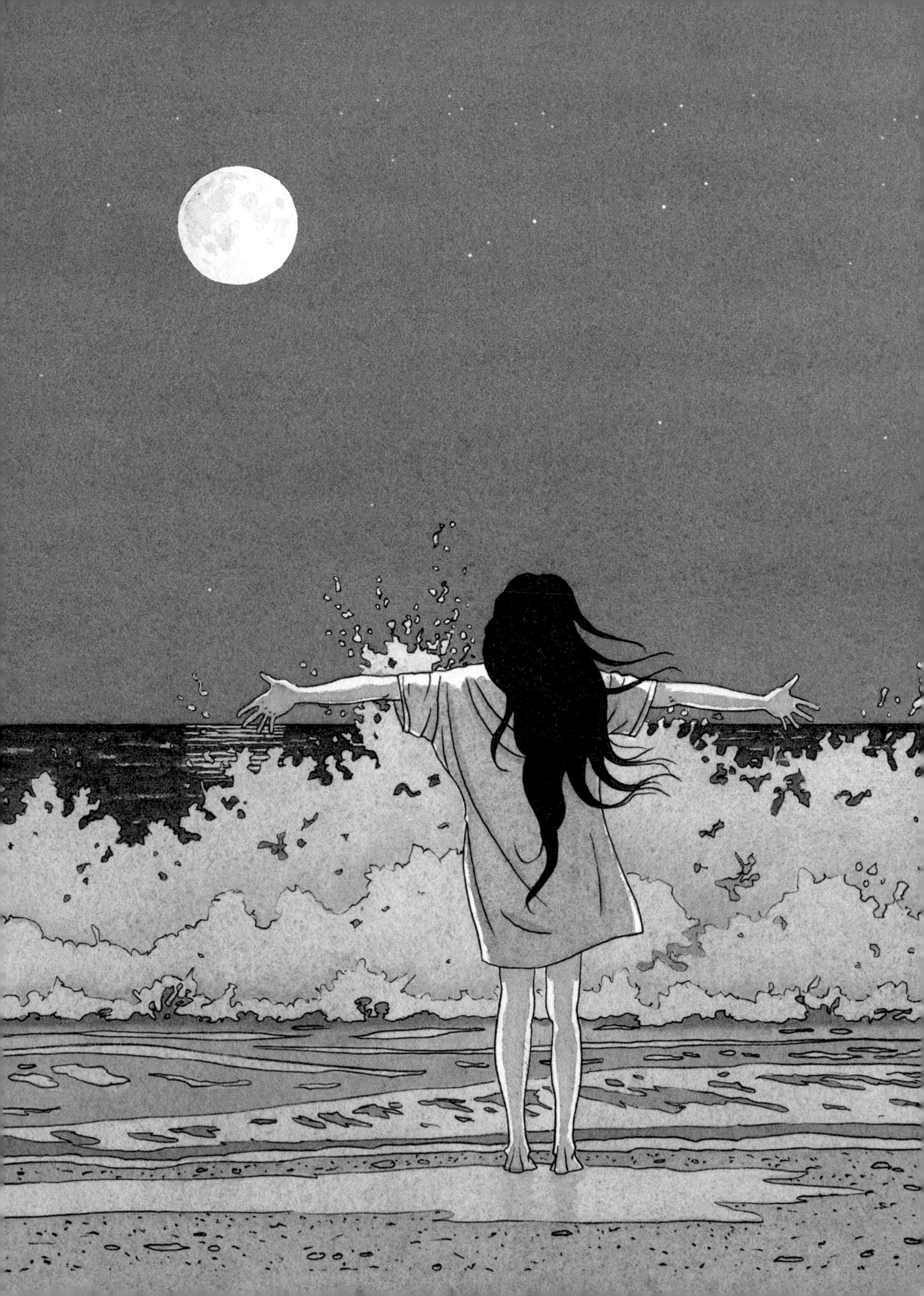

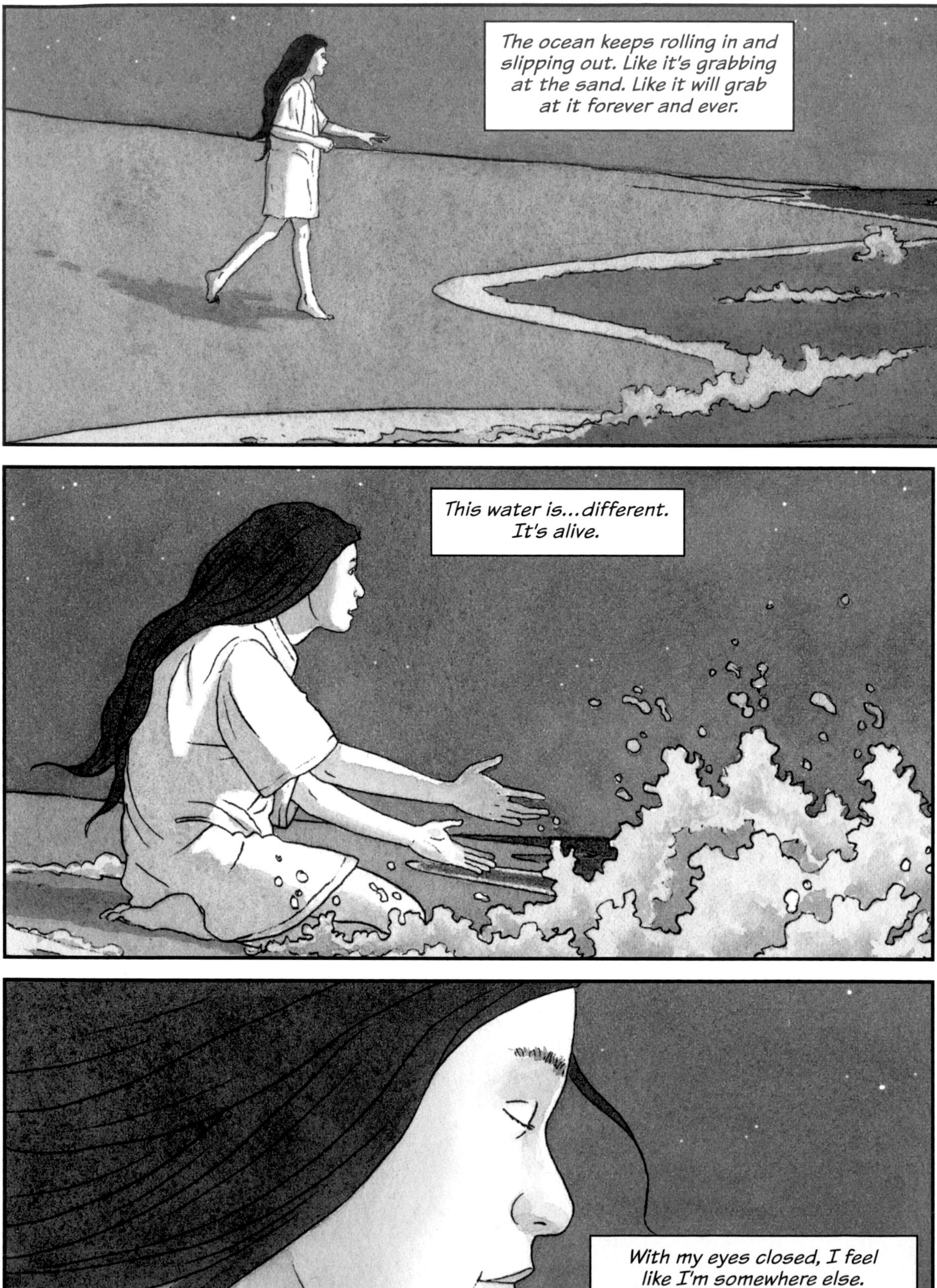
The ocean keeps rolling in and slipping out. Like it's grabbing at the sand. Like it will grab at it forever and ever.
This water is...different. It's alive.
With my eyes closed, I feel like I'm somewhere else. Somewhere I almost remember.

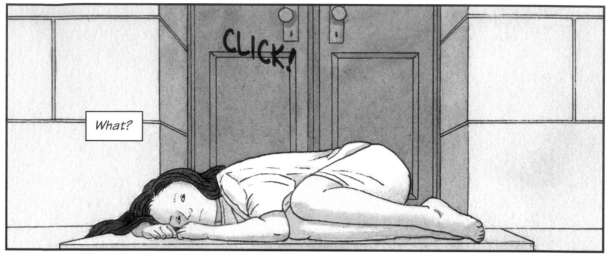

CLICK!

What?

Octopus, you waited up all night for me, didn't you?

I was so scared. It was almost a disaster. But I went out into the world as a girl!

There they go again—showtime. Octopus, he doesn't want anything from you except for you to be you.

But you're just as much a prisoner as I am. As all of us are. I wish we were free.

MMMMMMMMMMMMMMMMMM

"Storms." Ha.

Liar.

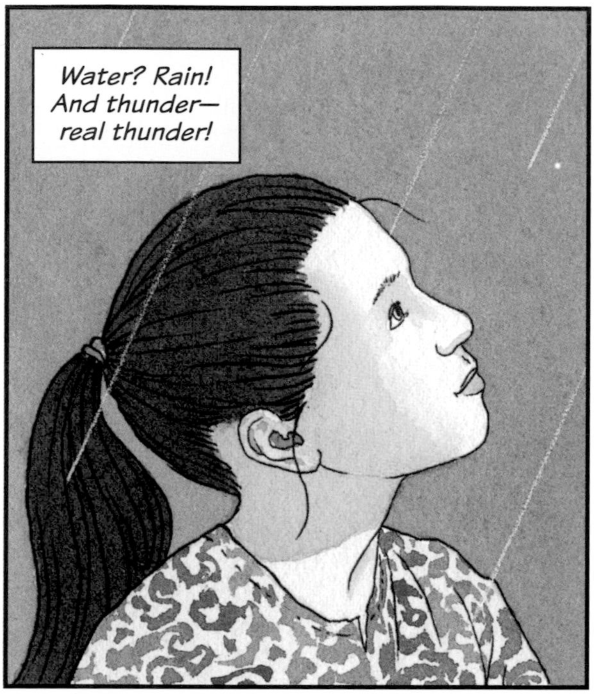
Water? Rain!
And thunder—
real thunder!

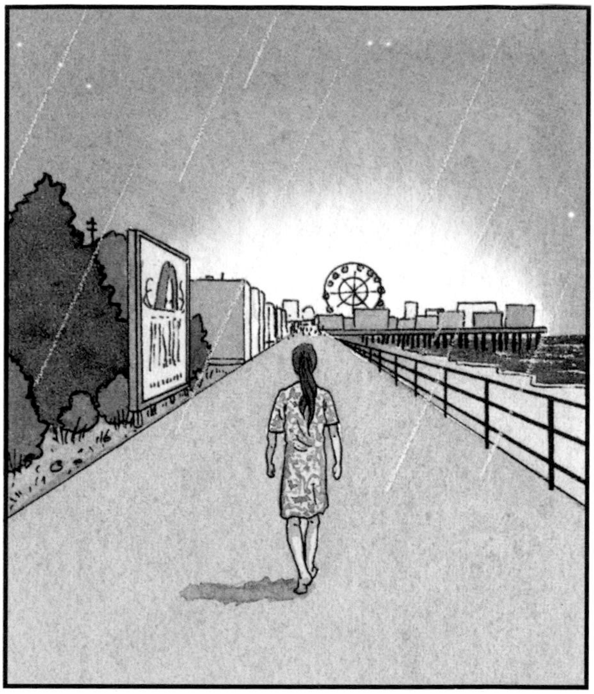

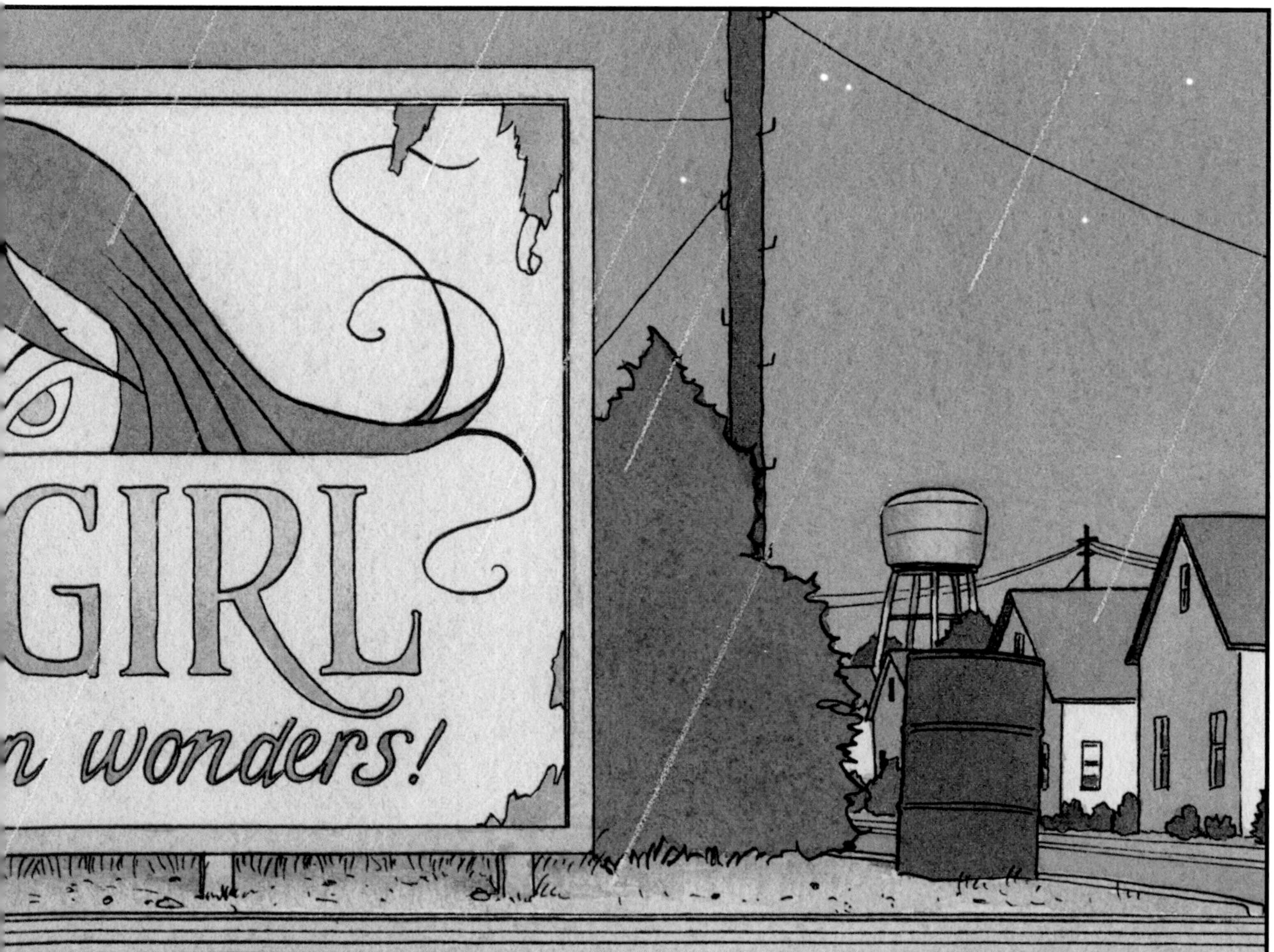
GIRL
n wonders!

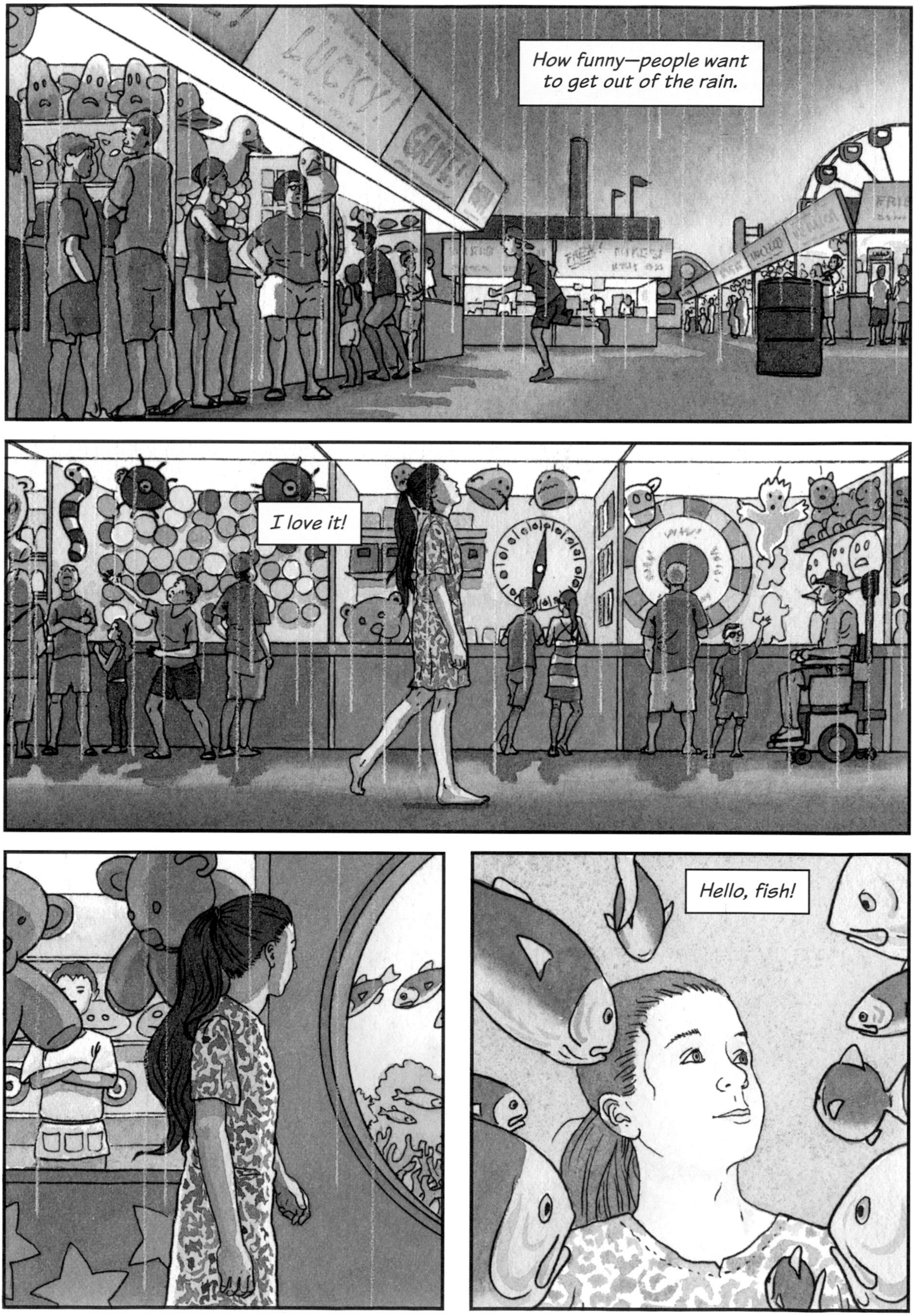
How funny—people want to get out of the rain.
I love it!
Hello, fish!

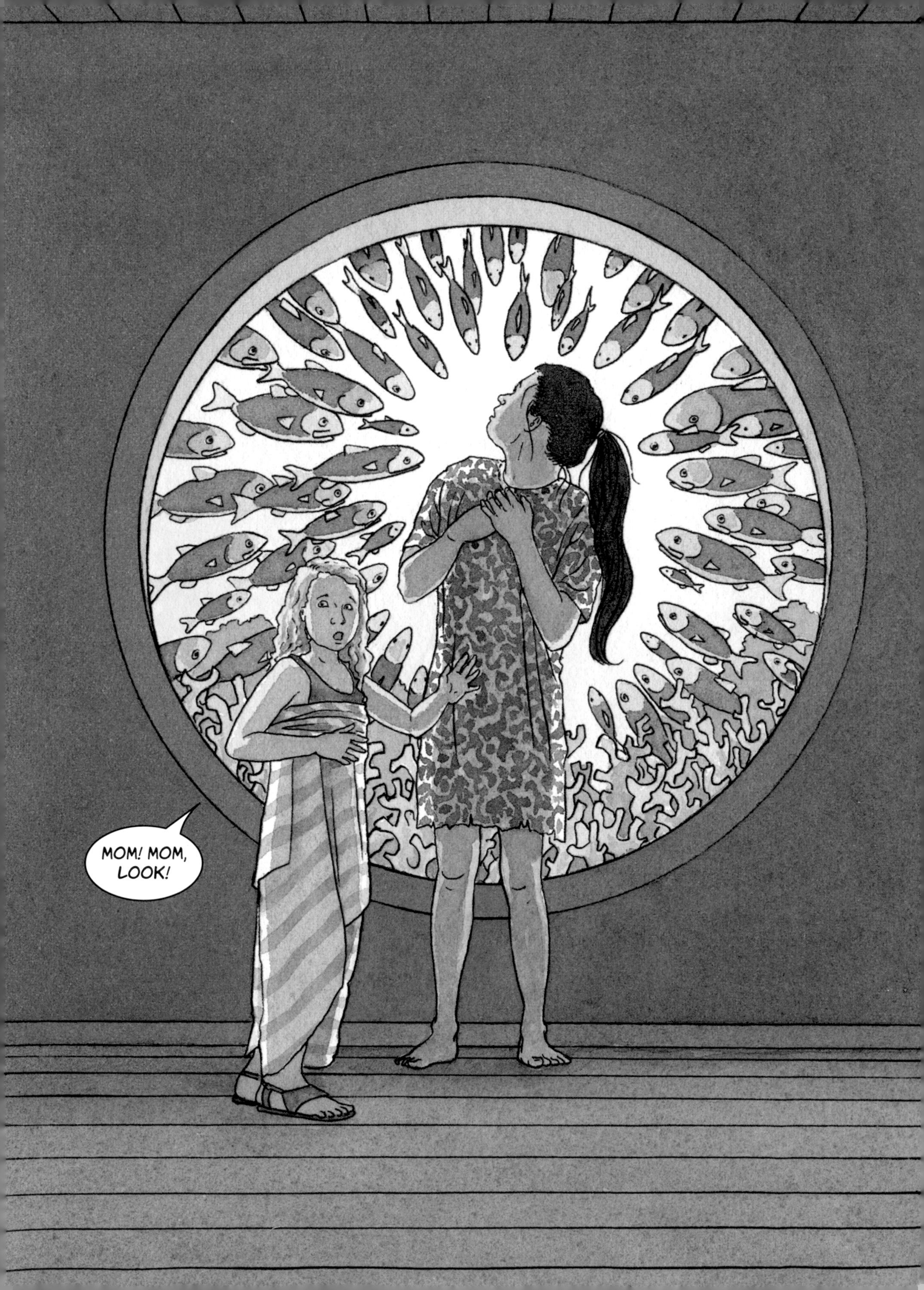
MOM! MOM, LOOK!

I should go home. Which way is it?

LOOKING FOR SOMEBODY?

YOU'VE GOT NICE HAIR.

Go away!

AW, I DIDN'T MEAN ANYTHING.

Leave me alone.

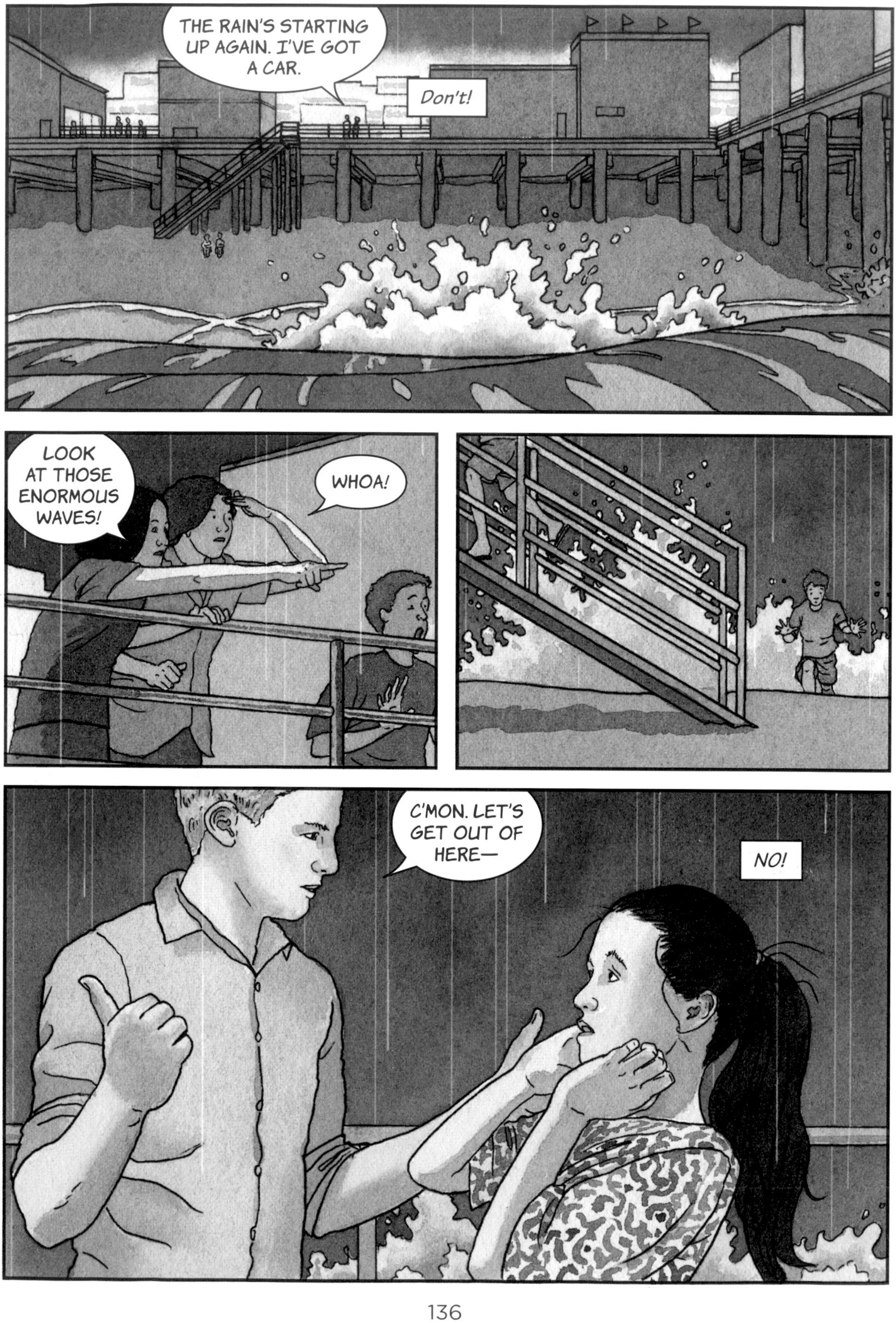
THE RAIN'S STARTING UP AGAIN. I'VE GOT A CAR.
Don't!
LOOK AT THOSE ENORMOUS WAVES!
WHOA!
C'MON. LET'S GET OUT OF HERE—
NO!

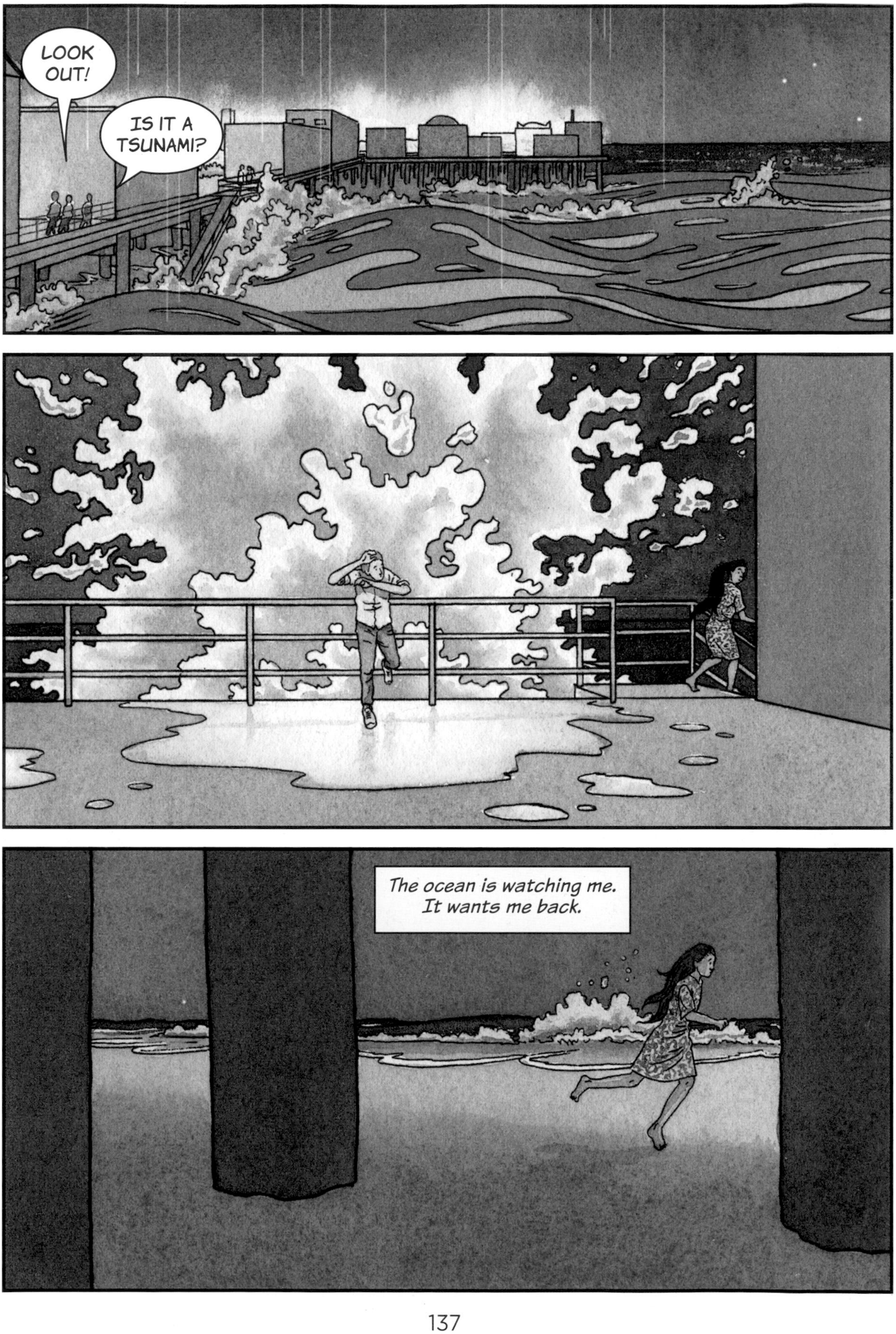
LOOK OUT!
IS IT A TSUNAMI?
The ocean is watching me. It wants me back.

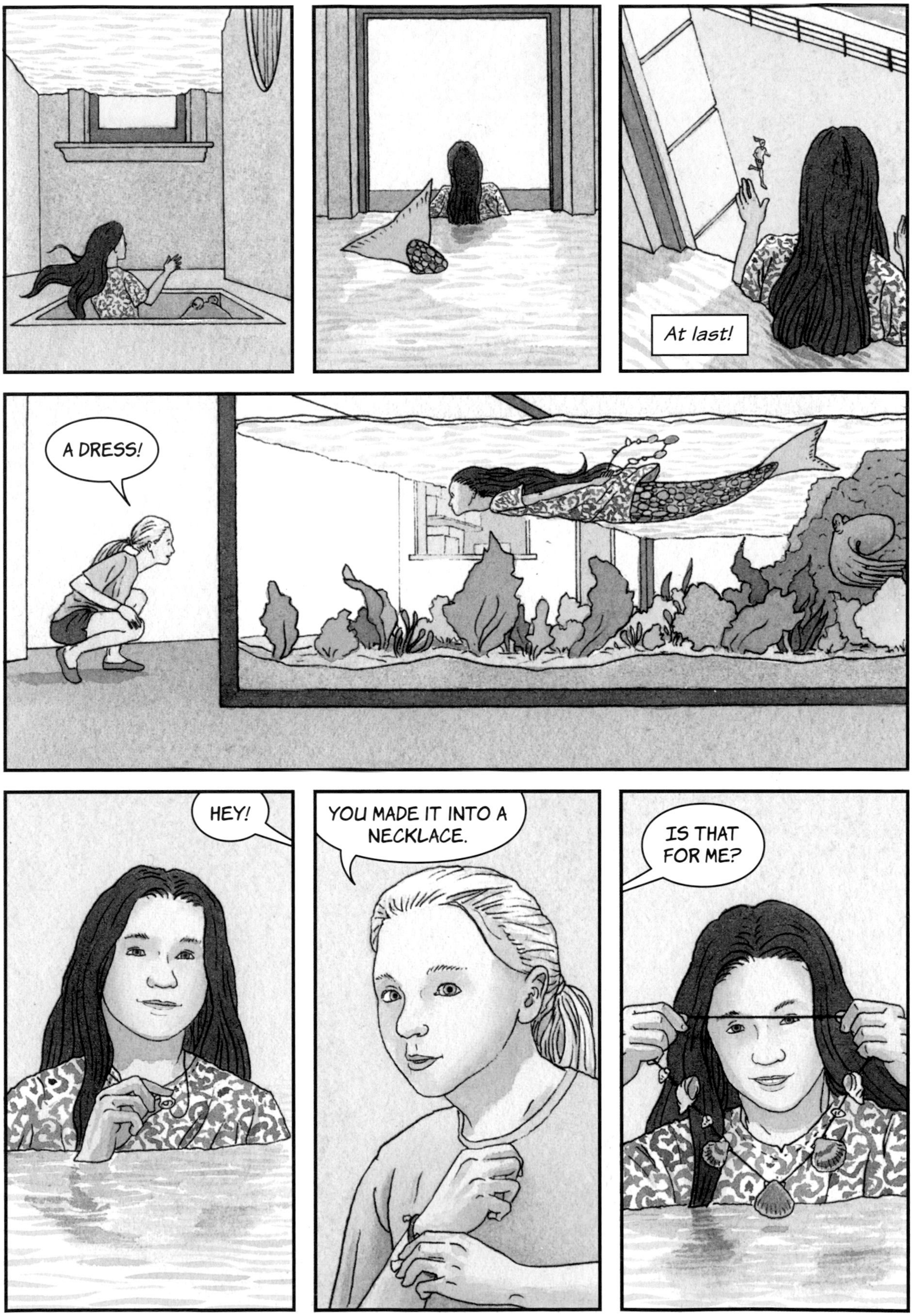
At last!
A DRESS!
HEY!
YOU MADE IT INTO A NECKLACE.
IS THAT FOR ME?

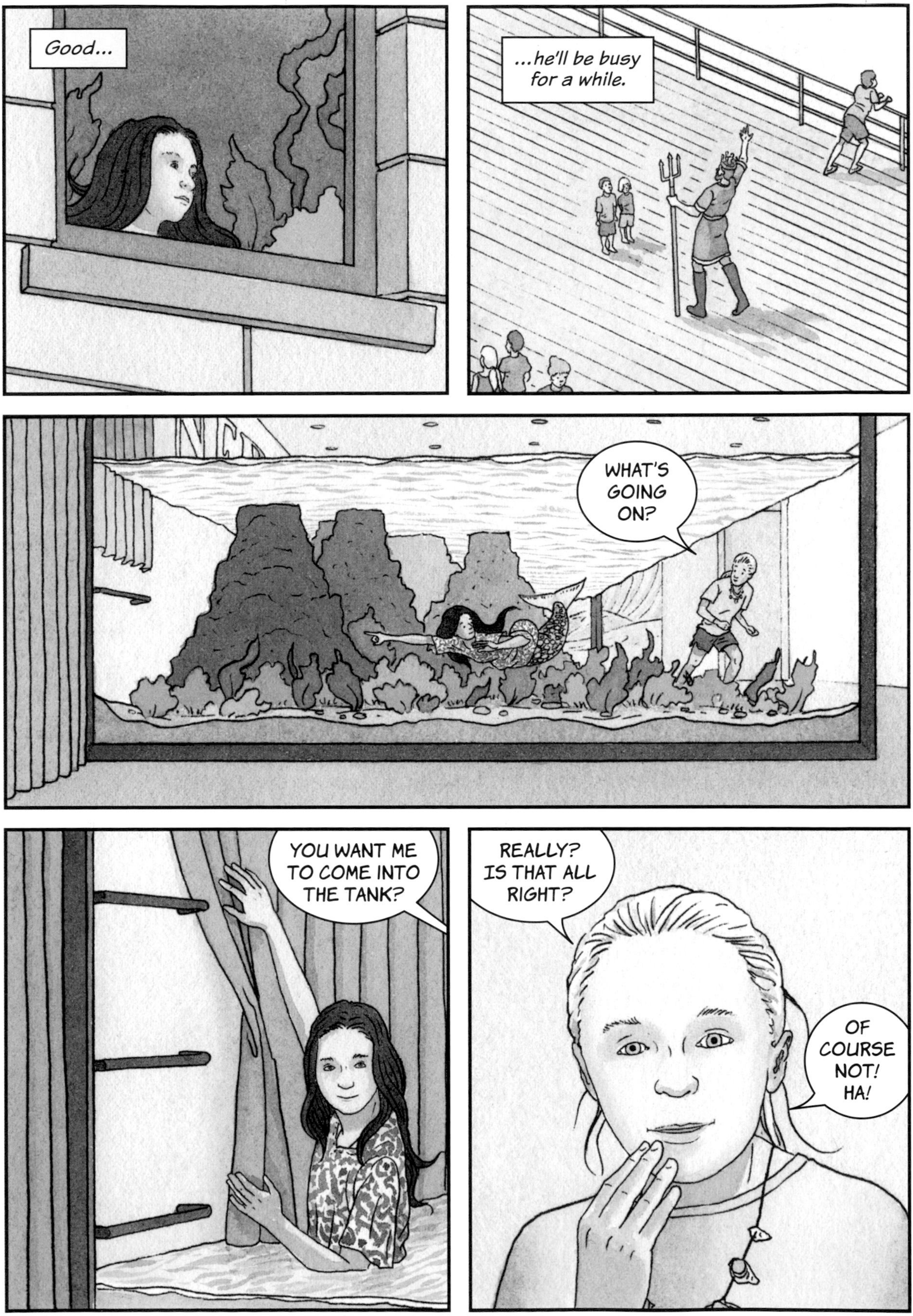

Good...
...he'll be busy for a while.
WHAT'S GOING ON?
YOU WANT ME TO COME INTO THE TANK?
REALLY? IS THAT ALL RIGHT?
OF COURSE NOT! HA!

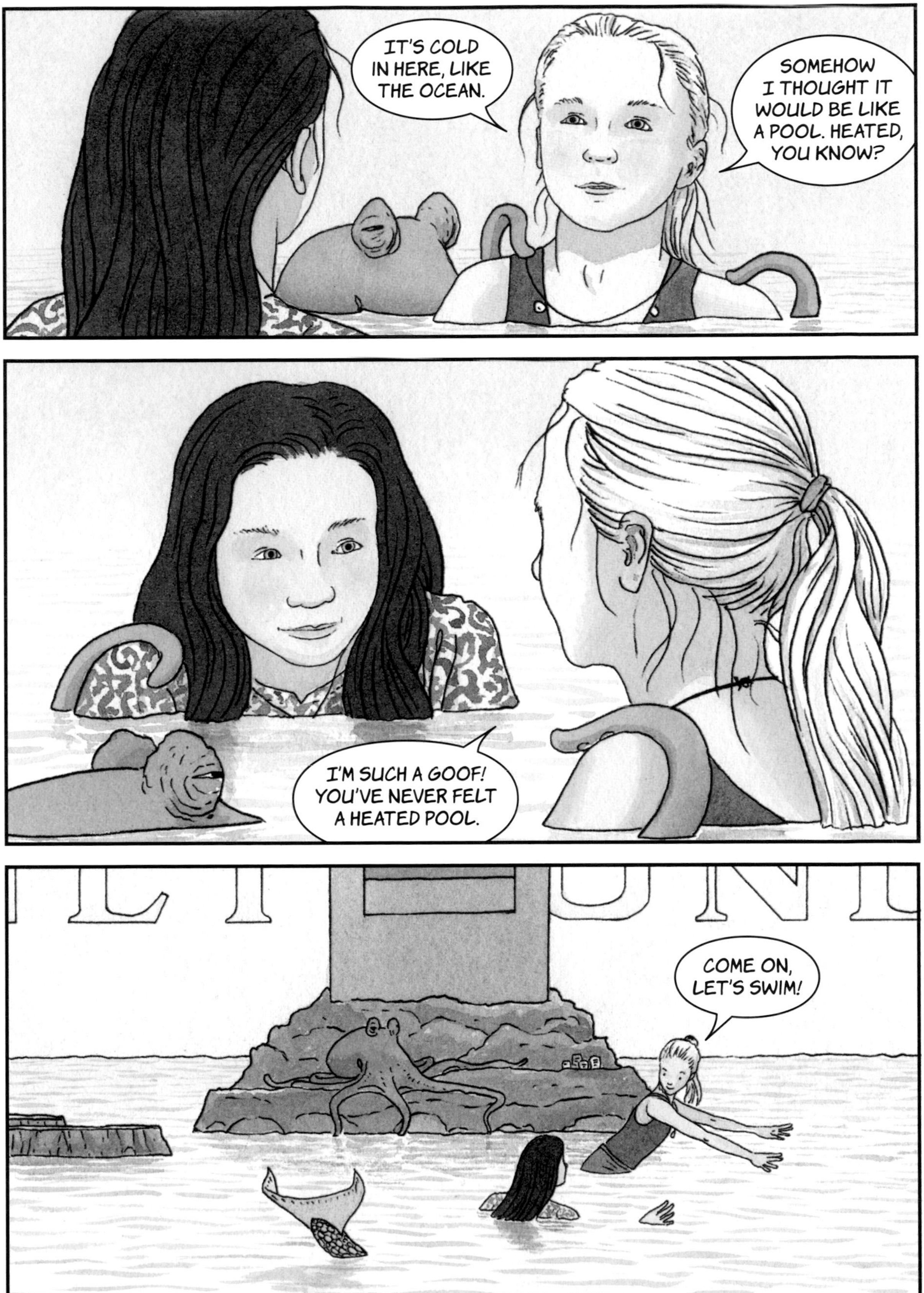
IT'S COLD IN HERE, LIKE THE OCEAN.
SOMEHOW I THOUGHT IT WOULD BE LIKE A POOL. HEATED, YOU KNOW?
I'M SUCH A GOOF! YOU'VE NEVER FELT A HEATED POOL.
COME ON, LET'S SWIM!

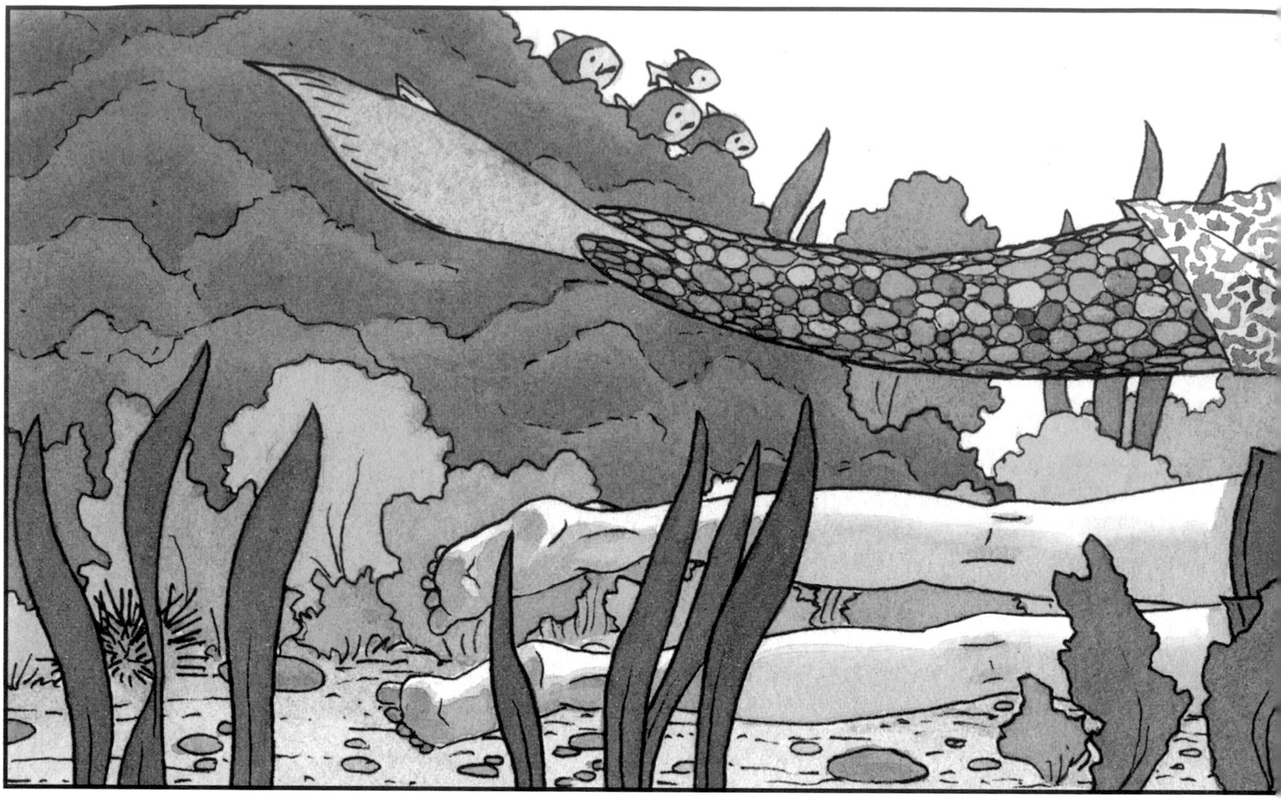

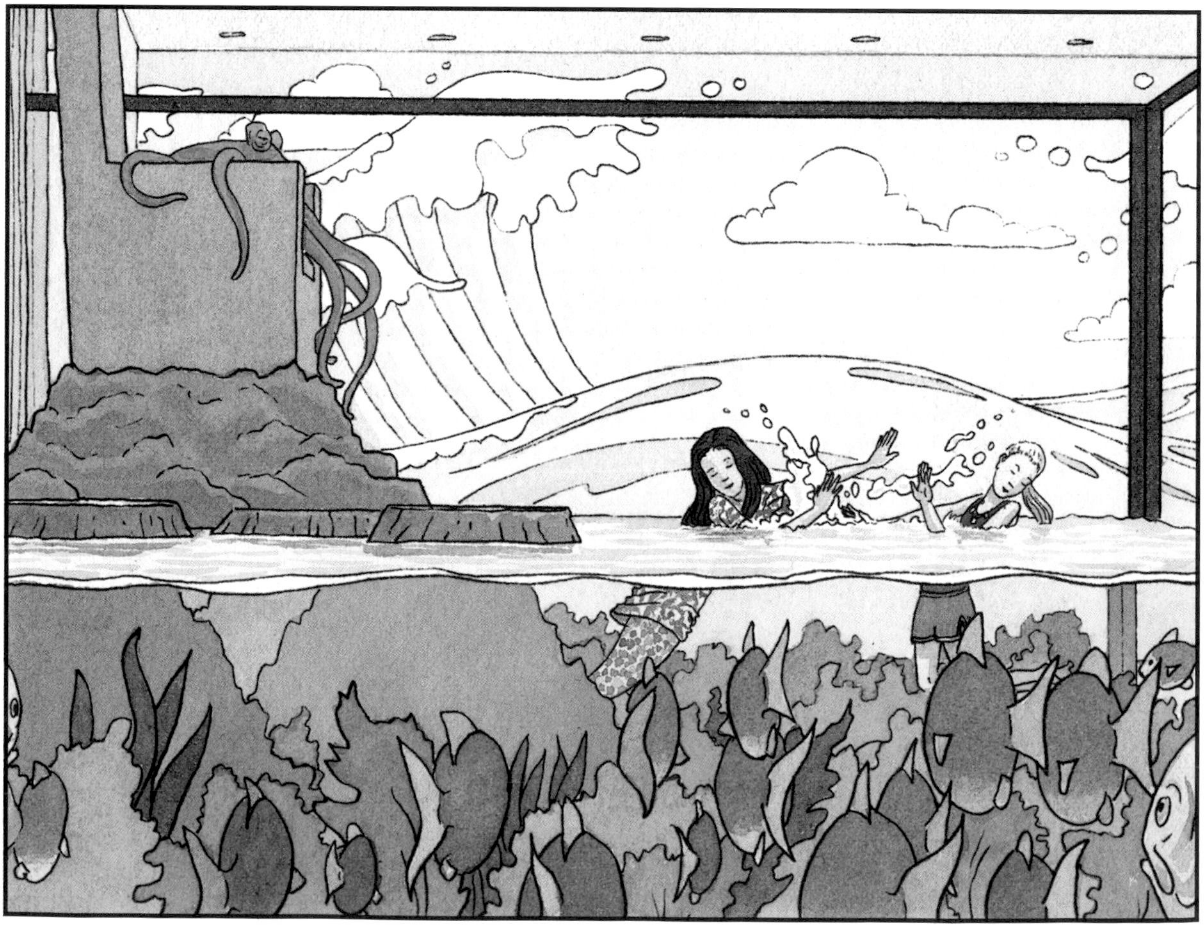

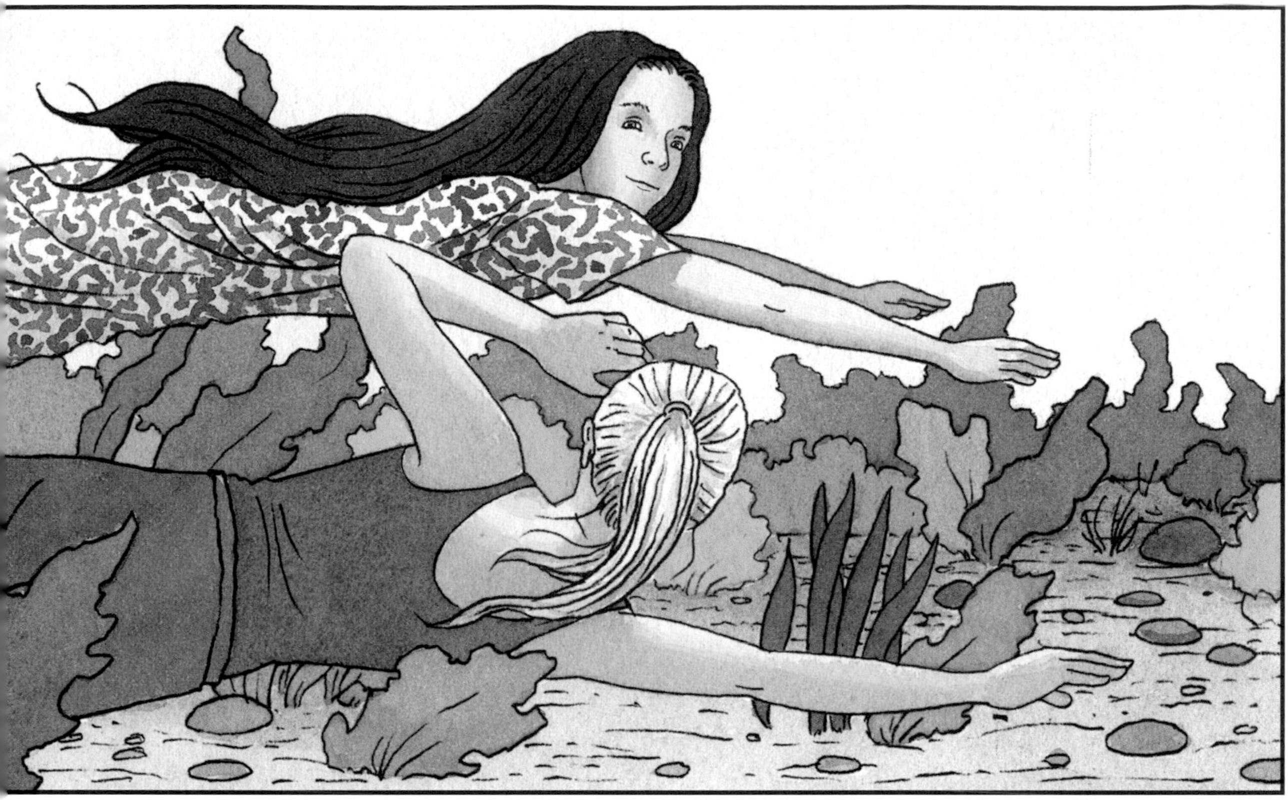

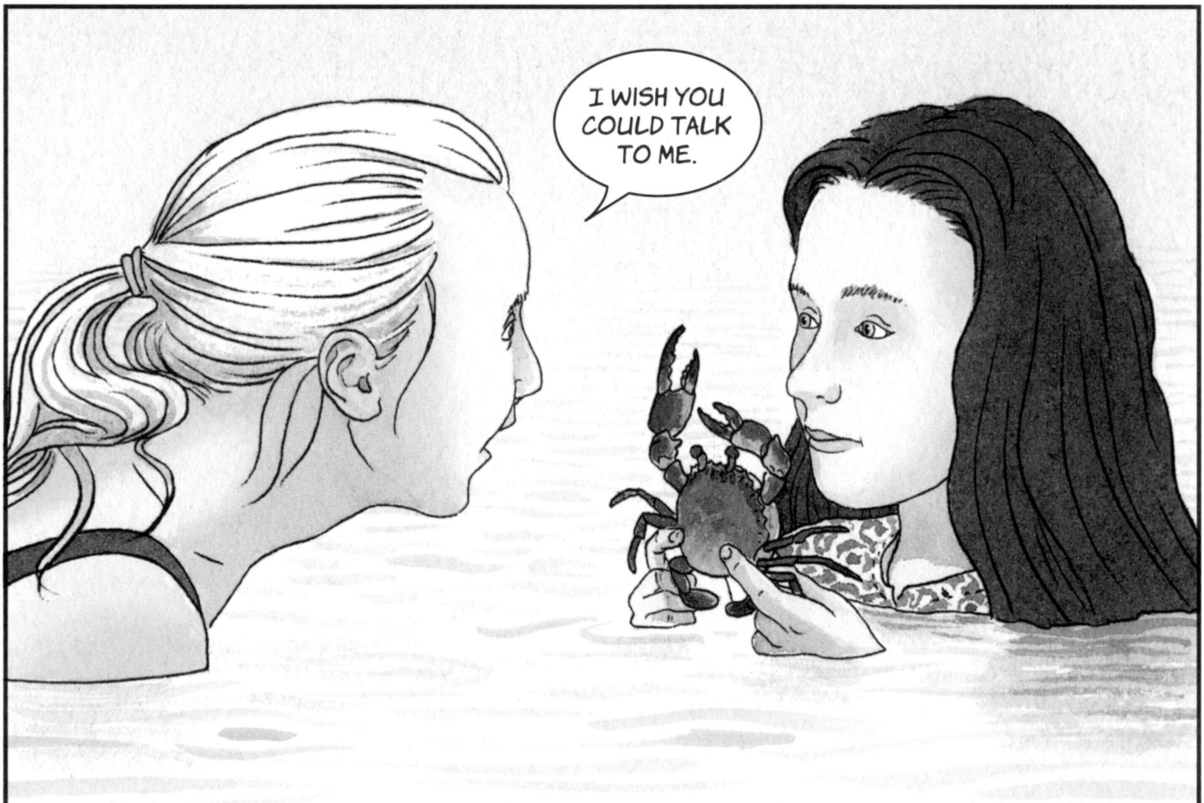
I WISH YOU COULD TALK TO ME.

150

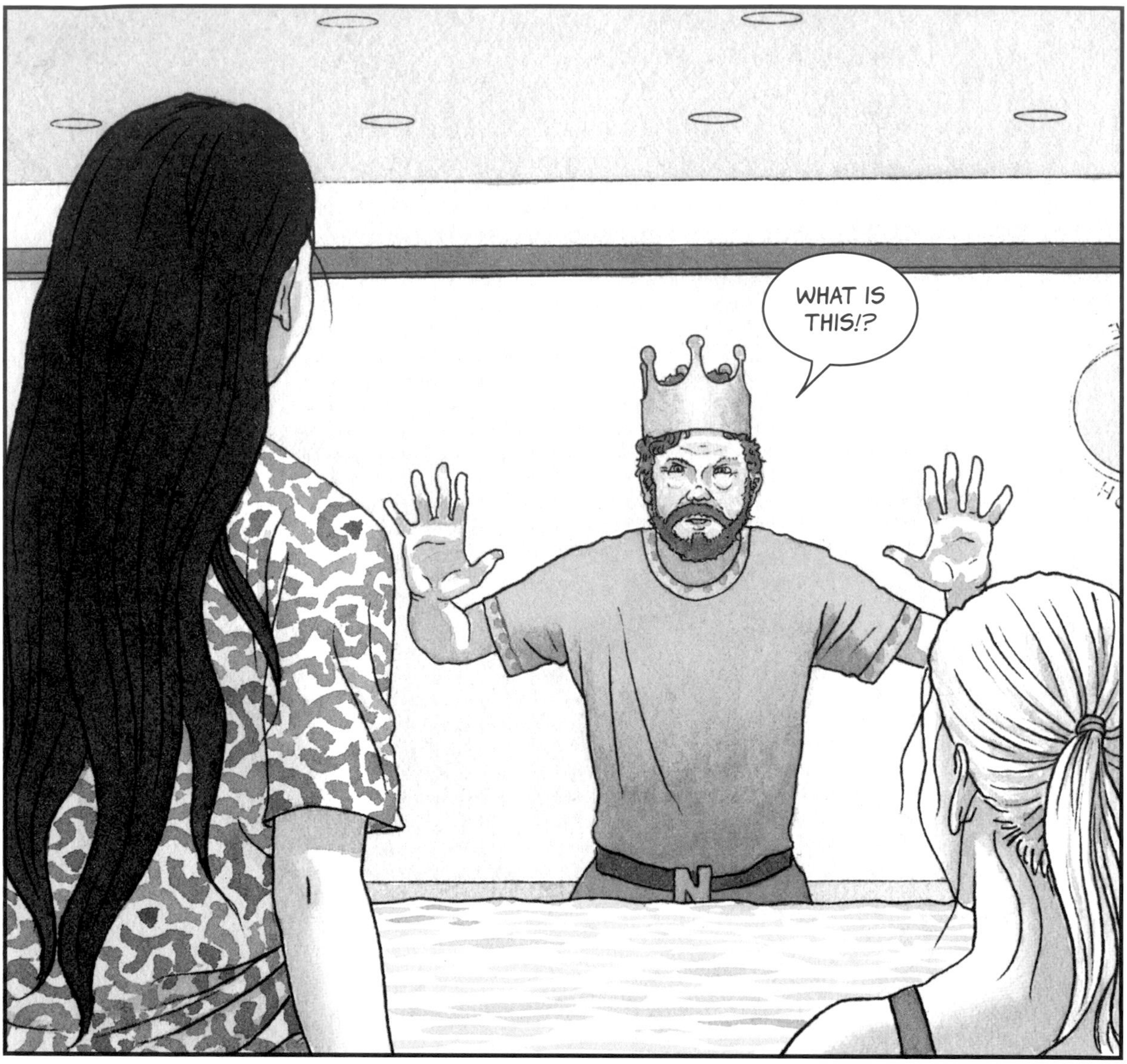
WHAT IS THIS!?

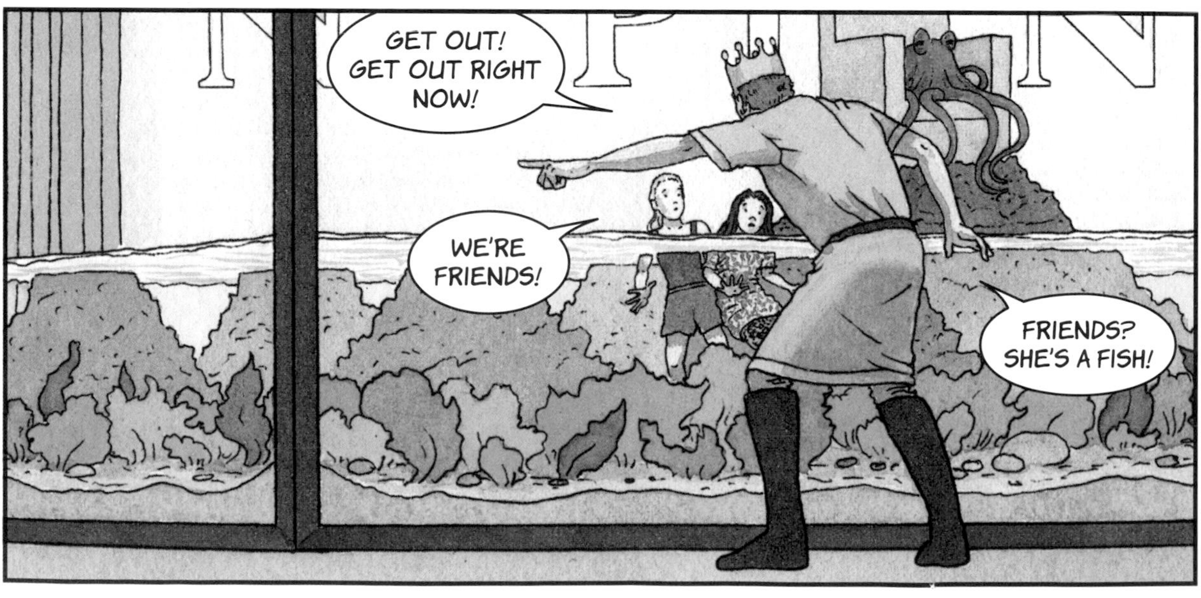
GET OUT! GET OUT RIGHT NOW!
WE'RE FRIENDS!
FRIENDS? SHE'S A FISH!

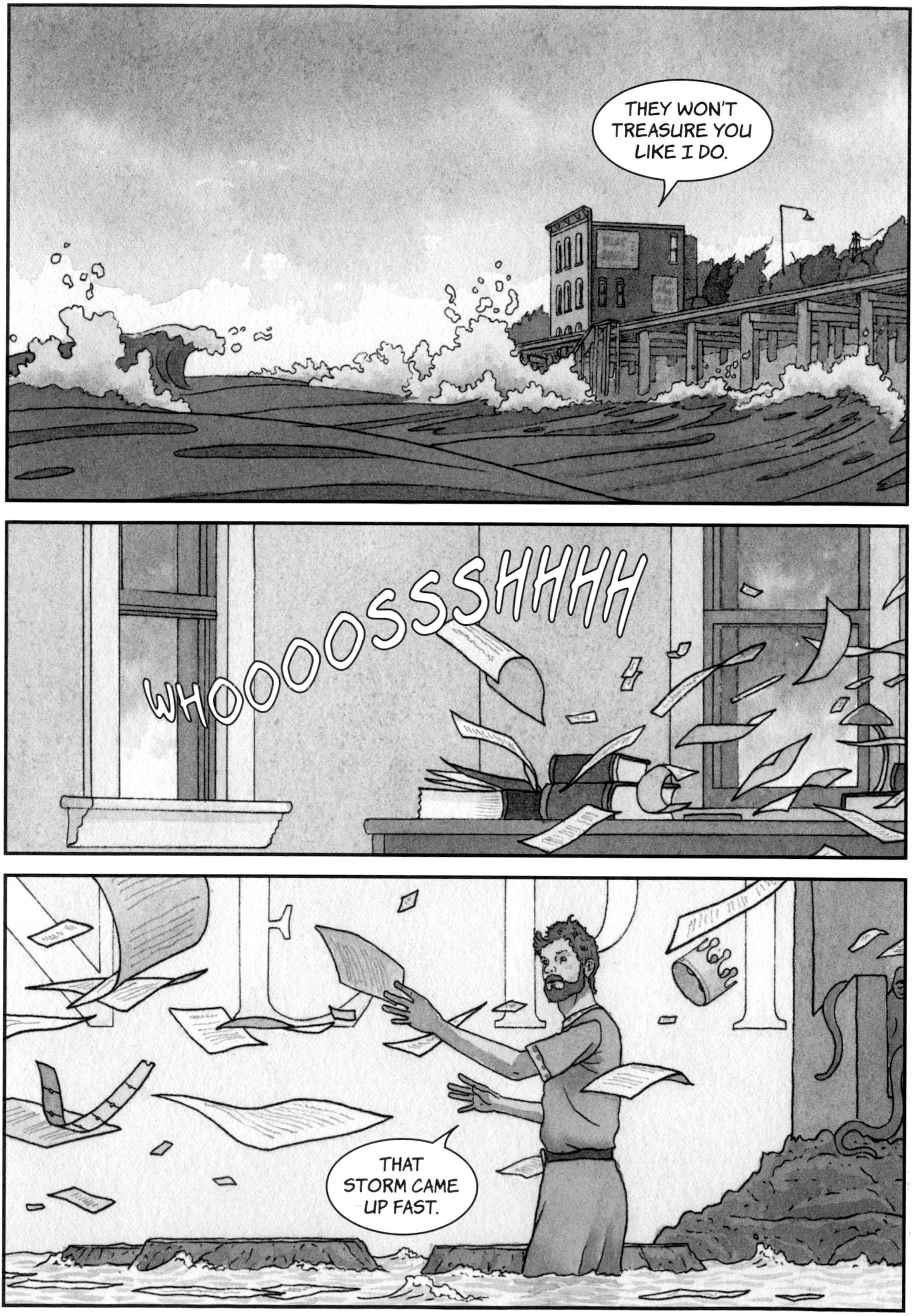
THEY WON'T TREASURE YOU LIKE I DO.
WHOOOOSSSHHHH
THAT STORM CAME UP FAST.

158

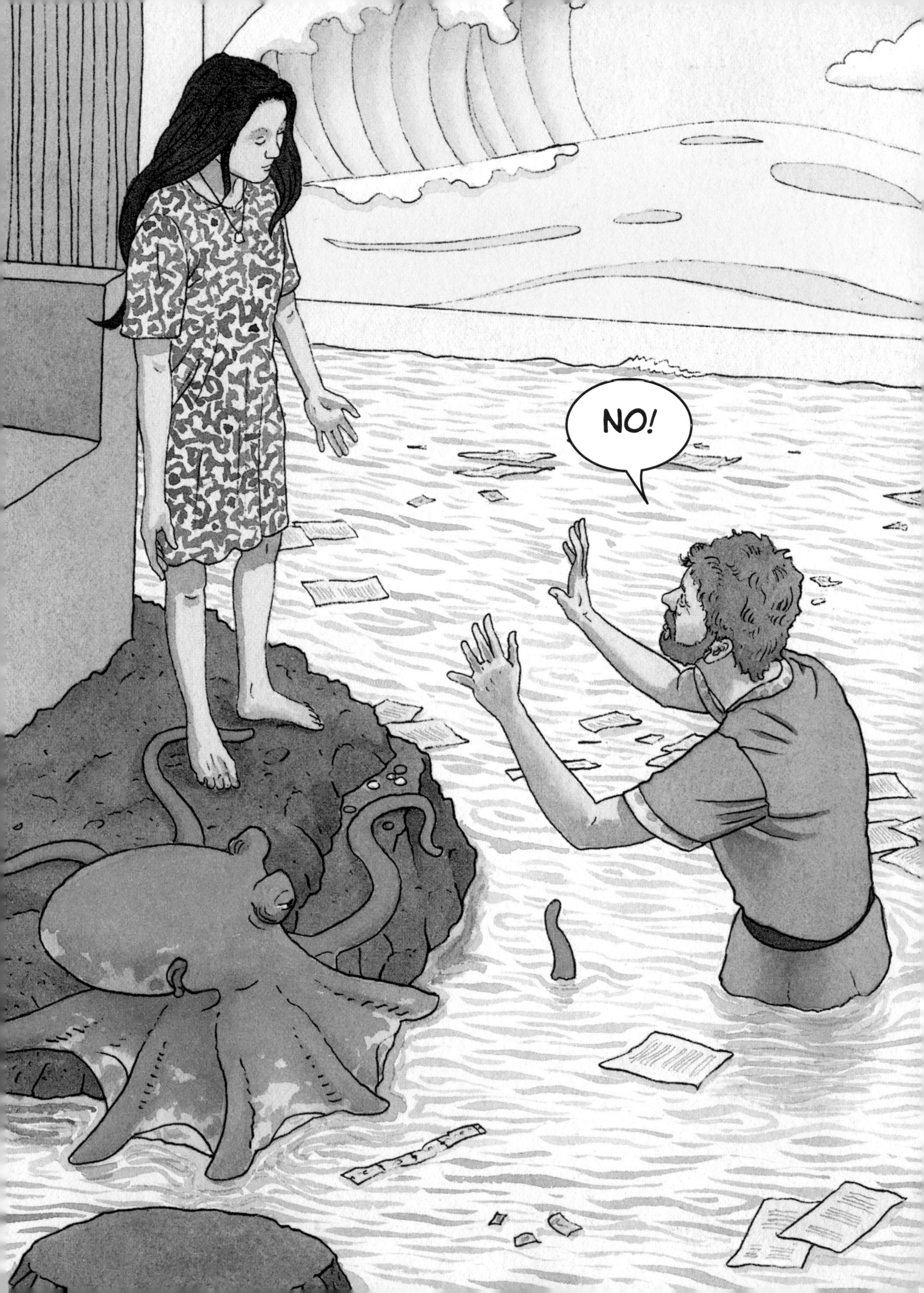
NO!

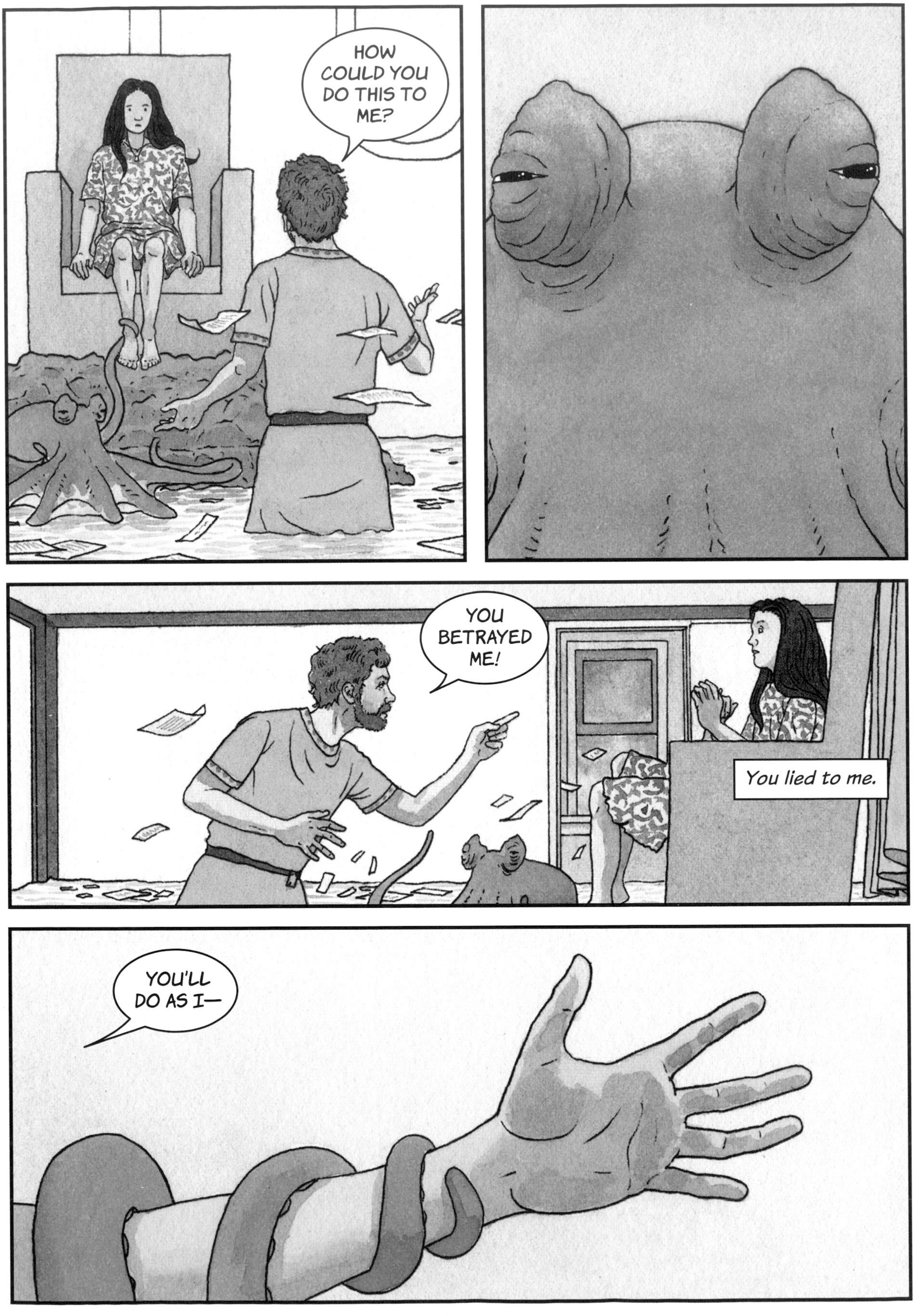
HOW COULD YOU DO THIS TO ME?
YOU BETRAYED ME!
You lied to me.
YOU'LL DO AS I—

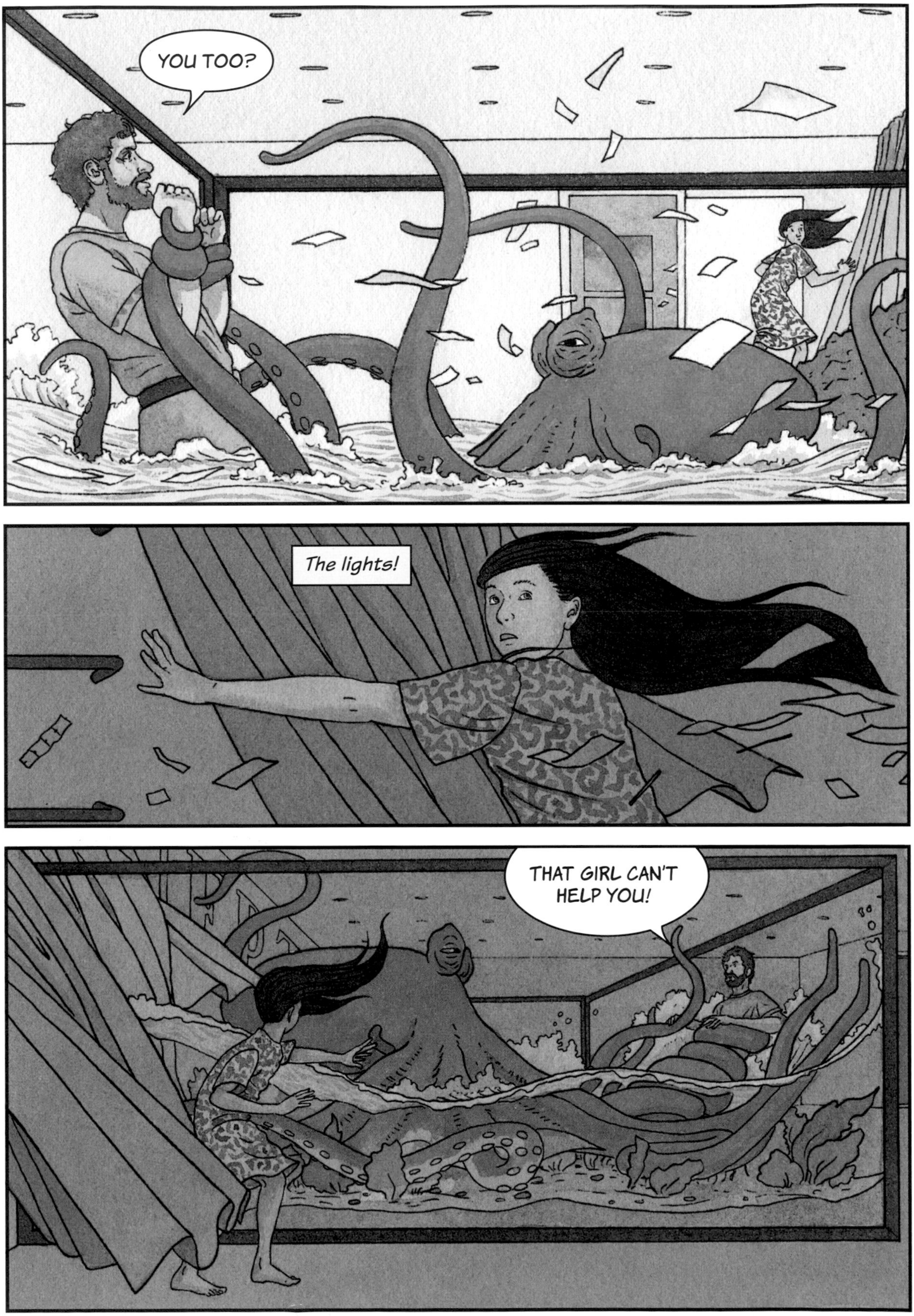
YOU TOO?
The lights!
THAT GIRL CAN'T HELP YOU!

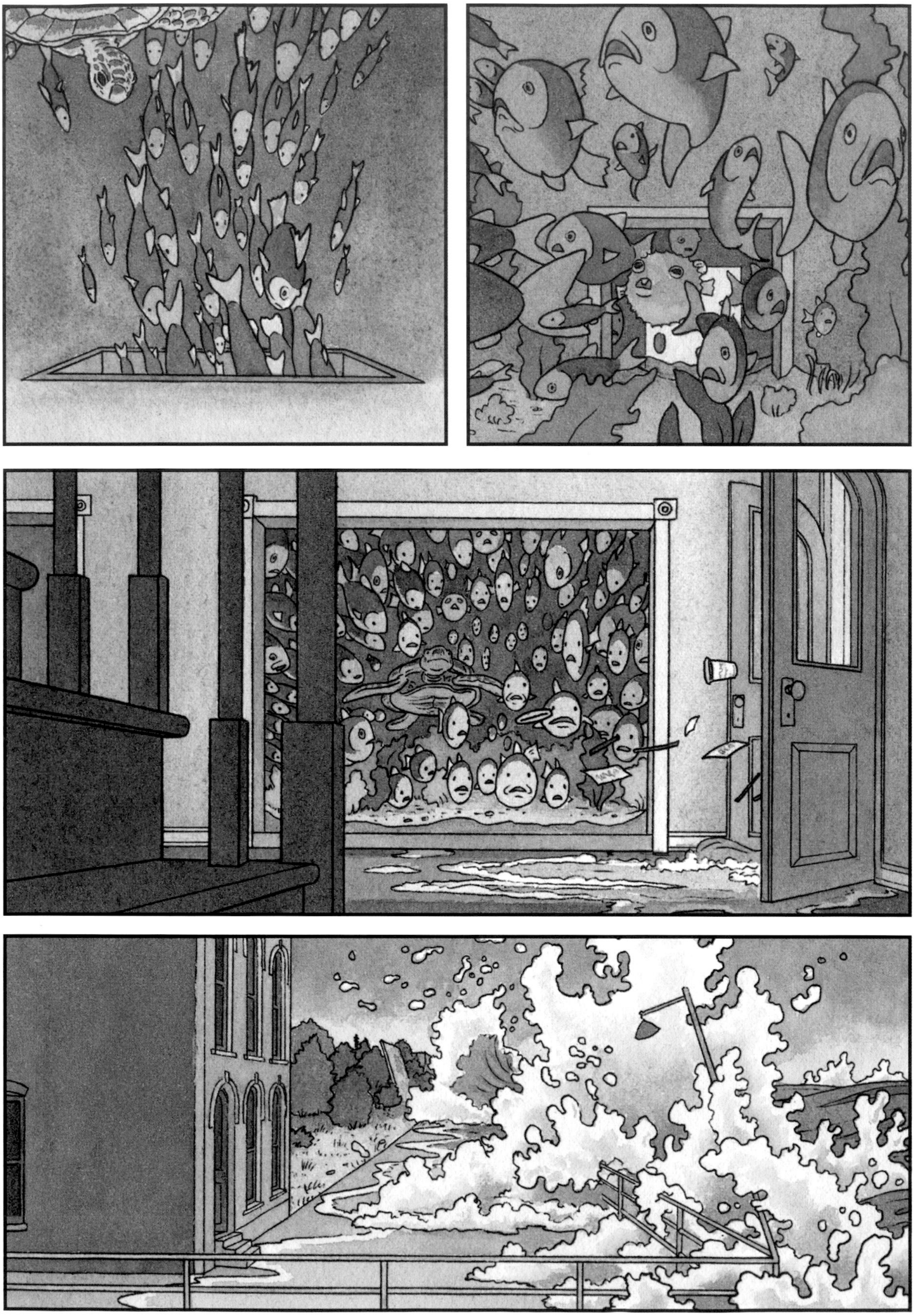

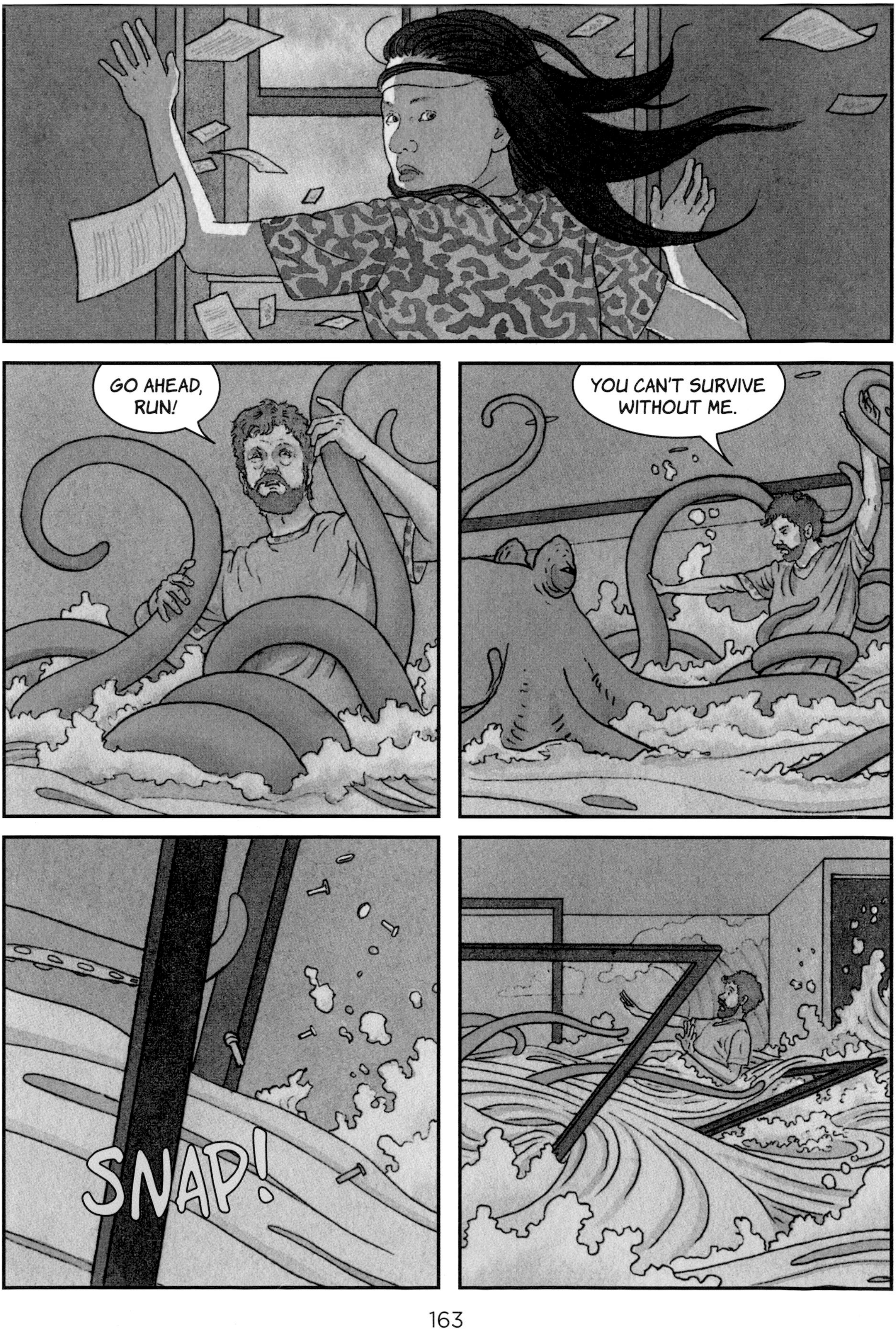
GO AHEAD, RUN!
YOU CAN'T SURVIVE WITHOUT ME.
SNAP!

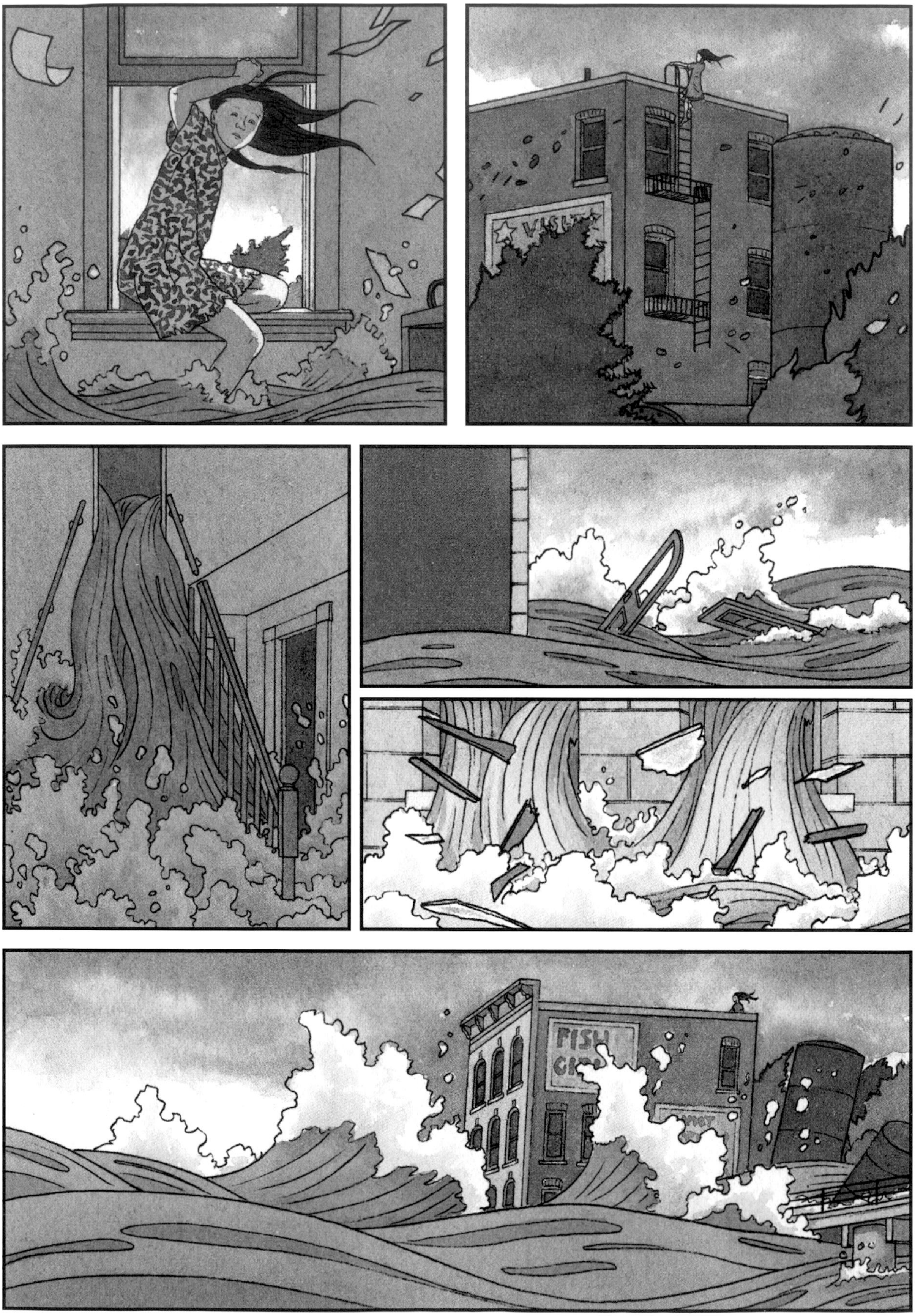
FISH

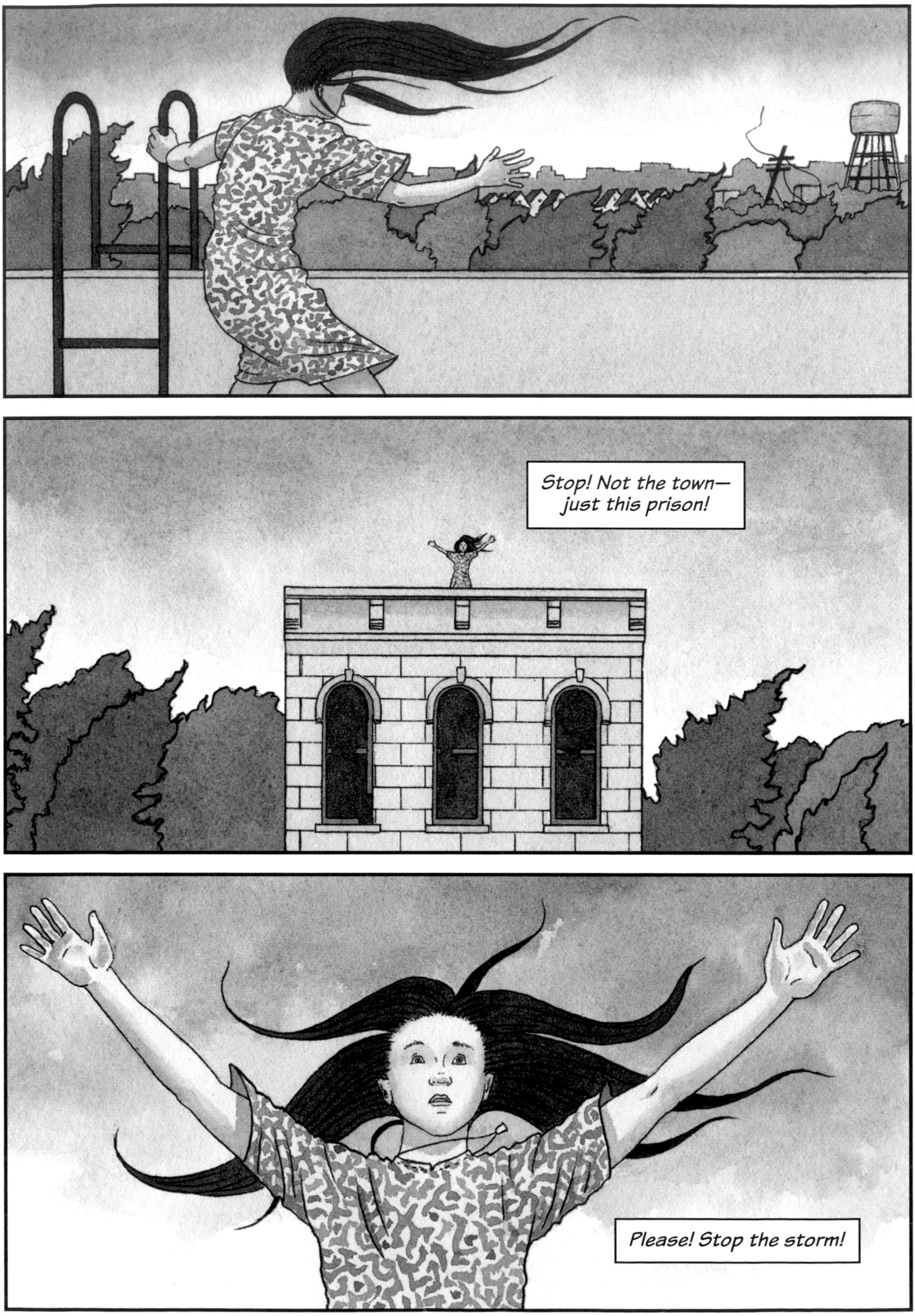
Stop! Not the town—just this prison!
Please! Stop the storm!

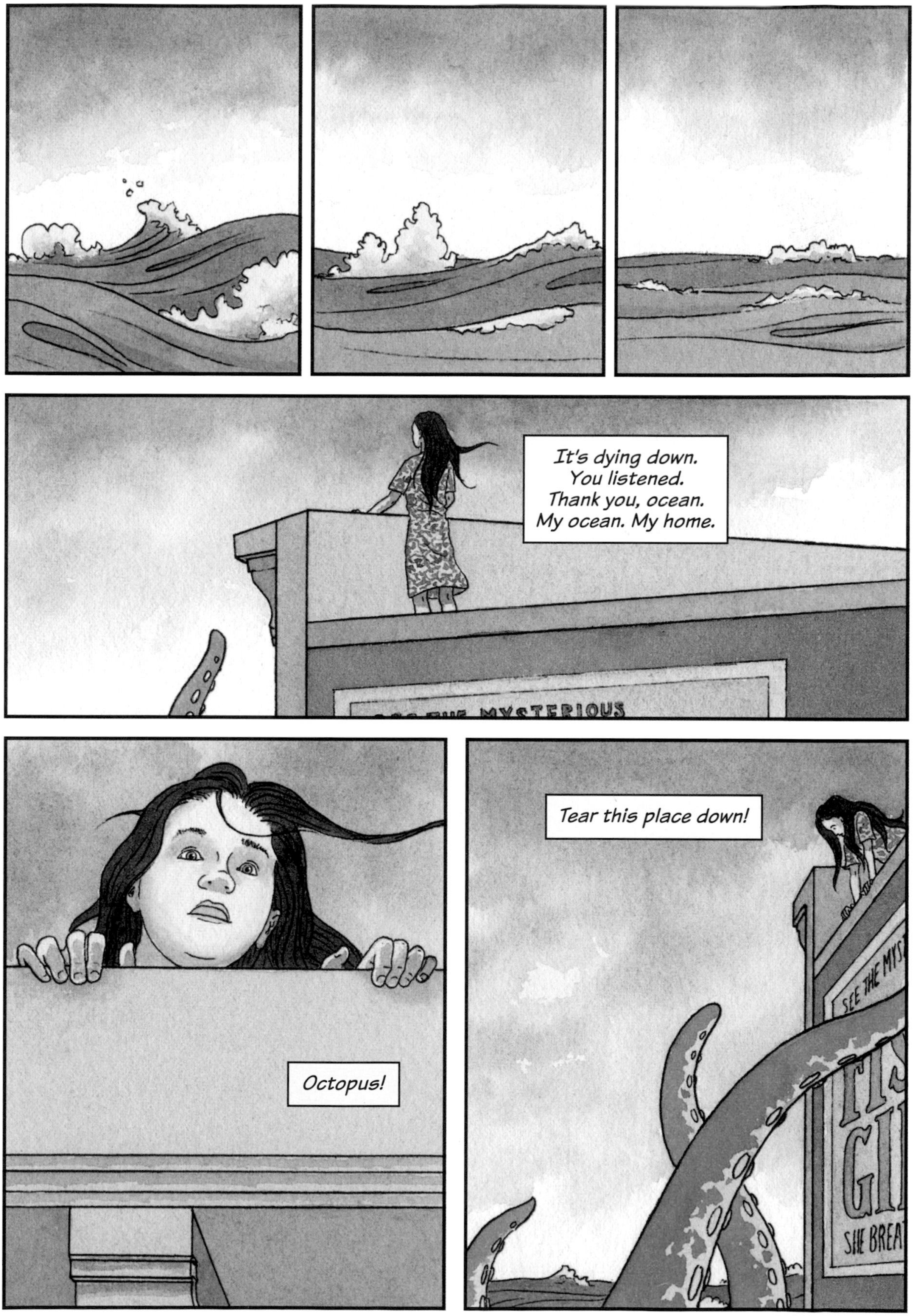
It's dying down.
You listened.
Thank you, ocean.
My ocean. My home.
Octopus!
Tear this place down!

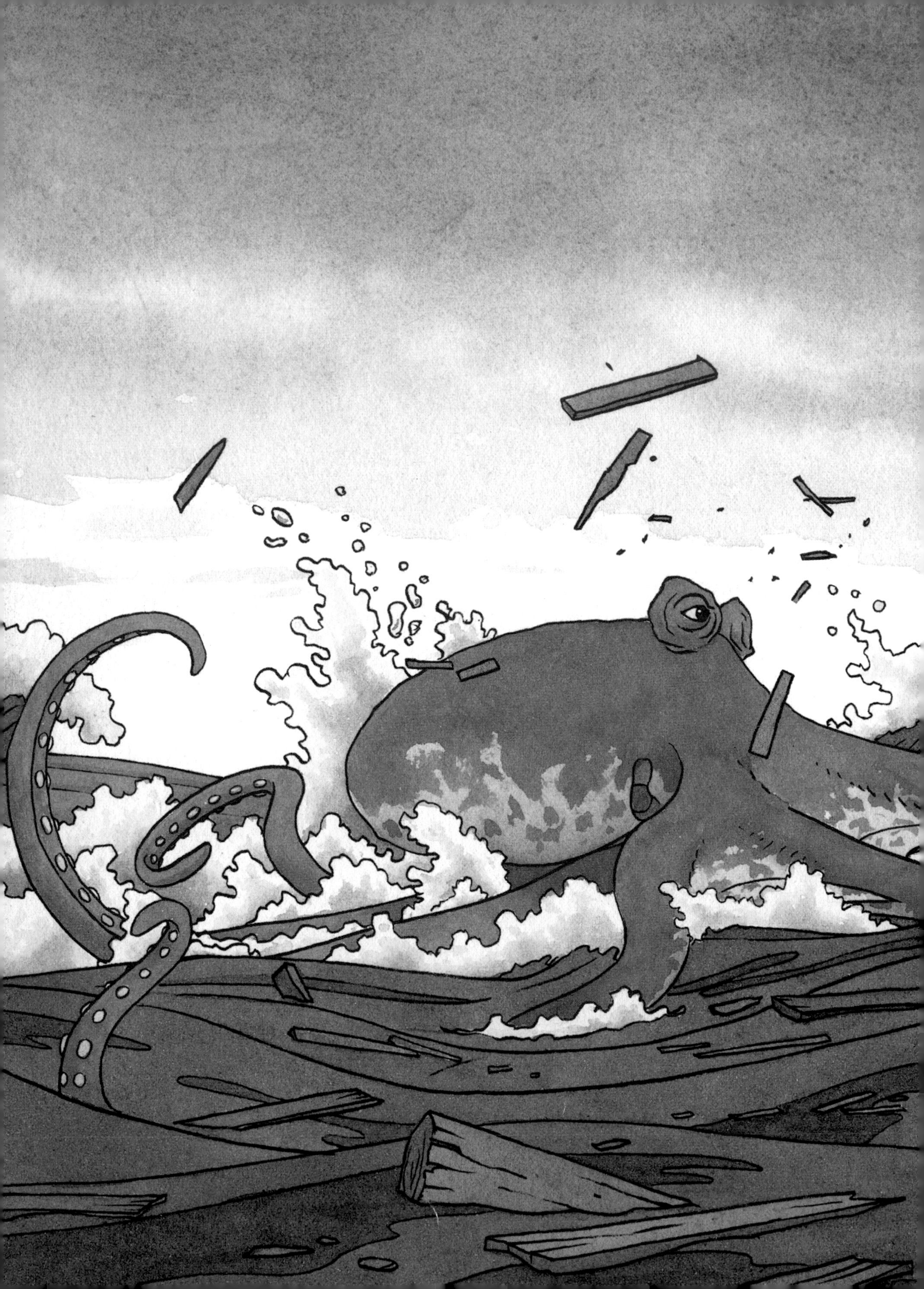

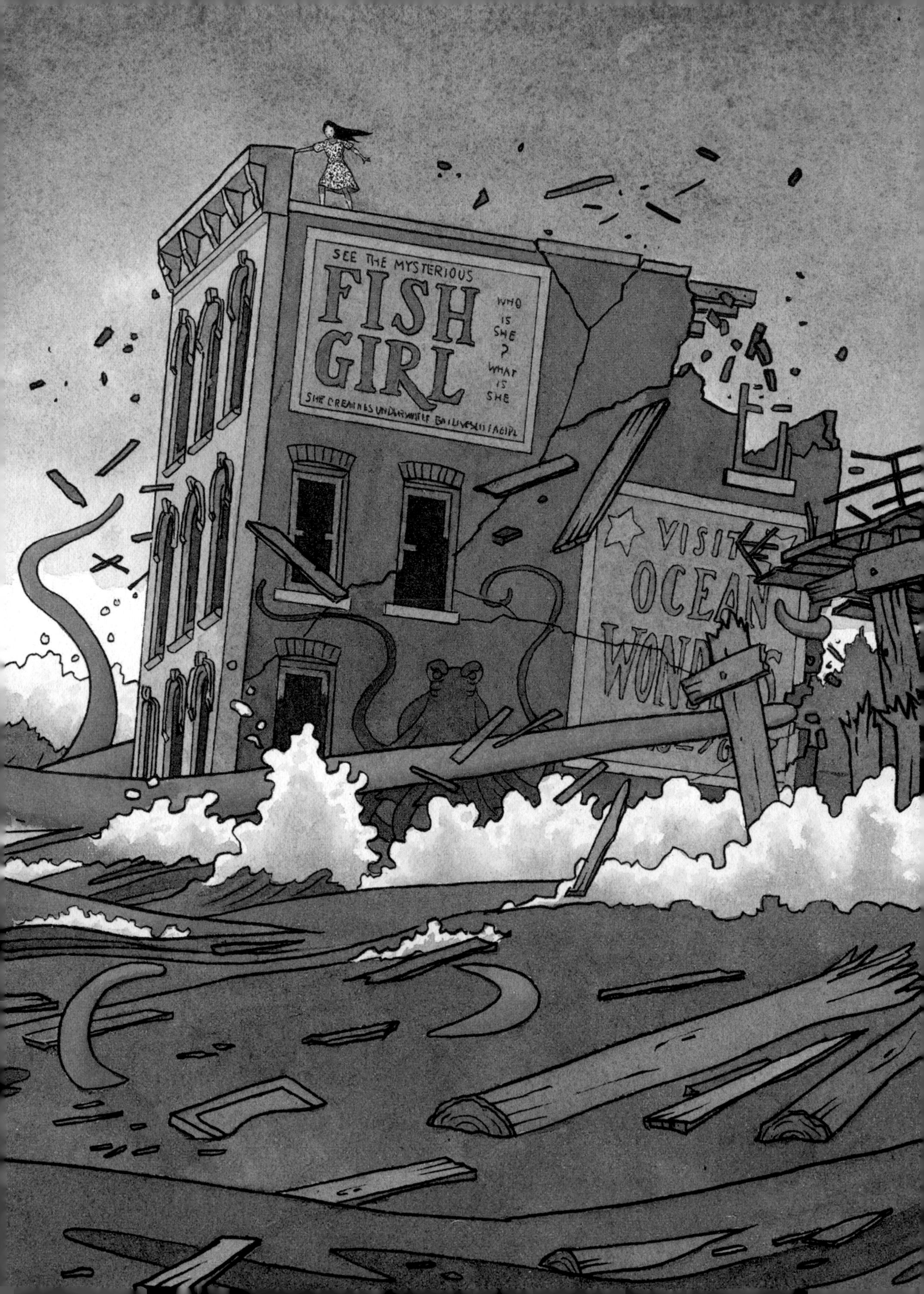
SEE THE MYSTERIOUS
FISH GIRL
WHO IS SHE ? WHAT IS SHE
VISIT
OCEAN

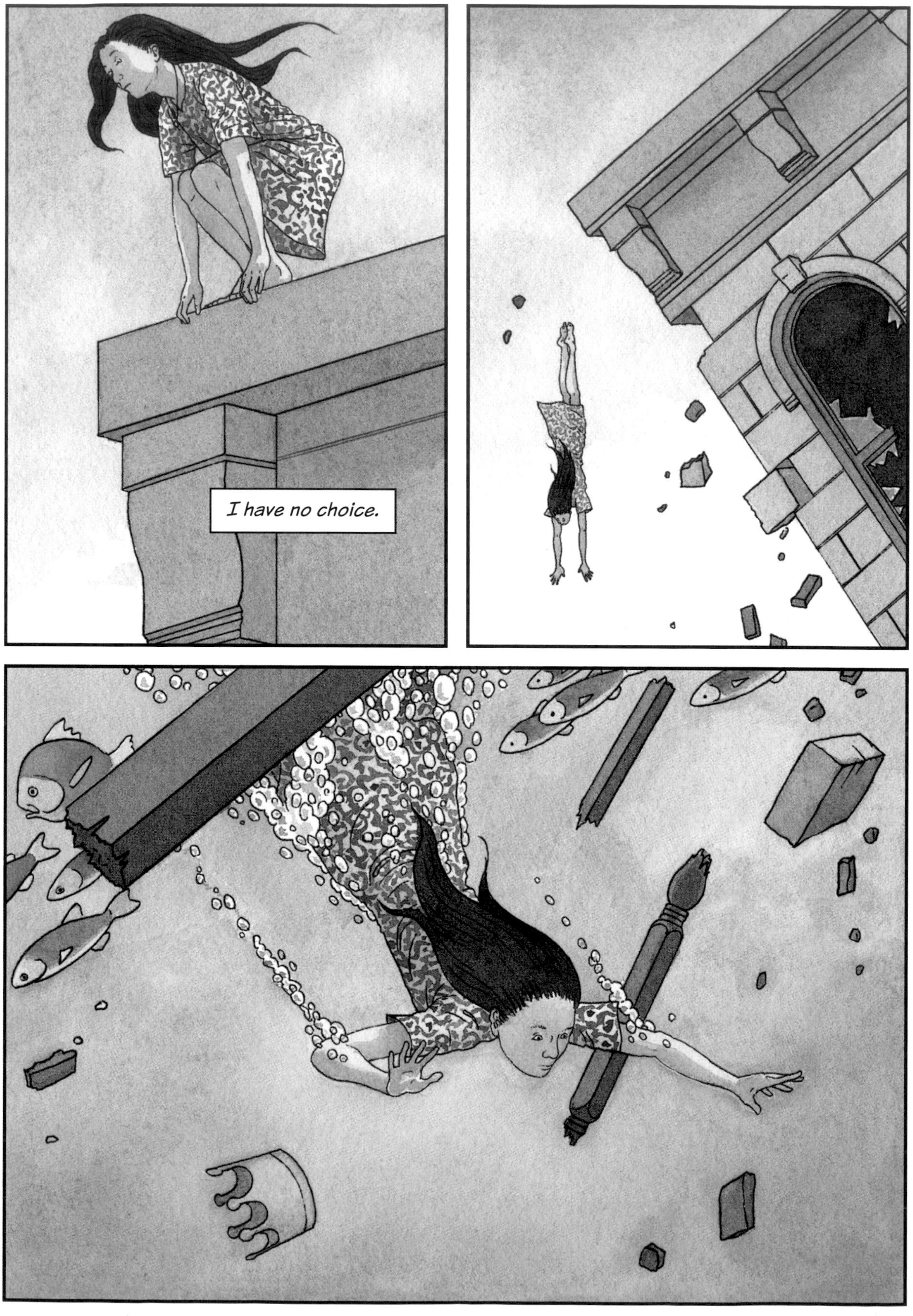
I have no choice.

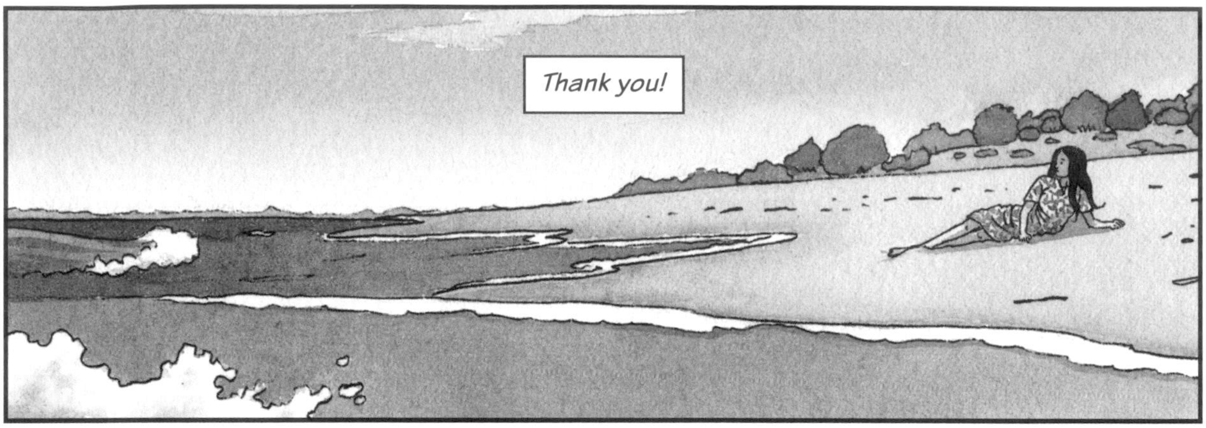
Thank you!

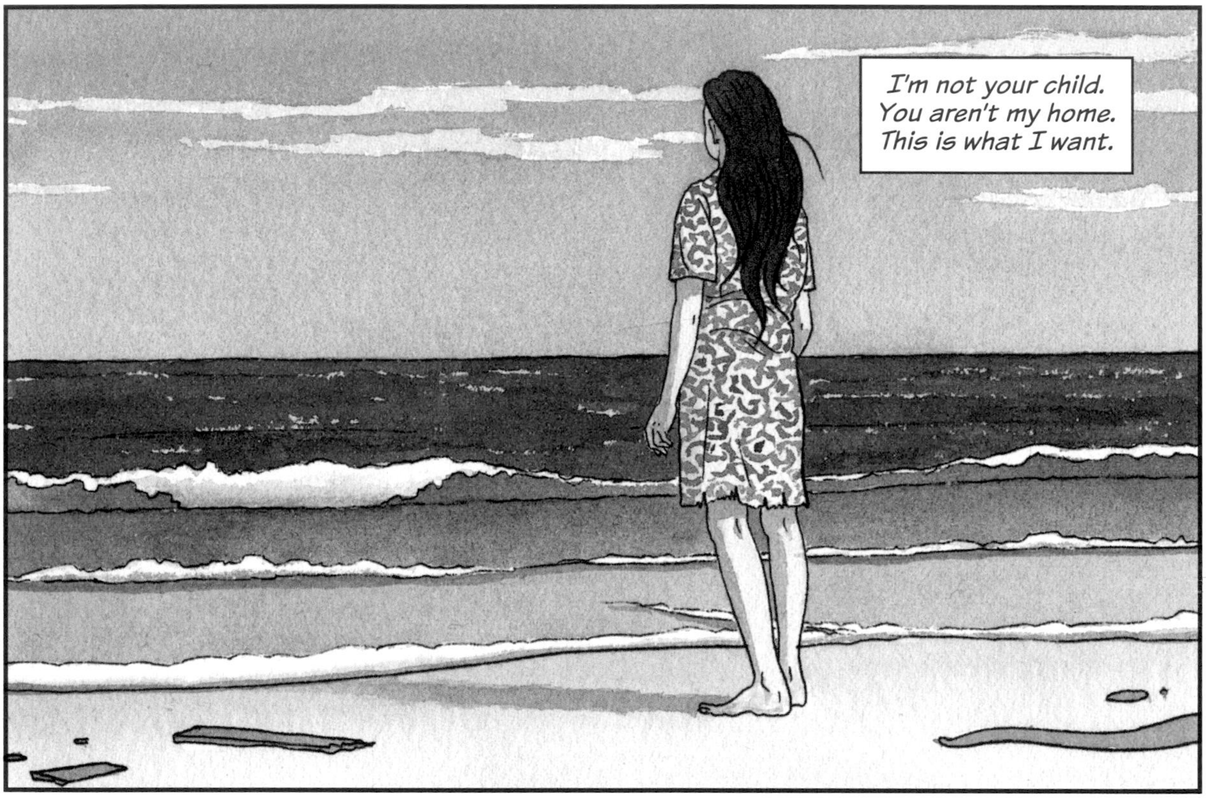
I'm not your child.
You aren't my home.
This is what I want.

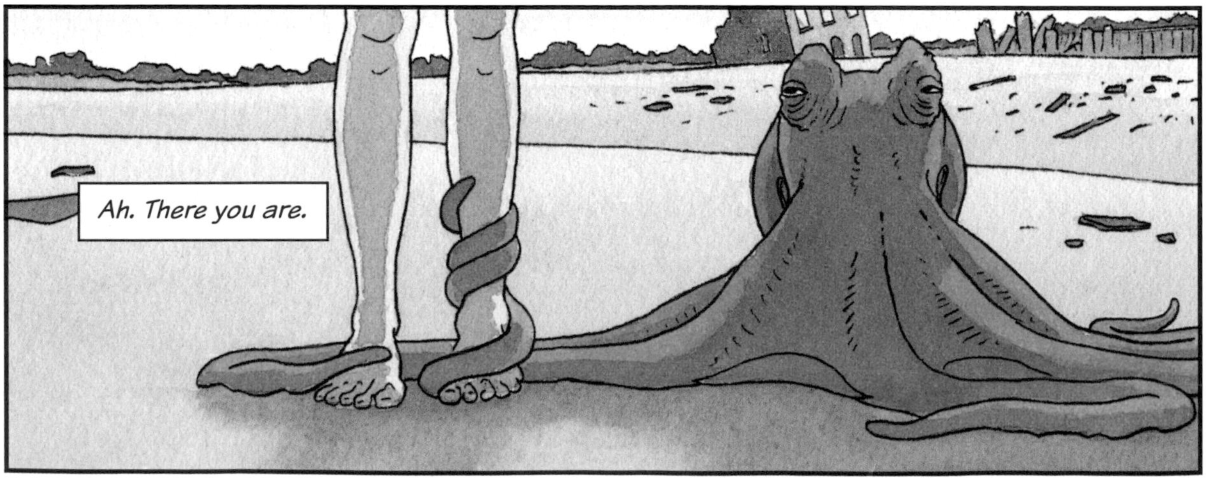
Ah. There you are.

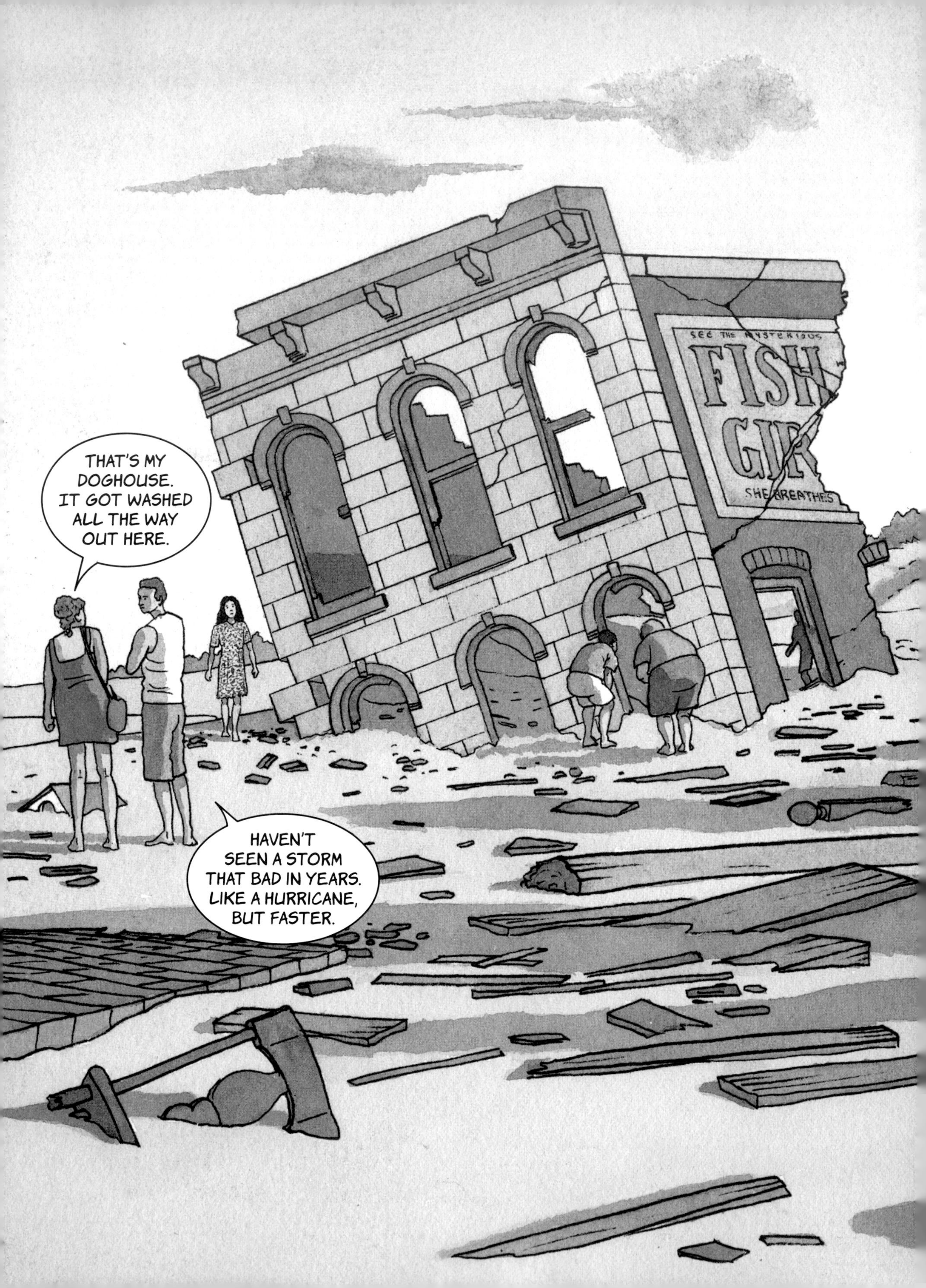
SEE THE MYSTERIOUS
FISH GIRL
SHE BREATHES
THAT'S MY DOGHOUSE. IT GOT WASHED ALL THE WAY OUT HERE.
HAVEN'T SEEN A STORM THAT BAD IN YEARS. LIKE A HURRICANE, BUT FASTER.

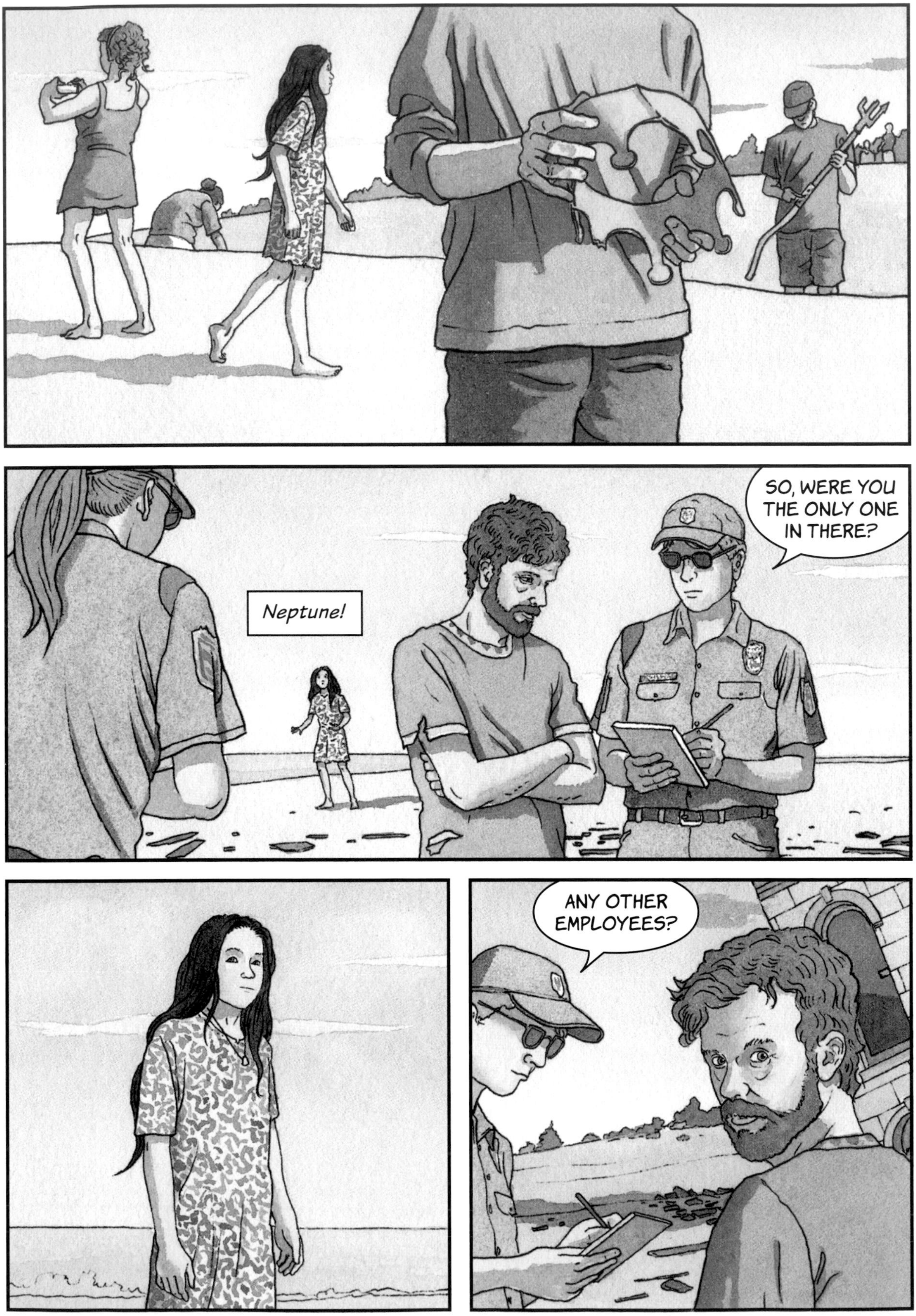
Neptune!
SO, WERE YOU THE ONLY ONE IN THERE?
ANY OTHER EMPLOYEES?

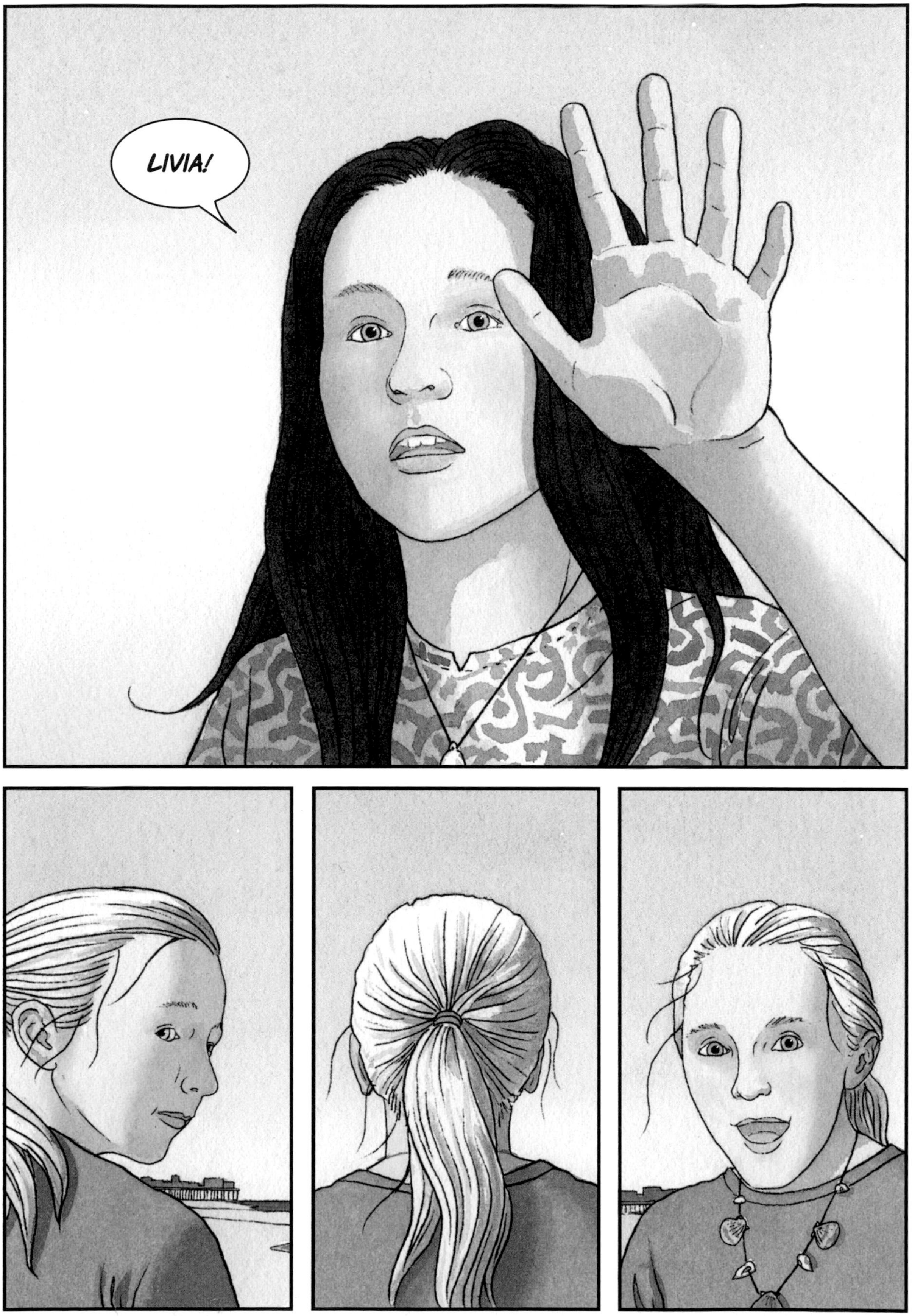
LIVIA!

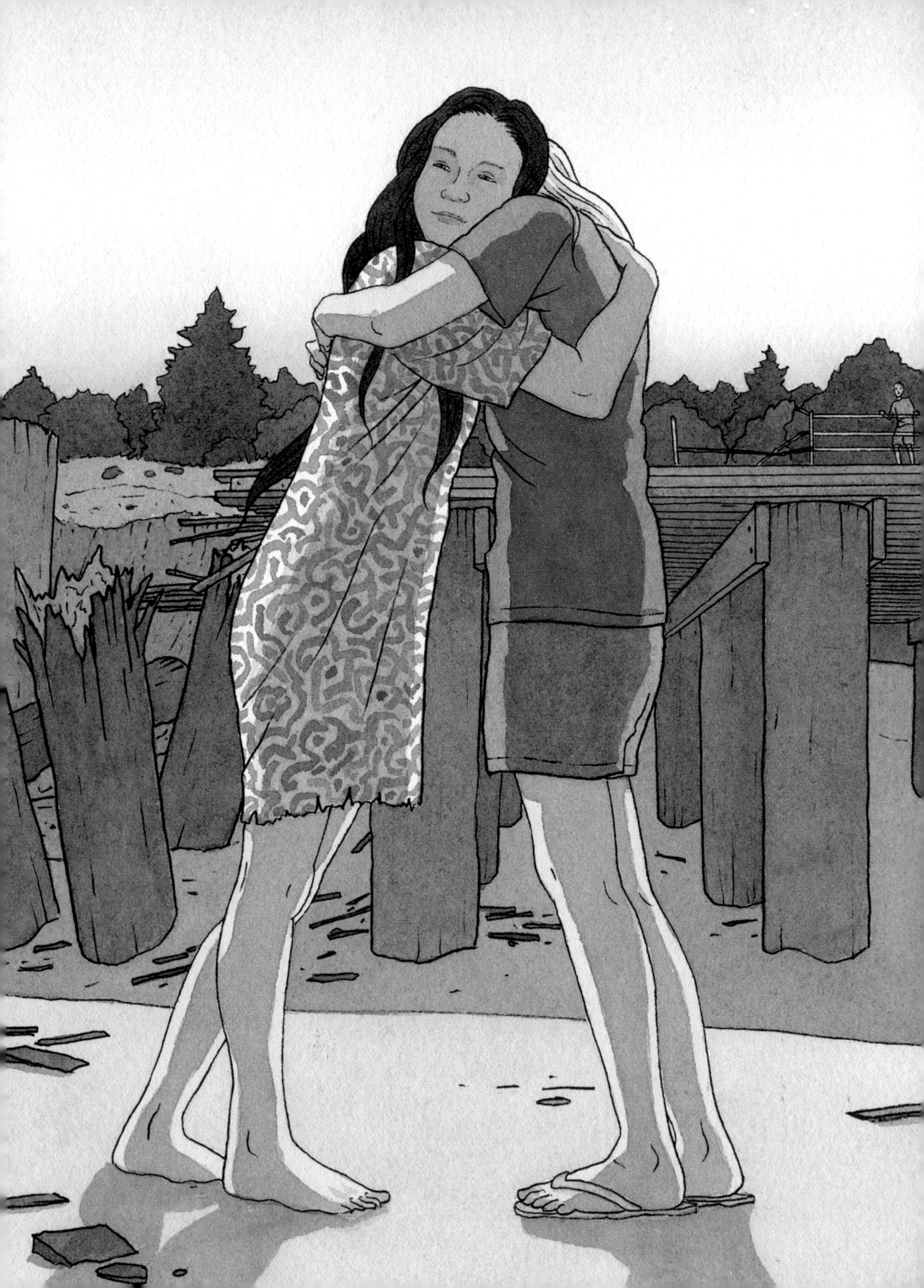

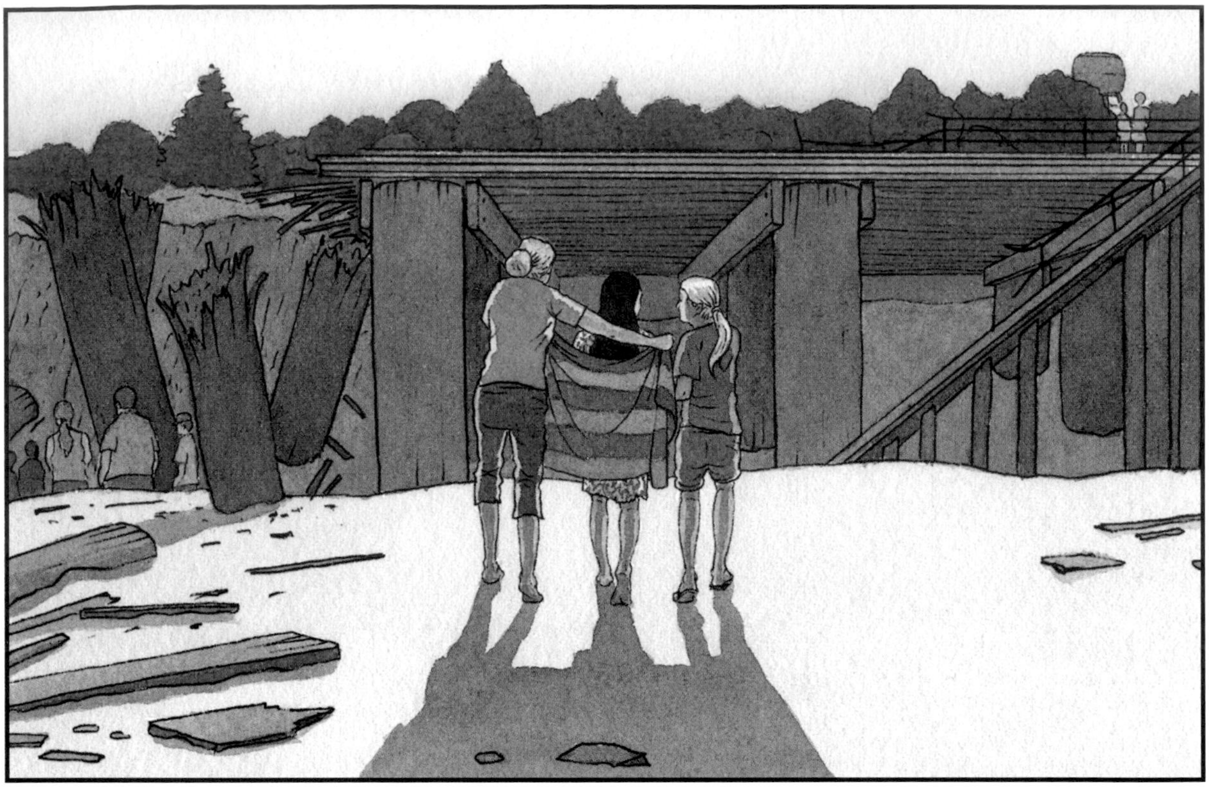

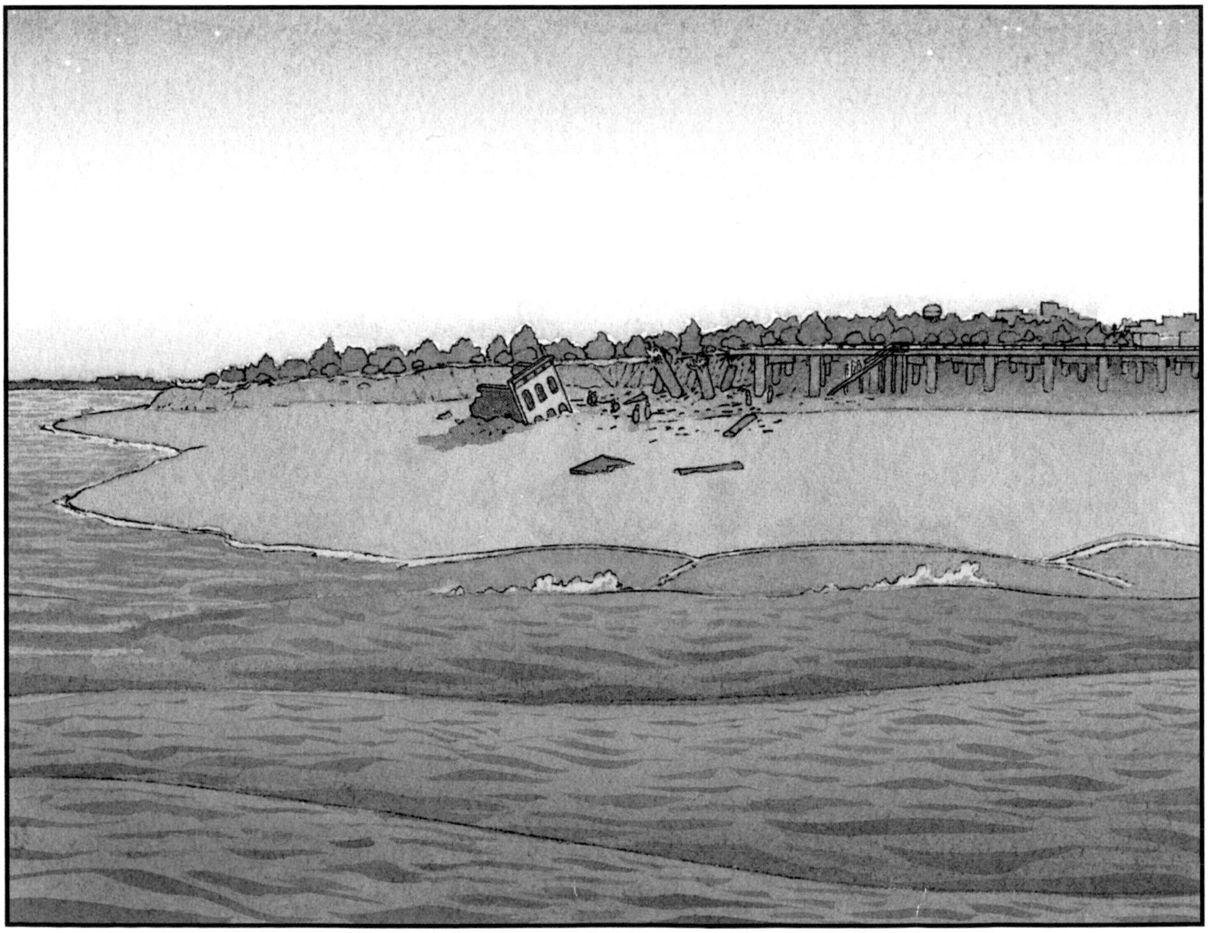

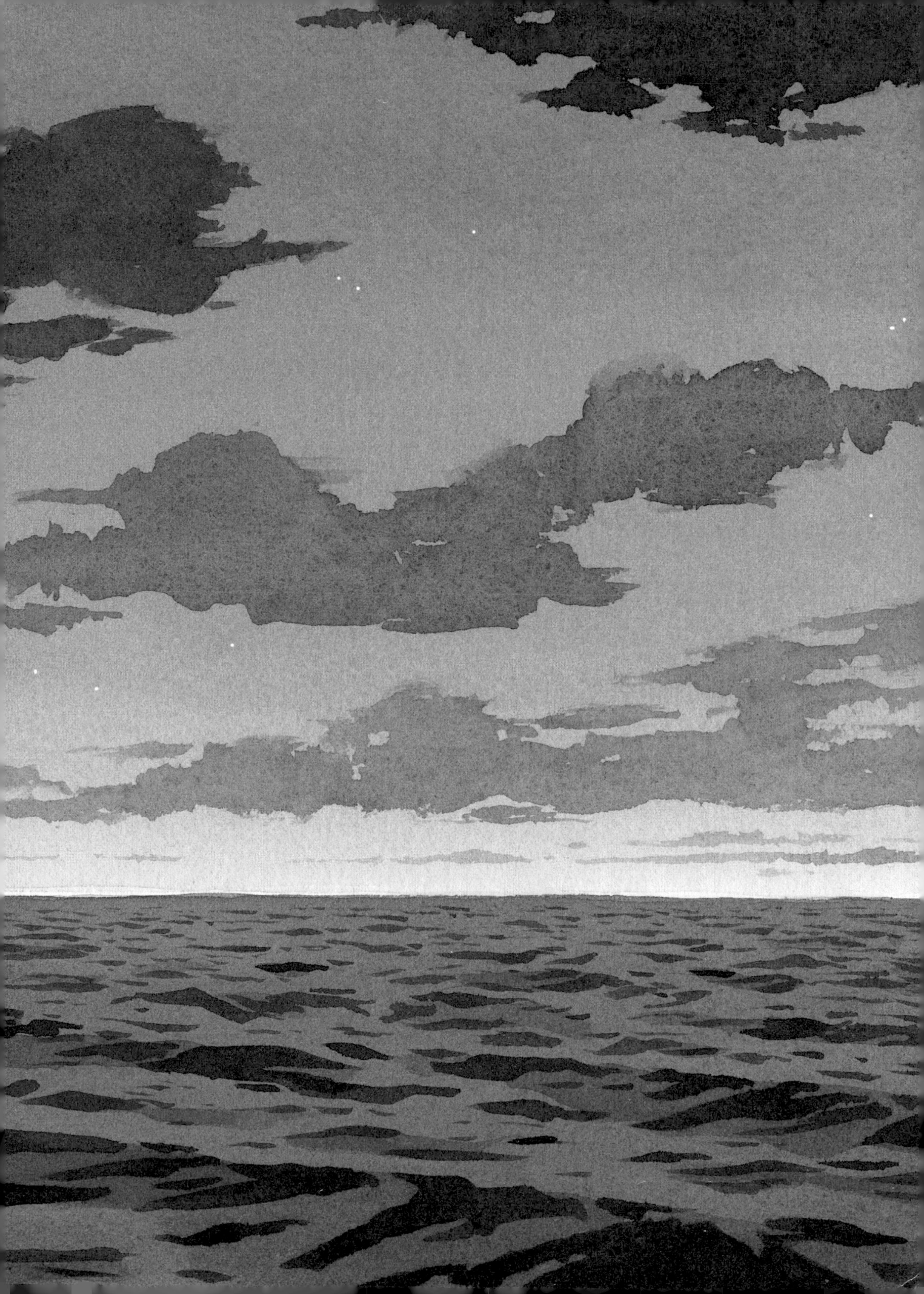

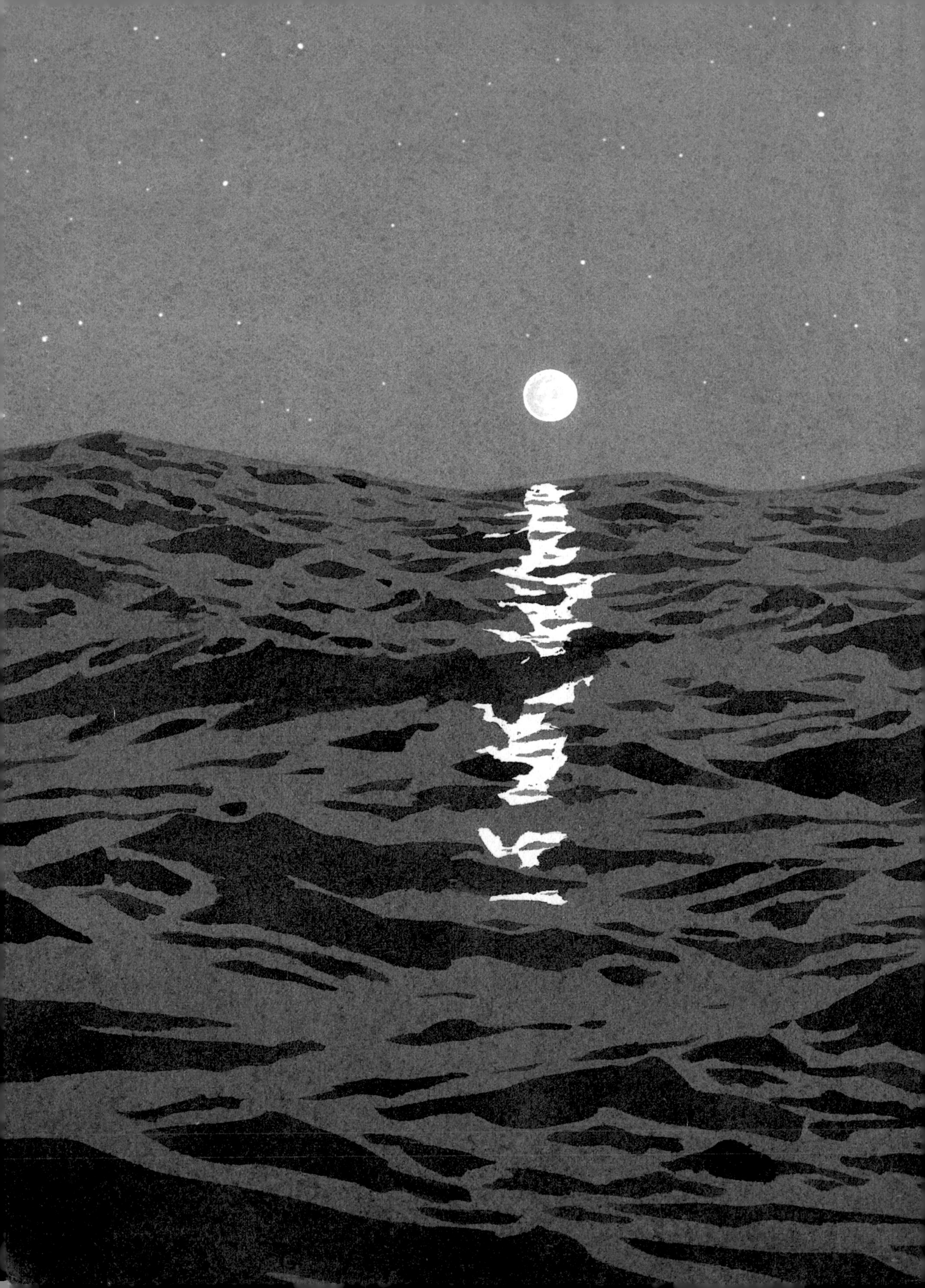

Acknowledgments

I want to thank the many people who helped me with this project.

First and foremost is my co-author Donna Jo Napoli, for agreeing to join me on this adventure—our adventure.

Those who graciously agreed to be models for the characters: Sabrina Shaffer, who readily logged much time in and out of the water; Margaret Harvey, who threw herself fully into character; Fred Brown, who now has a unique resume item; Caroline Putnam, who was a fine body double; Roni Anton, Joan Fox, and all the great kids at Project Learn in Mt. Airy—Dannan, Elise, Evan, Ian, Lily, Madison, Massimo, Nadja, Niko, and Tahmeer.

Moms Julie, Kathy, and Lois, for arranging schedules and transportation. Kate Garrity and David Kern for making the connections.

For their invaluable technical assistance, Mikelle Hicks and the mother/daughter tag team of Rebecca and Alice Thornburgh.

For their architectural help, Leonard Marcus, Jeff Block, Paul Zelinsky, and Craig Hofheimer.

For their infinite patience, wisdom, and cheerleading, Dinah Stevenson, Donna McCarthy, and Carol Goldenberg—Team Fish Girl!

David Wiesner

To my granddaughters, Aspen and Olivia
—D.J.N.

For Kim
Without her help, advice, and support, I would not
have made it through to the end.
—D.W.

Clarion Books
3 Park Avenue
New York, New York 10016

Text copyright © 2017 by Donna Jo Napoli
Illustrations copyright © 2017 by David Wiesner

Clarion Books is an imprint of Houghton Mifflin Harcourt Publishing Company.

www.hmhco.com

Art Direction by Carol Goldenberg
Lettering by John Green
The illustrations in this book were created in watercolor and line.
The text was set in Komika Text and Komika Hand.

Library of Congress Cataloging-in-Publication Data is available.
ISBN 978-0-544-81512-4 (HC)
ISBN 978-0-547-48393-1 (PA)

Manufactured in Malaysia
TWP 10 9 8 7 6 5 4 3 2 1
4500627546